PRAISE FOR S.T. GIBSON

"A painfully human tale about the price of ambition and the weight of pride, Gibson draws us into a multifaceted world of mysticism and magic, forcing us to confront the darkest questions at the heart of our souls – how far would you go for power, and what are you without it?"
K. M. Enright, Sunday Times bestselling author of *Mistress of Lies*

"A bruising and beautiful tale of devotion and desperation that explores the lengths people will go to for desire and ambition – and the anchoring power of multifaceted love, trust, and intimacy to always catch them when they threaten to fall too far."
Laura R. Samotin, author of *The Sins on Their Bones*

"Gibson has an uncanny knack for getting into the grit of a story and bringing it to life and love on the page. Between the vibrant prose, perfectly flawed characters, and exquisite tension, I was demanding more with every page and Gibson delivered. A stunning sequel that is quite simply a must-read."
Hazel McBride, author of *A Fate Forged in Fire*

"This treat of a character study is as lush as carmine velvet, as juicy as sun-warmed blackberries, and as rich as a glass of vintage port. This story of magic, love, spirituality, and ambition is not only a joy to read but the best depiction of polyamory I've seen."
Emma Sterner-Radley, author of *Snowblooded*

"A story as intimate as it is decadent, a delightful romp through occult society, grounded by all-too-human characters, the power of love is a real and vibrant force in this story and its effects are profound. Sincerity is scary and Gibson aims to thrill."
Elizabeth Kilcoyne, Morris Award finalist for *Wake the Bones* for *Evocation*

"Dazzling and compelling from start to finish, S.T. Gibson's Evocation crackles with magic and the strong chemistry between its three leads."
Morgan Dante, author of *A Flame in the Night* for *Evocation*

"Evocation *is the dark, sexy urban fantasy of my dreams. In David, Rhys and Moira's rich and twisty polyamorous relationship, S. T. Gibson conjures a remarkable romance that is often complicated, sometimes brutal, and always true. A sensual, bewitching read.*"
Holly Race, author of *Midnight's Twins* for *Evocation*

"*Romantic and delectable,* Evocation *is an entrancing start to a new series by S. T. Gibson. If anyone can make you root for three intricately crafted characters, it is Gibson. David, Rhys and Moira have ensnared me: I will be making a deal with the devil just to get book two in my hands.*"
Ben Alderson, author of *Lord of Eternal Night* for *Evocation*

"*Gibson pairs the old-world elegance of a secret occult society with the glitz and glamor of modern urban magic to create a dazzling world... The casual inclusion of polyamory within a committed relationship, and the positive reinforcement of love in different forms are terrific additions to what is already an engaging fantasy novel.*"
Booklist, starred review for *Evocation*

"*It's a pleasure to watch these three amusing characters fit together the puzzle of their relationship. An audacious and uncommon romp.*"
Publishers Weekly review for *Evocation*

ASCENSION
S.T. GIBSON

ANGRY ROBOT
An imprint of Watkins Media Ltd

Unit 11, Shepperton House
89-93 Shepperton Road
London N1 3DF UK

angryrobotbooks.com
The well of ambition

An Angry Robot hardback original, 2025

Copyright © S.T. Gibson 2025

Edited by Eleanor Teasdale, Athena Dixon and Shona Kinsella
Cover illustration by Eleonor Piteira
Cover design by Alice Claire Coleman
Tarot card descriptions by Adam Gordon
Set in Meridien

All rights reserved. S.T. Gibson asserts the moral right to be identified as the author of this work. A catalogue record for this book is available from the British Library.

This novel is entirely a work of fiction. Names, characters, places, and incidents are the products of the author's imagination or are used fictitiously. Any resemblance to actual events, locales, organizations or persons, living or dead, is entirely coincidental.

Sales of this book without a front cover may be unauthorized. If this book is coverless, it may have been reported to the publisher as "unsold and destroyed" and neither the author nor the publisher may have received payment for it.

Angry Robot and the Angry Robot icon are registered trademarks of Watkins Media Ltd.

ISBN 978 1 91599 805 7
Ebook ISBN 978 1 91599 811 8

Printed and bound in the United Kingdom by CPI Group (UK) Ltd, Croydon CR0 4YY

The manufacturer's authorised representative in the EU for product safety is eucomply OÜ - Pärnu mnt 139b-14, 11317 Tallinn, Estonia, hello@eucompliancepartner.com; www.eucompliancepartner.com

9 8 7 6 5 4 3 2 1

To everyone driven forward by bottomless ambition, Hozier said it best: Don't you ever tame your demons, but always keep 'em on a leash.

CHAPTER ONE
RHYS

The first time Rhys McGowan attempted magic, he was fifteen years old. Rhys had gone through a growth spurt that year, shooting up like a sapling, and he had developed a slouch to keep from sticking out too much in a crowd. That slouch benefited him most when he didn't want to be seen, like when he was trying to keep from getting picked to run a mile in gym class.

Or when he was attempting to avoid notice while breaking into the church's sacristy.

As he was generally considered an upstanding young man, no one batted an eyelash at finding him in the church after hours. Not the administrative assistant who nodded at him when he slipped in through the office door, and not the janitor who gave him a wave as he made his way through the carpeted halls. The McGowan boy was quiet and pious and paid attention during the homily. He probably had a good reason to be wandering the parish offices on a school night.

Rhys's reason, of course, was sorcery.

Rhys had slipped into the sacristy, a room that smelled overwhelmingly of citrus cleaner and myrrh, and walked towards the large wooden chest where the holy objects were kept. Inside, the gold chalices and polished offering plates winked at him, burning with the sacredness of the forbidden.

Rhys had run his little finger around the rim of the chalice and shuddered at the kiss of cool metal.

He had never broken a rule with such flagrant intention in his life.

Rhys retrieved a small silver chalice, a tin of communion wafers, and a bottle of port, then sat down cross-legged in a corner of the cramped little room. He shoved himself halfway into a vestment closet, just in case anyone walked by and peered into the room. Hanging albs brushed against his shoulders as he stole a gulp of wine, careful not to let his lips touch the bottle (his parents wouldn't let him drink at family dinners until he was sixteen, so he may as well enjoy this while he could), then splashed a bit in the chalice.

Rhys held one of the wafers a few inches above the chalice, then raised them both in front of his chest. He squeezed his eyes shut, blocking out every bit of light, and murmured the words of institution. The words of Christ himself, urging his people to eat and drink in memory of him.

If Rhys did this correctly, the wine in his hands would be transformed into blood, the particleboard cracker into the real presence of Christ.

Rhys put the wafer on his tongue and swallowed wine over it, savoring the slow-dissolving bread. He could almost taste the sweat of a laborer's body, the metal tang of a lip split open during roughhousing.

Rhys closed his eyes and willed it to be real, willed the magic inside him to catch fire instead of sputtering and dying out.

Transfigure, Rhys had commanded, wringing his consciousness dry of desire.

In the here and now, Rhys McGowan, High Priest and magician adept, stretched out his hand in the darkness of the conclave room and spoke a few words of Latin. The flickering candles laid out in a circle around him leapt and danced. It didn't always happen, the flames burning higher in response to his chanting, but Rhys was always thrilled by this small manifestation of his own power, the way he could push and pull on the oxygen in the room through sheer will.

The ring of Society members outside the circle stood in perfect silence, hands linked beneath the voluminous sleeves of their wine-red robes. They held him in breathless stillness, the entirety of their collective attention focused on Rhys's work.

"*Manifestus*," he ordered, his voice calm and clear.

Rhys, exceptionally gifted in the domination of spirits but bereft of any psychic intuition, couldn't see if his words sparked the desired manifestation. According to his research, his scryer should be looking for a roiling black mass, like a clump of shadows moving of their own accord.

"Black mass, two o clock," said David Aristarkhov, chief scryer for the Society. David was standing off to Rhys's right in the circle, the sleeves of his robe pushed up to reveal the *Monas Hieroglyphica* tattoo on his inner forearm. David was devil-may-care about protocol. He didn't need to triple-check his work and maintain the utmost decorum during a ritual like Rhys: he could count on his natural psychic prowess to buoy him through instead. "Watch your back."

Rhys pivoted his body to face the manifestation, one hand raised in command. A thousand things could go wrong in the circle, and as the acting sorcerer, he was particularly vulnerable. He needed to keep his head, maintain control of the spirit, and trust David if he wanted to get out of this working unscathed. If he lost his focus, even for a moment, the spirit would wriggle out of the ceremonial circle and disappear. Or worse, it would lash out by plunging the temperature in the room to freezing, or scratching up Rhys with phantom claws.

Luckily, Rhys had attempted much more dangerous workings on much less sleep before, and David, who didn't so much prepare as "get into the zone", was currently well within his zone of excellence.

"*Submit*" Rhys ordered, channeling the burning power in that single word down into his fingertips.

It was important that he *feel* this, really believe it. Without proper intention, spells were empty play-acting. Without correct execution, they were little more than a trick of positive psychology. A true magician adept drew upon both.

The electric tension in the air pulled taut as the spirit resisted Rhys's orders. Rhys couldn't see it bucking like a horse refusing to be bridled, but he could feel cold seeping into his hands in protest. His stomach lurched as that invisible force yanked on him as though straining against a lasso.

"It's getting testy," David said, pacing closer to Rhys. Rhys could feel David's body heat through the haze of power in the circle, smell the bite of his aquatic cologne. The effect was distracting, a markedly human detail in the ephemeral world Rhys had woven from ancient rites. Rhys tried to block out David's warmth and scent, and the visions they conjured of lazy Saturday mornings spent beneath rumpled sheets with David's damp-from-the-shower skin under Rhys's mouth.

"*Submit for me,*" Rhys said, in the sweetest Latin he could conjugate on the spot.

If commanding had fallen flat, cajoling the spirit into submission could work instead. The purpose of an evocation like this was to forge a relationship with a demon, and to convince it to grant boons when called upon, whether through a fair trade or flattery or intimidation. Some demons responded only to the pressure of a metaphorical boot on their throat, while others would grant their assistance only after being wooed with the correct offerings. This spirit, it appeared, needed to be seduced.

"Good," David said, crossing to Rhys's other side. "It's working. Keep buttering it up; it likes that."

Rhys repeated the request, as gentle as a lover. The energy in the room crackled, making the hair on the back of his neck stand up. The spirit was close to them now. He could feel it in the rapid-fire beat of his heart, the way his lips burned with electricity, the way David's breath caught beside him.

Rhys held his hand aloft in invitation, palm up.

"It's shrinking down," David said. "Getting smaller and smaller. It's almost–"

Rhys knew the moment it alighted in his palm. Dark, slick power coursed through him like an oil spill, dangerous and *delicious* and full of cosmic energy to be harnessed.

This, he thought in one grandiose rush, was the reason he practiced magic. The thrill of the moment when a spirit relented, bending itself to his will. The promise that all of his brutal hours of meticulous preparation had cumulated in the moment the universe re-aligned to grant him favor.

"Yes," David said next to his ear, fisting his fingers in triumph. "That's exactly right."

Rhys caged the spirit in his fingers, brought it up to his mouth, and whispered his request, just like when he was a child lighting candles for the saints in his parent's church. Only this time, he wasn't asking for his sisters to stop teasing him, or for his father to get a promotion at work. This was no saint, and it certainly wasn't an angel.

Rhys whispered his plea, focusing all his energy into the supplication. With his eyes closed, it almost felt holy.

And then, as soon as it had begun, the magical working was over. Rhys released the spirit back to whatever liminal realm it had come from with a few words and a pentagram drawn through the air, and David waved his hands to clear the circle of any residual energy.

One of the Society members turned up the lights in the ritual room, revealing a small, dingy room in the basement of a leased Cambridge building. The floor was stone, ideal for chalking out ritual circles and burning resinous incense without leaving a stain behind, and the walls were thick enough to (mostly) insulate the diners in the Cantonese restaurant above from the sound of ominous chanting.

A smattering of applause rippled through the room, along with a few approving murmurs, like a sorcerer's golf clap.

"We did it," Rhys breathed, his skin tingling with the knowledge that his request would be granted. It had to be. His evocation had been flawless.

"*You* did it," David said, clapping Rhys on the shoulder. His green eyes were bright, his wavy bronze hair catching the light like some forgotten Hellenistic demigod. He kissed Rhys on the corner of his mouth, quick and merciless, like a knife wound. David always kissed like he was trying to win a battle.

Rhys stiffened under the public display of affection.

"David," he began warningly.

David gave one of his blithe, golden laughs, the laugh Rhys would have moved Heaven and Earth for on any other day, when he wasn't being watched by his subordinates.

"Loosen up, babe," David said. "You're in charge here."

"Don't 'babe' me in conclave, please," Rhys said, but he couldn't stop smiling.

With the working over, the elaborate ceremonial circle chalked on the floor meant less than a children's game of hopscotch, and shoes scuffled across it thoughtlessly, smudging the yellow lines as Society members milled around the room. Antoni, the Society's treasurer, appeared at Rhys's side, his dark eyes shining with ferocious delight.

"Amazing work," Antoni said. "How did you get it to obey so quickly? That couldn't have taken more than two minutes."

"Practice," Rhys said. That was always his answer, not just because it gatekept all his precise tips and tricks for sorcerous advancement when he was in mixed company, but because it was honest. He would fill Antoni in on the dirtier details later, send over a PDF citing his primary sources and detailing the slight modifications he had made to the circle. Antoni could be trusted with the information, and more importantly, he would appreciate thematically, which made Rhys feel appreciated by extension.

"He's being modest," David said, slinging an arm around Antoni's shoulder. "He says practice, I say talent."

David leaned down to mutter something in Antoni's ear, causing the other man to laugh out loud. It was one of those infectious laughs, more treble than bass and clear as a bell. It reminded Rhys of good-natured arguing about dead occultists' sex lives over nachos in Southie bars. The glares from the waitstaff were worth how much fun it had been to loudly discuss whether Dee topped Kelly or vice versa, with Antoni playing Devil's advocate.

Rhys wanted to join in their chatter, to partake of a little gossip and swapping of field notes, but he had an appointment to keep. One he wouldn't miss for the world.

"David," he said, squeezing his boyfriend's wrist. "Dinner? Moira's waiting for us."

"I'm starving," David said, glancing down at his watch. His eyebrows shot up at the hour. Time had a way of warping in conclave, and they were already running five minutes late for their reservation. "Let's get out of here. Is she at the restaurant already?"

Rhys shimmied out of his robe until he was standing in his usual chinos and Oxford shirt, then hung the robe up on the ancient rolling cart that had probably held robes since the sixties.

"No doubt about it," he said, smiling fondly. "She's never late."

"High Priest," one of the older members said at Rhys's side, a little breathlessly. He was a father of two edging up on his retirement, a late-in-life occultist who was new to the Society. The honorific wasn't necessary, strictly speaking, but Rhys always warmed when he was called by his title. "Can we talk through that money-drawing ritual I proposed last week?"

"Of course," Rhys said, clapping him on the shoulder. "Email me and we'll find some time. But right now, I have to run."

Rhys settled his hand on David's back and politely excused them both from the swirl of conversation. There would be unwinding in the sitting room afterwards, which he usually made a point to stick around for, nursing a gin and tonic and keeping his ears open to any interesting rumors. But the High Priesthood afforded certain privileges, like occasionally being able to leave a Society meeting early to make a dinner date with his two favorite people.

CHAPTER TWO
RHYS

David drove them both in his Audi from Cambridge to the South End, one hand resting on Rhys's thigh. There were still a few leaves clinging to trees outside the window, the city's last gasp of vibrant autumn color. Already, the blanket of gold and orange on the cobblestone streets had started to turn brown, their edges curling and crisp. December would be here before any of them realized it.

Moira was waiting for them in the foyer of a trendy Spanish tapas restaurant, a vision in a tea-length fifties dress with a Peter Pan collar. She was wearing her hair in microbraids these days and sported chunky ceramic bracelets she had probably picked up from the bargain bin at the vintage shop where she worked. Currently, she was cradling the hand of one of the servers, who was watching her with open wonder.

"Hmm," Moira mused, tracing the lines on the palm of this perfect stranger. "A strongly defined life line, but some fractures in your fate line. You haven't had your heart broken recently, have you?"

"I have," the server said, tugging nervously on his ponytail. "My girlfriend broke up with me last week."

"Oh, poor thing," Moira said, in a tone that could have put a cornered wolverine at ease. This was her secret weapon – an uncanny ability to make anyone comfortable opening up within moments of meeting her. "I'm so sorry to hear that. Luckily, you've got good fortune coming your way, and a love line built for partnership. You'll find the right match soon, I'm sure of that."

"Moira," Rhys said, irrepressible affection in his voice. He never got tired of watching his witch wife at work.

Moira turned with a start, like she had been woken from a dream. When she saw Rhys, her brown eyes softened.

"There you are!" she said. "I was just entertaining myself, making some new friends."

David gave the server the kind of glance men in David's tax bracket generally gave to wait-staff, the sort that promised a big tip for privacy. The server nodded and disappeared, leaving the three alone in the foyer.

"Thank you for waiting," Rhys said. He bent down to kiss her, sweet and lingering, on the mouth.

"No trouble at all," she said in her soft Southern drawl. She extended her hand like a duchess to David, who kissed her knuckles, and Moira stood up a little straighter at the touch.

"You're excited about something," she told David. "I take it the summoning went well?'

"It was a thing of beauty," David said. He turned her hand over and kissed her palm with a mischievous smile, probably sending her another jolt of delight. David was better with the dead and Moira was better with the living, but they were both psychic people, bonded by their uncanny insight into the world beyond. "You should have seen him. The spirit never stood a chance."

"You don't have to ingratiate yourself to me anymore," Rhys said as he approached the hostess' stand. "You're already my second in command."

"A little flattery never hurts," David replied.

The trio were seated in an intimate table near the back, and Rhys positioned himself between David, who kept a hand on his knee under the table, and Moira, who held his hand on top of it. David pulled out his Zippo to light the candle on the table.

"Alright, spill," David said once Rhys and Moira had been served their sangria and David had been brought his sparkling water. "What did you ask that spirit for? The ritual was a bitch to plan, so I hope it was something good."

"I'm curious as well," Moira said. She was far from a layman, as she ran her own thriving astrology and tarot business, but she was still getting up to speed on the intricacies of Rhys's ceremonial style of magic. He and

Moira had grown closer in their practices over the last year, sharing more about the ways they interacted with the supernatural world. She even let him help her sometimes, asking him to wave incense around the room while she strained herbal tinctures, and he occasionally invited her to sit in his study with him while he thought out loud, using the assistance of her sharp analytical mind to sort through possible summoning formulas faster than he could by himself.

"What if it's like blowing out birthday candles?" Rhys asked, running his finger along the rim of his glass. "What if it spoils the spell if I say it out loud?"

"I don't think that's how it works," Moira laughed.

"Definitely not," David said.

"Which demon was it?" Moira asked. "That buzzard-looking one who makes people more interesting to talk to at parties?"

"Ipos," David supplied. "He grants charisma. No, we tied things up with him last week. This time, Rhys had us summon a notoriety demon."

Moira made a long humming noise and fixed her husband with a knowing look.

Rhys rubbed the back of his neck self-consciously. He was comforted by rules, formality, the structure of a plated meal to accompany complicated discussion. They had taken three hours over Szechuan once to hash out a schedule that would work for all of them. That meant flexible weekdays, a Friday Rhys spent sleeping over at David's house, and a Sunday that was kept sacred for quality time with Moira. It was enough structure to make everyone (mostly Rhys, who liked understanding social expectations to the letter) feel secure, while still leaving room for David and Moira's spontaneous psychic lessons and shopping trips to Neiman Marcus, or for David to sleep over at the Jamaica Plain house whenever Moira went to go visit her friend Chava in Providence. That wasn't counting all the events they showed up to as a trio, whether they were soaking up the last rays of summer on Nathan's boat or meeting Leda at an underground art installation that inevitably broke zoning laws and fire code.

Rhys took a bracing sip of sangria.

"Do you both really want to know?" he asked.

"Obviously," Moira replied.

"Say you won't make fun of me."

"Of course," Moira replied, at the same time David said, "I'm not promising that."

"I asked for every occultist in the country to know my name," Rhys said, his voice hushed despite the din of the restaurant.

Moira's expression was well-worn: part concern, part amusement. She knew Rhys too well to be impressed by his grandiose tendencies, or to assume that she had any ability to dissuade him from them. If anything, she found his outsized desire for power charming, like he was some kind of wild animal she had domesticated. No matter how Rhys might snarl and show his teeth when threatened, Moira never shrank away, and she was never particularly overwhelmed either. Rhys privately suspected that it excited her. Not his inner darkness itself, but the way she could always chasten him with a look, or entice him into bed and work him over until he was sweet as a lamb.

"Go ahead," Rhys sighed. "Say whatever you're thinking."

"Why in the world would you ask for something as volatile and thankless as fame?" she asked.

"I didn't ask for fame," Rhys corrected. "I asked for recognition within my own discipline. That's different."

"Alright, let's say it's different," Moira said, leaning across the table and latticing her fingers together. "Why ask for it?"

Rhys chewed on the inside of his mouth, re-formulating his words. He hadn't asked to be born with all this ambition inside him, just in the same way he hadn't asked to be born bisexual, or to be born with anxiety that flared up at the slightest provocation. Even as a small child, he had devoted hours to studying the rules of checkers and hopscotch to ensure he could become the best player possible, then dissolved into infuriated tears when other children broke the rules. By twelve, he was a straight-A student with his eye on a select handful of elite colleges, reading at an eleventh-grade level and often lying awake worrying that his science project wasn't up to par. By fifteen, he was the most dedicated altar boy at his parish, not to mention a budding occultist who spent nights reading Agrippa under the covers with a flashlight until his eyes stung.

Rhys had been called an "old soul" so often and from such a young age that he had started to believe there really was something ancient about him, something fundamentally ill-suited to the frivolities of childhood. Being the eldest child and the only boy in his family hadn't helped matters, either.

It had always been what set him apart, that drive, that need for *more*. It pushed him forward across every shadowy threshold and beyond every moving goalpost.

"I feel like I've stagnated in my own magical practice," Rhys said. "It's become rote. I'm not being challenged."

Moira snorted.

"You practice more than any other magical person I know," she said, stabbing a butter-basted mushroom with her fork. "You spend your days locked in your study, digging up progressively weirder rituals to try at the Society. You've got the Priesthood. Isn't that enough for you?"

David nodded at Moira's fork, asking for a bite. She stabbed another, smaller mushroom and fed it to him, as though he were a prize Persian cat being rewarded with a treat. David grimaced as he chewed and swallowed – he wasn't a big fan of fungi – but Moira looked pleased he had tried it.

"You could coast," David said, dabbing his mouth with a napkin. "I know that's pretty much antithetical to your entire existence, but most people would kill to be where you are now. You could just put your feet up and enjoy the spoils of your conquest, keep the gears of the Society turning while keeping up on your studies. That's what I would have done, if I was High Priest."

"And that's why you're not High Priest," Rhys said mildly. As Rhys's second in command, all David really had to do was back him up during split votes and sit in on meetings, occasionally offering his admittedly expert opinions. Other than the vanity title, David got free run of the Society, not to mention first dibs on scrying. It was all he had really wanted, at the end of the day.

"Fair," David said.

"Maintenance has its place, but as High Priest, it's my responsibility to make sure my skills stay sharp. How else can I be expected to lead others? I might have won the Priesthood, but now I need to prove I deserve the position. I'm not going to pretend that the Society is doing well for itself right now."

"Ya'll are doing fine," Moira said. She shot a look to David. He was the right person to go to if you wanted the truth without sugar-coating. "Right?"

"It's been a bit of a tight year, financially speaking," David said. "And we're not exactly swimming in new applicants. But that's just the way these kinds of organizations work, it's an ebb and flow."

"It's been ebbing for fifteen years now," Rhys said. David was the ultimate optimist, and Rhys was a born pessimist, which was one of the reasons they balanced each other out as a couple. But sometimes, like right now, it made it very difficult to get David to see the grave reality of a situation. "Wayne barely kept any records, and the records he did keep don't paint a very encouraging picture. We're hemorrhaging money."

"I doubt that," David said. "We're fine. We're always fine."

"We've only been fine because of huge one-off donations. How many times do you think your father bailed the Society out? Take a wild guess."

"I don't know," David said with a shrug. "Once? Twice?"

It was Rhys's turn to nod at the dish of mushrooms. Moira speared him a much bigger piece and fed it to him, then sucked the fork clean.

"Four times," he said after he had swallowed. "Your father kept the Society afloat as his personal social club for years, but he's dead now, and any money he donated has been spent. Our influence in ceremonial magical circles has waned so much we're basically a joke, and there are plenty of other organizations sniffing around who would love to absorb us."

"Then I'll just bail us out again," David said, seeing nothing humiliating about this offer. "Evgeni's money is my money now; what does it matter who signs the checks?"

Rhys swallowed down his knee-jerk impulse to swat David's generosity away. David was only trying to help. He had never understood why taking handouts was so hard for Rhys, and probably never would.

"I appreciate that, but it won't fix the problem. I need to completely overhaul the way the Society has been running in order to preserve it. This is my cross to bear, David. Not yours."

A sad expression crossed Moira's face.

"I love you very much," she said. "But sometimes I wish you would take up golf or tabletop roleplaying or something. You need a hobby."

"Magic is a hobby," Rhys said.

"Sure it is," David said, tone dancing on the borderline of bitchy.

Rhys scowled down at the table as the server brought out more small plates. Maybe the ritual had been a little self-serving, but he wasn't giving up on advancing his magical practice, not when he had so many people depending on him. If he couldn't set a shining example of what rigor and discipline looked like as High Priest, what was he even good for?

"Don't sulk," Moira said, passing him a plate of charred broccolini. "We're just looking out for your health. You promise you'll raise your hand if you start feeling overwhelmed? There's no shame in asking for help."

David nudged him encouragingly under the table, and Rhys lifted his gaze. David was giving him a look of affectionate knowing, and Moira leaned over to kiss him on the cheek. Rhys was suddenly seized with love for both of them, so strong he could barely breathe.

Good enough. He had to be good enough for them.

"I promise," Rhys said.

In that moment, he almost believed he wasn't lying.

CHAPTER THREE
MOIRA

The bell over the door to the Botanica De La Curación dinged merrily as Moira shouldered her way into the metaphysical supply store, cradling a to-go order of spicy carrot soup to her chest. The comforting scent of Lorena's shop filled her nostrils; candles rubbed down with peppery protective oil, sweet tobacco smoke, wooden prayer beads, and of course, that inescapable carnation and currant perfume that always followed Lorena around in a cloud.

"I made it!" Moira called, her voice carrying easily through the modestly sized – and at this time in the morning – totally empty shop. It was frigid outside, and Moira was grateful that Lorena always kept the heat cranked up in here. Moira always missed Georgia most in the winter, especially summers on her family's hobby farm. She missed fried green tomatoes served with her mother's spicy pepper preserves and the sound of her father plucking out guitar melodies on their front porch in the muggy twilight. She ached for August thunderstorms and lazy afternoons walking the wildflower-speckled trails into town.

Moira ambled down the nearest aisle, careful not to knock anything over.

"Lorena, are you here?"

"Herb wall," Lorena called back in her Spanish accented alto, to-the-point as always. Moira often wondered if David's directness had come built-in, or if it was something he had picked up from Lorena, who was his godmother in every way that mattered.

Moira weaved through the shelves of tinctures and holy oils and hand-painted plaster statues to the very back of the store. Lorena balanced on an ancient stepladder in orthopedic shoes, up on her tip-toes to reach for the top shelf.

"Let me help," Moira fretted, setting the soup down on the counter.

"I'm a foot taller than you and I can barely reach," Lorena said with a chuckle, carefully arranging the mason jars of dried peppermint and stinging nettle on the shelf. "No sense in both of us breaking our backs."

"You'd better not even break a nail up there," Moira said, but left it at that. She had developed a good rapport with Lorena during her monthly trips to the botanica to pick up yarrow and candles, but Moira still minded her manners when she was around the older woman. As an importer and purveyor of magical supplies, Lorena was one of the most well-connected occultists Moira knew, not to mention a priestess of Santeria and a devotee of the powerful folk saint Santa Muerte. Lorena was kind, she was wise, and she was patient. But she didn't suffer fools, and she certainly didn't tolerate disrespect.

Lorena waggled her fingers down at Moira with a mischievous expression, showing that her acrylic manicure was already chipped. But then, having adjusted the jars to her standards, she carefully dismounted the stepladder.

Lorena gave Moira a warm hug, and Moira pushed up on her toes to kiss the older woman's cheek.

"Have some soup," Moira said. "How's your cough?"

"Oh, I'll live," Lorena said, in that half-joking world-weary way that reminded Moira so much of her late grandmother. "It's just a winter cold. And there's nothing soup can't fix. Thank you for picking that up for me."

"Any time," Moira said, trying to sound breezy. To tell the truth, she had been thrilled when Lorena had texted her to say her custom oil order was ready, then texted her *again* to ask her to run an errand on her way over. It seemed like an invitation into deeper friendship, and it felt good to be relied upon by someone so powerful. That made Moira feel powerful too, a sensation she liked quite a bit, even if she pretended that she didn't.

Lorena took a seat behind the register and propped her feet up on a little cushioned stool, unwrapping the plasticware that came with her lunch. She nodded at an upturned wooden crate with a padded blanket folded tidily on top, bidding Moira sit.

22   ASCENSION

Moira took her seat, smoothing the pleated skirt of her 80s dress, which she wore layered over thick tights and a turtleneck sweater.

"Don't you have young people on staff who can do the grunt work for you?" Moira asked.

"Daniella is out sick with the same cold, and Jude is at his little sister's baptism. Thank you for playing errand girl in their stead." Lorena popped the plastic lid off her soup, inhaling the aroma. "Ginger, turmeric, and cayenne. That's good medicine."

"We don't want you to be sick on your flight," Moira said. There would be time to gather and pay for her order later. She was Southern; she knew the value of a little unhurried chit-chat. "Are you excited to see your family for the holidays?"

"Very much," Lorena said, taking a dainty bite of soup so as not to disturb her lipstick, the same brick-red color she had been wearing every day for years. "I miss my sister and her little ones every day. We always have such a good time gossiping and cooking together, even though she always gets distracted and burns the plantains. I'd like to make the pilgrimage to the shrine at Rincón as well, to petition Babalú-Ayé and San Lázaro for my health. And maybe, if the kids are lucky, I'll take them out to watch fireworks. I hate the noise, but through prayer and earplugs, all things are possible."

"You absolutely deserve a rest," Moira said. "Will you be visiting your husband's family in Guatemala as well?"

"Not this year. Too little time and too little money, but isn't that always the case?"

From what Moira understood from Lorena's scattershot stories, she had spent the first twenty-five years of her life sweeping floors and stocking shelves at a grocery store in Cuba while diligently studying Santeria. After being initiated into the tradition, she had begun working at a botanica, assisting with rituals and continuing her study until she became a santera, or priestess.

"How did you meet him, anyway?" Moira asked. "I don't think I ever asked."

"A better question would be to ask me how I met Santa Muerte," Lorena replied. She was making short work of the soup, and there was more color in her face now. "I was happy in Havana, but my heart was restless. I went to Guatemala to clear my head. One night I saw a group of my neighbors praying at a little street shrine to the Bony

Lady. Someone's son had been killed by the police. They gathered to cry together, to pray for his soul, to ask Santa Muerte for justice. Their devotion moved something deep inside me. I came back to that shrine day after day, simply to admire her. On the third day, I offered up my own prayer, for luck in love. Not two hours later I turned a corner and ran headlong into this handsome young man selling flowers. He spilled lilies all over me, and splashed water on my dress. He was so embarrassed. He insisted on buying me a soda and sitting with me until my clothes were dry. That was Jorge. We've been together ever since, and I've been loyal to Santa Muerte since that night."

"That's a lovely story," Moira said, warming as ever in the light of someone else's love. She reminded herself to leave a small offering at Santa Muerte's altar when she left the shop. Moira didn't understand everything about the saint, and she was still a little wary of the skeletal, veiled figure, but she understood that Santa Muerte had protected Lorena, her family, and her business for decades, and that was worth Moira's respect. "But selfishly, I'm glad you and Jorge moved to Boston. We'd all be lost without you."

"Rhys would have a much harder time getting his hands on those obscure incense cones he's always ordering," Lorena said good-naturedly. "And David would have no idea what to do with himself. I believe I owe you a dominating oil, however."

Lorena reached behind her towards the shelf where brown bags of magical supply orders were kept. She retrieved a small square bottle from one of the bags, holding it up to the light so Moira could see the herbs suspended in the murky green oil. Dominating oil was most often used to soften other people's wills, typically through making the magician more persuasive, threatening, or authoritative. Lorena sold a perfectly serviceable dominating oil to her customers every day, batching it up monthly. But Moira had placed a custom order for a blend with a little extra juice.

Specifically, a domination blend strong enough to work on other occultists.

"Now who is this for?" Lorena asked. "Should I be concerned that you're casting spells on my other customers?"

"It's just a little peace of mind," Moira said, offering her sweetest smile. "I'm married to a High Priest now. The Society has enemies, which means Rhys does too. I hope I don't have to use this on anyone, but it makes me feel better knowing it's in my kitchen cabinet."

Lorena hummed thoughtfully, giving the bottle a shake for luck before handing it to Moira. The glass was warm in her hands.

"Take my advice, *nina*. But remember that most often, the best way to overcome your enemies is to keep yourself in their good graces. Why do you think I took David in when he was sixteen and sour and useless at stocking shelves? Out of the goodness of my heart?"

"I assumed you were friends with David's father," Moira said, tucking the oil away in her purse. It was unlabeled, just as she requested. If Rhys discovered the oil while looking for sugar in the cabinets she could just pretend it was for protection, or drawing money, or something similarly benign. She didn't like keeping things from her husband, but she was willing to fudge the truth a little if it meant not worrying Rhys about his wife quietly stockpiling magical weapons.

Besides, she was probably being overly cautious. It wasn't like she was ever going to need to use this.

Lorena barked out a laugh, then reached for her lighter. It was an ancient brass thing, emblazoned with a snake and roses. She produced a cigarillo from the drawer of the register then tore open the packaging and placed the fragrant miniature cigar between her lips.

"You know David lectures me for smoking these, every time?" Lorena said, taking a few puffs. "Says I'm going to keel over from a heart attack. I've been smoking for forty years, and he still goes and stands outside to have his cigarettes, rain or shine, just so I don't breathe in the fumes."

A warm bloom spread through Moira's chest. David could be an asshole, that came with the territory, but no one who really knew him could ever say that he wasn't also deeply kind to those he loved.

"But no," Lorena said, sobering slightly. "I was never friends with Evgeni. Contemporaries, certainly; we were the same age in the same city at the same time. But he never respected me, and I didn't have a very high opinion of him. He could be charming, and he was level-headed in a crisis. But he was a cruel man, humorless and miserly. And he ran David into the ground, always making him channel spirits after school late into the night. I gave David a safe place to go because he didn't have one, and because I thought I could help him, but also because I knew if Evgeni owed me a favor, he was less likely to move against me, magically or otherwise."

"I never knew that," Moira said, disparate puzzle pieces coming together neatly.

"And," Lorena said, smoking thoughtfully, "I had hoped to talk some common sense into this boy who stood to inherit such a powerful legacy. I liked David right away, and I loved him quickly afterwards. He loved me too, and I think Evgeni saw that. David must have been speaking too highly of me, or coming over too often, because Evgeni forbade David from visiting for quite some time. I didn't see him for years, not until Evgeni finally died."

"But he found his way back to you in the end, didn't he?" Moira asked. She was aware that her instinctive positive outlook could chafe against more practical people, that sometimes there was simply no silver lining to be had. But Lorena gave her such a soft, sincere smile that Moira knew her perspective was appreciated.

"I suppose he did."

Lorena's phone chirped, and she flipped it up from where it sat, face down, on the register.

"Ah, there's my little mage now," Lorena said, then pulled the phone to her ear. She then said, as brusquely as if she had not just been talking sweetly about her wayward godson: "What, you can't be bothered to call an old woman back until it pleases you? I needed you hours ago."

"I was in court, Lorena," David said, sighing extravagantly. "I'm on my lunch break now. Do you still want soup? I'll pick you up some pho and run it over."

"I already got my soup," Lorena sniffed. "You've been replaced. Moira, say hello."

"Hello," Moira said, leaning forward to speak into the phone Lorena proffered.

"Is that Moira?" David asked, sounding offended and delighted at the same time. "Listen, don't do that old witch any favors, you'll just end up owing her your firstborn child."

"Don't be a pill," Lorena said. "Will you still come see me today?"

"Of course I will. And let me fix that goddamn awning over the door, it drips all over me every time it rains."

"I'll let you," Lorena said, eyes sparkling with mirth. "See you soon, *mijo*. Be safe. I love you."

"Love you too," David replied. Then, raising his voice so Moira could hear. "Bye, Moira!"

With that, the call disconnected. Lorena chuckled as she rose to her feet, patting Moira on the shoulder.

"He's always so much nicer when you're around. I'm amazed you managed to tame that little pit viper."

"Oh, he barely bites," Moira said in her most syrupy drawl.

"I was serious about that oil," Lorena said, ashing her cigarillo into a clamshell and counting the money in the till and ordering the rosaries hanging behind the counter by color, like a many-armed octopus with a single-minded dedication to managing inventory. "It's the most potent stuff I sell, and it will knock anybody on their ass, no matter how well they're warded or what gods they pray to. Dominate responsibly."

"Yes, ma'am," Moira said, kissing Lorena's cheek one more time. "And you finish that soup."

"Yes, ma'am," Lorena said, already lost in counting change.

On her way out the door, Moira dropped into a baby-sized version of her best cotillion curtsey in front of the altar to Santa Muerte, set up in a place of honor away from the other statues. Then she fished around in her brocade purse for two quarters and a Werther's Original, and placed them respectfully at Santa Muerte's feet along with the other offerings. After a moment of thought, she untied the lavender ribbon holding back her braids and offered it as well.

"Bless Lorena with good fortune," Moira whispered under her breath, then slipped out of the shop.

CHAPTER FOUR
RHYS

Rhys knew the results of a ritual took time to manifest, even if the ritual had been done perfectly and to the letter, but that didn't spare him the very human frustration of impatience. Like a child on Christmas Day, he awoke each morning to check his email and his mailbox for any interesting invitations, and to log into various occult discords to see if anyone had mentioned the Society (or him) in any context that wasn't just poking fun at that dusty Golden Dawn offshoot barely holding on to life in Beantown.

Each morning, Rhys was disappointed.

The Society could be doing much worse: most occult brotherhoods dissolved within decades due to ideological schisms, sex scandals, and embezzlement. The fact that the Society had been holding on this long – since 1968! – was a testament to its endurance. But the Society wasn't exactly influential, and it certainly wasn't chic. Older practitioners steered clear of Rhys's organization, knowing they were too stubborn to welcome friendly criticism, and young occultists congregated on TikTok, not in basements. When they did meet in person they gathered in private homes where they could discuss Wicca or chaos magic or lucky girl manifestation without bothering with membership dues.

Rhys knew that ceremonial magic, with its regimented operations and strict hierarchy and endless lists of expensive ingredients and tools, wasn't exactly twenty-first-century friendly. But that was exactly why Rhys loved it: its antiquated sheen.

Still, it would be nice if they had a bigger budget, or a larger space to meet, or perhaps any charismatic spokesperson outside of David. David had no interest in trading on his father's name for clout, despite the dozens of pleading invites he got every year to speak at occult conferences or appear on podcasts. He had a vested interest in keeping the Society small and intimate, just the way he liked it. It wasn't malicious, David's desire to keep his friends close and strangers far away. He just liked things as they were, and that was no crime, but Rhys was hungry for expansion. Influence. *Reputation.*

And he refused to sit on his hands while he waited for the demon of notoriety to do its work.

Rhys spent a few days calling around other occult societies to formally introduce himself. Wayne hadn't bothered with introductions before absconding to warmer climates, and Rhys had been so swamped in getting up to speed on running of things over the past few months that he hadn't had much time for rubbing elbows. So, Rhys went hunting for phone numbers in the leather address book Wayne had abandoned in his office.

"Is this Wayne?" asked a woman, presumably the head of the Rosicrucian order, Rhys has dialed.

"No, actually," Rhys said brightly. "My name is Rhys McGowan, I'm the current High Priest and I thought I might call to–"

"When Wayne gets back will you please tell him I'm still waiting for him to return my book on geomancy?"

With that, the line disconnected. Rhys called a handful of other local leaders, meeting outright suspicion and hostility at worst and, at best, empty promises to "get lunch sometime". Unlike David, his name didn't carry enough weight to open doors, and his youth certainly wasn't doing him any favors. Even the most pleasant conversations invited him to read between the lines: Rhys had been tapped in to steer a sinking ship, and he would spend the rest of his twenties doing everything within his limited power to keep it from running aground.

Only one person gave him the time of day: the leader of the New York City branch of the Ordo Templi Orientis.

"I'm not sure how much help I can offer," said the man on the other end of the phone. He had that polished, clipped way of talking that spoke a life lived mostly within the confines of the Upper East Side. "But I sympathize with you. I was apprenticed into my position. I couldn't imagine trying to figure it all out myself."

Rhys opened his mouth to say, politely but firmly, that he wasn't looking for help or a handout, but the man on the other end just kept talking.

"Maximilian is up there, though. He might be able to steer you right."

Rhys didn't want a mentor, or worse, someone to pity him while he floundered, but he didn't exactly have many options, so he clicked his pen.

"What's that name again?"

"Maximilian Markos. He's in art, I think. As I understand it, he's back in Boston for work, but he's also a senior leader in the OTO. We answer to the same frater superior. I'll give you his number. Ready?"

Rhys dutifully wrote down the number, then said thank you twice before he hung up to avoid embarrassing himself further.

Rhys glanced back in Wayne's address book. That was the last occult leader's number he had on file. He sighed, slipped the phone number into the address book, and snapped it shut. His face burned with humiliation. He knew making a name for himself would be hard, but he didn't expect people to actively refuse to take his calls.

Inadequacy haunted his steps like a starving hound, nipping at his heels.

Rhys pinched the bridge of his nose and sighed heavily.

He had been convinced that if someone had just given him the chance to step into a leadership role, he would shine, but instead he felt like he was drowning. The role was more demanding than he could have ever imagined, and now that the crown had been lowered onto his head, he was gripped by the belief that he didn't deserve it. He still made mistakes in his own practice, for God's sake. Just last week he had burned copal incense during a ritual that called for frankincense, then spilled holy water all over his desk when he rushed to smother the smoldering mess.

How could he expect to guide others if he wasn't himself above reproach?

He didn't have the privilege of someone like David, who had been born into occult royalty and raised up as a prodigy. Unlike his wife with her witch's intuition, Rhys had no inherent magical abilities, and he didn't have the edge of bottomless energy that Antoni's youth gave him. Hell, he didn't even have his Society friend Nathan's near-supernatural ability to broker peace wherever he went, or Nathan's wife Kitty's family tradition of magical excellence to lean on.

At the end of the day, Rhys only had the strength of his own mind and the scope of his own ambition to rely on. In the dark of the ritual room, where the physical world fell away and he stepped heedless of consequence into the shadows, it was all that stood between him and ruination.

Not to mention all that prevented the lives of those he loved from once again falling in jeopardy.

Last summer, Rhys had watched his oldest friend writhe in agony in a ceremonial circle, sobbing and begging for death. Rhys had never felt so hopeless as he had standing over David's convulsing body, crushed by the realization that he wasn't strong enough to break the centuries-old chains around David's soul.

David had survived on a technicality alone, a loophole Rhys had barely been quick enough to exploit, and it had taken Moira's level-headed might to pull David back from the brink. That loophole had passed the Aristarkhov curse on to Rhys, but Rhys had inherited none of David's supernatural charm in the tradeoff, only the ticking clock counting down to Rhys's thirtieth birthday. That felt fitting, if in a cruel way.

There had to be a more permanent way to wiggle out of the Aristarkhov deal, one David assured him they would find as he fried up eggs for breakfast in his condo. Moira kept Rhys company while he read through historical exorcism accounts, her feet in his lap as she embroidered glyphs onto charm bags and helped him sort through his options. Both his lovers seemed to think he would live to see thirty-one, and they both seemed to believe that he deserved to.

The only thing Rhys felt he deserved was this infernal albatross around his neck. It was his fault David had very nearly died, his fault Moira had drained herself to the point of exhaustion.

If any of them had to bear this burden, Rhys would rather it be him.

Rhys's phone vibrated his pocket.

"Jesus, Joseph and Mary," he swore under his breath, irritated to be pulled out of his thoughts.

Rhys retrieved his phone. It was his mother.

"Hey Ma," Rhys said, his hereditary Southie accent creeping in. He had worked hard in college to round out his flattened vowels and drop some of the Boston slang he grew up with, but old habits died hard. "How are you?"

"Oh, I'm good, John Michael," Mary Ann McGowan said on the other end. Rhys bristled at his given name but said nothing. He had been going by his middle name since he was eighteen, but he couldn't very well hold his parents accountable for not calling him Rhys when he had never been brave enough to tell him that he preferred it. John had been his grandfather's name, and Michael was his confirmation saint. Telling his mother to call him Rhys would feel like betraying his family, somehow.

"You sound out of breath."

Mary Ann was perpetually frazzled. She had raised one boy and three girls while holding down a part-time secretary job for most of Rhys's life, plus she was on the flower committee of their local parish and headed up the yearly food drive and the women's knitting circle. Rhys's childhood memories of his mother were of a woman perpetually in motion, never at rest.

"Oh, your father was just giving me grief for burning the dinner rolls, but what can you do?"

"I am not," Rhys's father Arthur called distantly. Mary Ann and Arthur's durable affection for each other was built on a foundation of mutual ribbing and dry sarcasm.

"You always leave them in too long, I keep telling you that," Rhys said. "You can't trust what they say on the box, you've got to eyeball it."

"What can a woman do except her best, by the grace of God?" Mary Ann said, martyred.

Rhys smiled despite himself. Talking to his mother was like walking a tightrope, but if he managed to stop worrying about slipping up and tumbling into her disapproval, it was enjoyable.

"Anyway, how are you?" Rhys's mother asked, and he could tell from the quality of the audio that he had been put on speakerphone.

"Doing fine. Busy with work, as always."

As far as his traditional Catholic parents were concerned, Rhys spent most of his working hours in the library, and he was part of an extracurricular circle of scholars in his field. It wasn't the biggest lie he had ever told them. It was almost the truth, if he squinted and ignored the demon-summoning.

If you put a gun to Rhys's head and told him to choose between telling his parents that he was a sorcerer, that he was bisexual, or that he was polyamorous, he would tell you to pull the trigger and get it over with.

"Alright. That's good," Mary Ann said. She didn't sound convinced. Rhys could practically see her face, pinched with worry.

"Is something wrong?" he asked, too anxious to do anything but cut straight to the chase. "Did Dolores fail the SAT again?"

"No, nothing's wrong. We just haven't heard from you in a month, and we thought we'd check in. Everything good with the job? Good with Moira?"

"Everything's great," Rhys said, forcing brightness into his voice. He shouldn't have gone so long without calling home. He would set a reminder next time, stay on top of it. "Moira and I are doing well; still planning on coming down for Christmas. Work is great; I actually, uh... got a promotion."

"That's right!" Arthur put in from somewhere in the distance. "About time they took notice of you and did something about it."

Rhys plastered on a smile, even though his parents couldn't see him. It made the dishonesty easier.

"We're proud of you," Mary Ann said, her voice so warm that Rhys felt sick. "We never worry about you, you know that? You've always been such a high achiever."

"Thanks, Ma," Rhys said, his throat dry.

It wasn't that his parents had a track record of reacting poorly when he fell short of their expectations. It was just that he had never done it before, and he wasn't about to start now.

"I'm sorry to jump off," he went on. "But you caught me in the middle of something. I'll give you a call this weekend and we can catch up properly. Sound good?"

"Wonderful. Give our best to Moira! We love you, John Michael."

"Love you too," Rhys said, once again resisting the urge to correct her. It was somehow always easier to be whoever they wanted him to be.

The line went dead, and Rhys tossed the phone down on his desk, sighing heavily. On the one hand, lying got easier the longer you did it, but on the other hand, lies tended to compound and grow heavier over time. It would be nice to be known fully by his family and accepted for who he was, but Rhys was a pragmatist. He lived in the real world, and all the data pointed to coming out of any closet going poorly.

It didn't usually bother him, carrying around the weight of a decade of secrecy, but for some reason, probably because he was already exhausted and frayed, that day it made angry tears prick at his eyes.

Rhys swore under his breath and blinked skyward, refusing to lose precious time and even more precious pride to crying. Instead, he flipped open the next grimoire in the stack.

Rhys splayed his fingers over a Latin evocation, his eyes skimming the spell as fast as his grasp of the language would allow.

If the demon of notoriety was going to drag its feet giving Rhys what he wanted, he would just have to do it himself. God helped those who helped themselves, right?

Strictly speaking, Rhys was already at capacity. There were half a dozen demons in his stable, and it took an immense amount of energy to keep them placated, disciplined, and on call. They each required different boons to keep Rhys in their good graces; offerings of incense smoke and hand-peeled fruit and strong whiskey, and little supplications written out in blood-red ink and burned by candlelight. He spent almost an hour a day tending the offering plates set up around his study and warding the house to keep it safe from the nastier demons on his roster. It was probably excessive, but he justified it by telling himself that most people spent that much time a day on social media. Besides, he wasn't willing to gamble with Moira's safety and spiritual wellbeing, especially since she operated her business out of the house.

An old sorcerer's superstition capped the number of spirits any one magician could comfortably control at seven. Any more than that, and the spirits would start running the show. The stories weren't exactly clear on what that entailed. Sometimes they suggested garden-variety descent into lunacy or moral decrepitude, while other tales warned of mysterious physical ailments like bloody tears and a preternaturally shortened life span.

But that seven-spirit-rule was more a guideline than a commandment. Besides, Rhys had heard legends of occultists who had commanded entire armies of demons.

If they could do it, so could Rhys.

He was daring enough, he was smart enough, and most importantly, he wanted it badly enough.

Rhys drew the curtains, shrouding his study in darkness, and took a deep breath.

Then he retrieved a stick of white chalk from his desk drawer, knelt onto the creaking floorboards, and began to chalk out the ceremonial circle for his new evocation.

CHAPTER FIVE
DAVID

David tapped his fingers rhythmically against the underside of the bistro table, antsy for a cigarette after close to three hours of strategizing. He wanted to excuse himself for a walk around the block, but he wasn't willing to miss a minute of the rapid-fire financial discussions currently going on between Rhys and Antoni. His role as second in command was mostly ornamental, with few real duties – David didn't do well with bureaucracy – but he still never skipped a meeting. It felt good to be consulted.

"What's your opinion on pursuing alternative investments?" Rhys asked, taking a sip of his Turkish coffee. Rhys and his chosen council were seated in a booth at Sofra, the Middle Eastern bistro where they had been brunching for years. Many in that group had been promoted into administrative roles after Rhys's ascension, including David, Nathan, Kitty, and Antoni.

Antoni Bresciani leaned forward in his seat, sorting through the contents of a thick manilla envelope. He was short and sturdy, from Italian stock that had gifted him with thick dark hair, skin that tanned bronze in the summer, and expensive taste in imported suits.

"I've done as you asked and transferred most of our assets into more aggressive investment portfolios already," Antoni said, in his loan officer day job voice. Nothing tempered Antoni's spitfire personality quite as much as math. "So far, they're holding well, although some market fluctuations are to be expected. We're likely to feel them more with these riskier investments, so I wouldn't suggest pursuing alternatives at this time, certainly not more than one or two percent of total allocations. We could easily find ourselves overleveraged."

Rhys pushed papers around on the table, surveying the printed numbers with quick efficiency. David watched his hands as he worked, admiring the long, agile fingers, the short, clean nails. He used to steal these appreciative glances at Rhys surreptitiously, but now David could look as much as he wanted.

However, it would be more fun watching Rhys at his most competent and therefore most sexy if the air wasn't so tense. Brunch used to be a time to unwind, but things had changed after Rhys had become High Priest.

Rhys ran a tighter ship than Wayne, which David supposed was necessary, but Rhys didn't have Wayne's easy charisma or gregarious nature. Rhys brought the laser-focus of an academic to his work as High Priest, never dropping a detail or overlooking a mistake, whether it was his or someone else's. David missed the old days, when the rules were looser, and they could all get away with cutting more corners.

"How's the endowment looking?" Rhys went on.

"Before or after adjusting for your salary?" Antoni replied.

"Salary?" Nathan asked, plucking his sunglasses out of his perfectly coiffed black hair and tucking them into the front of his shirt. Nathan Vo was a California transplant from a wealthy Chinese American family and the Society's chief recruitment officer. Which was a fancy way of saying that Nathan was the most personable out of all of them and the most likely to be able to rope in new recruits.

"I'm going to make a public announcement at the next Society meeting," Rhys said. "But I'm quitting my position at the library. Running the Society is my full-time job now."

The only sounds that broke the ensuing silence were the shuffling of feet under the table and the rustling of napkins in laps. David's hand slid towards the Parliaments in his pocket before he remembered that he was indoors, and so, robbed of his usual response to awkward silences, he stared at Rhys in disbelief.

Rhys smiled at his compatriots, but it was a thin, unconvincing smile. Unlike David, charm was not among his gifts.

"We need someone putting in at least forty hours a week of magical and admin work, not to mention the social side of things," Rhys said. "It just makes sense."

"I admire your dedication," Nathan said.

"It's going to be good for the Society," Antoni said, gathering up his equities printouts without meeting Rhys's eyes.

Kitty, who tended not to speak when she didn't have anything nice to say, offered a diplomatically neutral expression.

"I've taken the time to think this through," Rhys said, sighing. A little of his kingly mask slipped, revealing the sullen teenager beneath. David preferred him this way, honest even when it was unflattering. "Come on, you all know I'm good for it."

"And you've run this by Moira?" David asked. Irritation, hot and prickling, built in his chest.

"Of course. I ran it by you too."

David remembered. Rhys had been standing on his condo balcony, dreaming out loud about quitting his job while the wind rustled his curls. David had indulged his scheming, swept away by the charming scene and sure that it was just a pipe dream.

"Hypothetically, sure. And I told you it *might* be a good idea in the new year. I didn't know you were pulling the trigger now."

Rhys's shoulders sagged. Only an inch, but David caught it.

"I'm telling you now, all of you, ahead of anyone else."

"How much are you paying yourself?" David asked. He'd rather get right down to brass tacks instead of watch Rhys's halfhearted attempts to backtrack. David was getting better at keeping his head when Rhys pissed him off, and he tried to remind himself that this slight wasn't monumental in the grand scheme of things.

But on the other hand, David had never known Rhys to do anything without an ulterior motive, and Rhys lied most when covering up one of his schemes.

"Nothing extravagant," Rhys said. "Fifteen percent more than I got paid at the library, all above board and run by Antoni. It's in the budget."

David took a long sip of his sparkling water and didn't push the issue. This was something to be hashed out in private, without Kitty smiling behind the fingers pressed to her mouth and without Antoni and Nathan exchanging nervous looks across the table. In the past, David and Rhys had been known for airing their dirty laundry publicly. David was intent on not making that mistake again.

"David?" Rhys prompted. It was a gentle inquiry, more lover than superior, more friend than Society brother. An invitation to open up, if David was willing to accept it.

David didn't bite.

"Congratulations on the raise," David said.

Rhys watched him a moment more, uncertainty flickering behind his eyes, but then it was gone.

"How are recruitment numbers looking?" Rhys asked, in control once again.

David breathed deeply through his nose and turned inwards, screwing a lid on his feelings. He was in no position to preach to anyone about greed. Still, he wished Rhys would have given him a heads-up sooner.

Kitty Vo set down her butter knife and straightened in her chair. The first female initiate in the Society's history, Kitty was one of the city's most sought-after interior designers, not least of all because she incorporated traditional feng shui energy manipulation techniques into her designs. Because she was so new, she didn't have a dedicated role in the Society yet, but she had thrown herself into learning everything she could about goetia, and she was an immense help with their recruitment efforts.

"Nathan and I are having a potential new applicant over for coffee next week," Kitty said, hooking her sleek black bob behind her ears. "We're hoping to sway him into throwing his name in for the Society instead of the Rosicrucian order. And I'm in talks with a TikToker who specializes in folk magic. She's interested in branching out into ceremonial magic. I told her I would bring her as my guest to the next Society social, so she could introduce herself to the members."

"Thank you, Kitty," Rhys said. "I'm hoping to initiate at least five new members by the end of the quarter."

"Five?" Nathan said. "I thought we were aiming to take two or three a year."

"If we want to be able to fund all the new initiatives Rhys is pushing through, we're going to need to see an uptick in membership dues," Antoni admitted.

"Why don't I just fund us through the fiscal year?" David said, swirling around his San Pellegrino. He didn't like the idea of a tidal wave of new blood rushing into the Society. It might be where David went to hone his magical skills, but it was first and foremost his own private social club. In his mind, it was already full enough.

"That won't be necessary," Rhys replied.

"My father–"

"You're not your father. And I'm not Wayne. I can handle it."

Arguing with Rhys when it came to money was a losing battle. Rhys's pride still didn't allow him to accept cash or large gifts from David, even though he had mellowed out enough to let David pay for dinner now and then.

"What's the verdict on Cameron?" Nathan asked, sipping on his gooseberry soda. The divinity school professor hadn't been able to join them that day, but he was, as always, with them in spirit.

"I'm going to keep him on retainer as a researcher," Rhys said. "He can translate new spells for us, or cross-reference sources to make sure we're using the most historically accurate version of rituals."

And, David thought, *it allows you to keep all your friends close at hand*. That would cement Rhys's intimate companions as essential fixtures of the Society, shoring up Rhys's power even more.

David had never been above a little nepotism. He was a legacy inductee himself, after all. But still, something about the whole situation made him uncomfortable. There was a strained quality to the proceedings he couldn't put his finger on, a tension beneath the wide smiles and friendly chatter.

He tried to catch Rhys's eye to no avail.

Maybe David was overthinking. Maybe Rhys wasn't overstepping boundaries after all. Maybe this was just what High Priests did, and maybe that was fine.

David's phone vibrated in his lap, and he glanced down to a text from his sister. Older than David by seven years and bonded to her brother by their shared hatred for their now-dead shared father, Leda was still living wild despite pushing forty. She ran a chain of goth nightclubs, kept a bevy of lovers in constant rotation, and spent her weekend doing ecstatic rituals with her dedicated following of chaos magicians.

She had also been doing her best to be more present in David's life since his brush with death over the summer, even though it hadn't exactly been an easy transition. Leda didn't understand the concept of boundaries, and David wasn't good with intimacy, but after stepping on each other's toes a couple of times, they had ironed things out. Leda knew not to call in the wee hours or invite David out to events where the main activity was drinking, and David had learned to welcome her random appearances as affection, not intrusion. He was also getting better at texting her back in a timely fashion, and sending her memes that appealed to their joint gallows humor. The electric joy that had crossed her face the one time he had showed up on her doorstep unannounced with a large spinach calzone and a bottle of Sprite, a childhood favorite, had made him decide to drop in on her again sometime soon.

How goes the politicking? Leda's text read. *Are you bored out of your skull yet?*

Turns out politicking is mostly just talking about how to spend the endowment, David typed back.

Boo, numbers. I'm playing a short set tonight at the Black Swan. Wanna come?

Crowded nightclubs generally just reminded David of how old and how sober he was. If anyone else had been asking, David would have declined without a second thought. But music was something the Aristarkhov siblings had always had in common. During the few years they lived together in Russia, David would often sneak into Leda's room to listen to her contraband rock records while gorging on the chocolate she stole every time she went into town. Leda had made a career out of music while David had contented himself with using his proficiency on the piano and his membership in a men's acapella group in college to flirt with boys. Still, it felt good to be invited back into that part of Leda's life, even just as an audience member.

Thanks for the invite. I'll make an appearance, so long as that club of yours stocks sparkling water.

We just got in a shipment of San Pellegrino with your name on it. See you later!

David was independent by nature and had recalibrated his emotional needs from a very early age to rely on others as little as possible. But some things that had felt so stiff and foreign to him only six months ago, like keeping up regular correspondence with his sister, were starting to feel easier. More right.

Rhys brushed his fingers across David's knee beneath the table and David settled his hand on top of Rhys'. Rhys didn't look at him, keeping his gaze trained on Kitty as she spoke, but he rubbed his thumb in a circle along David's wrist.

David hated how light of a touch he was sometimes under Rhys' agile hands, but he had to admit the gesture was soothing. Maybe they would all catch up to whatever wavelength Rhys was on, or bring him back down to theirs, whichever came first.

Maybe, everything would be alright.

CHAPTER SIX
RHYS

Rhys had spent most of his life waiting for the other shoe to drop. The moment too many pleasant synchronicities started aligning, he began looking over his shoulder for the looming specter of tragedy. He was aware that bad things happening to him were just as random as good things happening to anyone else. There was no cosmic scale being rebalanced when Rhys had walked beaming off his high school graduation stage, only to be informed that his grandfather had died suddenly of a stroke, or when he had broken his ankle a week after meeting David. It was just life, just luck, as miserable as it was mundane.

Believing anything to the contrary was childish.

Still, it was hard to shake the conviction that, since he had stolen so much happiness for himself, he deserved any pain doled out in return. He had cheated God countless times and the Devil even more than that. Ergo, he shouldn't be surprised when the universe reared back to bite him.

Rhys had been so incandescently happy during his wedding that he had refused to let Moira out of his sight for most of their honeymoon, convinced that some awful accident would snatch her away if he didn't keep sleepless watch. And now, with David back in his bed and his good graces, and Moira at his side smiling up at him brighter than the sun, and both of his beloveds finding companionship in each other, that fear had returned tenfold. Rhys nearly jumped out of his skin every time

David texted, or every time Moira called his name from the next room, convinced that this was the moment misery would descend.

Still, he had not yet been punished for hoarding not one but two happy endings for himself. His increasingly demanding Society duties vied for his time, but he still enjoyed lazy Sundays with Moira, trading kisses and window-shopping while walking hand-in-hand through their neighborhood. He still cooked bread in David's kitchen (Rhys's rosemary focaccia was the only carb David was willing to betray his diet for) while they playfully sparred about misremembered trivia from those campy action movies David liked so much.

These moments of domesticity served to remind Rhys that he was human, that there were things worth paying attention to that weren't written in grimoires. For a while, he was happy.

Then, with the inevitability of a storm cloud breaking into rain, Rhys's good fortune ran out.

He was sitting shoulder-to-shoulder with Moira at the kitchen table, an arm looped around her waist and his chin resting on her shoulder as she idly scrolled through her phone. He breathed in the scent of the cruelty-free designer perfume he had bought her with his new salary. She smelled like neroli and vanilla and precious sweet woods, like Bathsheba brushing out her hair in a rose-strewn bath.

"Whoa," Moira breathed, leaning in closer to her phone.

Rhys stirred from his reverie, paying closer attention. He rubbed at his eyes, reminding himself for the hundredth time to get himself fitted for reading glasses, and peered at her phone. A headline from the *Boston Inquirer* hovered near the top of the screen.

GRISLY SCENE DISCOVERED ON BOSTON COMMON.

The noose of tragedy tightened around Rhys's neck, nearly choking the air from his lungs.

There it was, the familiarity of pain.

Moira scrolled quickly downward, and Rhys skimmed the article. Something about an occult cabal terrorizing the city, leaving signs of their rites out in public. Rhys's spine straightened instinctively, like he was back in parochial school trying not to get his knuckles rapped for slouching.

Someone had spraypainted a summoning circle on the grass of the common, just big enough for one magician to work in. Rhys couldn't name the spirit it was supposed to summon, the paint was corroded from rain and footsteps, but he recognized a few symbols from the Lesser Key of Solomon.

It was a classical goetic evocation, exactly the kind of thing he did every week in conclave at the Society.

As much of a traditionalist as he might be in other regards, Rhys knew the age-old magician's code of secrecy didn't exactly hold water in the modern world. In the past, open discussion of alchemical principles was enough to get one excommunicated, turned out of royal court, or even burned at the stake. Now, the worst someone in Rhys's privileged position could expect was getting cancelled on Twitter, or a tense conversation at Thanksgiving dinner, or perhaps losing their employment because of a superstitious boss.

Still, while much of a magician's power came from the will to grasp for something beyond the mundane, the power of having the will to keep silent couldn't be overstated. Plenty of modern practitioners made a tidy living selling spiritual services on the internet, but there was still an unspoken understanding among most magicians that the bulk of magical work was to be done in private. There was a reason that the word "occult" was derived from a Latin word for "hidden"; most magic was not meant for the masses.

It felt indecent, seeing those symbols spraypainted in a public park.

Even more strangely, there was a human form in the center of the circle, although a moment's examination proved that it was not, indeed, a dead body. It was a life-sized model of person lying with their arms crossed as though in death, made of papier mâché, with a dead-eyed painted face.

"What in the blue blazes?" Moira muttered, squinting. "What tradition is that even from? Those symbols look goetic, but I've never seen a voodoo doll or a witch poppet that big, or one made from paper…"

Rhys's skin prickled with the numbing TV static of anxiety. An air of secrecy didn't just safeguard magic's efficaciousness and protect the practitioner, it protected the entire magical community at large. This was bad. Not just for whatever magician had been stupid enough to work a ritual in public, but for anyone in the city associated with the occult.

Fate swung above Rhys like a pendulum, threatening to slice him open. He could see it now, the Satanic Panic-style headlines that would bring Rhys and everyone he loved under a microscope that, historically, had not been very forgiving.

"The press is going to have a field day with this," Moira muttered. "And God forbid the police get involved. The common's public property, so I suppose this constitutes a crime. They're going to need someone to hold liable. We should call somebody. David? Antoni?"

44 ASCENSION

With their idyllic morning ruined, the mantle of responsibility settled heavily on Rhys's shoulders.

"You text David, I'll ring the other Society members," Rhys said, reaching for his phone.

He was High Priest. High priests cleaned up supernatural messes, no matter the cost. High priests weighed the cost of their actions, and they made sacrifices accordingly.

This was the sort of challenge he had asked for when he all but begged for the Priesthood. Now, he needed to rise to the occasion.

"Nathan," he said into his cell as soon as the other man picked up. "Are you at home right now?"

Rhys's clique met at Nathan and Kitty's to discuss damage control. The airy Back Bay apartment had been meticulously decorated to Kitty's taste, with low-profile furniture in shades of cream and slate, and large abstract paintings by emerging global South artists. It was lavishly large, by Boston standards, and the sunken living room accommodated all seven of them easily. Moomin, Kitty's snow-white Persian cat, was nowhere to be found. He was probably spooked by all the commotion.

Rhys couldn't possibly sit still, so he paced the length of the living room and pretended to be admiring the art, desperate to cultivate an air of intentionality to cover for his nervous wandering. David was having some kind of hushed conversation with Kitty about optics and how much money it would take to shut up every newspaper in Boston, while Nathan chatted on the couch with Moira about breezier things, like the new crime drama on streaming. Rhys wanted to involve himself in the conversation, if only for the sake of being polite, but he couldn't stomach it. It was just Nathan's response to stress, to weave an illusion of normalcy with breezy pleasantries. Nathan and Moira were similar in that way, offering kindness in a crisis when most people could barely keep their head.

Antoni, who was well-adjusted enough to have hobbies outside of magic, had gotten into cocktails recently, and was doing something mysterious at the bar cart that involved cracking large format ice with a long metal spoon. In addition to bartending, summoning demons, and weightlifting, Antoni also ran a menswear Tiktok account where he rated celebrity street styles based on whether the men in question had "sauce or not". Rhys had no idea where he found the time.

Antoni fluidly combined champagne and absinthe to craft six Death in the Afternoons, plus an elaborate second drink that involved nonalcoholic bitters and soda water for David. Rhys lost himself for a moment in the repetition of Antoni's movements, not unlike his own when he prayed the rosary. It calmed something forever restless inside him, that agitated animal within that could only be lulled to sleep with the trancelike focus of research or prayer.

Rhys smiled tightly as Antoni pressed a champagne flute into his hand. Antoni, not fooled for an instant, said:

"Sit down, Rhys. You look ready to crawl out of your skin."

"I'm fine," he replied.

"You're not," Cameron put in from his seat in the armchair. He was flipping through an honest-to-God print edition of that morning's *Inquirer*, analog as ever. The rest of them had read the offending article digitally, then vented about it in a group chat Antoni had started. Cameron had been included, of course, but he didn't participate in group chats; they moved too fast and stressed him out. He would probably opt to send them all handwritten letters by carrier pigeon if that was an option.

Cameron primly folded the paper and laid it across his knee.

"Well, the *Inquirer* certainly isn't out to make any friends with this one," he said. "I guess sensationalism still sells."

Rhys ground his teeth. Because the Society was secret only in the loosest of terms (they hosted an annual public gala for God's sake) the *Inquirer*'s suspicion had fallen squarely onto them. The paper had, very boldly Rhys thought, asserted that Boston was being overrun by shadowy supernaturalists. A few local Wiccan covens also came under fire, and freemasons were briefly mentioned as possible culprits, but the paper seemed to know as well as Rhys that the masons were more concerned with raising money for charity and preserving heritage sites than they were with summoning infernal powers.

The *Inquirer* didn't call Rhys and his ilk Satanists outright, but it was heavily implied.

Rhys put away a third of his drink in one swallow, then drifted over to his wife and settled a hand on her shoulder to steady himself. Moira covered his hand with her own and continued her chat, accustomed to Rhys's nervous tics.

Rhys shot David a glance, inclining his head slightly toward the center of the room as though to say *the floor is yours*. David possessed a poise that never wavered, and Rhys needed to anchor himself in that poise now. He needed David to step into his role as second in command.

David, to his credit, didn't roll his eyes at being asked to work. Instead, he stood, pitching his voice perfectly to carry through the room and over the chatter without startling anyone.

"I appreciate everyone making it here today," he said. A few of the muscles in Rhys's shoulder unknotted. This was David's courtroom voice, slower than his rapid-fire social prattle. It conveyed ultimate calm, enveloped in honeyed masculine composure. "I know it's early, and I know it's a Sunday, but I'm afraid this is an all-hands-on-deck situation. Personally, I'm not a fan of jumping to conclusions. We don't have all the details here and I don't want to be too reactionary. It's possible that this is just some publicity stunt for a horror movie."

"Or the project of an art student from RISD," Moira put in.

"That's a good point, Moira, thank you," David said. "But on the off chance this is a rogue occultist, or some new coven that we know nothing about, I think we should treat this seriously, at least for now. Mostly because the papers seem to be treating it seriously."

Rhys grimaced. News traveled faster than wildfire in the occult community. They had an hour, maybe two, before every magician in Boston came to their own conclusions about who was at fault. Rhys would have hoped the Society had brokered enough goodwill among their colleagues to prevent people from pointing fingers, but he knew better. While many of the other magical organizations in the region were polite to the Society, that didn't preclude them from waiting in the wings for their downfall. Occultists were poachers by nature. Greedy for an extra drop of power here, a leg up on research there, and as much social influence as they could broker. If the Society dissolved, their supplies, ritual space, and members would be up for grabs.

"This obviously wasn't anyone of ours," David went on.

"That we know of," Antoni put in.

"Do you really think a Society member did this?" Nathan said.

Antoni shrugged a shoulder, uncommitted to any one theory.

"I'm saying we don't have all the facts. Cam, let me take a look at that."

Cameron passed Antoni the newspaper, and he flipped it open, squinting at the photo included with the article.

"I'm going to be honest with you," Antoni said. "The papier mâché human sacrifice freaks me out."

"We don't know if it's a sympathetic magic stand-in for a real person," Cameron provided. "It may not signify sacrifice."

"It could be apotropaic," Rhys conceded, gnawing on his thumbnail. "Meant to repel evil, not elicit a corresponding change in the material world. Passive instead of active."

"Either way, it's certainly a choice," Antoni went on. "And these symbols *are* goetic. They're mismatched and poorly drawn, but there's a Solomonic ritual circle here underneath the scribbles."

"Just because somebody did it wrong doesn't mean they weren't trying to do it right," Kitty mused. "A determined amateur is sometimes more dangerous than a competent adept."

"Is that paint or blood?" Antoni asked, leaning down to show the picture to Nathan and Moira.

"Blood," Moira said, at the same moment Nathan said, "Paint."

"Let's hope it's not blood," Rhys said. "The moment you bring blood into a ritual working, everything gets more volatile. It heightens every potentiality and consequence... It's an important part of certain religious traditions, but I hope that's not what we're dealing with here. Even I wouldn't touch it."

"Evgeni always said blood magic was more trouble than it was worth," David said, half to himself.

Rhys pulled a flake of skin from his lip with his teeth, tasting iron. It was impossible not to remember the scent of candle smoke and terrified sweat, or the warm, sticky sensation of David's blood splattering across Rhys's lips in the ceremonial circle. The taste of Moira's mouth mingling with copper when she kissed him.

The memories rushed back, almost forcing Rhys to take a seat. He swallowed hard, waiting for them to abate.

Blood magic was the only thing that had helped David wriggle free of his family curse, but the process had been painful, and it had left its mark on all of them. Rhys rubbed the thin pink scar running through his palm. It was fading now, but it still ached sometimes, especially when Rhys stopped working long enough to regain awareness of the curse rattling around in his bones.

"Sounds like all we know is a whole lot of nothing," Moira said.

"Realistically, this is probably going to blow over," Nathan said, draping his arm over the couch behind Moira's shoulder. She accepted his offer of comfort now, angling her shoulder into his. "I say we lay low and ride it out."

"I like that strategy," David said, pointing at Nathan as though he had just offered to buy everyone dinner.

"We can't just do nothing," Rhys said.

"I'm not saying we do nothing," David said. "I'm just saying we might get lucky. There could be a triple homicide or a sex scandal tomorrow that completely derails the news cycle for days."

"Very cheery," Nathan muttered, as Moira rolled her eyes.

"I'm just being pragmatic," David sighed. "But Rhys, if it makes you feel better, we can brainstorm some sort of response, just in case we end up needing one. It's possible that journalists will start snooping around the Society asking questions, or that the police start knocking on doors, God forbid. Did you see the way the *Inquirer* talked about the Wiccans? Dion is probably pissed."

"Oh, he is," Moira said, tapping her phone alight. "He DM'd me this morning."

"This is bigger than just the Society, Rhys," Cameron said. He removed his glasses and cleaned the lenses with his shirt tail, fixing Rhys with his perceptive eyes. Rhys was grateful that Cameron almost always wore his glasses; otherwise, his scholar's gaze cut too much. "There are other people's necks on the line, but because you're High Priest of the Society at the center of the crosshairs, they're going to look to you for guidance."

"For starters, someone's got to talk to the paper," Moira said. "David, you're Rhys's second, and you have the most public speaking experience."

"Truthfully," David said, polishing off his drink fast, like he was hoping it had suddenly been alchemized into something alcoholic. "I'd rather sit on a tack."

"And why is that?" Kitty scoffed. She had gotten friendlier with David after her induction into the Society, and David, to his credit, had been more welcoming of a new face at meetings than Rhys expected. But they weren't exactly a perfect personality match. "Let's not play coy here. You love the spotlight."

"I love my job," David corrected. "And I love mediumship. But those two worlds don't intersect. If I go on record in an interview discussing the Society, every normie in Boston, and more importantly, *the entire district attorney's office*, will know that I talk to the dead for fun."

"Your family is famous," Kitty said.

"Microfamous," David corrected.

"Macrofamous in certain circles. How likely do you think it is that none of your coworkers know? They've at least heard rumors. All it would take it one Google search and the cat is out of the bag."

"Thanks," David said flatly. "That's comforting."

"I just don't see why you can't put your pride aside in this one instance, when you could be so much help. Why hide? It strikes me as cowardly."

"And you're striking me as picking a fight right about now, Kitty."

"We'll table it for now," Rhys said, knowing better than to get into a back-and-forth with David when there were more pressing issues at hand. David would do nothing unless he was convinced it was his own idea, and Rhys didn't have time right now to work that particular magic. "Nathan, anything to add?"

Nathan held his palms up as though Rhys had just pointed a gun at him.

"I'm just a recruitment officer, Rhys. This level of disaster assessment is beyond me."

"We should get our ducks in a row before anyone makes any statement," Kitty said, recovering smoothly from her tiny tiff with David. He could never quite get under her skin the way she got under his. "Like Nathan said, everything will probably be fine, but we may as well batten down the hatches, just in case."

"Antoni, what do you think?" Rhys said, turning towards his friend. Bonded by their working-class upbringings and the impressively young ages at which they had been inducted into the Society, Rhys trusted Antoni implicitly.

"This might be a good opportunity for the local occult community to close ranks." Antoni said. "If we can rely on each other, and maybe even agree on how to handle this, all the better."

"Not a bad idea," Nathan offered. "Except for the fact that most occult leaders are so self-obsessed they would rather die than fall into line with anyone else. No offense, Rhys."

"None taken," Rhys said. He ran his thumb along the rim of his glass, over and over again. His anxiety had become so omnipresent in recent weeks that he barely noticed the tingling in his fingertips, the numbness creeping into his tongue.

"You've already got Leda on your side," David said. "Chaos magicians don't have leaders, exactly. But if they did, Leda would be one of them."

"And Dion," Moira said. "He knows what it's like managing a bunch of strong personalities, with that coven he runs. I'm sure if you made it worth his while he would agree to meet."

"Great idea," Rhys said, tucking a braid that had come loose from Moira's ponytail behind her ear. She looked up at him, her lovely face so open and trusting, and he was seized with the need to protect her. To protect all of them. "I've got a few other people I could call, folks who were on good terms with Wayne, at least. Maybe I can kill two birds with one stone; establish myself as the new High Priest while strengthening our ties with other magicians."

"I think that's all we can do at present," David said. "If the heat gets turned up on this situation, we'll deal with it. For now, we take care of our own."

"You sure picked a hell of a time to ascend, Rhys" Antoni said.

Cameron merely hummed in agreement. Then, as though dismissing the congregation after a sermon, he picked up the paper from his lap and went back to reading.

CHAPTER SEVEN
DAVID

Rhys elected to call the meeting of occult leaders on neutral ground, in the courtyard tearoom of the central branch of the Boston Public Library. The airy room was filled with tables draped with white tablecloths, where tourists and locals alike chatted over steaming cups of breakfast tea and towers of finger sandwiches. The French doors, white crown molding, and bulbous golden light fixtures were almost oppressively cheery, at stark odds with the dark subject matter they had all met to discuss.

Antoni hadn't approved of throwing money around for high tea service during a business meeting that could have been an email. Rhys had insisted the setting cultivated the right image, and Antoni said the only image it cultivated was that of grandmother with a pocket-sized chihuahua in her purse. The pair had refused to speak to each other for an hour after that.

David just thought finger sandwiches and scones and cakes were kind of stupid, especially since he couldn't eat most of them, but he kept his mouth shut about it. Right now he was sitting with Rhys and Moira at a large circular table in the corner of the tea room. Irritatingly, it was right by a bar, but it was the only table big enough to seat six.

"Ready to face the wolves?" Moira asked her husband. She raked her acrylic nails lightly across his scalp, finger-combing the curls into place. Her pinky traced the shellwork of his ear.

52 ASCENSION

Rhys smiled back, his eyes dropping briefly to Moira's mouth. Rhys and Moira had a relationship dynamic that walked the line between saccharine and scheming, which David found amusing, if a little strange. It was like watching a medieval arranged marriage that had blossomed into a love match, or a puppy dog infatuation that had grown teeth.

"Born ready," Rhys said, flirtation in the flash of his smile. Rhys wasn't usually someone for public banter, much less public displays of affection, but something about Moira melted him.

"Are we a party of three today?" David asked, gently shaking the couple from their reverie. "Should I be worried we're being stood up?"

"We're always a party of three," Moira teased. She nudged him with her foot under the table, as though apologizing for being lost in her husband for the last five minutes.

David smiled without his brain telling him to. Maybe Moira had a way of melting him too.

"They should be along any time now," Rhys said, glancing at his watch.

David hadn't bothered asking Rhys for the guest list, knowing it would probably change a dozen times before the actual meeting. This was a preliminary gathering, anyway, just a light snack between influential occultists who may or may not have to band together in the near future to smother a Satanic panic. This would no doubt be the first meeting of many.

"There's Zachary now," Rhys said, face brightening as he glanced over David's shoulder.

Zachary Horowitz brushed freezing rain from the shoulders of his peacoat as he walked towards them. He was dressed in a crisp blue blazer that complimented his eyes, so brown they were almost black, and he wore his customary kippah. Zachary was only thirty-three, but shouldering the duties of running a large synagogue in Brookline had given him the distinguished bearing of someone a decade older. So, probably, had dedicating the last ten years of his life to the study of the esoteric mysteries of Kabbalah. David knew him from a seminar Zachary had taught at the Society last year about Western hermeticism's Kabbalistic influences and how to minimize mistranslation and appropriation, but hadn't had much of an opportunity to talk to him beyond that.

"Rhys," Zachary said, reaching to shake his hand. "And you brought Moira; what a treat. I don't think we've been acquainted."

"We haven't," Moira said. "But it's nice to meet you."

"I've heard you're Boston's premier expert on the stars."

"I wouldn't go that far," she said with a wry smile, but David could tell from the way her eyes sparkled that she was pleased.

David gave Zachary's hand a firm shake and then gestured to an empty chair.

"Good to see you again, Zachary," David said. "Make yourself comfortable. How's Sasha?"

"Great, thanks for asking," Zachary said, getting settled at the table. He scrubbed a hand across his short beard, the only indication that he was tired. "We just had our fourth anniversary; can you believe it? Sasha's mom is in town helping us out because the baby's been keeping us up more than we expected. What a lifesaver."

"First baby?" Moira asked.

"Our second. But each child is a new blessing and a new challenge."

Before pleasantries could continue, Leda breezed into the room. She was wearing those platform boots that made her modelesque legs look about a mile long, but had forgone the usual ripped denim and leather in order to appease the tea room's "smart casual" dress code. She wore a chunky gunmetal sweater over black cigarette pants, and the side shave in her long black hair looked fresh.

"Wow, you almost look presentable for polite society," David said by way of greeting. "Who died?"

"Probably the same person who left you that dumb pinstriped shirt," she responded, sitting down with a jangle from all her silver jewelry. "Anyway, what did I miss?"

"We're just getting started," Rhys said.

Leda bumped David with her knee under the table, her best estimation at a companionable greeting. Things were getting easier between them, more natural, but their interactions still had that quintessential Aristarkhov awkwardness. They could talk shit about other people and text about music or magic all day, but they still faltered over whether to go in for a hug when they saw each other.

"Leda, this is Zachary Horowitz," Rhys said. "He's a local rabbi and a very accomplished kabbalist."

"That's probably an exaggeration," Zachary said modestly. "I consider myself more of a lifelong student of the sacred. Leda, it's very nice to meet you."

"Oh, a holy man," Leda said, wiggling her shoulders like a cat poised to bat into a koi pond.

"A *married* holy man," Rhys put in. "Settle down."

"Leda's a chaos magician," David said, unable to resist bragging on his sister, just a bit. He loved shining the spotlight on people he admired, especially because a little of that light tended to bounce back onto him. "One of the best. She practically has her own mystery cult going out there in Allston."

"I was gifted with charisma and cursed with notoriety," she responded. "A dedicated following comes with the territory."

Zachary smiled into his glass of water, and David got the impression that he was a bit charmed by Leda despite himself. Most people were.

"How many more are we expecting?" Moira asked, smoothing the skirt of her pleated dress. She had told him all about how she had taken it out to accommodate her hips on the ride over. David knew absolutely nothing about garment construction, but he enjoyed listening to Moira update him about her sewing projects all the same.

"Just one," Rhys replied. "Everybody else couldn't make it."

"Well, trying to get a bunch of magicians together in one place is basically herding cats," Leda said, glancing over the menu.

David opened his mouth to shoot back a quip, but then the door opened, and the words died on his lips.

The man who strode into the room was tall and brawny, equal parts muscle and softness. His olive skin was offset by black waves of hair, and he wore a day blazer over a simple T-shirt. But it was the eyes that made it suddenly hard to breathe.

David knew those eyes.

He had been pinned in place by them like a butterfly under glass years ago, pierced by longing.

"Maximilian," David blurted.

Maximillian Markos looked at David with a stranger's surprise, his full lips parting. Then recognition sparked behind his eyes.

"My God," he said with a laugh. "Is that David Aristarkhov?"

David stood and extended his hand for a shake, hoping it wasn't clammy with sweat. The room was suddenly summertime-warm.

"The one and only," David said with a glib bravado he didn't feel.

Maximilian shook his head in delight. "It's been fifteen years. I can't believe it. You look well."

Heat coursed through David, wild and antsy. He recognized this feeling from his adolescence, when he would trail after older men trying to catch their eye to no avail. In retrospect, it was probably for the best no one had ever taken him up on any of his fumbling offers, but at the time he had felt martyred by their lack of attention.

But Maximilian was different. He was the blueprint. The originating point of all David's desires. He wore the same cologne as when he had breezed into David's father's house on that first day, cedar and sea salt and fir, but now there was silver threaded through his hair, and the smile lines around his eyes had deepened into elegant crow's feet.

The last time they met, Maximilian had been twenty-two and David had been a surly, hotheaded sixteen-year-old aching for attention. Maximilian, ever honorable, had never given it to David in the way that he so desperately wanted. But he had been nicer to David, nicer than David probably deserved, and David had never forgotten that.

In the here and now, Maximilian shook David's hand.

"Am I missing something?" Rhys said, looking from David to Maximilian and then back again.

David lurched back into the real world.

Right. Weird goetic ritual. Public relations crisis. Rhys.

"We know each other," David said.

"I was colleagues with David's father," Maximilian provided. "I spent a summer at their house in Beacon Hill years ago while I was completing some research."

"Oh, how nice!" Moira said.

"Nice is right," Leda said, eyeing her brother. Sibling instinct would have no doubt cued her into the fact that he was falling all over himself – if that wasn't already blatantly obvious to everyone else at the table.

"How do you know Maximilian?" David asked Rhys.

"We were put in touch by an old colleague of Wayne's," Rhys said. "This is the first time we've met, actually. Thanks for being good enough to join us on such short notice, Maximilian."

"I was pleased to be invited," Maximilian replied. "It's a warm welcome back to the city, even if it isn't under the best circumstances."

Maximilian took the final seat, right between Zachary and David. He was close enough to reach out and touch, if David decided to absolutely lose his mind and do *that*.

"I appreciate you all making the time to meet," Rhys said, dragging

David's attention back to the issue at hand. Rhys leaned across the table, lacing his fingers together with a serious look on his face. He might as well have been ordering a mafia hit in the back of a bar, not discussing spiritual politics in a sunny tearoom. "As you know, there was an incident last week that has, justified or not, implicated many of our communities. I asked you to join me today because you all hold sway over certain groups. Leda is influential among chaos magicians, and many of them look to her for direction. Zachary, you're a fixture in both religious and occult circles, and your community trusts you. Maximilian was chosen for obvious reasons."

"What reasons?" David put in. He regretted not quizzing Rhys about the guest list.

"I'm on the leadership team for one of the largest branches of the Ordo Templi Orientis in the States," Maximilian responded.

"He's the vice president, specifically," Rhys said. He never liked faux modesty.

"I've been working out of Seattle for the last five years," Maximilian said. "But a job with the MFA brought me back to Boston."

A Thelemite. David's interest was beyond piqued. When Maximilian was twenty-two, he had been new to the occult, and he hadn't settled into a practice or a tradition yet. But apparently, he had since become a disciple of Crowley, or at least an adherent to the controversial sorcerer's philosophical worldview. Thelemites believed in the axiom "do what thou wilt shall be the whole of the Law", which encouraged them to pursue their highest actualization heedless of social standards or conventional morality. To some, this condoned hedonism or naked self-interest. To others, it was an invitation into deep self-knowledge and altruism. Some Thelemites practiced solo, studying and integrating the writings of Crowley on their own. Other Thelemites gathered in branches of Thelema's occult order, the OTO.

Thelema was controversial in occult communities for a number of reasons, from the religion's historical proclivity for cherry-picking sources and systems, to the inclusion of sex magick in its rituals, to its general disregard for whatever anyone, Thelemite or not, thought of it.

David was agitated to realize that he found this new development unspeakably sexy.

He tore his eyes away from Maximilian and looked to Rhys, his *actual* boyfriend, the reason he was even sitting here in the first place. Rhys looked perfect as ever: sharp cheekbones, a smattering of freckles, eyes bright enough to burn. David's desire for Rhys was not diminished in the slightest, nor was his admiration or his care. But Max was also very much *here*, inexplicably tanned despite the weather and still smelling of ocean and forest.

David didn't know where to look, what to say, or what to do with his hands.

Moira nudged him under the table with her foot, seeking insight into his emotions. Her bare ankle brushed against the band of skin exposed between his sock and cuff. David didn't draw back fast enough, and she undoubtedly got a straight shot of his adolescent lust.

Moira raised her eyebrows at him across the table. David covered his embarrassment with a hasty swallow of tea. He didn't even like tea.

"I know that we've all generally given each other a wide berth," Rhys went on, twisting his wedding ring on his finger. "Occultists can be territorial. But it would be worth all of us building a stronger sense of community, just in case we end up facing a crisis."

"Are you talking about drafting up a joint statement?" Zachary said.

"Or getting our stories straight in case the police haul one of us in for questioning?" Leda asked.

"A bit of both, if I'm being honest," Rhys said. "But primarily, I'm interested in information. Have any of you heard chatter about who might be behind the public ritual? Anything, even a rumor, could lead us to the culprit. Personally, I'm hoping to put this issue to bed quietly without involving the police."

"That sounds a bit reactionary," Maximilian said levelly. David had never known Max to lose his temper, not even when he was up at 2am debating alchemical theories with Evgeni as they worked through a bottle of Glenfiddich. David had sometimes lingered on the stairs on his way to bed, listening to the murmur of voices through the walls. "What exactly is it you're afraid of happening? None of us are likely to get burned at the stake."

Rhys looked at Maximilian as though startled, like it hadn't crossed his mind that anyone might take issue with his perspective on the situation.

"You know what happens to people like us when the public believes that we're holed up in a basement summoning Satan," Rhys said.

"That's very close to what we actually do, babe," David put in. "If some reporters clutch their pearls about it, who cares? People barely read the paper these days anyway."

"It was *your* idea to figure out who did this," Rhys responded.

"No, I suggested a team-building exercise, and then you jumped to extrajudicial vengeance."

"Who said anything about vengeance?" Rhys asked, completely focused on David now, everyone else at the table forgotten. This was one of David's guilty pleasures; demanding more of Rhys's attention by getting under his skin. "Maybe we have a firm conversation with them once we find them, maybe we hex them, I don't care. I just want this over and done with."

"If we're having this conversation, Dion should be here," Moira said, steering them all back on track. "You can't expect to get anything done without the Wiccans on your side."

"I called him," Rhys responded. "He couldn't get out of Salem. Something about a love spell gone wrong he had to clean up. I was going to make a house call next week."

"I'll come with you," Moira said. "

"Are you sure you want to go? Salem always wipes you out, between the weird energy in the metaphysical shops and the fact that the town is crammed with occultists and tourists. You've told me before you're too sensitive for it."

"Dion is my friend, not yours. I'm coming."

David took a sip of tea so Rhys wouldn't see him smirk. Rhys had always had difficulty making friends, and tended to pick up Moira's by proxy, but he wasn't very good at maintaining those connections without her gentle prodding. Rhys probably hadn't spoken to Dion since his ascension, whereas Moira and Dion were always chatting on Instagram, liking each other's selfies and comparing notes on the properties of various herbs.

Rhys might have a reputation for being the tactician in the relationship, but Moira could very easily outmaneuver him when she wanted to.

"I've never met Dion," David said, raising his hand as though asking to be called on in class. "But I'd like to. Besides, I need a new crystal ball."

"You're sure you're not just chasing the high you get from being around all that psychic energy?" Rhys asked. "I've been to Salem with you, babe. Sophomore year, remember? It keys you up like two Adderall and a shot of tequila."

"Once an addict, always an addict," David quipped. "But I'm serious. You don't need to do this alone. Let us help you."

The waitress appeared with more earl grey, and Maximilian smiled at her. David couldn't help but watch the interaction out of the corner of his eye, trying to parse if it was flirtatious or not. Did Maximilian like women? Men? Both? David had never asked. Talking about something like that out loud would have been unthinkable all those years ago, especially when David's burgeoning homosexuality was a secret he guarded with his life.

"Dion is the most likely of any of us to know something," David said, forcing himself to focus. He was letting his imagination run away with him. There was nothing between him and Maximilian Markos, never had been, and they certainly weren't going to start something now, at a glorified networking meeting. "He always has his ear to the ground for gossip. Leda, have you heard anything in the backchannels?"

"Just a lot of speculation," Leda said, pouring two sugar packets into her tea.

"Zachary, anything?" Moira asked.

"Nothing on my end. Practitioners are talking about it, sure, but it's just flavor-of-the-week small talk. I don't think anyone's seriously concerned. And, for what it's worth, I doubt the person who did this was anyone I know."

"A Thelemite might go that far," Maximilian said thoughtfully. "The discipline can attract provocateurs. That said, there were no distinctly Thelemite symbols at the scene of the crime, no evidence of any of Crowley's writings... To be honest, Rhys, the photographs I saw looked much more like a traditional goetic summoning. That's your wheelhouse."

"I know," Rhys said, gnawing on his thumbnail. He was getting irritated.

"Are you absolutely sure it wasn't someone connected to the Society?" Maximilian went on.

"I'm positive," Rhys said. "Most of the Society members aren't even advanced enough in their studies to design a ritual like this, much less have the guts for it. If I had a fox in my henhouse, I would know it."

"Fair enough," Maximilian said mildly, sipping his tea, but still with a challenge in his eyes. Maximilian was the only one at the table with a title that superseded Rhys', since Rhys was only a regional leader. David sensed that the two men were attempting not to get drawn into some kind of supernatural dick-measuring contest.

Moira, no doubt picking up on the same energy, placed her hand over her husband's.

"Thank you for your input, Maximilian," she said diplomatically.

"I still think it's worth our time to go over some talking points to share with the people under our care, and maybe the press," Rhys said, breaking a scone into tiny pieces without eating any of it. He was definitely irritated. "We could draft up a letter, if everyone is on board. Put forward a unified front."

"I'm still not convinced this warrants a public response," Zachary pressed. "Addressing it could just throw gasoline on the fire."

"I'll sign my name on something if it comes to that, but I'd rather not," Leda said. "I run a nightclub and host ritual orgies, so needless to say I like my privacy."

Rhys chewed on his lip, looking for all the world like a twelve-year-old who had gotten picked last for dodgeball. David, who could indeed feel pity despite cultivating an image to the contrary, swooped in to save him.

"Rhys, you're a strong writer, and you have the authority to represent the Society. Why don't you work on drafting a letter, just in case? We can all look over it and sign off on sending it to the paper if we agree to run it."

"You're giving me homework to keep my hands busy," Rhys said.

"I am," David conceded. "But I also think it will be helpful. Are you up for it?"

Rhys glanced at him, dark eyes still suspicious, but David could tell from the way his tightly pressed lips softened that the olive branch had been accepted.

"I am."

"Good," David said, squeezing his shoulder. It was then he noticed that Maximilian was watching him with a small, approving smile on his face. David, who was not good at subtlety, especially as far as men were involved, asked: "What?"

"You're as persuasive as your father was," Maximilian said. Now it felt like David and Maximilian were the only people in the room. "But it appears that you're much kinder."

David opened his mouth, quickly realized that if he said anything he would stutter, and closed his mouth again.

Rhys and Moira exchanged one of those we're-talking-about-this-on-the-drive-home married couple glances. Leda made a sound halfway between a giggle and a scoff into her tea. Zachary politely studied his menu.

"Thanks," David said, finally settling on a response. All those seconds of shellshocked silence for one word.

"If you think drafting a statement is a worthwhile effort, Rhys, I'll support it," Maximilian went on, like he hadn't peered into David's heart like the inner workings of a grandfather clock moments ago. "In the meantime, please let me know if there's any way I can assist you, or the Society. I don't know everything, but I've been in occult leadership positions for a decade and I'm happy to share notes."

"I'll be sure to take you up on it," Rhys said, in a polite but toneless voice that clearly telegraphed he would not. "At any rate, do we want to order another round of tea? Moira, do you still want that cranberry scone?"

Conversation ebbed and flowed back into something approaching normal social chatter, but David barely processed what was being said.

He was too focused on the sensation of Max brushing his fingers across David's knee under the table for a microsecond, just as Rhys firmly – and perhaps a bit performatively – settled his hand on top of David's in full view of everyone.

CHAPTER EIGHT
MOIRA

Rhys's new salary could cover all their bills with a little left over for flowers and lipstick and wine, but Moira wasn't the type to live off her husband's allowance. Rhys would never lord it over her, and his deeply entrenched sense of Catholic masculinity would probably be thrilled to be able to cater to her every need, but she still needed her own saving and spending money. Her mother, an accountant by trade and by temperament, had instilled in her daughter the importance of a woman being able to make her own way in the world.

So, Moira started that week with deep stretching, journaling, and a single-card tarot pull for herself, then got down to work. Working did the body good, working kept income flowing into her home, and working, most crucially, helped her not worry about the ritual on the common, or about Rhys's increasingly long hours spent at the Society, or about whatever was going on with David.

David had dashed out of the tea house before she got a chance to ask him about the warm rush of desire she had picked up from him under the table, but she suspected it had something to do with Maximilian. Maximilian, who had gallantly walked at her side all the way back to the car.

"You have my number," Max had said to Rhys, who stood with one arm around Moira and his car keys in the other hand. "Please don't hesitate to reach out. I know how overwhelming inheriting a leadership position can be."

"I appreciate it," Rhys said with a smile. His sunglasses hid the fact that the smile probably didn't reach his eyes.

"So if you'd like me to come in and help you organize records, strategize policy, balance the budget for the new year, anything at all..."

Maximilian's voice trailed off in invitation. Rhys just kept smiling.

"Got it," Rhys said.

After they had said their goodbyes and Max had disappeared into his own car, Rhys slid into the driver's seat beside Moira and let out a huff.

"That was pushy, right?" he asked. "I feel like he was being pushy."

"I like him," Moira said with a shrug. At almost forty, Max radiated an easy authority that came from calm and experience, and he didn't have to throw his height around to let people know he was in charge. Rhys could learn something from that. Just the way he could learn something from the reminder that other people possessed wisdom that he did not. "David seems to think he's alright."

She didn't bring up the way David had been staring at Maximilian between every sip of tea with an interest that almost crossed the line into ogling. Moira knew from Rhys's college stories (as well as David's own self-admission) that David had a bit of a wandering eye, but the attention he showed Max seemed more intense than any passing flirtation with a barista. Moira wasn't sure if it that spelled trouble or not.

"Mm," Rhys had said noncommittally, peering up at the sky through the windshield as though evaluating the threat of a storm.

Rhys had kept busy after the meeting in the tea house as well, mostly with that clever piece of extracurricular work David had given him. Rhys would wander out of his study occasionally to read her a few sentences, or to ask for her input on phrasing.

"Should it be 'we firmly disavow' or 'we strictly disavow'?" Rhys asked, chewing on the end of his pen as he stood in the doorway of Moira's meditation room.

"Why don't you just say 'we don't support'?" she asked, pushing herself up into cobra pose on her yoga mat. "Sounds a little bit more plain-speak."

"Disavow is plainly spoken," Rhys said, with total sincerity. "People say "disavow" all the time. I most certainly do."

"Keep workshopping it," Moira replied, pushing herself back into child's pose and resisting the urge to point out that people didn't often say "most certainly" either. The unique combination of antiquated language, modern slang, and the edge of an almost-hidden Boston accent that came out of Rhys's mouth delighted her, and she didn't want him to feel self-conscious about it.

Rhys chewed his pen harder, leaving vampire bite marks on the cap.

"Are you gonna want any dinner?" Moira asked. "Or are microplastics dinner?"

Rhys took the pen out of his mouth, chastened.

"I'm still full from breakfast," he replied. "I'll think about eating when I'm done editing this paragraph."

Moira believed her husband had been locked in his study going over the same paragraph again and again with a perfectionist's eye (she had heard David's stories about Rhys losing all interest in sleep, sex, conversation, and food during exam week in college) but she wondered if that was all he had been doing in there. He smelled strongly of copal, just like when he emerged from his study dehydrated and bleary-eyed after an arduous summoning. And there had been a strange energetic static clinging to him for days now, like he was wearing the darkness of the summoning circle like a cloak.

"Suit yourself," Moira said, letting her husband keep his secrets for now. At any rate, it was almost time for her to meet David.

Moira arrived first to the Beacon Hill House and let herself in with the spare key David had gotten pressed for her. He had acted blasé about it, but Moira had been delighted to be gifted the tiny golden key. Six months ago, David had guarded entrance to his family home as ferociously as he guarded his heart, and now, she was free to come and go as she pleased.

She hardly had time to set down her purse and place a foil-wrapped plate on the parlor table before David swept in with the November breeze, debonair in his wool coat and cashmere scarf. Standing on the gleaming parquet floors, flanked by the arching doorways of his childhood home, he looked absolutely princely.

It made her feel mixed-up inside, the way her heart sometimes leapt into her throat when he walked into the room. She knew he felt it too, whatever "it" was. Sometimes she caught him staring at her, always when he thought she wasn't looking, as though she were a priestess guarding the secrets of the universe.

"Tell me that doesn't have sugar in it," David said, pointing to the foil-wrapped plate as though it had insulted him.

"Only a little," she said, batting her eyelashes.

"Don't bat your eyelashes; that doesn't work on me," he went on, stripping off his coat.

"It works a little," she corrected. "And they're just brownies with candied lavender. At least have one."

"You know these don't fit my macros," David said, lifting the edge of the tinfoil and retrieving a brownie all the same. He broke it in half, kept the smaller half for himself, and handed the bigger half to her. "Lavender alleviates stress, right? You're not feeling stressed about our lesson, are you?"

"No," she lied, then sighed when he arched a skeptical eyebrow at her. "Sorry, I've just got a lot on my mind. I'm still adjusting to Rhys's new job. To the tell the truth, I'm getting irritated with him."

David couldn't have looked more shocked if she had told him she was running for president, or joining a convent.

"What?" she demanded.

"It's just that I've never heard you talk shit about Rhys, not even when I've tried to bond with you by talking shit about Rhys."

"That's not how I bond. And you weren't in my inner circle then, you were just some rich boy asshole making sheep eyes at my husband. I don't open up my marriage to any stranger off the street. You've got a vested interest in this now, so I trust you."

"I'm honored to have made it onto your list of vetted people," David said drolly, but the sparkle in his eyes told the truth. He *was* honored. "What's going on with you and Rhys?"

Moira paused, working bits of candied lavender out from between her teeth with her tongue. Maybe talking to David about this was a mistake. Maybe he was actually *too* close to the subject, no longer impartial enough to be a safe listening ear.

"Never mind. I'm not going to make you listen to me bellyache."

"When you submit your application to the department of homosexuality they make you sign an affidavit stating you will offer relationship advice to any straight woman in need," David said, delivery flat as though he were relaying a fact. "It'll be my charitable deed for this quarter."

"Oh shut up, you hate it when people whine to you."

"I do. But you're not people. You're Moira. So spit it out and then we can get down to talking to the dead; we don't have all day."

Moira used to be annoyed by his no-nonsense affect, but now she saw the value in it. He might not be the most cuddly, compassionate person in the world, but he was hard to throw off balance, and he knew how to keep his priorities straight. His practicality grounded her.

"I'm afraid the Priesthood is gonna eat Rhys up and spit him back out, and whatever is left in the end will barely be recognizable to me," she said.

"Oh, one hundred percent," David said with a nod, breaking off another tiny piece of brownie from the plate.

"One hundred percent like you feel the same, or like you think that's going to happen?"

"Both, unfortunately," David said. "But you know how he is. He needs to fly too close to the sun and get burned before he learns any kind of lesson. I'm not wishing him ill, and I don't hope he fails. I'm just waiting for him to get a little singed so he settles down and we can all find some equilibrium."

"You really do know him, don't you?" Moira said, marveling at this bone-deep recognition of similarity within opposites that David and Rhys found in each other.

"I do," David said, and for once, it wasn't sarcastic.

"I'm just mad, more and more these days. I want to be patient with him, but he gets so absorbed into what he's doing that it's like I barely exist. And he's lying to me about something, I know it. Something magical he doesn't want my hands in."

"Sounds like Rhys. One time he grew mushrooms in the closet of our apartment for three months because he thought a hobby would be good for him. He didn't tell me until they started to stink, because he didn't want me disturbing the ecosystem or whatever. Another time he hid one of those Catholic embroidered things, what are they called, a *scapular* under our bed to keep us from fighting. I didn't find that one until he moved out."

"He knows I'd take his secrets to my grave," she said, frustration rising within her like a hot gust of desert air. "Why pull away now? What did I do wrong?"

"It's not about you, peach. It's about Rhys. Always has been, always will be. But if he makes you cry, I'll kick his ass. You just let me know."

"You sound like an overprotective boyfriend," she said, sort of joking and sort of not. It was silly when David did this, and probably mostly performative as he would never actually hurt Rhys, but she still liked it. It still made her feel cherished. Chosen. Loved.

"Yeah well," David said, taking yet another bite of brownie. This was a winning recipe; she would have to remember it. "I basically am."

Moira just raised her eyebrows at him, letting silence speak for her.

"Well," he said, quickly covering for himself. "If we're getting technical I'm your boyfriend-in-law."

"Sounds like you've thought this through very thoroughly," she said, slow and serious, doing her level best not to laugh. David scowled at his shoes, which only made her want to laugh more, or hug him, or both.

"Don't make it weird," he huffed.

"I'm not making it weird. I think it's very sweet. Does that make me your girlfriend-in-law?"

"I mean, if you want to be, I–"

"I want to be," she said, and stuck out her little finger to him like they were children playing jacks on the playground, promising not to cheat.

David hooked his little finger through hers and gave a decisive shake, sealing the deal.

"Glad we cleared that up." He leaned down and gave her one of those quick, sharp kisses on the cheek, the ones he used like punctuation. "Now are we going to stare into the abyss together or what?"

"And what if it stares back?" Her cheek buzzed where David had kissed her, electrified with solidarity and hope.

"We flip it off," David said.

Moira gave him a smile of mutual challenge as she tied up her braids into a high ponytail. If Rhys felt like diving into the ocean, wrapping herself up in enveloping, luscious depth and regulating calm, David felt more like the summer sun beating down on her while she sunbathed topless. He got her drunk on optimism and made her feel like the winter would never come, like she could live bold and brazen and free forever.

"After you, Mr Aristarkhov," she said.

CHAPTER NINE
RHYS

Rhys stalked down the cobblestone streets of Witch City with his yawning wife and his hyperactive boyfriend at his side. He thanked his lucky stars it wasn't October, when it was absolutely impossible to find parking or navigate the city because of the crowds. David would not be corralled, and kept stopping to look in shop windows, but Moira, at least, let Rhys take her hand and guide her through the throng of people gawking at historical reenactors on Essex Street.

After getting turned around twice, Rhys ducked down a side street and slipped into a shop with a triple moon carving over the door.

Rhys was enveloped by the scent of dragon's blood incense burning in a small altar dedicated to the Horned One, and he relaxed instinctively. During a brief rebellion against Catholicism in his college years, he had explored Wicca. He had found the carnality of the religion thrilling, the ethical framework of the Rede grounding, and the idea of a feminine Divine comforting. While Wicca no longer fit him, it was like a beloved coat worn threadbare that he still kept in his closet for sentimental value.

Dion Masters was tending the altar, sprinkling some aromatic herbs over a candle flame. He was a slender Black man and wore his hair in shoulder-length locs, and he was dressed mostly in black except for the moss-green scarf looped around his neck. Bloodstone and black tourmaline crystal bracelets clattered on his wrists, and a thin silver ring glinted in his nose.

"Well," Dion said in his soothing bass. He had a voice for the stage, or for audiobooks. "It's an honor to be in the presence of a High Priest."

Rhys smiled and extended his hand for a firm shake. It was an inside joke, as Dion was also a High Priest in his own tradition. Dion had made a name for himself with love spells and ex-banishing rituals, finicky magic that was incredibly difficult to get right without any backfiring. His specialty with relationships made him sought after as an officiant for weddings and home blessings, but Rhys knew better than to discount Dion's power just because he busied himself with the matters of the heart.

Moira had a supervisor once at the vintage store who always cut her hours and made snide comments about the way she dressed and wore her hair. The woman had quit after coming down with a mysterious rash and backing her car into a pole in the same week, and when Rhys had asked Moira about it, she had simply smiled and told him Dion had handled things.

"It's been ages," Rhys said, hoping Dion could feel a *mea culpa* in Rhys's firm handshake. "So good to see you again."

"Dion!" Moira squealed and tossed herself into his arms. Dion groaned with surprise, then laughed good-naturedly and folded Moira into a tight hug. Dion was half a head taller than Rhys, which meant he towered over Moira.

"Nice to see you too, Miss Moira," Dion said.

"Hi," David said with a little wave, bouncing on his heels and popping a bubble of mint gum. "I'm David. Rhys'—"

"Boyfriend," Dion supplied pleasantly, shaking David's hand. "Pleasure to finally meet you."

Rhys tensed, tendrils of embarrassment spreading through his chest. It was by no means a secret that David and Rhys had picked their relationship back up where they left off, or that Moira and David had a connection of their own. Rhys knew people talked, and he wasn't exactly worried about their friends finding out, especially Dion, who was a diehard romantic and trustworthy as they came.

Rhys had already calmly walked himself through all possible outcomes of his "lifestyle choice" (as his mother would call it) in his diary, but he was so used to code-switching and slipping in and out of closets depending on who he was around that he still felt like he had been caught committing a crime. Anxiety started to build inside him. If everyone in the occult community already knew, that meant that people outside of the magical community might know, which meant his parents might find out, which meant–

"I was going to say scryer," David said, shaking Rhys from his panicked visions of being disowned. He snaked an arm around Rhys's waist, and Rhys let him, even covering David's hand with his own and giving a grateful squeeze. There was no point in hiding, at least within the protection of Dion's shop. He was overreacting.

Dion draped an arm across Moira's shoulder in a brotherly way, and she leaned on him heavily. Rhys had bought her a double espresso at Odd Meter a half hour ago and it had done nothing to shake off her sleepy haze.

"Salem taking it out of you?" Dion asked. "You seem tired."

"Honestly, I'm zapped," Moira said, yawning. "How do you put up with all this energy all the time?"

"Your body adapts, eventually. I used to get splitting migraines when I first moved to town."

"Do you have any place I can sit down?" Moira asked, her lashes drooping.

Dion pulled back the velvet curtain that separated the small psychic reading room from the rest of the shop. Inside, there were two overstuffed armchairs crowded around a tea table, each just big enough to curl up in.

"Go ahead and lie down," Dion said. "I'll keep the customers away."

Dion closed the curtain behind her, turning over the sign so it said, "Reader out to Lunch".

With Moira gone, Rhys spun his wedding band awkwardly on his finger. It was easier to socialize with her at his side. Without Moira, he had more trouble deciding where to look when talking to others, how much eye contact to make, or even what to say.

"I'm going to look at the crystals," David said, dropping a kiss to Rhys's temple as he strolled over to the table where malachite, selenite, and amethyst were tidily laid out.

"What about you?" Dion asked, hands clasped loosely in front of him. Rhys had never known Dion to look anything but perfectly at ease, even in situations where he knew no one, or during difficult conversations. Rhys envied him. "Can I help you find anything?"

"I was hoping to talk to you, actually. Do you have a minute?"

"For Boston's top ceremonialist? Always."

Dion led Rhys into the storeroom in the back, which smelled of sawdust, candle wax, and orange peel oil, and swept a few gift-wrapped orders to one side of a battered wooden table. Dion took a seat, sweeping his feet up onto the edge of the table. Rhys perched primly on the edge of the only other chair in the room.

"What's going on, Rhys?" Dion asked, voice somber, brown eyes soft. "Something tells me this isn't a social visit."

"No," Rhys said, feeling that familiar twinge of guilt in his stomach. He should visit Dion more often. He should try to maintain any friendships outside of work at all. "No, it's not."

"Alright," Dion said, nodding thoughtfully. "Let's talk High Priest to High Priest, then."

Right to business. That felt better. It wasn't that Dion wasn't easy to talk to, it was that Rhys had forgotten how to talk to pretty much anyone about anything unrelated to Society matters. He spent so much time with spreadsheets and grimoires that human beings were starting to feel foreign.

"There was a very showy ritual in Boston last week, as you know. The press are having a field day."

"I saw that," Dion said. "The way they talk about us irritates me, but they're just doing their jobs."

"My concern is that where the press go, the police will follow. There's already so much misinformation out there about magic... I don't want anybody getting caught in the crossfire. You haven't had any trouble, have you?"

"Not me. I heard the owners over at Portent got a couple of phone calls from police, but I'm not inclined to feel sorry for them."

Rhys simply nodded, not taking the bait. Magicians in Salem were famous for holding grudges against each other, a vice even Dion was not immune to. Rhys knew Portent had a reputation for mistreating their staff and starting edgy rumors – claiming that the owner drank bat's blood to stay young, that sort of thing – but Rhys was an elder emo: he knew shock-rock showboating when he saw it. Still, he wasn't interested in getting drawn into whatever beef Dion had with the owners. Rhys would take Dion's side in any dispute, but he needed to at least attempt to maintain neutrality as High Priest.

"You don't have any theories as to who might be behind something like this, do you?" Rhys asked. " No one's taking credit for it."

"It's no one in my coven. The symbols don't line up, and we're very conscious about preserving our collective reputation. We live by the Wiccan Rede. That it harm none–"

"Do as thou wilt," Rhys finished.

"Are you sure you aren't a Wiccan?" Dion said with a smile. Common ground. Rhys could work with that.

"Not anymore."

"What a plot twist! Moira never told me. How long were you Wiccan?"

"I mostly dabbled, just a couple years in college. Catholicism got me, in the end."

"I've heard it often does. Cradle Catholic?"

"How could you tell?" Rhys shot back, dry humor shining through the awkwardness. "Was it the Saint Michael medal or the ambient aura of guilt?"

Dion's smile grew, showing a few more teeth. Rhys felt as though he had scored a point with the other man.

"Here," Dion said, retrieving a small, unmarked vial of oil from a nearby cardboard box. "This is for you."

Rhys unscrewed the cap and identified the scent immediately.

"Basil?"

"To boost your success and protect your heart against the trials to come," Dion said, as though it were obvious.

Rhys rubbed a bit of the oil between his thumb and forefinger, filling the room with the sweet smell of crushed greenery. A memory came to him, unbidden.

"There's an old story that basil grew at the foot of the true cross. They say the scent led Saint Helen right to it."

"Isn't that something?" Dion said, fixing Rhys with a knowing look. Rhys screwed the cap back on and pocketed the gift. When Dion spoke again, it was with a sigh. "I wish I had an idea who was behind that ritual, but it could be anyone. There are people drawn to the darker side of magic in every sect, and I'd even argue making peace with darkness is part of spiritual development. Still, this reeks of foolishness, maybe even malice. Why do a ritual out in public like that if you don't want the attention, or if you aren't trying to drag the entire city into it?"

"I agree," Rhys said, rubbing the smear of basil oil into his palm in a near-unconscious gesture against evil.

"Whoever did this, I hope they're caught soon. The more paranoia there is around magic, the worse off folks are, especially folks with the most to lose. If the witch trials taught us anything, it's that. I've got a lot of members of my coven who don't need the police sniffing around their lives, not because they're bad people, but because they're the sort of people police aren't inclined to play nice with."

"I understand. I'm going to do everything I can to deflect the attention away from your coven. In the meantime, will you let me know if you hear anything?"

"Of course."

"Well," Rhys said awkwardly. "I appreciate your time."

To his surprise, Dion didn't stand to politely usher him out the door. Instead, he said:

"It's a full moon tonight. Come to the circle. You and Moira and David."

"I couldn't possibly impose–"

"It's not an imposition, Rhys, it's an invitation," Dion said with a chuckle. "Don't you know how to recognize one of those? I haven't seen you in months, and I haven't seen Moira since the autumn equinox. I'd like the chance to get to know David, too. You're my guests tonight. I insist."

Everything in Rhys longed to make a discreet Irish exit from the conversation, or to conjure some excuse about having a standing appointment. But he should nurture his few friendships before they withered on the vine.

He should try harder to be a person.

"I'll ask them. If they both want to stay, we will."

"Fantastic," Dion said. He stood and clapped Rhys on the shoulder. "Let's go see what they're up to."

To Rhys's dismay, David was juggling three small crystal balls to the gobsmacked delight of a pair of young children. David, who had as much paternal instinct as a king cobra. David, who Rhys didn't even know *could* juggle.

"David," Rhys said gently, touching his elbow. "Time and place."

David rolled his eyes, but he returned the crystal balls to their shelf all the same.

"How would you feel about sticking around for a full moon circle tonight?" Rhys asked. "Or is that not your speed?"

It was hard to tell which parts of occultism David found cringeworthy and which parts he enjoyed, mostly because he had been submerged in the magical world since he was five years old. He was jaded by nature.

"Love a good Wiccan circle," David said. "Who doesn't go in for a little chanting by the light of the moon?"

David was so punch-drunk on Salem's energy that he probably would have agreed to anything, but Rhys could work with that.

He pulled back the curtain of the reading nook and found Moira fast asleep in one of the chairs, curled up like a cat. He kissed her forehead to wake her, then helped her to her feet.

"Feel better?" he asked.

"I do," she replied, delicately rubbing her eyes so as not to disturb her smoky makeup. She had gone traditionally Salem for this trip, in a tiered black dress, oversized gray cardigan, and moonstone choker necklace. All she was missing was a pointy hat.

"Dion invited us to stay for his circle tonight. Would you like that?"

Moira's eyes lit up like two stars.

"Oh, that sounds *wonderful*."

How could Rhys ever deny her anything, when she looked at him like that?

The coven was out in force that night. Rhys counted over thirty people – some full members, some new initiates, and some guests – gathered around the flickering light of a bonfire. Dion disappeared a few minutes before the circle kicked off, then reappeared looking kingly with a willow wand in his grasp. Rhys held hands with Moira on one side of him and David on the other, falling into the familiar rhythm of casting a ceremonial circle.

No matter the tradition, Rhys was good at this: cultivating sanctity.

Together, they repeated the chants Dion led them in, in an ebb and flow of call and response. Rhys tipped his face up towards the moon and gave thanks to the feminine and masculine divine, to the powers of the earth, sea, and sky, and to the spirits of the land. One by one, the participants of the circle stepped forward to burn their written petitions in the bonfire. Dion sprinkled fragrant green sage and rosemary into the flames as he whispered his private words of power. The flames sparked and danced before him, as if performing for his special delight.

Then, with the ritual over and done with, it was time for the festivities to begin.

Everyone stuck close to the fire's warmth with their plates of potluck dinner, but the weather was blessedly mild for November. An older Wiccan couple, a man and a woman, played the guitar and sang a folksy hymn to the Goddess, and Rhys watched, enraptured, as Moira danced with a crown of dried nettle and chamomile in her hair. She was Inanna, she was Aphrodite, she was Oshun, she was every deity of love, and renewal, and terrifying might, all wrapped up into one perfect woman.

Rhys waited until she danced close to him, her gaze teasing, and then he caught her by the waist and kissed her firmly. David's laughter pealed from somewhere across the bonfire, and when Rhys looked up, he saw that his boyfriend was doing what he did best: dazzling Dion with sheer charisma. David glanced over at Rhys, his eyes green as seaglass in the firelight, and winked.

Rhys loved them both painfully, and for a moment, his treacherous heart longed for it to always be as simple as this. Good food, good friends, and the closeness of his two favorite people.

But he was High Priest now, and that came with a level of responsibility and scrutiny that even Rhys couldn't have imagined. If he got too comfortable, he might trip up. If he tripped, up he could lose all the ground he had gained, jeopardizing everything from his reputation to his finances to the safety of his loved ones.

Rhys knew what it felt like to watch someone he loved slip through his fingers because he had been too weak and too afraid to act quickly enough. It was never something he wanted to experience again.

Until the danger of this public inquiry into their previously private subculture had passed, Rhys was determined not to let his guard down. He would keep his head above water. More than that, he would excel.

And he would harden, if he had to, into stone or into steel.

CHAPTER TEN
DAVID

David had been raised with an atrophied sense of righteousness. His father, Evgeni, had used every underhanded method imaginable when it came to managing his money and acquiring his rare books, and he had lectured David on the finer points of wire fraud as though it was something that should have been covered in school. Evgeni had friends, even close ones, but he wasn't above selling them out if it meant he could advance in his own occult studies. He had cheated on every wife and girlfriend David had ever been aware of – including David's own mother – with a sort of blasé openness, as though carrying on affairs was a foregone conclusion. And of course, he had responded to any emotional outburst or softness from his son with violence.

If Evgeni never did anything more criminal than that, it was simply because he didn't want to deal with the mess of cleaning up blood and the hassle of paying off the police. On the few occasions David had expressed equivocation at the way his father chose to do business, Evgeni had simply stared at him as though he could not recognize his own son.

It was perhaps this frustrated sense of justice that led David to become a prosecutor in the first place. Or maybe David was no more altruistic than any other Aristarkhov. Maybe he just liked the prestige and liked proving Evgeni – who always said David was good for nothing more than channeling spirits – wrong.

Still, David wondered if there was something fundamentally misshapen about his moral compass. If perhaps ethics had not been instilled in him at an early enough age for them to take hold.

Admittedly, he didn't actually care about the incident on the common, not in the way Rhys and Moira did. Moira was fretting up a storm about the way this thoughtless act would jeopardize the safety of innocent people. Rhys was consumed by a scholar's zeal for the truth, spurred into action by the insult of having such a dereliction of responsibility happen right under his nose.

David's natural instinct was to ignore the papers and the problem, since it had nothing to do with him. What did he care, when his money insulated him from consequences? If things got really bad, he could just take Rhys and Moira up north to his family's hunting lodge in Vermont. It wasn't a bad fantasy: dozing on the couch under an Afghan with Moira while Rhys baked bread, a crackling fire lulling them all into a comfortable domestic haze.

But David knew that impulse was *objectively* wrong, even if it didn't *feel* wrong, and he also knew it was precisely the reason he would have made a bad High Priest. He was trying to turn over a new leaf, and while it was difficult to summon deep empathy for strangers, it was easier to focus on taking care of the small number of people he actually cared about.

So, David took it upon himself to help Rhys re-emerge from his ascentic hermitage built entirely from books and theories and Society meetings.

What Rhys needed was to be re-acquainted with the pleasures of the flesh.

David goaded him into a date at an expensive French restaurant and insisted Rhys try at least a bite of every one of the seven courses – David suspected he hadn't been eating much. Then, after they got back to David's apartment, David got right down to doing the second-best thing his mouth was good for, after putting people in jail.

The pressure of floorboards beneath David's knees was familiar, as was the way Rhys's breath hitched as David took him into his mouth, but there was a persistent tightness in Rhys's thighs that belied stress. David wanted Rhys unable to conjure even the faintest memory of the things that were bothering him, so he laid Rhys down naked in his sheets, pressed a firm hand between Rhys's shoulders, and eased inside Rhys's body, working him over until they were both panting and spent.

Rhys lazed in David's bed afterwards, his brow smooth. David loved seeing him like this, undone and unguarded, partly because it was so rare. Rhys almost never dropped his defenses. Even in the bedroom, he preferred to be in control, setting the pace and giving the orders and administering just the right amounts of well-timed pain. But David could occasionally maneuver him into a posture of receptivity, of accepting pleasure as a freely given gift.

"Thank you," David said, nestling closer to Rhys under the sheets. Rhys was lying on his stomach, the sweat still drying in his curls.

"For what?" Rhys responded drowsily, his chin pillowed in his arms.

"For letting me spoil you. You usually put up such a fight."

"I don't deserve to be spoiled," Rhys mumbled. This was an old argument. Rhys simply did not view himself as worthy of special treatment, and David simply thought Rhys was one of the only people in the world who should be shown such handling, and this was one of their great impasses.

"Sure, sure," David said, trailing his fingers along the freckles and moles decorating the pale skin of Rhys's back. When they had first picked up their relationship again, Rhys had looked out of place tangled in David's dark blue comforter, like a ghost from the past who might evaporate along with the morning mist. But David had grown accustomed to seeing Rhys in his bed, in his apartment, in his *life*.

Rhys rolled over and fixed David with a pointed look. This was more like the Rhys David knew, all suspicion and those sharp edges that David delighted in sanding down.

"I think you're too nice to me, sometimes," Rhys said.

"It's amazing how nice I can be when I'm not drunk off my ass. Or trying to undermine you in meetings."

Rhys ran his palm along the curve of David's bicep. Mere months ago, this would have been an anathema, unthinkable. Now it was just a regular Friday.

"Can I ask you something?" Rhys said. "Something I've been thinking about for a while?"

"Always," David said.

There were half a dozen things Rhys could bring up: premier among them the way Rhys was still carrying around a curse that had been meant for David all along. They didn't talk about it much, not really, the wound still too fresh and raw to sustain the prodding needed to find a real solution. But maybe whatever was on Rhys's mind had nothing to do with the curse. Maybe Rhys needed space. Maybe he was already getting bored with their routine, with the way it had become steady and domestic so quickly. Or maybe David, who had finally talked himself into dropping the performative animosity and being as sweet with Rhys as he wanted to be, had miscalculated.

Maybe Rhys only liked David when they were at odds, when their friction created sparks.

"It's about Moira..." Rhys said, voice trailing off.

David thought he and Moira were in a good place, that they were successfully nurturing their friendship and their magical connection and the weird grey area of whatever else was going on when you put Moira and David in a room together. Had he fucked something up between them?

Or maybe Moira had just gotten tired of indulging David's relationship with Rhys. Maybe she had asked Rhys to break things off. David didn't think any of them had the power of veto over the others, but on second thought, that was probably a delusional assumption to make. Of course Rhys would always choose his *wife*, the person he had joined his life with, over David, an auxiliary player.

"Sure," David said, too quickly. "What's up?"

Rhys stared up at the ceiling for a long moment. David wanted to cut out the middleman and get straight to climbing into his own grave, but he somehow managed to wait quietly.

"Are you... in love with her?" Rhys asked.

David burst out laughing, in that uncontrollable way that only happened when he was nervous, the way that usually got his ears boxed by his father when he was a boy. He didn't want to talk about this with Rhys right now, maybe not ever, but the wistful somberness in Rhys' voice was a little bit laughable, so David laughed.

"Have you ever seen me, even at my most blackout drunk, take a single woman home?" David asked sarcastically. "Take your time; I know it's a lot of math."

"Be serious. You know that's not what I'm asking."

David did his best to be serious. Navel-gazing about his sexual orientation was not a pastime he enjoyed, not as a teenager and not now. Once his undeniable attraction to men surfaced during puberty, all of David's awestruck childhood hero worship of older boys made sense, as did his disinterest in forming any sort of connection with a girl outside of a playground alliance against a bully, or a quiet lunchtime partnership sitting in the grass sharing a fruit cup. He had spent plenty of time as a teen worried about someone finding out he was gay, but there had never been any question that he *was* gay. Even as an adult, when good-natured banter with a woman started feeling a little bit too much like genuine flirtation, it would be so strongly eclipsed by the emotional and physical draw David felt to other men that the contradictory data became negligible.

David kept stumbling across that friendship-flirtationship line with Moira however, often without really knowing where the line was to begin with.

He had allowed himself one serious journaling session in his notes app about this, and had come to the conclusion that he didn't want to sleep with her (the thought didn't disgust him, but it didn't excite him either, and it felt like a recipe for mutual embarrassment), and getting into the song-and-dance of anything resembling heterosexual dating with Moira sounded like a prison sentence, wonderful though she was.

But that didn't mean she wasn't nice to look at, the way a watercolor painting or an orchid was nice to look at, and that didn't mean he didn't like spoiling her with gifts and surprising her with outings, and that didn't mean that he didn't feel alive in a very unique and undefinable way during their magic lessons. And, gun to his head, it didn't mean that sometimes getting a rise out of her and making her blush didn't make his blood heat in a confusing way.

It *had* to have something to do with their psychic connection, electric and unspoken and communicated through touch. It must just be wires getting crossed. That was his best working theory.

"Maybe you should ask Moira how she feels," David hedged.

"I can ask Moira any time I want because I live with her, ass," Rhys said, with deep affection. "Right now, I'm asking you."

Generally, David didn't really define relationships. He just hooked up with people he liked until he stopped liking them or started liking them so much that he tricked them into dating him for perpetuity. The situation with Moira was more complex, because David hadn't led with sex, and yet, some days, whatever was going on with her felt an awful lot like dating, especially when she threaded her arm through his when they crossed a busy street or tugged him down to whisper something in his ear while they were at an event together, dressed to the nines and waiting for Rhys to retrieve them a wine and sparkling water.

Even more strangely, it felt good.

David, predictably, had said nothing about this to his boyfriend, convinced that Rhys probably wouldn't notice… whatever was going on. Rhys, predictably, had noticed right away.

David didn't need any curveball identity crises catching him off-guard at the age of thirty.

But maybe it didn't have to be a crisis. Maybe it could be an expansion of something he already knew about himself, like a plant reacting to shifting weather patterns by growing deeper roots.

"I want to make Moira happy," David said, forcing himself not to soften the truth with a joke. "I could spend my whole life learning new things about her and not get bored. She's so… I don't know. Vivacious. Looking at her makes me feel alive, like warming up by the fire after being in the snow for hours."

"I see," Rhys said.

"There's nothing weird going on, though. I'm not, like, trying to seduce her. Ask her, she gets it. I just want to hang out with her all the time and buy her Prada and kill anyone who makes her cry."

"So yes?" Rhys asked, cutting through the equivocation. "You love her?"

David stared up at the ceiling, resigning himself to the mortifying ordeal that never got any easier: admitting – out loud! – to having a heart.

"Yes," David said. "I love her, whatever that means these days. Is that alright?"

"I think it's good," Rhys said with a dreary sigh, like a Dickensian child watching snow fall out the orphanage window.

"It doesn't sound like it," David said, taking the obvious bait. Rhys loved to brood and then be asked what was wrong.

"You two just have such a strong psychic connection. It's something I don't fully understand. It's not a bond I have with either of you. I feel on the outside of things sometimes."

"Yeah well, maybe that's good for you. Far be it from me to be the one dispensing this advice, but it's not always about you, Rhys. What Moira and I have is special, just like what you and I have, or what you and she have. You don't see me getting jealous about your weird married person thing."

"You absolutely do," Rhys said with a bark of a laugh. "That's why you call it our 'weird married person thing'."

"Okay fine, shoot me! Maybe it's alright to feel insecure sometimes. Maybe we all do it and we take it out on each other in different ways and maybe parts of us even like it. But I promise I'm not having some kind of paranormal affair with your wife behind your back. Feel better?"

"I do," Rhys admitted.

"And since it's honesty hour..." David said carefully. They had to address it sometime. "Can we talk about what happened at Dion's?"

"What do you mean?"

"Dion called me your boyfriend, and you looked like you had seen a ghost. I thought we were beyond ducking in and out of the closet. That's kid stuff, Rhys."

"I don't care about anyone knowing I'm queer," Rhys protested, too strongly. "I just think it's best to be discreet about the three of us in public."

"That's just another closet. You're almost twenty-seven. You're High Priest. Who gives a fuck what anyone thinks?"

"Nobody in our circle is going to treat us any differently; I know that. It's just that you know how fast rumors spread, and my parents still live in the city–"

"Right," David said flatly. They had started this conversation a half dozen times in the years they had known each other, and it always ended in a fight. "But I didn't emigrate from Russia and live under my father's thumb for years to sneak around with you."

"I know," Rhys said, closing his eyes and taking a deep breath.

"Do they at least know you're bisexual?"

"No."

"You told me you would tell them."

"That was years ago. Things changed."

David nodded slowly, chewing on the inside of his mouth. If he said anything else, it would be something he regretted.

Rhys lasted two seconds in the silence before he turned towards David, dark eyes wide.

"I'll tell them," Rhys said. "I'm serious, babe."

David scoffed. There was no use getting his hopes up where Rhys's family was concerned. He had met Rhys's parents twice in college and had been introduced both times as Rhys's "roommate". It was so cowardly and so *passé*, so totally nineties. David had barely believed his ears.

"You're going to tell them we're dating?" David pressed.

"I'm going to come out to them, at least. Soon. Let me start there."

David hummed suspiciously, a tick he had picked up from Moira, but he let Rhys win this round. Maybe Rhys wasn't lying, to himself or anyone else. Maybe he was finally ready.

"Anything else you need to talk about?" Rhys asked, arching an eyebrow. "Since it's honesty hour?"

David's gut response was to clam up and smile. That's what he would have done in college, the first time they tried their hand at this. But he was trying to be better, no matter how much healthy communication felt like having teeth pulled. And Rhys was looking at him with such earnestness that it seemed criminal not to voice the question that had been biting at the back of David's brain for days. It was a question he should have asked months ago, but there was no avoiding it now.

"Is our relationship closed?" David ventured. "You, me, and Moira. Or could other people become involved under certain circumstances?"

Rhys pressed his lips together, and David resisted the urge to kiss him, to cover up the question hanging in the air with an easier sort of intimacy.

"Is there someone else?" Rhys asked.

"No."

Rhys didn't need to know about the teenage giddiness David felt around Maximilian. That was private to David's inner world, and it wasn't like anything was going to come of it anyway. Maximilian didn't wear a wedding ring, but that didn't mean that he was available to David, and David had his hands full enough with the Society and his law career and Rhys and Moira anyway. He wasn't looking for an excuse to pursue Maximilian; he was seeking clarity on the subject in general.

"Are you still into hooking up with other people when we're out?" Rhys asked. "Or when you're by yourself on trips?"

"I'm not as interested in that anymore, and I know it stressed you out."

"It was risky."

"I was always safe. I'm talking more about actual dating, not just blowing strangers at a bar. You know, real grown-up shit."

David loved Rhys to the point of abjection. He would do damn near anything for him and commit a whole host of atrocities for Moira besides. But David had never been built for ironclad monogamy. Even during their first relationship, when David was trying much harder to be the kind of person Rhys might want to keep around for a long period of time, they had an unspoken agreement that if David happened to find himself in the bathroom with someone else at a nightclub, Rhys would look the other way while he ordered another round of drinks. It wasn't healthy, strictly speaking, but it was functional.

David was really trying to be healthy. He was trying to be good.

But he wasn't interested in betraying himself to get there.

"What if, hypothetically, Moira fell in love with someone else?" David went on.

"We've talked about it," Rhys said, fiddling with his wedding ring. "We've agreed it's fine, so long as I can meet him and hopefully be on good terms. I think it would make her happy. She's got such a big heart. Are you okay with that?"

"She's not my wife, what do I care? Go to town, live a little."

"I'll tell her you said that," Rhys said with a smirk. That smirk softened the next question David wanted to ask, the one he had been trying to ask the entire time.

"Okay, so what if I wanted to date other people? Hypothetically."

"Hypothetically, I would want you to be happy too. But hypothetically, I would probably feel pretty jealous at having to share either of you. But I can't stop you from doing what you want."

"No, you can't. But I'd rather have your blessing."

"Just be truthful with me," Rhys. "If there's someone else, I would rather know."

"Of course," David said, relief crashing over him like a wave.

"That doesn't mean I won't still be jealous," Rhys said, a dark cast in his voice and a wicked smile on his lips. He leaned over David, who laid back against the pillows obligingly. "I just got you back and I don't want to lose you again."

"Lucky for us all, I like you when you're a little jealous," David said, then made a satisfied sound as Rhys's fingers curled around his throat. Rhys applied the faintest amount of pressure, a tantalizing promise of what was to come.

"Thank God for that," Rhys said, and lowered his head to kiss David deeply.

David lost himself in the sensation, every single other person in the world besides Rhys forgotten for the time being.

CHAPTER ELEVEN
RHYS

Rhys typically avoided downtown. It took ages to get there on the T or in the Lincoln, and he didn't enjoy weaving through the crowds of theatergoers and office workers to get to his destination.

That said, he probably would have swum across the Atlantic for Brattle.

The Brattle Book Store boasted three floors of rare and antiquarian titles, not to mention an open-air alleyway of used books that only cost a dollar. Rhys had spent hours browsing through those bargain paperbacks in college, when he barely had two pennies to rub together. Although his budget had changed since then, his enthusiasm for the written word had not.

Especially not when certain hard-to-obtain texts held the key to his success as High Priest.

Rhys had managed to survive flaunting the seven-spirit superstition so far and had grown his demonic stable to nine entities. There were his longtime standbys: Stolas for insights into the properties of herbs and stones, and Eligos, who equipped Rhys with the fortitude he needed to triumph in personal conflicts. The rapport Rhys had with those two was careful but convivial, bolstered by the occasional chant or candle dressed in cedar salves. Crocell was more difficult to manage, as slippery and changeable as water, but Rhys needed his assistance with sacred geometry, since he had never been perfectly steady-handed when it came to chalking out ceremonial circles. Balam was a newer addition, one Rhys was still wrestling with. When properly cajoled, Balam improved Rhys's otherwise shoddy ability to grasp the future through divination, but he also appeared in Rhys's dreams as a fearsome three-headed creature with flaming eyes, who roared his demands for more wine, more incense. Rhys often woke in a cold sweat, heart pounding, and had to sneak out of bed to blearily wave frankincense around his study as quietly as possible to avoid waking Moira.

He hadn't told her about courting extra demons, and he certainly hadn't mentioned it to David. Rhys also hadn't mentioned the tiny altars erected to each individual demon in his study. These altars acted as pinch points between the seen world and the unseen spirit realm, allowing him to quickly make requests of the demons without casting an entire summoning circle. It was fast and effective, but less formal and therefore less secure.

And of course, altars demanded to be fed.

Rhys always had trouble getting back to sleep once awake, so he would sit in his pajamas at his desk, drafting and redrafting that just-in-case statement David had asked him to write. Rhys would shuffle words around until his eyes burned, trying to find the right way to express what the Society did and didn't do without giving away too much of their secrets, and trying to make it all sound very pleasant and casual and not at all frightening.

Rhys had shared the working document with the group of leaders who had gathered in the tea room. Moira and David had made encouraging noises about the whole endeavor but hadn't looked at the document very closely, confirming Rhys's suspicion that this task mostly just to keep his mind busy so it didn't devour itself with worry. Zachary had opened the document, at least, and Maximilian had left a few irritatingly helpful editorial notes in the margins. Leda hadn't even sent a confirmation of receipt.

Those sleepless nights were becoming so frequent, however, that Rhys decided he needed to find something to do with himself at midnight besides work. A new book about the Magna Carta had just been released by one of his favorite academics at Cambridge A little light reading on royal charters would help soothe him back to sleep after getting up to feed his demons. Hopefully.

Rhys ducked into Brattle a half hour before closing, determined to pick up his international order right away without indulging in a meandering browse. There would be time for that another day, and he didn't want to make the shopkeeper stay late.

Well… Maybe he could check the spiritualism section, if he was quick.

Rhys ducked down the familiar aisle and almost ran headlong into a middle-aged finance type. He was wearing a suit and insipid aftershave, and he was loitering *right in front* of Rhys's favorite section.

Rhys stood a polite distance away, scanning the shelves over the man's shoulder. Then he saw it, an honest-to-God antique edition of *La Science Des Esprit*s by Éliphas Lévi. It was a rare text from one of Rhys's favorite magicians, and though Rhys didn't speak French, Nathan was more than proficient and would be happy to help. Rhys squinted over the man's shoulder to make out the number written on the price tag. Miraculously, it was within Rhys's budget.

Rhys took a step forward, fingers itching to pluck up the book, but he didn't move fast enough. The man snatched the book from the shelf, barely gave it a cursory glance, and then nodded as though he found what he had been looking for.

Rhys had to bite the inside of his mouth to keep from groaning in frustration. Why did this always happen to him? The moment he thought fortune was going to turn in his favor, it was snatched away.

Rhys sullenly followed the man up to the counter. There was no time to look for anything else, and no point in doing so when his luck had turned so rotten. He would just pick up his order and leave, burning off his anger with the frigid walk back to his car.

The woman working the register was young, perhaps freshly out of college. She had the unpainted soap-scrubbed face and tired eyes of an academic who had stayed up too late parsing data points or translating texts. She could have been a researcher, or an adjunct in training, or maybe even a magician.

Or maybe Rhys just saw his reflection everywhere he looked.

Rhys seethed as the man ahead of him made inane small talk with the shopkeeper. He tried to remind himself that this stranger had just as much right to cosmic secrets as Rhys, that he might be in a tight spot and in need of supernatural aid, and that, just like Moira always said, everyone you met on the street was fighting their own invisible battle. Unfortunately, Rhys only ever believed in the inherent goodness of the world when Moira was pouring her honey into his ear. When left to his own devices, he was much more misanthropic.

Finally, the man inserted his card into the chip reader. In a hot flash of petulance, Rhys hoped it declined.

The card declined.

The man inserted his card again, brow furrowing, and again the transaction was rejected. Rhys stood a little straighter, openly staring now.

Had he done that? It seemed impossible, and yet…

"I'm not sure what's wrong," the man admitted. "I can step outside and call my bank?"

"Normally that would be fine, but we're closing soon," the cashier said,. "Maybe you could come back tomorrow? We can hold books for twenty-four hours."

"That won't work," the man said, trying his card a third time to no avail. Chastened, he returned the card to his wallet. "I'm going out of town on business tonight. You're sure you can't hold it for me until next week?"

"Sorry, no. That's our policy."

The man muttered a terse thanks and exited the shop, the door banging shut behind him. In his absence, the room was somehow warmer, more charged. Rhys felt almost like he was standing in a ceremonial circle, like he could feel the shadows moving over his body and dripping off him like water.

"That's a shame," the woman said, shaking her head. She turned to Rhys, offering a perfunctory smile. "How can I help you?"

Rhys placed a hand over the antique book on the counter and handed her his card.

"I'm picking up an order for McGowan. And I'll take this home with me too, if you don't mind."

"One man's misfortune is another man's gain, right?" she said, handing him his history book from under the counter and scanning the occult text one more time

Rhys should have felt guilty, and he so often did when any stroke of luck befell him, but the victory coursing through his veins was stronger than shame. It felt like downing a whole glass of champagne, like a pretty girl smiling at him when he walked past, like his very existence was charmed. Is this what David felt like all the time?

"The card reader might be down," she said apologetically, and swiped Rhys's card.

It went through instantaneously. She smiled, relieved.

Rhys smiled back at her, wide with all his teeth.

It was finally working. Rhys was finally the universe's favorite, and all it had taken was pinning the universe's arms behind its back and commanding it to obey him.

Rhys gathered his book on the Magna Carta along with his treasure written in French, then ducked outside, his parcels tucked under his arms. He never broke rules, but that had felt deliciously illicit.

Rhys pressed through the midday crowd to get towards the train station, but a streak of black in the corner of his eye caught his attention.

He glanced down an alleyway and saw a large, slender dog silhouetted at the other end. The dog was panting heavily, staring right at Rhys. Trepidation trickled down his spine, even though he wasn't afraid of dogs and never had been.

Rhys couldn't look away, even as an eerie feeling started to build.

A delivery driver on a bike cut close to Rhys as they swerved down the street, nearly clipping him in the shoulder, and he stumbled out of the way just in time to avoid being knocked to the ground. He swore under his breath, clutching his books tight so as not to drop them, then looked back down the alleyway.

The black dog, if it had ever been there, was gone.

Despite his insistence that he didn't go in for garden-variety superstition, Rhys took the incident at the bookstore as a sign that he should double-down on his magical practice. If nine demons were manageable and serving him so well, surely ten would be better, especially if he poured more time and energy into feeding his hungry helper spirits.

He cancelled his standing plans to go boating with Nathan and sit in convivial silence reading in a cafe with Cameron, opting instead to lock himself in his study and experiment with new evocations. He tried to protect the plans he had made with Moira and David, but ultimately, even those took a hit. Moira nodded with understanding when he apologized for having to cancel their date to browse the Christmas market in the Seaport, but there was disappointment in her eyes. David, less prone to niceties, responded with a curt "that's fine" text when Rhys flaked on going over to David's to watch a horror movie. No emojis, no punctuation.

Rhys pretended not to be bothered by this. Routine changes happened as people undertook new responsibilities, and relationships naturally recalibrated to accommodate that. There was the Society budget to balance, the new candidates to interview, the rituals to plan and lead, not to mention the social functions to make a smiling appearance at.

As his calendar spiraled further and further out of his control, Rhys called on his demonic assistants more and more.

Orias, who assisted the sorcerer in the study of planetary hours, was bombarded with offerings day and night until Rhys's ability to interpret cosmic transits improved to near-faultless accuracy. Naberius was placated with music in exchange for boosting Rhys's infinitesimal natural charisma. If Rhys offered up tracks from the self-soothing My Chemical Romance album he would have been playing on repeat anyway, so be it. He needed all the help he could get with so much public speaking ahead of him.

Despite his bottomless ambition, Rhys's time and energy was bound by human parameters. He was sleeping less these days, and he didn't often have much of an appetite, though he forced himself to eat handfuls of trail mix and string cheese sticks at varying intervals to keep from crashing. His already concerning caffeine intake had doubled, which probably wasn't very good for his heart, but he needed the buzz of cold brew and espresso to keep himself focused.

This breakneck pace finally caught up with him one Thursday in conclave, when he was back-to-back with Antoni trying to summon a minor demonic marquis. The demon was supposed to bolster Antoni's mathematical abilities to help him study for his series seven license. It was a simple evocation, one Rhys had completed successfully multiple times before, and with Antoni acting as scryer, it should have been a breeze.

If David was a summer electrical storm in the summoning circle, soaking Rhys to the bone with pure magical thrill, Antoni was an autumn rainfall, all-enveloping and tinged with the mystical. Normally, Rhys trusted Antoni enough to lean into that dark, moody undercurrent and let Antoni set the pace of their summoning.

But today Rhys was itchy and keyed up, like he was wearing skin two sizes too tight. The magic words were clunky in his mouth, and he kept losing his place in the ritual. He hadn't been drinking enough water, and since conjuration required sweat and breath and physical exertion, dehydration was impacting his ability to successfully draw the spirit into the circle. Antoni tried to patch over the holes Rhys left in the summoning, slowing his pace so Rhys could catch up, but it wasn't enough. Rhys was off his game.

When the demon slipped through his fingers for a second time, refusing to settle in the triangle in the center of the circle designed to capture entities, Rhys let out a groan. The dim light of the ritual room and the overpowering scent of resinous incense, usually so comforting, was giving him a headache. And he was painfully aware he was being stared at by the Society members gathered around the circle.

Rhys clenched his jaw and swallowed through a dry throat. They were probably already whispering about him behind his back, insinuating that he was not fit to lead. Maybe they thought he never had been.

"It's alright," Antoni said, squeezing his arm. "We'll try again. From the top, OK?"

"No, I'm tapped out," Rhys said, unzipping his robe halfway down his chest. He felt suddenly suffocated. "Are you good to keep scrying?"

"Sure," Antoni said, looking concerned but thankfully not arguing. As much as Rhys would have liked the contrary to be true, magic was an art, not a science. Sometimes, evocations fell flat, and sometimes, sorcerers hit a wall halfway through a summoning. It happened.

Rhys glanced around the room, doing a quick head count. David was there, lingering at the edge of the circle with his arms crossed as though waiting for Rhys to tap him in, but Rhys was trying to show less favoritism towards his boyfriend, and moreover, David was a lousy sorcerer. He needed more opportunities to practice keeping steady and patient in the circle, but this wasn't the time. And Rhys wasn't confident David had done his homework about this particular spell.

Actually, Rhys wasn't sure any of them had.

Except one person, who could always be relied upon to pursue their own advancement.

"Kitty," he said. "Do you want to lead the summoning today?"

Kitty's eyes brightened. She had been applying herself to her studies with ferocious dedication, but she had yet to lead a formal summoning. Rhys was keeping a close enough eye on her progress to know she was capable of it, but she hadn't been tested yet.

"You think I'm ready?" she asked, not an ounce of fear in her voice. Nathan glowed with pride at her side.

"I know you are," Rhys said. "Are you comfortable working with Antoni in the circle?"

Kitty looked at Antoni, a smile pulling at her perfectly painted pink lips.

"I am."

Rhys glanced to Antoni, seeking his perfunctory consent, and was surprised to see Antoni staring at Kitty with a strange, slightly pained expression. There was something wild in his eyes. Or maybe it was just the reflection from the candlelight.

"Are you alright with this?" Rhys asked his friend, pitching his voice low so that only Antoni could hear.

Antoni blinked a few times and then he was himself again, all boyish bravado.

"Always," Antoni said.

Rhys swept a hand towards Kitty as he exited the circle, ceding the floor to her. She stepped into the matrix of chalked symbols, kitten heels clicking softly on the stone floor, and Rhys held his breath.

Make me proud, he thought.

Antoni extended his hand to Kitty in a show of good sportsmanship. The formality wasn't necessary. Most of the Society members skipped the opening handshake that total propriety demanded. But Kitty seemed to appreciate it, and gave him a firm shake before assuming the position, back-to-back in the center of the circle.

Kitty smiled at her husband, sharing a private moment of triumph, and then she began her evocation.

Her Latin was flawless, which wasn't surprising. Kitty was a Columbia graduate who had split her childhood between New York and Beijing and summered in Nice; languages weren't a problem for her. Rhys also wasn't surprised by her natural command of the space. But he couldn't help but be impressed by how intuitively she worked with Antoni, seeming to know exactly when to press forward and when to pause, waiting for Antoni to tell her what to do next.

"It's manifesting above you," Antoni said, guiding Kitty's eyes towards the ceiling with two fingers. "Draw it down."

Kitty shifted her tone from polite to effortlessly dominating. It sounded like a gleaming stiletto pressing down a heaving chest, or a dozen lighters jostling for the honor of igniting a single cigarette.

An involuntary shudder crawled up Rhys's spine, responding to the presence of power.

Every sorcerer brought their own style of command into the circle. Rhys went the traditionally kingly route, invoking religious authority and the language of fealty, while David shone when he played the part of the petulant prince, demanding demons obey him for the sake of his own amusement. Antoni did well by leaning into the archetype of the renaissance sorcerer, relentless in his desire to uncover the secret sciences that powered the universe, and Moira, on the few occasions Rhys had seen her order a demon around, was the dark side of the moon, all feminine rage and undeniable gravitational pull.

Apparently, Kitty was an Iris dipped in titanium.

The demon pushed back against Kitty with an unseen blow that made her feet skid on the stone floor.

"Find your center of gravity," Rhys said, trying not to pace. He wanted Kitty to succeed, so earnestly that he almost forgot that he had failed. She was the first initiate inducted under his reign, but more than that, she was a friend. He *wanted* her to win. "Don't let it talk back to you."

Kitty widened her stance, chanting with renewed intensity. Antoni circled her, closer and closer as he directed her gaze. Kitty's fingers twisted through the air, somehow elegant in their brutality, and Antoni's breath caught in his throat as the spirit was drawn down towards the triangle. Rhys couldn't see any distinct manifestation, but he could see the way Kitty strained against that supernatural pull, and he could feel the temperature of the room rising, along with the humidity. Within moments, it felt like they were in a hothouse.

Rhys had never seen anything like this. He had only read about it, when a scryer and sorcerer invoked lightning or caused earthquakes with their sheer might.

The energy Kitty and Antoni raised together had transformed the atmosphere.

A bead of sweat trickled down Kitty's brow, a streak of shine in her perfect makeup, and she all but snarled as she yanked her fist through the air, demanding the demon submit to her.

"Almost there," Antoni said, eyes burning with focus. "You're so close, Kitty."

"She's running too hot," Nathan said at Rhys's side. There was a worried crease between his brows. "She could get hurt. Rhys, pull her out."

"Let her cook," David said. He cupped his hands around his mouth and raised his voice. "You've got this, Kitty!"

Kitty crouched, drawing the demon down further, and Antoni followed her, the knees of his slacks smudging the chalk. They were inches away from victory.

"*Now*," Rhys breathed, mostly to himself.

When Kitty slammed her palms on the ground, trapping the spirit inside the triangle, an electric sizzle went through the room. Static lifted Rhys's hair and fizzled along the hem of his robe.

For a heartbeat, no one said a word. The only sounds were Kitty and Antoni's exerted breaths. A haze of steam rose from their skin and clothes, as though they had just emerged from a hot spring on an ice-cold day.

Antoni broke into a grin, huffing out a laugh, and then Kitty giggled, delirious and proud.

Rhys brought his hands together in a brisk clap, igniting an avalanche of applause. Kitty and Antoni stood and stared at each other in wonder. Kitty put her hand out for a shake, but Antoni stepped forward and grasped her by the upper arms instead. She swayed slightly and then righted herself, grounded by his touch.

Antoni said something to Kitty, snatched away by the sound of cheering, but Rhys could almost read the words on Antoni's lips.

It looked like:

You're a revelation.

Rhys' shoulders dropped with relief, and for a moment all he felt was bone-deep admiration for his talented and tough friends.

Then, like the snake slithering through Eden, doubt crept in.

Kitty was more than competent, that much was obvious, but she was still new. If Kitty had managed in one attempt what Rhys couldn't do in two, that didn't bode well for Rhys' spiritual abilities, nor for his esteem in the eyes of his peers.

He was slipping. He could feel it, the ground slowly but surely giving way beneath him like sand.

Rhys swallowed down his bitterness and kept clapping, over and over again until his palms stung.

CHAPTER TWELVE
DAVID

David had learned over the years that, sometimes, you had to let Rhys get a little megalomaniacal. Whether it was swearing vengeance under his breath against an academic who had lifted his research, or barricading himself in his dorm room after a tiff to summon demons until his eyesight got blurry, or losing himself in fantasies of English foxhunting summers as he browsed the Jo Malone cologne counter with David's black card in hand, it was, all in all, good for Rhys. These dalliances with grandiosity were Rhys's way of letting off steam, of indulging the darker aspects of his ambitious nature without letting them rule him entirely. He always reigned himself back in after a couple hours, or a couple days, and then returned to David chastened and kind.

David was currently trying to figure out where they were in that capture and release cycle as far as the High Priesthood was concerned. Something had shifted in the Society since Rhys had taken the helm. The atmosphere in meetings was more tense, more focused, more, well… Rhys.

The summonings Rhys guided them through were longer and more arduous than anything Wayne, the former High Priest, had ever expected. David hadn't been pushed so far in his psychic abilities since he was living under his father's draconian rules, and while Rhys's leadership was far less cruel, sweetened by praise and stolen kisses, it was still demanding.

David wasn't sure whether he should be concerned about that or not.

The answer crystalized when David was awoken one morning by an email from the High Priest, with all Society members CC'd, outlining a set of new policies. There would be no more skimming off the endowment for expensive parties and outings, besides yearly functions like the gala and the winter social. In addition, there would be no more unauthorized after-hours use of the ritual room for personal practice. All rituals had to be greenlit and scheduled by the High Priest's office, all business expenses had to go through Antoni, and all new proposals for events had to be sent to David for review.

David was barely awake enough to be irritated, but the sensation still pricked through his sleepy haze like a needle. He hated paperwork; he got enough of that at his day job. He was offended that Rhys had volunteered him for more bureaucracy without running it by him first.

David pulled up Rhys's name on his phone, but the call rang through to voicemail.

"Rhys McGowan. Leave a message and I'll get back to you as soon as I can."

David rolled his eyes, then tossed his phone down and threw back his duvet. He had to be at the office earlier than usual to put out a fire, and the law waited for no man. Strange that Rhys, who was usually the nocturnal one, had been up at 5:45 sending emails anyway.

David attempted to put these matters out of his mind as he splashed water on his face and brushed his teeth. He slapped on the industrial-grade sunscreen he hoped would prevent him from having to succumb to his own vanity and get Botox before thirty-five, then began getting dressed.

An email lit up David's phone as he made his way through the kitchen towards the door. He nearly dropped his phone when he read the sender address, then slammed his hip against the counter of his kitchen by making too wide of a distracted turn. He should be getting his ass to the office to stand impatiently on the steps while they unlocked the front doors, but instead, David tapped the email open immediately.

David,

Hello! I hope you're keeping well. It was so nice to connect in the tearoom with you and the other representatives. I wasn't able to speak with you directly after the meeting, so I'm following up here.

I'd be interested in hearing any more insights you have, as a psychic or as a Society member, into the ritual in the common as well as into the state of the occult scene in Boston in general. I think keeping in touch as the situation progresses could be wise, and it might be nice for us to play catch-up, since I've been living on the West Coast and don't have my bearings totally on the city yet. Moira mentioned you've lived in Boston for fifteen years, so you seemed like the natural choice for a local guide.

Lovely to be back in touch after all these years!

Warmly,

Max

Max. He'd signed the email Max. Did that mean something, or was David reading too much into it? And *warmly*, what did that mean?

Trying to figure it out made David's head hurt, so he marked the email as unread and went about his week, promising himself he would respond when he had mentally composed an answer.

David sent one more text to Rhys as he pulled on his suit jacket, just to cover his bases.

Hey. I tried to call, but you weren't picking up. Work has been crazy. How are you holding up over there?

It was limpid, but it was the best David could do right now.

To Rhys's credit, he responded quickly.

It's been madness over here as well, sorry I've been MIA. I'll see you at the Society meeting tonight?

David wrinkled his nose. If Rhys had been in a better place, he might have offered to call, or even to grab an after-work coffee at one of their favorite bistros. This felt dangerously close to getting blown off, which David hated more than almost anything.

Obviously, he texted back, not caring if he sounded bitchy. *You know I don't skip meetings. Talk soon.*

The atmosphere in the clubhouse was palpably tense. The conversation was more frenetic yet more hushed, as though members were afraid of being overheard. The younger clique, David's group of friends, weren't seated in their usual semicircle of overstuffed chairs in the back corner. Instead, they were scattered through the room, harried as they carried on individual conversations.

David made a beeline to Antoni, who was lingering at the buffet table, looking somewhat out of place as he nibbled on salami and cubed cheese.

"Antoni, your macros," David reminded him.

Antoni grimaced but put down the cheese. Antoni and David kept each other accountable as far as fitness was concerned, so David knew that Antoni was a nervous snacker. The damage he had done to the charcuterie board probably didn't bode well. "Where's Rhys?" David asked.

"On the warpath," Antoni responded, his dark brows pulling together in a scowl.

"What's that mean?"

"You tell me. Did you get his weird email?"

"Of course I did. I don't know what he was thinking, putting me in charge of holding everyone's hand and wiping their asses. You know I didn't ask for that."

"Listen, he was texting me at two a.m. last night, asking for exhaustive financial reports. Do you know how long it takes to pull reports like that together? I have a job, David. This isn't my only commitment. Remind him of that, will you?"

"I'll talk to him."

"He's holed up in his office," Antoni said, waving a hand in that general direction. "Good luck getting an audience, but he might agree to see you if you say you've got Society business."

David passed Cameron on his way to the office, who looked like he was trying to placate a red-faced older brother who was waving his finger in the air. Kitty was poised as motionlessly as a coiled snake on one of the couches, placing some very serious calls in quick succession. David shot her a questioning look, and she merely shook her head.

The vibes were, to put it plainly, fucked.

The Society consisted largely of two basement rooms: the siting room which was decorated with heavy wood paneling and tarnished oil paintings and outfitted with a very illegal smoking section; and the ritual room, where the actual magic was performed in conclave. A narrow hallway running between the two rooms featured a small collection of offices, most notably the High Priest's.

David stopped in front of the door to the High Priest's office, with its brass nameplate and frosted glass window, and knocked twice.

No response.

"Rhys, I know you're in there," David said. "It's me."

"Give me fifteen minutes, David," Rhys said through the door, like David was a PhD student trying to get his advisor's attention during office hours.

"We've got a time-sensitive issue on our hands," David lied.

Rhys unlocked the door, ushering David inside. He was formally dressed in a wine-colored blazer and slacks, and had even done something to his curls to make them slightly less wild, but there were bruised circles under his eyes.

Obviously, somebody hadn't been sleeping.

"What's the problem?" Rhys asked.

"You are," David said, shutting the door and locking it behind him. Under better circumstances, he would have loved to be acting out a power exchange fantasy behind the locked door of the High Priest's office with his boyfriend, but this wasn't the time. Moreover, David wasn't in the mood.

"I beg your pardon?" Rhys said.

It appeared he didn't have a sense that he might have gone off the rails, but David didn't find this innocence endearing. If anything, it irritated him more.

"What were you thinking, making me your point person for all this? I don't have the time, Rhys."

Rhys waved away David's complaint like it was nothing more than a gnat.

"You're good with people, and you have a head for details. And you agreed to be my second. I assumed I could count on you to step up when I needed you to."

"And I assumed you would do me the courtesy of *asking* me instead of *telling* me to step up."

Rhys sank down at his desk. He had attempted to corral Wayne's complete lack of an organization system into folders and file cabinets, but there were still grimoires and receipts and membership applications spread out all over the desk. Rhys kept talking about digitizing all of it himself. David knew that would take a designated staff member months at minimum.

"OK, you're right about that," Rhys said. "I should have asked. But there wasn't time."

"It's sorcery, Rhys, not heart surgery. Things can wait."

Rhys kept lacing and unlacing his fingers and bouncing his knee under the desk. He was acting like he had just done a line of coke; an explanation David might have believed if it was anyone other than Rhys.

"Wayne left a lot of loose ends when he retired," Rhys admitted, and there it was, the tiniest flicker of vulnerability. "He wasn't exactly running a tight ship. I'm just doing my best to help us all regain equilibrium."

"Which I appreciate. But it seems like some of the members are irritated with the... swiftness with which you implemented these new policies."

"They'll adjust. Come on David, we used to talk about this when we dreamed about the Priesthood. Leading by example, encouraging everyone to take their studies seriously."

"Not by running yourself into the ground."

"I'm happy," Rhys said, in the exact same tone of voice he used to lie to his mother over the phone.

David had come in here hoping to talk some sense into Rhys, but it was becoming rapidly evident that it was a fool's errand.

Rhys reached across the desk and squeezed David's hand, and the security of touch thawed David, if only slightly. Maybe Rhys was just having an off week. Maybe, after instituting a few bylaws and threatening to whip them all into shape, he would mellow out.

"Let me know if there's any way I can help you," David said. "*Outside* of doing paperwork."

"Actually..." Rhys said, with bright hope. David knew where this was going, and he regretted offering to help. "Did you have a chance to look at that drafted statement I sent you? I know you're busy, but I would appreciate any notes. The more I think about it, the more I think establishing a pseudo-presence in the public eye might be a good idea. Ratify the Society as a venerable Boston institution, you know?"

"Babe," David sighed. "Are you still hung up on this public sacrifice thing? I know it freaked us all out, and I know you're convinced it makes you look bad or weak or whatever, but drawing attention to it will only make it worse. Trust me on this."

A hurt look passed over Rhys's face, and David wanted to kick himself. His irritation had bled through into his words, and now Rhys felt like a fool.

Rhys glanced down at his watch, then flipped shut the thick folder of files he had been reviewing. Rhys obviously felt misunderstood, but David had never been good at smiling and nodding along to bad ideas.

"I'll have someone else look it over for me. It's almost time to move everyone into the conclave room, anyway. Will you walk with me?"

"Always," David sighed.

David drifted after Rhys and began to round up the Society members for their ritual. Drinks were abandoned, conversations were cut short, and everyone filed into the ritual room.

"Where are the robes?" Nathan wondered aloud. There was usually a rack of wine-red ritual robes stashed in the corner. David's robe still had his father's name written above his on the polyester tag in sharpie, so faded it was almost illegible.

"I got rid of them," Rhys said with easy smile. It was all casual New England charm, like a working-class Kennedy, but David had seen that smile enough times to know it was something Rhys had studied and learned to imitate when he wanted to appear relaxed. "They were so hard to work in. I figured we could do away with one old tradition, at least."

The Society members drifted to their places in their street clothes, if a little awkwardly. Only Antoni lingered behind near the door next to David, his full lips pressed into a displeased line.

"What's wrong?" David asked quietly. He shot a glance over his shoulder to make sure Rhys wasn't paying attention to them. They had maybe sixty seconds for a chat before people noticed they were missing from the circle.

"He's lying," Antoni said.

"Who, Rhys? About the robes? Why?"

Antoni turned his keys over in his hands. An embossed keychain winked at David: STWHS stamped in serif font onto polished bronze. It was the abbreviation for the Society's full name, a mouthful of antiquated keywords that were only ever printed onto letterhead and tax forms. David probably knew the whole thing, if he racked his brain, but they all just called it "the Society" for a reason. It was simpler that way. Antoni, however, knew the whole name by heart and with pride.

He cares, David thought, heart twisting. *He takes this seriously.*

Maybe David should start taking things more seriously too.

"Think of it the way Rhys thinks of things," Antoni said, unbuttoning his cuffs and rolling his sleeves up past his elbows. "Think of it symbolically."

"No logic games, please, I get enough of that at work."

Antoni took off his watch, tucking it away in his pocket as though anticipating a particularly strenuous spell.

"If the High Priest presides over members in plainclothes, what does that communicate?" Antoni went on.

Across the circle, Rhys was saying something to Cameron, a convivial smile on his face. David looked at him for a few moments, chest aching with that old love, and then tore his eyes away.

"Straight talk, Antoni," David said. "Now."

"It means he's extending his influence as High Priest. If he tells us what to do out of robes, he tells us what to do twenty-four seven."

It was so subtle, so antiquated in its Machiavellian aims, so quintessentially *Rhys* that now that it had been pointed out to David, there was no way not to see it. Rhys was sending a clear message:

I'm in charge here.

Alpha and omega, forever and ever, amen.

Rhys caught David's eye for just a moment, offering him one of those tiny smiles that reminded David so much of when they were young together, in those precious early months before they had been thrust into rivalry.

They were on a different path now, but David wasn't sure where it was heading, and somehow, he felt even more out of control then before.

David swallowed through a suddenly dry mouth, then straightened his tie and took his place in the circle.

CHAPTER THIRTEEN
MOIRA

"You look tired," Moira said as she heated water for a fresh pot of oolong. Rhys sat at the kitchen table, staring off into space. "Get enough sleep last night?"

"Mm?" Rhys asked, startled. "Oh, I'm alright. Just had nightmares."

"I heard you up at midnight," Moira said carefully. She had been awoken by the gentle rocking of the bed as he tried to slide back in beside her as quietly as possible. She wasn't sure exactly what he was doing in his study in the wee hours, but he came back to bed smelling like myrrh and nervous sweat. Rhys had always been private, which was fine because Moira had always been independent, but as far as he was entitled to his privacy, she was entitled to the truth. "I thought you might have been in the kitchen making yourself a drink with that sleep tonic I brewed. But it sounded like you were in your study."

"I was," Rhys admitted. This was a good first step; at least he wasn't outright lying.

"Doing research?" she asked, giving him the grace of an open-ended question.

"For the Society, mostly. Just sorting through my thoughts in the quiet."

Moira poured two steaming cups of tea, never breaking eye contact with her husband.

"And that's all it is, right, baby?"

104   ASCENSION

Rhys' phone lit up with a notification, and he glanced down at it thoughtlessly before snatching up the phone and taking a second, harder look.

"Jesus *Christ*," he said, like he had just been bitten by something.

"What is it?" Moira asked, bumping him with her hip so he would tilt the phone screen towards her.

"That's my letter," he said. He was white as a sheet. "The open letter I wrote to the *Inquirer*. They ran it. How did they even get their hands on it?"

Moira peered at Rhys's phone, recognizing her husband's polite, if a bit formal, language in the letter. It outlined the occult community's ethical commitments, as well as the innocence in the matter of the public ritual. The accompanying article wasn't exactly a hit piece, but the paper treated the letter with skepticism, as proof of some larger ulterior motive or perhaps, even a veiled admission of guilt. They had somehow managed to get statements from two police officers, a professor of religion at Harvard, and, Moira saw with dread in her stomach, Dion. His statement was perfunctory, no doubt a soundbite he had offered up in exchange for being left alone: *Magic isn't about fear. It's about freedom.*

Her heart stopped when she took a closer look at the names included at the bottom of the letter. It was signed not just by Rhys, but by Zachary, Leda, Maximilian, David, and Moira.

"Why is my name on it?" Moira asked, worry heating into anger. "I never signed off on this. I told you I didn't think it was a good idea, Rhys."

"I know!" Rhys said. He looked genuinely baffled, threading his fingers through his curls and tightening in distress. "I was never going to run it without written approval from everyone. I would have taken anyone's name off if they asked. David's going to be so pissed. And what if my parents see this?"

"Mary Ann can't watch the news without working herself into a state, and Arthur only reads the *Globe*. Let's stay focused alright? This isn't just about you."

"Only six people had access to the document," Rhys said, tapping furiously at his phone. "I keep everything encrypted. You don't think this is David trying to help, is it? Or Leda pulling some kind of prank? I swear to God, if either of them went behind my back and–"

Rhys's voice dropped off as though he had just walked off a cliff. He tapped twice on his phone, then tapped again.

"That's not–" he muttered, eyes round and agonized like the paintings of Saint Sebastian Moira had seen in museums. "I didn't–"

"Let me see," Moira said, holding out her hand for her phone.

It took a moment for Moira to parse what she was looking at. It was an email, sent from Rhys's business address to the editor's desk at the *Inquirer*, with the open letter attached. The body of the email was brief but damning.

Hello,

My name is Rhys McGowan; I'm the High Priest of the Society for Theurgic Work and Hermetic Study. The Society, along with other local spiritual organizations, was recently profiled in an Inquirer *article. Please find attached a joint statement on the matter.*

Sincerely,

Rhys

"You sent this?" Moira demanded. She didn't think Rhys was capable of doing something so foolish, but that was his name. The syntax even sounded like him.

"I don't think I did," Rhys replied. His cheekbones looked particularly gaunt, like he was slowly losing the sort of weight someone with his bird-bone build couldn't afford to lose. "I wrote the email, sure, but it was just a working draft. I must have hit send without meaning to, or accidentally scheduled something, or–"

"Or maybe you were sleepwalking, or astral projecting," Moira said, with a meanness she couldn't take back. "Doesn't much matter now, does it?"

Rhys winced.

"Moira, I'm sorry. I haven't been sleeping well, and I shouldn't have been on my phone so late–"

Rhys's phone began vibrating insistently. Moira glanced down at the caller ID, then held the phone to her ear and said:

"David?"

"Did you see the *Inquirer*?" David demanded. "Can you believe they called me an entertainer, like what I do is some kind of party trick? Me playing piano, *that's* entertainment. They made me sound like a bachelorette party stripper. Where's Rhys? I'm going to kill him. I *told* him not to do this."

Moira held the phone slightly away from her face to put some distance between herself and the verbal barrage. Rhys, who could hear every word, looked like he wanted to melt into the floor.

"I just had a huge séance booking pull out because they didn't want to be associated with a possible criminal," David went on. "No one at the office will stop asking me questions. Suddenly I'm not just the gay lawyer, or the Russian lawyer, I'm the lawyer who *talks to dead people*. And now all my dead dad's friends, who were convinced I had gotten out of the psychic business altogether, are blowing up my phone asking if we can do a mastermind over coffee, whatever the fuck that is."

"It must be hard to be heir to a fabulously wealthy occult dynasty that stretches back centuries," Moira said. Stress made her snappish.

"I just got outed at my job Moira, take it down a notch, Jesus."

"Don't you tell me to take anything down."

"Listen, I don't want to yell at you, I want to yell at Rhys. Put him on, I can hear him breathing."

Moira handed her husband the phone. Rhys held it to his ear with the grim resolve of a man walking to the gallows.

"David, I didn't do this," he said. "Or maybe I did, but I didn't mean to. You know I wouldn't go against you and Moira on something like this, especially not with your names included. I'm furious at the paper for running that article alongside the letter. I'd burn down the *Inquirer* if I could."

"Don't let anyone hear you say that," David shot back. "They're liable to print it."

"If the *Inquirer* wants to escalate things, we'll just have to show them that we're all normal, law-abiding citizens who vote and pay our taxes," Moira cut in, leaning over Rhys to speak into the phone. Rhys put it on speaker.

"The press won't care," David said. "Trust me, I deal with these people all the time. They just want a story. Wait until they find out we're all dating. I can see the headline now: depraved Satanist swingers terrorize pious New England town."

"Nobody is a Satanist, and nobody is a swinger," Rhys said firmly. He had regained a bit of his composure and was talking slower now, with more resolve. "I'm going to handle the paper, I'm going to find whoever is behind that ritual and bring them to heel, and I'm going to have this all sorted by the winter social. That's it."

"The winter social is two weeks away so you'd better work fast." David took a long breath, as though counting down from ten on the other end. When he spoke again, he had simmered down a bit. "How did this happen, Rhys?"

"The most likely answer is that I was working on the document late at night and sent it without realizing. I'm sorry. I've been so..." Rhys faltered, his voice thick before he recovered himself. "I haven't been feeling super well lately."

"I'm aware. Just... let's get this cleaned up and make it go away, alright? I'll pay off whoever I need to."

"We aren't bribing the fourth estate, David," Rhys replied.

"Fine, but never say I don't offer to help you. Rhys, listen, I love you, OK? I do. But you've got to be more careful."

"I know," Rhys said, clenching his jaw. "I love you too. I–"

An incoming call cut in. *Antoni Bresciani.*

"Put him through," Moira said.

"Rhys, I need to talk to you," Antoni said. Moira knew Antoni primarily as a good-time-guy, someone who was the first to order a round of drinks or start a chorus of "happy birthday", who always smelled of hair pomade and cinnamon gum. He was happiest when he was laughing, or flirting, or both, but right now, he sounded downright grim.

"Talk to me," Rhys said. "Moira's here. I've got David on the line too."

"I'm going to preface this by saying that I'm not an expert in running a not-for-profit fraternal organization, which, according to the IRS, is how the Society is categorized," Antoni said. "Wayne was the one filing the paperwork and reporting expenses every year, and we all know he didn't leave the best records. But from what I can tell, we're in fiscally dangerous waters."

"Uh, how so?" Rhys said, shooting Moira a baffled look. She was sure Antoni had been calling to chew Rhys out about the letter. Had something else gone wrong in the last hour?

"We have to follow certain guidelines to maintain our tax-exempt status. That includes allocating any net earnings we make in a given year to approved purposes. Education, donations to the community, maintenance of the building, that kind of thing. And it looks like Wayne just... wasn't doing that. Between your salary and the retainer fees you've allocated to me and the rest of your immediate staff – which I appreciate, don't get me wrong – we've attracted the wrong kind of attention."

"None of us know what that means," David said.

Antoni sighed on the other end of the phone, like he was being forced to explain death to a child.

"We're being audited. Or we're going to be, if I don't placate them with documentation and promises to behave ourselves better in the next quarter."

Rhys dropped his head into his hands.

"I don't need this right now, Antoni."

"This isn't Antoni's fault," Moira said. "He's only trying to help.".".

"I might be able to work some magic to make this go away," Antoni went on. "And I mean that literally; I've got a regulus talisman that could help. It will take some finessing and it will take working overtime to organize Wayne's records, but I can do it."

"I'll pay you double," Rhys said.

"I don't want double. I want you to cool it on the spending, OK? No more expensive luncheons or guest lecturers or hiring more staff, and no more renovations. Not right now."

"But we talked about repaving and soundproofing the ritual room–"

"Yeah, and the bank denied our request for a loan. We're not solvent, Rhys."

Moira didn't think it was possible for her husband to turn any paler, but somehow, he managed it. Rhys's phone rang again. Nathan Vo this time. Rhys made an irritated tsking noise, then tapped Nathan into the conference call.

"You're on speaker," Rhys said by way of a hello. "What is it?"

"Oh! If this is a bad time, I can call back–"

"There's not likely to be a better time any time soon," Rhys said drearily. "Tell me you have good news for me."

"Uh, listen big guy–"

Rhys groaned. Nathan only called him "big guy" when breaking bad news.

Moira leaned over the phone, speaking crisply.

"Expediency is close to godliness in this case, sugar, so get it out quick."

"Remember the handful of Society applicants Kitty and I were courting? They all pulled out, except for one. They're not comfortable being associated with the Society right now. I don't think that letter in the *Inquirer* did us any favors."

"There's still one though, right? Can we move forward with them?"

"Um, about that... Kitty did some digging and found out that they're a journalist with a newsletter dedicated to infiltrating insular groups and then writing exposés about them. I think they're more interested in Substack clout than in the occult."

Rhys covered his face with his hands and tipped his head back in his chair, as though surrendering himself to the torrential downpour of bad news. Moira settled her hand on Rhys's shoulder and gave a reassuring squeeze. Static crackled over her fingers, evidence of her husband's stress, but there was something else under the anxiety. A heavy, slick darkness, staining her skin like motor oil.

She didn't like that one bit.

"We need those membership dues," Rhys said.

"I know," Nathan replied. "But the other candidates have already been snapped up by rival orders. I'm sorry."

"You know Rhys," David said, with nonchalant lightness, "you might consider outside help. I've been emailing with Maximilian–"

"No," Rhys said with a scowl. That sticky, dark aura emanated from him even stronger, and Moira removed her hand from his shoulder before her fingers went numb.

"He's not even asking for you to pay a consulting fee; he's offering to come in and keep the ship from sinking *pro bono*. It would only take him a couple weeks."

"And when I give Maximilian access to our private records and rituals, what then?" Rhys demanded. "He feeds them back to his Thelema friends? Pick up a history book, David; this is how orders collapse. By bringing in an outsider with an ulterior motive."

"That strikes me as paranoid," Moira said. This meeting was quickly running off the rails, and The Society was clearly in worse shape than Rhys had let on. "And uncharitable to your second in command."

"Then offer me a better alternative," Rhys said.

"You need to focus on building trust with the rest of the occult community," Moira replied. He might not want to hear it, but she knew she was right. "The endowment, the police investigation, the newspapers, that's all out of your hands. And if you keep pushing through new initiatives and demanding deference, it is not going to endear you to other leaders. Magicians are by nature self-interested. They need to feel esteemed to give esteem back. You've been throwing your weight around instead of laying the groundwork of friendship. If you find yourself in a bind with money or magic or the law, I can't think of anyone in our community, except maybe Dion and even that's a stretch, who would offer you protection or aid."

Rhys looked at her for a long while, black eyes gazing into brown. Moira almost believed that he would listen to her. But then his gaze shuttered, and he shook his head, and Moira's heart fell into her shoes.

"If I roll over and show my belly now, they'll eat me alive, and the Society will be collateral damage." Rhys worked his thumb into the thin scar running through his palm, rubbing an anxious circle. "We aren't strong enough to survive a power vacuum. You're not understanding my position."

"What don't I understand?" Moira responded, cold anger trickling down her breastbone. How dare he speak to her like a wife cheering from the floor seats rather than an active player on the court? "My business is on the line. Some of us don't have fancy titles and endowments. Some of us need to get by on the work of our hands and the quality of our character."

"That's not what I meant," Rhys said, frustration rising in his voice.

"I'm getting the feeling you don't actually want advice from any of us," she said, loud and clear for everyone on the call to hear. "I think you just want an audience for your own self-destruction. And I hate watching men fall on their swords. Good job reporting in, everyone. Hold the course unless you hear otherwise from Rhys or David. Take care now."

With that, Moira ended the call. Rhys glowered at her, his arms strapped across his chest.

"You call that helping?" he asked.

"I call it doing your job for you," she said, crossing her arms across her chest right back.

Rhys glowered at the floor, the expression made all the more adolescent by last vestiges of baby fat still clinging to his face. Moira was starkly reminded of the fact that he was not yet twenty-seven, and that she was only twenty-four. Most women her age were worried about student debt and getting along with their roommates, not navigating the politics of the city's occult underbelly. Most of them didn't have husbands at all, certainly not husbands holding up the Sisyphean weight of an entire magical order on his shoulders. And none of them had lived through the sort of enchantment and terror she had borne witness to in the last year alone.

Was she missing out on life, she sometimes wondered? When she had thrown in her lot with Rhys and let him put that ring on her finger, had she given up the last bit of her youth in the process?

"I'm sorry," Rhys said. He seemed truly chastened, but he had already gone and pissed her off. "I shouldn't have talked over you like that, I'm just... overwhelmed."

"Looks like you got that notoriety you wanted," Moira said, mad enough to sting like a wasp, over and over again until she either tired herself out or her target begged for mercy. "If you're so overwhelmed I'll give you some space to collect yourself. I'll be in the meditation room on the phone with Amari. No need to come find me; I'll find you when I'm good and ready."

"Moira," Rhys groaned. "Love, come on–"

"Only place I'm coming is to my senses about trying to be a good partner to you when you won't do the same," she said, already taking the stairs two at a time and hoping that Amari was up for a vent session. "Groceries for dinner are in the fridge. Figure it out."

Moira sequestered herself away in her meditation room, surrounded by her potted plants and rose quartz and knitted pillow poufs, and tried not to hear Rhys swearing downstairs, like he had just broken something priceless.

She tried even harder not to hear him grab the keys, leave through the front door, and slam the door to his Lincoln outside.

CHAPTER FOURTEEN
RHYS

Rhys had never been very good at prayer. From the outside, he was sure it looked like he was, as he could hold stock-still on his knees with his back straight and his head bowed for long periods of time. Rhys was good with self-punishment, with the meditative clarity that came with pain and denial. Through some masochistic death drive, he actually yearned for the weight that was lifted off him as he let his consciousness be annihilated by total submission. But that didn't mean his mind didn't wander when he was in that twilight space of surrender, and it didn't mean the petitions of his heart weren't selfish.

As he lowered himself onto the kneelers in Saint Cecelia church and clasped his chipped red rosary beads, Rhys knew he looked the part.

But internally, his mind was a maelstrom.

He should be thinking holy thoughts. He should be asking for selfless things, for Moira to continue to heal after the loss of her grandmother, for Antoni to get his Series 7 license, for his sister Dolores to pass her exams. But all Rhys could think about was how angry his wife was with him, the way his mother would stare at him with horror if she read that article, the cutting edge of betrayal in David's voice over the phone.

And of course, pressing in from all directions, were thoughts of his demons. He was up to ten now and considering adding one more (Shax was said to siphon money from the rich to bestow upon an adept magician, which may help the Society's finances) but that didn't mean he wasn't feeling the strain.

Rhys pressed his lips together, willing himself to focus on the words of his Hail Mary. His mouth moved silently, forming the prayer with brutal efficiency. As if he could conjure penitence with perfect pronunciation.

As a well-catechized Catholic, Rhys knew the dangers of working with demons. There was a reason official Church teaching forbade it, and why many magician-priests who had trafficked with demons renounced the practice later in their lives, or didn't live long enough to die peacefully in their beds. Rhys' ritual technique was perfect, but he worried that God was getting tired of protecting him in the circle. Why should the creator of the universe continue to guard his wayward son from infernal consequences when Rhys insisted on striving for more than his already generous lot? How far could Rhys wander into the dark until the cord tying him to his heavenly Father pulled tight and then snapped behind him?

Flaunting the order of the universe had always filled Rhys with a perverse thrill, there was no denying that. Turning ancient spirits into lapdogs that licked obediently at his palms made him feel like a true adept, not so different from a holy man who could drive a spirit out of a possessed person with a single benediction.

But lately, Rhys was feeling more and more like a child toying with a Ouija board at a Halloween sleepover: playing with fire and in way over his head.

His demons were getting unruly, knocking over expensive items in his study or turning the temperature down in the room so much that Rhys could see his own breath. His sleep and nerves had not improved, and his dreams took on a darker tinge, bleeding over into the waking world in a way that made every synchronicity feel like an ill omen. He was even seeing things while he was awake, jumping at shadows that moved in the corner of his eye.

Like sharks scenting blood in the water, his demons were circling him, seeking out any weakness.

Rhys ground his teeth together, realizing he had lost his place in his Hail Mary *again*, and started over again at the beginning of the decade. He continued like this for some time, grasping impotently for prayers he could barely form, until he released himself from his punishing posture, sagging forward against the pew in front of him.

Rhys opened his eyes, neck burning from the weight of the metaphorical crown bearing down on his head. He looked up at the triumphant scene of the ascended Christ, painted on the wall behind the altar in soothing hues of beige and salmon and cream, and his stomach twisted.

When was he going to stop pretending to be a good person?

Guilt washed over him, as familiar and cold as the waters of the Atlantic Ocean. Rhys wished he really could step into the ocean and wash away all that shame, emerging as someone completely new. Someone who wasn't so broken and weak.

Rhys pressed his palms together and dug his thumbs into the twin furrows between his eyebrows, trying to summon discipline. Or maybe just a little self-respect.

"Father," he prayed in a whisper, like he was afraid that God might actually hear. "I'm not a holy man. I know that. I'm selfish and vain and greedy. Kindness has never been easily for me. But please, for the sake of everyone I love, I need you to make me strong enough to be the leader the Society deserves. I need you to help me figure out what to do. Grant me power, and bravery. Turn me into…" Rhys swallowed hard. "Someone else."

Rhys waited for some revelation, for God to crack open his ribs and pour supernatural peace into his heart like cool water. Anything to quench the fires of *wanting* that burned inside him.

But God stayed silent, and the fire inside Rhys raged on, spreading from his chest to the points of his fingers and the tips of his toes. Rhys stayed on his knees until he could barely stand it, until his muscles were screaming and the flames had made their way into his skull, and then he stood with an irritated huff.

"Amen," Rhys said, polite even in his rage.

He didn't know what else he had expected.

He crossed himself before turning his back on Christ as he exited the pew.

Rhys made it halfway down the aisle to the door, when one hand came up unconsciously to touch the Saint Michael medal around his throat. He had worn it nearly every day since his confirmation at the age of twelve, one year earlier than planned because he had begged his parents to let him receive the anointing oil before his birthday. When every other form of devotion failed, Rhys could usually trust in the prayer to Saint Michael. God's heavenly general, His mercilessly martial but ultimately fair sword of righteousness who had cast Satan out of heaven.

Rhys wasn't sure where he stood with God, or with Satan for that matter. But Michael had never abandoned him. Maybe he should to seek assistance where he was mostly likely to find it.

Rhys turned back towards the altar, and brought his hands together in prayer one more time. He took a deep breath and launched into the familiar words of the prayer.

"St. Michael the Archangel, defend us in battle. Be our defense against the wickedness and snares of the Devil..."

Shame twisted in Rhys's gut, so strong he nearly vomited. How could he possibly ask to be delivered from the wickedness of the devil when he relied on demonic assistance to get through his day? He couldn't get through this, not without perjuring himself.

Rhys liked extemporaneous prayer, but sometimes a fumbling but honest petition from the heart was more powerful than recitation. So Rhys switched his tactics.

"Saint Michael the Archangel," Rhys prayed, feeling a bit awkward as he made this up as he went along. "You who cast down the evil one and worship forever at the foot of the throne of God. I call on you. I call on your strength. I need your assistance, and I need your intercession. Please."

He huffed out the last word, more tinged with desperation than he would have liked, and he waited for the comfort of Michael's presence. There was nothing ecstatic or transcendent about the swelling of courage in his heart that sometimes made him believe that Michael was real, and near, and that he cared about Rhys. It might just be wishful thinking, and Rhys was prepared to take any spiritual comfort he could get right now, even if it was mostly a trick of positive psychology.

Rhys stood on the floor of the drafty church until his feet started to ache, until the stillness became too much to bear. Then, letting his shoulders drop in defeat, he turned to go.

He wasn't able to make it to the door, however, because the atmospheric pressure shifted, like the air was pushing in all around him.

He took a gasping breath, the air of the church suddenly impossibly desert-warm, and when he swallowed, he tasted hyssop and sand and sweat-soaked leather.

Rhys swayed, suddenly dizzy.

Then the angel appeared.

Rhys could not express even to himself what he was seeing, because while it was true in one sense that the sanctuary remained completely empty, it was just as true in another that he was assailed by blinding golden light. In one sense there was perfect silence, and in another, Rhys clearly heard the metallic creak of a set of ancient scales, the responding ring of a sword being unsheathed.

When the angel spoke, pouring a shapeless, formal salutation into his fevered brain in a thousand-voiced murmur that Rhys understood without being able to linguistically parse, Rhys dropped to his hands and knees.

The church floor was cold beneath him, but he pressed down further, unable to get low enough to show enough terrified deference. He pressed his cheek against the dirty stone, squeezing his eyes shut and struggling to breathe.

Rhys had met only a few occultists who worked directly with angels, and he had been a little afraid of all of them. They had radiated a strange, unsettling calm, and an energetic signature so strong that even Rhys could pick it up, like they were throwing off heat from being haloed by divine fire.

Demons were puzzle boxes, crucibles of rules and loopholes that could be studied and leveraged. Angels were nuclear batteries hooked up directly to the universe's Divine power source, created to serve their respective functions to the unflinching letter.

And unlike a demon, an angel could take the measure of your soul simply by looking at you.

Michael had come. *Really come*, in a way that rent reality in two. And Rhys, with his sin-stained heart and ink-stained fingernails, was not ready to receive him.

"Please," Rhys rasped, huddling into fight-or-flight mode. "Mercy. Please."

The angel regarded him as though he were a pitifully small lizard taking refuge beneath a rock to escape heatstroke. It spoke again, a rumble of many tongues that resonated within Rhys's rib cage as though his body were nothing more than a rough-hewn instrument for divine fingers to play.

Make your request, the voice said.

Rhys opened his mouth, but no words came out. Twin beads of sweat trickled off his brow and splashed against the flagstones below. How could he ask anything of the embodiment of God's righteousness? How could he possibly hope that divine mercy would be extended to him, driven as far as he was into the shadows of his own devouring heart? And how in the hell was he supposed to remain calm when an entity he believed in mostly theoretically was *present* with him in this space?

"Mercy," Rhys said again, trying to melt into the stone.

Dark spots danced behind Rhys's eyes as the angel rumbled another phrase, more insistent this time.

What battles are you fighting, boy? What aid do you require?

Heat crawled across his skin, like the storybook flames of hell that had kept him from sleeping soundly as a child. Rhys bit his tongue, drawing blood in his panic. He could not pull back his skin and muscle and bones and expose his beating heart to this angel. He could not tolerate being so seen, so known in all his wretchedness, he could *not*.

"Leave me," Rhys begged. With a wince, he yanked up his last bit of resolve like he was uprooting the bulb of a flower, and barked out, "Leave me!"

Rhys swore the foundation of the church shook beneath his bruised knees, but then, moments later, the world righted itself.

The heavenly light winked out.

The church was empty.

He was utterly and completely alone.

With shaking fingers, Rhys wrenched the Saint Michael medal from around his neck and hurled it into the darkness of the church. It skittered under a pew, perhaps to be rediscovered later by some young man with stronger faith, someone worthy of the protection of God's attack dog.

Rhys hauled himself upright, wiping his mouth with the back of his hand. He felt filthy, but no amount of holy water could save him now. He had been confronted with the divine and he had failed its test. Instead of responding to the angel with perfect courage, he had succumbed to his own cowardice and banished the only olive branch God was willing to extend to him.

Rhys had been abandoned. Panic and tears rushed in at the thought.

Rhys bit down reflexively into the fleshy part of his palm and stifled a cry. Hurting himself to calm himself down was a shameful habit he very rarely indulged, but this was all that had worked when he was a child and trying to stop himself from crying. His father always refused to speak to him when he was crying, and sent Rhys to his room to "pull it together" before he was permitted to join the family again.

The sting of his own teeth jolted him back into sense, and Rhys hissed in pain as the tears dried up.

He needed to pull it together. He needed to think straight.

Rhys blinked back the haze of dissipating glory in his eyes and tried to get his bearings. For a moment, it appeared like the shadows of the church were stirring, sliding over his shoes like an oil spill stretching across pavement.

There was angel left to intercede for him. The only spiritual aid he could rely upon was the only aid he was worthy of: the cruel favors of the demons he had tied his soul to.

Rhys squeezed his eyes shut, swallowing hard. When he opened his eyes, he was himself again. Perfectly calm, brutally practical, dry-eyed and unsmiling.

He would push forward with his infernal practice, out of the house if he had to, where Moira wouldn't ask questions and couldn't be hurt if things went wrong. He had access to the Society's ritual room, and he could use that as much as he needed, again and again until any demon he summoned bowed at his feet.

Neglecting to cross himself as he left, Rhys strode out of the church, letting the door swing shut behind him.

CHAPTER FIFTEEN
DAVID

David tried to bounce right back from the awkward-as-fuck conference call, but he wasn't very successful. He was irritable with everyone in the DA's office, especially when he caught them staring at him like an animal in a zoo. He left work an hour early with some bullshit excuse about a headache, then seethed the whole drive home.

Rhys's micromanaging had driven a wedge between them in college, souring into a pettiness that only worsened as David's drinking and high-risk behavior escalated in response. David didn't like being reminded of that miserable first breakup, that awful nightmare afternoon when he walked into his apartment to find that Rhys had simply packed up and left, and the vodka-fueled spiral that had nearly totaled the speeding car of his life directly after. But Rhys always tightened control when he felt helpless.

David's phone dinged as he pulled up to the corner store grocer on his block. His stomach did a little flip when he saw who the text was from. Max.

They had been emailing back and forth for days, keeping in professional touch as they discussed the best steakhouses in the city, but Max had never texted David before. Not even after David had slyly provided his cell number in his email signature.

Max here! I saw the paper this morning. I wasn't aware that Rhys was going to run the letter without edits. Did he talk to you about it?

Hey! David texted back in the car. *No, Rhys didn't talk to me. We just got off the phone. He didn't mean to run it; I think it was on autosend or something, but it's out there now lmao.*

Got it. I guess what's done is done. How are you doing?

They texted back and forth while David headed into the grocer and picked out his oranges and broccolini and three-color quinoa. After a bit of small talk, Max segued into talking about work, which is how David learned that Max worked in art conservation, and was engaged in some kind of consulting work for the BMFA.

David volunteered information about his own job, as much as he could share without breaking client confidentiality. Max replied with interest, sprinkling in just enough praise to make David catch himself smiling as he read the messages.

David and Maximilian kept texting as David carried the groceries into his building, took the stairs for the extra burned calories, and put everything away in the fridge. They kept texting as David tidied up the living room and organized his Google calendar, and then they just... didn't stop.

Professional conversation quickly became personal, and David learned how Max had inherited his love for impressionist paintings from his mother, as well as her miniature pinscher, Alfie. David mentioned wanting to get back to Capri that summer for a week of genuine vacation, no emails or grimoires allowed, and Max, whose family hailed from Greece, tried to convince him to add a stopover in Athens.

David barely noticed how much time he spent over the next couple days formulating or typing out responses. He was so caught up in the pleasurable tennis match of volleying texts back and forth that he didn't think to silence the phone during his next gym session.

"Why is Maximillian Markos blowing up your phone?" Antoni asked.

"Why are you looking at my phone?" David shot back, trying to ignore the fact that he was at a disadvantage, since he was on his back with Antoni spotting him during his bench press, and since Antoni had a clear view of his phone, which David had stupidly left face-up on the ground.

"Two more reps and you're done," Antoni said, tossing his sweat-streaked curls. The upscale gym where they met up three days a week was bustling with the after-work crowd, an outdated Rhianna song blaring through the loudspeakers.

"I've got five more in me," David said.

"No, you don't."

"Watch me."

David struggled through the final five reps, but his form never wavered. He smirked at Antoni in triumph as he set the barbell down with a clang.

"One of these days," Antoni said, "I'm gonna drop those weights on your face, just to take you down a few pegs."

"You're bluffing," David said, wiping off his forehead with a towel.

David's phone dinged again, and he snatched it up before Antoni could, switching the device into airplane mode.

"It's just Society stuff," he said. "Squats next?"

"I thought Rhys told you not to involve Maximilian in Society stuff."

"Rhys doesn't own me."

"Yeah, but you're his second."

"OK then, maybe it's personal stuff. What do you care?"

Antoni swung his water bottle from left to right on his thumb, an irritating metronome that wore away at David's resolve.

"Spit it out, Bresciani," David said.

"Moira said he's hot," Antoni said, as though this explained everything.

David sometimes forgot how old he had gotten until he found himself talking about dating with Antoni, who approached the pastime with a libidinous enthusiasm and powerful fear of commitment only found among people in their early twenties.

"Why do you have Moira scoping out guys for you?" David asked.

"If I want to achieve my goal of running through every eligible single in the city, I need intel."

This was braggadocio and nothing more, and they both knew it. Once Antoni had realized that he couldn't escape the reputation he had developed for going through Hinge matches like water, he leaned into the bit. It was sometimes hard to tell when he was joking, but David knew Antoni had no real interest in Maximilian Markos, or anyone else outside their immediate circle for that matter. Antoni was only trying to get a rise out of David.

Unfortunately, it was working.

"She's cute," David said, nodding towards a woman across the gym as she dropped into a deep lunge. She was age-appropriate for Antoni, with botanical tattoos across her strong shoulders and long legs that even David could appreciate, at least in a dispassionate, aesthetic sense. "I see her in here every week. No wedding ring. You should go talk to her."

Antoni barely spared the woman a passing glance.

"Eh. She's not my type."

David rolled his eyes.

"Right. You like them, what? About five seven, brunette, mind like a barracuda?"

Antoni shot David a forbidding glance. David wasn't deterred.

"And can't forget married," he went on, precise and sharp as a dart.

Antoni's face fell. Bullseye.

"Squats," Antoni said, already striding towards the weights. "Now."

They all had their ways of avoiding talking about their feelings. David had cut out the drinking and the binge shopping, and Antoni was getting better about controlling his temper. They met in the middle on punishing exercise, which they mutually, if silently, agreed was a healthy enough coping mechanism.

So, when Antoni added two extra plates to the barbell and got into position, David let him.

"Widen your stance," David said.

"I know what I'm doing," Antoni said, but widened it anyway.

David spotted Antoni through a full set, but when Antoni dropped the barbell to the ground, slightly more aggressively than was necessary, David saw that he was still upset.

Maybe he had pushed the joke too far.

"Hey," David said.

Antoni ignored him, taking a swig from his water bottle.

"*Hey*," David repeated, layering just enough charm into his voice to get Antoni to look at him.

"What?"

"You know that I know, right?" David said, treading lightly. "I'm not judging you. It's fine, is what I'm saying."

"I wouldn't call it fine," Antoni muttered. "It's actually pretty fucked."

"So what? We're all fucked. Just don't... I don't know. Don't do anything stupid about it."

"I haven't yet, have I? What's another year of keeping it to myself?" Antoni wiped his mouth with the back of his hand. "Just don't tell anyone."

"Antoni," David sighed, clasping Antoni's shoulder. "You annoy the hell out of me sometimes, but I have no intention of humiliating you. You'll figure it out. You always do."

Antoni glanced up at him, brown eyes soft. Antoni had big, thick-lashed eyes set into a classically handsome, trustworthy face, a combination that won him no small number of free drinks and freer sympathy among men and women alike. David, admittedly, was not entirely immune.

"Thank you," Antoni said, with full sincerity. And then, without changing his expression at all, he deadpanned, "So how long have you been hooking up with Maximilian?"

"We're not hooking up," David said, tossing Antoni back. Antoni snickered, happier than David had seen him all day. "Don't start rumors."

"OK, but you *want* to hook up with him, right? Don't you guys have history?"

"Ancient history. Another set, go."

Antoni huffed but obeyed, probably regretting the extra weight he had put on. To his credit, he managed to get through the set without dropping anything or pulling his back out of whack.

"I might have had a thing for him when he stayed at the Beacon Hill house the summer I was sixteen," David admitted. "But nothing happened between us."

"Sure it didn't."

"I'm serious. He barely looked at me. He was way more interested in my dad's books. It was no Call me By Your Name situation, which is probably for the best."

"And now?"

"Well, now I'm not sixteen anymore, am I?"

"Word to the wise," Antoni said, leaning over with his hands braced on his knees to catch his breath. "Don't fuck around with Maximilian behind Rhys's back. There's something going on with him, I don't know what, but the last thing we need right now is Rhys going off the deep end. Especially when he's currently steering the ship we're all stuck on."

"Fair," David said, the closest thing he could give Antoni to full assent. "I'll think about it."

"That's all I'd ever ask. Sweetgreen?"

"Sweetgreen," David agreed, grateful that they had tabled the conversation for now.

CHAPTER SIXTEEN
MOIRA

"Square or almond shape?" Amari fretted, clicking her tongue. She peered at her perfectly moisturized, ring-laden hands. "Gosh, I can't decide."

"Almond," Moira and Chava chorused. They were all sitting in a row like little ducklings at their favorite nail salon, where the employees always played *Days of Our Lives* in the background and offered them complimentary Styrofoam cups of Lipton tea.

"You're sure?" Amari asked. She had come straight from her marketing job in the Seaport, and was wearing a Zara blazer, a pastel blouse, and a skirt short enough to be fashionable without getting her written up by HR. Her silk press was pinned up with a lotus flower claw clip while she pondered the high-stakes decision.

"You always get almond," Moira said.

"Literally every time," Chava chimed in. Her set was already halfway done, since she didn't bother with acrylic. A little gel on her short nails was all Chava, who packed grocery bundles for families in need and carried around toddlers at her literacy nonprofit job, needed. She was still based in Providence, but was gracious enough to make the monthly train ride up to Boston, where Moira and Amari lived, for manicures and gossip.

Moira had called them both few days ago in a tizzy, frustrated with the Society and the *Inquirer* and most, of all, Rhys. She hadn't said much about why she wanted to get together so badly, but the girls had cleared their

Thursday to see her. Just as well, because Moira didn't want to sit around the house wondering how tyrannical Rhys was getting at the Society meeting, or if the stress was going to make him have a breakdown in his office.

"Almond then," Amari said, smiling at her nail tech. Amari had one of those megawatt pearly-white smiles. It was surprising she hadn't pursued a career as a QVC host or weather girl. "Short, please."

"I'm waiting for you to ask for two short and the rest long," Chava teased, leaning forward to shoot Amari a devilish look around Moira. "Just get the full lesbian manicure."

"How are things with your lady, anyway?" Moira asked. "Still dreamy?"

After a score of boyfriends in college who treated her like an inanimate trophy, Amari had gone through a dark night of the soul that made her realize she was exclusively interested in women. Not a month later, an older butch who just happened to be a very successful client of Amari's firm had swanned into her life. Amari was currently in the enviable position of never having to work again if she didn't want to, and getting put to bed most nights with a back rub and an orgasm.

"I love her so much," Amari said, with the sort of reverential awe that, on any other day, would have made Moira's heart swell. Now it just made her feel bitter. She had used to sound like that when she talked about Rhys. "I get crazier about her every day. And I feel like if anything does go wrong, I can just talk to her about it, and it will all be OK."

Must be nice, Moira thought sullenly.

"What about you?" Amari asked Chava. "Solo poly still treating you well?"

"I'm so into it," Chava said, beaming down at her nails as tangerine lacquer was applied. She wore a matching scrunchie in her curly dark hair, which had grown all the way down her back since she and Moira had met in drawing class. Moira had gifted her a handmade apricot detangling oil for her birthday last year, and Chava, who was so stalwart she didn't even cry during *Steel Magnolias*, had teared up on the spot. "It's just, like, giving me the space to be me, you know?"

"Are you still seeing that bartender?" Moira asked.

"Nah. He moved to Toronto. But things are heating up with the aerial silks instructor! I'll report back after our date this weekend."

Amari giggled, the sound washing over Moira like warm ocean waves. It had been too long since she had unplugged from the ever-churning magician's gossip mill to spend time with her favorite non-magical people, and it was a balm on her soul.

Despite their differences, Amari and Chava and Moira had been a tight little crew since they were all twenty. No matter where the winds of life blew them, they always found time to meet up for manicures, or oysters, or a drive up the coast. Amari was an avowed agnostic and Chava was culturally Jewish, but they didn't make Moira feel like the odd girl out for her spiritual pursuits.

Honestly, it was nice to hang out with people who had loved her for years without caring one whit about magic. They loved her whether her astrological predictions were correct or not, they loved her when her Scorpio moon made her jealous of their time spent with others, they loved her when she didn't answer texts for days because she was doing a full-blown ritual cleansing of the house.

And that made Moira love them both even more. "And what is Rhys up to these days?" Amari asked, flexing her fingers so the nail tech could more easily press a rhinestone into her thumbnail. Amari was unflaggingly gracious to every service worker she had ever encountered. "He's still working at the library, right?"

Moira had known this was coming, but she still didn't have a prepared reply. She didn't want to smile and lie about how her love life was just as perfect as Chava's and Amari's, but she knew if she tried, even obliquely, to express her frustration with her husband, the floodgates would open. Rhys had apologized afterward disregarding her advice in his party call war room, sounding truly sincere and smelling like church incense, but Moira wasn't entirely convinced. An apology was one thing, a commitment to not making the same mistake in the future was another.

"Oh, you know," she said airily. "He's pretty busy, and–"

Her phone trilled, cutting her off. As slid her free hand into her saddle bag and brushed her fingertips against the phone, a persistent buzzing began in the base of her skull.

Her witch's intuition.

A portent of danger.

Moira retrieved her phone and swiped open her texts, heart beating fast. It was Nathan. That, already, was a red flag. Nathan always called her, when he was running late for a group dinner or when he needed advice on what to get Rhys for his birthday. He only texted when discussing something he was too nervous to speak about, like when he had asked her for a woman's opinion on how to make up to Kitty for forgetting their anniversary after getting his time zones scrambled while traveling.

Hi! I hope you're doing well. I'm sooooo sorry if this comes across as weird, but there's something going on with Rhys I think maybe you should know about? Kitty thinks so too, fwiw.

The buzzing in the back of her brain turned into burning. The phone nearly slipped from her hand as she rushed to type out a response.

Not weird at all. What's up?

Moira held her breath as three little bubbles appeared while Nathan typed.

You know Rhys is like a brother to me. But sometimes your brothers piss you off! So, apologies in advance if I overstep here.

Chava and Amari chatted on about how excited they were for the first snow of the year, which was due any day, but Moira barely heard them as she typed under the table.

It's OK to be frustrated. What's going on?

More bubbles. More agonizing waiting. Then, the breathless paragraph she had been bracing for.

I don't know how much you know about what's been going on behind the scenes at the Society, but a lot of us are having trouble keeping up with the changing bylaws and the long hours. I thought Rhys would mellow out once he got settled, but I feel like he's just getting worse. I did some snooping (which I know is wrong! I'm sorry!), and Rhys has been booking himself into the ritual room frequently. Like, multiple days a week. Always after hours. I've got no idea what he's been summoning in there, but whatever it is, it's taking up a lot of his time. I'm telling you this because I'm worried about him. I think he's having a hard time right now, and I don't think magic is helping.

Moira took two deep breaths through her nose to try and steady herself, but her feelings were too big to vanquish with mindfulness. She was terrified, with that stomach-lurching surety that could only mean she was experiencing some kind of presentiment of doom, and she was *pissed*.

If this was what had been pulling Rhys away from her during the day and keeping him awake at all hours of the night... If he had been dabbling with something too dark to even share with her, much less summon in the house, she thought she might kill him.

Something terrible was gathering in the air above all of them, an electrical storm of strife that would soak them all to the skin if Moira didn't get everyone inside the metaphorical house, *fast*.

"I have to go," Moira said, pushing up from her chair with the pink acrylic on her nails still wet.

"Baby, what's wrong?" Amari said, so sweet that Moira could have cried. There was no way she could explain all of this to Amari and Chava, not her marital problems, not her foreknowledge of onrushing tragedy, not the complicated webs of sorcery and intimacy that tied her to the Society. "You look freaked out."

"I'm sorry," Moira said, leaning down to press her cheek against Amari's and give her a big hug. Amari smelled, as always, of Flowerbomb perfume and hairspray. Then Moira slung an arm around Chava and squeezed, kissing the top of her curly head. "I love you guys. I'm going to make this up to you, but there's something personal I need to take care of right now. I'll fill you all in later. I'll be alright, it's just complicated."

"OK," Chava said, a line of concern between her brows. "Text us when you're home?"

"I promise," Moira said, flipping through her wallet for whatever she owed her nail tech, plus a hefty tip.

"I'll cover your tab this time; it's no trouble," Amari said as she waved Moira out the door. "Get out of here and go do whatever you've got to do. Love you so much!"

"Loveyoulotsdrivesafe!" Chava hollered, fast enough that Moira heard every word before the door swung shut behind her with a clang of a bell.

She walked as fast as she dared back to the car, resisting the urge to break into a sprint. Angry tears pricked at the corner of her eyes, but she blinked them away. There would be time to cry later.

As Moira tossed open the door and slid into the driver's seat, she texted Nathan back. Soon all the Society members would be in their underground clubhouse, where reception was spotty, or in the ritual room, where phones were forbidden.

If she moved fast, she might be able to catch her husband before disaster struck.

Or perhaps, before he turned into the disaster that befell someone else.

Thank you so much for telling me. I'm going to try and get in touch with Rhys. Is he with you?

I haven't heard from him today, came the reply. *I tried calling him earlier, but his phone was off. I think he's in the ritual room. The meeting is in two hours, so I'll see him then but idk where he is now.*

Typically, Moira left Rhys to wrestle his own demons, figurative or literal. But that strategy was obviously not working.

I'm on my way to Cambridge. Don't say anything to him, OK? I appreciate you!

Moira pulled up her GPS app and made a smothered shrieking sound when she saw that, between rush hour traffic and construction on the bridge, it would take her ages to get to the Society. Maybe, if she didn't take a single wrong turn, she would still be able to catch Rhys before the meeting started.

Moira turned over the engine, backed out of her spot, and did something she hadn't done in a long time.

Under her breath, in a mutter punctuated by curses she began to pray.

CHAPTER SEVENTEEN
RHYS

"Come on, you son of bitch," Rhys said through gritted teeth, widening his stance as he attempted to drag the demon into material reality for the fourth time.

Three times he had tried to get Paimon to manifest, and three times he had failed.

A trickle of sweat dripped down Rhys's temple, and his feet ached from being on them all day, but he didn't care. He couldn't quit now. He needed this to work.

He was aware, if in a way he was working hard to ignore, that summoning Paimon was punching above his weight class. Rhys had never been able to successfully summon Paimon before, and sorcerers who had completed the ritual described the experience as arduous and terrifying.

But Rhys was desperate enough and hungry enough and most of all *upset* enough to try and get this to work. If his body was forfeit in the process, so be it. If Paimon fought back and Rhys found himself temporarily blinded, or so nauseous he emptied his stomach on the ritual room flagstones, or unable to string together a sentence for days, fine. It would all be worth it if Rhys could get him to obey.

Moira was still mad at him. And David was ignoring him and Antoni kept looking at him like there was something wrong with him. They could all see how weak and scared he was, and they were starting to resent him for that.

Paimon offered him something no other demon could, something that Rhys hoped desperately would make him strong enough to hold The Society and his relationships and himself together.

The power to bend others to Rhys's will.

If he could, with a word, just get the police to stop looking into the Society, if he could call the newspaper and convince them to drop the story, if he could strike down infighting from within the Society and sabotage from without, he would be secure. He would finally have enough, *be* enough, and everyone he loved would be safe. Then he could rest.

Electricity crackled across his skin, a surefire indication that his invocation was working, and Rhys pulled harder, *demanding* that the spirit manifest for him. His voice echoed off the walls of the ritual room, bouncing Latin back at him. His arms were shaking from being held extended so long, and his skin was slick with cold sweat, but he kept going. The temperature in the room plummeted downwards, colder and colder until Rhys could see his breath.

A dull rumbling grew around him, rising from the stone beneath his feet. It grew louder until he felt it rattling his bones, until it made his teeth chatter. As the sound became less diffuse, Rhys was able to put a name to the noise.

It was a roar, like a caged animal straining against its chains.

According to the historical record, that meant Paimon had arrived.

An image took shape in his mind's eye, hazy at first and then aflame with clarity. There was a crown before him in the air, perfectly circular and scintillatingly golden, with jewel-encrusted peaks sharp enough to pierce his skin. It rotated slowly, captured somewhere between the law of dreams and the law of gravity.

Delirious from exhaustion but emboldened by this manifestation(he saw it, *really* saw it, in the way only mystics and madmen and David could see) Rhys reached out to seize the crown.

This was his moment, his reward for all the suffering. Paimon was offering him aid. Glory was there for the taking, if he could just extend his hand far enough to claim it.

His fingers touched the phantom crown, and the metal sizzled against his skin as though it had just been pulled from a blacksmith's fire. Rhys yelped, yanking his arm back and staring down at his hand. There must be scorch marks there, or angry red blisters torn open and weeping.

His skin was unmarred.

132 ASCENSION

He was hallucinating.

Someone slid a key into the door of the ritual room and opened the door, ripping a hole in Rhys' web of magic.

Rage, usually so unfamiliar to Rhys, caught fire in his chest.

"*What is it?*" he snapped. He turned to face the intruder, ready to eviscerate them for this disrespect.

Antoni stood in the doorway looking at Rhys with wide eyes. One of his hands was still clutched around the doorknob, knuckles white.

"Antoni," Rhys said, the word coming out of him in a rush of air.

"What are you doing in here?" Antoni asked. He didn't even have the decency to sound apologetic. If anything, he made it sound like Rhys was the one who was trespassing.

Rhys scrambled for an excuse, an explanation, throwing his eyes around the room. It was hard to pass this off as anything less than a high-risk unauthorized summoning. The jagged chalked circle under his feet, the lingering frigid temperature in the room, and the undoubtedly wild look in Rhys's eyes all told the truth.

"The meeting isn't for hours," Rhys said. "Can we talk later? I'm working on something."

"The meeting is in a *half hour*," Antoni said. He closed the door behind him and walked into the room, which was exactly what Rhys was trying to avoid. "You must have lost track of time. How long have you been in here?"

Once again, Rhys dodged the question.

"Who let you in?"

"I've got keys, Rhys. You had them made for me, remember? It's my turn to cleanse and prep the ritual room. You asked me to."

Rhys swallowed hard, biting back the encroaching edges of a panic attack. He couldn't deal with his anxiety right now, not on top of everything else. He needed to keep it together – *smile for God's sake* – and do damage control.

Antoni's eyes scanned the Solomonic seal chalked onto the ground. If it had been anyone else, Rhys might have been secure in the knowledge that they wouldn't be able to match the seal to the demon it summoned. But Antoni had a talent for memorizing occult symbols. It was one of the things that had always made him great, the part of his initiation exams that had taken Rhys's breath away and convinced him that he *needed* to be friends with Antoni.

"Paimon?" Antoni huffed out a disbelieving laugh. "Just last year you told me not to waste my time summoning him. You said he was too unpredictable."

"Everything is fine," Rhys said, as though trying to soothe a spooked stallion. "I'm testing a new evocation I wanted to share with everyone next week. It's nothing, OK? It's research. Just... chill out."

"Chill out?" Antoni took a few more steps forward, more sure this time, and Rhys resisted the urge to shrink away. He needed to stand his ground. "Don't patronize me. Why are you using the ritual room alone to summon *Paimon* without a scryer? That's so dangerous it's stupid."

The walls started closing in around Rhys, blackening his vision at the edges.

"Does Moira know you're here?" Antoni pressed. He retrieved his phone from his pocket. "Does David? I'm calling him."

Like a light switch being flipped, the anxiety won, and Rhys was gripped by reactionary panic. He couldn't involve David, or Moira. They would just worry, and worse, they would try to stop him. He had never been closer to greatness than he was now. He could still feel the crown burning his hand, and the scar through his palm screamed in pain, as though reminding him that his soul was already corroded, already tainted by an ancient curse. He was marked by the darkness anyway, what was another demon, or three?

Rhys was drunk on the circle, he knew that, inebriated by the dark slurry of shadows slithering around him and worming their way into his heart, but he couldn't stop now. He couldn't crack.

If he cracked, it would probably be into so many fragments that no one, no matter how much they loved him, would ever be able to put him back together again.

"Don't," Rhys said in his sternest sorcerer's voice, snapping his hand up. The shadows in the room shuddered, as though responding to his command.

"You can't boss me around like I'm a spirit," Antoni said, lifting the phone to his ear. "You've spent too much time in the circle, Rhys." "I'm telling you not to, as your High Priest," Rhys went on, words coming faster now. The room was so cold he could barely feel his fingertips, but Antoni seemed unaffected. That rumbling was growing around him again. Antoni couldn't seem to hear it. Was Rhys still hallucinating? It didn't matter. Nothing else mattered except convincing Antoni to *hang up*. "That's an order, Antoni."

Antoni shot him a dirty look, not moving a muscle.

The phone kept ringing.

Rhys balled his fingers into fists at his side, and some nasty survival instinct, so deeply buried he didn't know it was there, took over. He spoke before he even had a chance to consider whether this was a line he wanted to cross, the words slipping from his mouth like oil. He could almost see them dripping onto the floor, staining the stone so dark there would be no scrubbing things clean again.

"Put the phone down or I'm telling Nathan about the winter social."

"What?" Antoni said, with such quiet vehemence that Rhys immediately regretted what he had done. Clarity rushed in, along with shame. Antoni was his treasurer, and moreover, Antoni was one of his closest friends, maybe his best friend in the world if Rhys didn't count David. He didn't deserve this.

"No," Rhys said, clenching his fists as though he could physically yank his words back out of the air. His head was spinning. "I didn't mean that, forget it. God, I'm sorry. I just meant…. I'm sorry."

"You did mean that," Antoni said, more hurt than Rhys had ever seen him. "You *did*. Or else why would you say it?"

Rhys remembered that winter social clearly. It had been their first party as Society brothers, and Antoni was still riding high on his successful initiation exams, emboldened by gin and the esteem of his peers. He had pulled Rhys aside beneath the glittering Christmas lights in the rented ballroom and gushed that he had just met someone.

The most amazing girl, is what Antoni had called her.

It had, of course, been Kitty. Nathan hadn't come that year, called away to California to sit at the bedside of his ailing grandfather, but Kitty had shown up by herself, wearing a silver dress that dripped off her body like melting ice.

Rhys had taken Antoni's shoulder in his hand and gently explained that this was Nathan's girlfriend, the woman he intended to propose to by year's end and marry the following summer. Antoni had taken it in stride, even made a joke about it, but Rhys had seen the anguish in his eyes.

Antoni had only fallen more in love with Kitty since then. Rhys knew that, and so did David, and Cameron. The only reason Nathan didn't know was probably because he didn't want to.

Antoni ended the phone call.

"You were going to blackmail me," Antoni said. He was looking at Rhys like Rhys was some monster who had just shed the human skin he had been wearing around like a costume. "That was something that crossed your mind and you actually considered it."

"Antoni, please, I don't know why I said that. I'm not myself right now, I–"

Antoni stepped right into Rhys's space, looking up at him in challenge. For a moment Rhys thought Antoni was going to hit him, or yell. But when Antoni spoke, it was deathly quiet.

"I really hope you know what you're doing, Rhys. Because I am not going to be there to protect you when people start getting sick of you. I don't know what the fuck is going on with you, but frankly I don't care anymore. You don't have the decency it takes to lead; you don't even have the decency to be a good friend. When you're finally forced to step down, and trust me, you will be, I am going to be more than happy to step up. Do we understand each other?"

Every word pierced Rhys's heart like a sword, but all he could do was nod. In one fell swoop, he had destroyed his relationship with Antoni and planted the seeds of bitterness within him that could flower into all-out mutiny. Rhys had only been able to manage the Priesthood in the first place because he had Antoni to support him. Without Antoni as his advisor, Rhys had no solid ground to stand on.

And without Antoni as his friend, Rhys was relegated to a world without sunlight, without warmth.

"Perfectly," Rhys said hoarsely.

"Pull yourself together and wipe that seal off the ground," Antoni said, striding towards the door. "Everyone else is going to be here soon. I'm not scrying for you today, and probably not for a while. Get David to do it."

Antoni slammed the door behind him, making Rhys jump. Finally alone, Rhys's face fell into his hands, shoulders tightening as a sob threatened to break through.

He was so *exhausted*. And he felt guilty, more guilty than he ever had in his life, like he was filthy inside and out.

Rhys' head spun faster, and faster, until he was so disoriented he was on his knees.

He didn't even realize he had collapsed until his cheek was pressed to the cold flagstones of the ritual room.

* * *

When Rhys opened his eyes, seconds or minutes later, the dark room was thick with an oppressive presence he couldn't categorize. It might have been Eligos creeping in, or Shax, or any of the other demons he had bound to him by short lengths of metaphysical rope. Any of the hungry mouths that were always demanding more offerings, more words of power, more pieces of Rhys broken into bite-sized pieces and tossed into their open mouths.

He felt his demons circling his throat like a noose, threatening to suffocate him with their attention. His demons didn't love him – he didn't think they were capable of such a banal, mortal feeling – but they did need him. And they would devour whatever was left of Rhys the moment he stopped being of use to them.

Rhys didn't want to think about what that would look like. Financial ruin, the destruction of his reputation, the dissolution of his closest relationships, perhaps even the decay of his own body.

He hauled himself to his feet, shoulder and hip screaming from where he had been pressed against the ground.

The muffled scuff of shoes moving around in the next room filtered in through the walls, along with the amiable chatter of Society members arriving to their weekly meeting. Everyone would be here soon. He didn't have time for this.

Letting out a snarl of frustration, Rhys uncapped his water bottle and splashed the contents across the floor of the ritual room, dissolving Paimon's seal into a useless blur.

CHAPTER EIGHTEEN
DAVID

Something felt energetically off the moment David stepped into the clubhouse. But Gerald, the Society's ancient footman who came out of retirement one day a week to take coats and clear plates, didn't seem bothered.

"Good to see you again, Mr Aristarkhov. A very sharp choice of coat today."

"Thanks, Gerald," David said, divesting himself of his trench coat. David had known Gerald since he was a boy, and even though their relationship wasn't exactly familial, it was familiar. David had never once seen Gerald lose his professional composure, not even when a younger David had shown up to meetings drunk and combative. "How are the horses this week?"

Gerald was privately fond of betting on horse races. David only knew this because Gerald used to gather Evgeni's bets and call the racetrack during social hour, back when you had to phone in to place your wager.

"Bully Pulpit hasn't had as strong a showing as I would have hoped, I'm sorry to say," Gerald said, shaking his head. "But Rum Runner still has some fight left in him, so I'm optimistic."

David nodded encouragingly. He had no idea who these horses were. But it didn't really matter. He asked about the horses because it cheered Gerald.

138 ASCENSION

While sorting through his father's old financial records, David had discovered that Evgeni had covered Gerald's salary for an entire year when the Society's finances weren't strong enough to keep him on payroll. It was a baffling act of generosity that David would never understand, a gesture that didn't benefit his father at all. Perhaps some things about his father would always remain a mystery, and perhaps even monsters had their moments of kindness.

"Well, you never know which way the winds will turn," David said. "Have you seen Rhys today?"

"Not yet. I assume he'll be here any moment, but it's strange. He's not usually late."

David made a suspicious sound, then thanked Gerald and strode into the meeting hall.

Rhys being late to a meeting was nearly unheard of. He had skipped one meeting in college because he and David had been having a fight and lost track of time, and another last year to stay home and take care of Moira when she had strep throat. Twice in all of history.

David glanced down at his phone, wondering if he had received a text from Rhys with any sort of explanation. But there was nothing there, just an unread text from Moira that was probably a continuation of their conversation about the best ways to scan a building for ghosts. David resolved to respond later, then caught Antoni as he stormed past.

"What's eating you?" David asked. "You look like you just swallowed a salamander."

"It's nothing," Antoni said. He was a worse liar than Rhys. "I'm just stressed. Listen, today isn't a good day for me to scry. Can you do it?"

"Absolutely," David said. He didn't need to ask why. If Antoni needed him, David was there.

"Thanks. It's Valac today; he's easy. Just direct Rhys through the summoning and use it as a teaching example for the other members. Nothing fancy. Ritual should be starting soon. I'll see you in there."

With that, Antoni strode off to round up the other members. He was speeding through social hour tonight, cutting it mercilessly short, which didn't put David any more at ease. And gathering the members was Rhys' job, not Antoni's.

What the hell was going on?

David drifted towards the ritual room with the other members, spinning his phone between his fingers. Phones were forbidden in conclave, but David thought it was a stupid rule so he had never followed it.

David stopped in his tracks the moment he stepped foot into the ritual room.

Rhys was there, a haunted look in his eyes, his sleeves rolled up past the elbows. The stone beneath his feet was still wet, drying in uneven patches as though he had just scrubbed away a seal.

"What are you doing here?" David asked. David thought it was a pretty fair question considering that Rhys had been totally AWOL all day. Judging from the wrinkles in Rhys's clothes and the sleepless sallowness to his face, he had been here for some time. His eyes were flat and dull as a shark's, as though all the life had been sucked out of them.

"Nothing important," Rhys said. Liar. "You good to scry today?"

"Duh," David said, too annoyed to be nice. "Antoni already asked me. What is going on with people today? Everyone's vibes are fucked. Are you OK, babe?"

"Don't 'babe' me in conclave," Rhys said, running a hand through his bedraggled curls as he got into position in the center of the circle. "And put your phone away, please."

David moved to shut his phone off, but then he stopped. Why should he extend Rhys deference when Rhys wasn't willing to do the same for him, when Rhys could barely be bothered to call him back or keep his promises about meeting up? Rhys always complained about having to be the one to clean up David's messes, but David had been trying very hard not to make a mess of anything lately, and now he was the one being asked to cover Rhys's ass in the summoning circle.

Petulantly, David began typing, taking his sweet time even as the other members fell into place around them. He should be more present right now, gauging the spiritual energy in the room and checking in with Rhys before launching into the ritual, but he couldn't be bothered.

Rhys paced a tight circle-within-a-circle, pressing his hands to the small of his back as he waited.

David continued to type.

"There's no reception down here," Rhys reminded him. He gestured for the gathered Society members to start their chanting. The sound of droning Latin enveloped David, as familiar as a lullaby.

"Then the text will go through later," David said. "Just let me finish, one sec."

"Who are you talking to?" Rhys pressed, unable to help himself.

David considered lying or softening the blow somehow. But he wasn't in the mood to coddle Rhys's feelings, not when this was the one of the first things Rhys had said to him all day.

"Max," David said.

"*Max*," Rhys repeated, disdain dripping from his voice.

Good, David thought. *Let him stew in his jealousy.*

David hadn't let Rhys know about his romantic interest in Maximilian, because he had already gotten permission to date other people, and because nothing worth reporting had actually happened between David and Max since then. He hadn't done anything wrong, and he wasn't going to be made to feel bad about it.

The chanting reached a crescendo, and David's body responded to his cue to move into the innermost part of the circle, right onto his mark. The phone disappeared into his pocket as David took a deep breath.

He and Rhys stood back-to-back, flanking each other in magical defense. It was a position that usually felt safe and powerful. But now it made him itchy, like Rhys might spin around at any moment and drive a knife into his back.

When Wayne had forbidden them from working together in the circle, all those years ago, he had said something David had never forgotten.

Stepping into a ceremonial circle with someone you don't trust is more dangerous than stepping into one alone.

Rhys began his invocation, his Latin clear and confident. They had done this a hundred times before, David reminded himself, and there was no reason to think that this time was going to be anything but a run-of-the-mill educational ritual. It was mostly performative, an opportunity for the less experienced members to observe and take notes.

David closed his eyes, letting his consciousness drift into that twilight space where he could see clearly with the eye of the mind. This was his moment to shine. This was what he had been born to do.

"Manifestation on your left, eleven o clock," David said, pointing at the clump of shadows over Rhys's shoulder. They were taking the shape of a skinny, naked child with tattered wings, or at least that's how the manifestation appeared to David.

"Who is it?" Rhys asked. The child bared its teeth, chipped and rotted, but David was unimpressed. He had summoned this demon a dozen times, and his bark was far worse than his bite.

"Valac, as intended. You're good to proceed. Just don't–"

"Insult him, I know."

David pressed his lips into an irritated line. Rhys was so focused on the working that he was getting ahead of himself, cutting David off in his breakneck race towards the climax. If Rhys had been a worse magician, this would be where he got messy, mispronouncing a crucial binding word or losing focus at a decisive moment.

"You know how to address him, then," David muttered. "Go on."

Rhys spoke the divine names that would bind the demon to his will, his voice low and sure. Something was off, however, maybe the timbre or the pitch. Valac let out an aggressive, high-pitched chitter that only David could hear, and David winced as he pressed two fingers against his ear.

"He's getting agitated," David supplied. "Try the binding again, slowly this time. You need to calm him down."

"That's what I'm trying to do."

Rhys' cheeks were pink with embarrassment, and his aura, usually a mellow teal, was embroiled in darkness. David could usually ignore most people's auras, and looking at them so closely gave them a headache, but there was no denying what he was looking at now. David had only seen this murky indigo color on people a few times before, usually during a a battle with grief, or, in the case of his father near the end of his life, a complete surrender to the darkest of supernatural forces.

"Don't panic or else you'll lose him," David said.

He would talk to Rhys about the aura as soon as they were done. Maybe he could get Lorena to take a diagnostic look at him when she was back in the States, or have Leda cleanse Rhys of this heaviness by painting her sigils on his skin.

"Just let me do my job, David, and you focus on doing yours," Rhys snapped, like David was useless to him if they couldn't get this summoning right. Like all he was good for was scrying.

That *did* remind David of Evgeni.

Rhys was sleep-deprived and overworked and strung out from anxiety, and on any other day, David's better nature might have let Rhys get away with speaking to him like that. David would remember to be gracious, to be forgiving, to be so much more like the person his therapist believed he was and so much less like himself.

But this wasn't any other day, and most importantly, David was at the end of his rope. Rhys had pushed him too far, and now he was fucking *mad*.

"If you're going to act like a bitch I'm going to stop scrying for you," David snapped.

Rhys rounded on him, dark eyes wide with shock. Apparently, even though David had trouble maintaining Rhys's interest these days, he could still get his attention when he really wanted to.

Rhys's focus was so thoroughly destroyed that the apparition fizzled out of existence, leaving David and Rhys alone in the circle.

"I beg your pardon?" Rhys said.

This was David's out. If he really wanted to smooth things over, he should walk it back immediately and do a full public *mea culpa*. Bend the proverbial knee to Rhys's bruised ego.

"I said you're acting like a bitch," David said. "It's not that serious, Rhys. It's just a summoning."

Rhys took a few short steps forward until he was close to David, almost close enough to kiss. He pitched his voice low, angling his face for privacy.

"Are you seriously undermining me?" Rhys asked, almost inaudible. "Right now? I just want to get through this ritual and go home. We can talk through this later, but not now."

Rhys's body language was familiar, just like when he leaned over to whisper a joke to David when they were in conclave, or quietly ask if he was ready to leave a party. But Rhys was not inviting him into any kind of intimacy right now. He was trying to intimidate David into shutting up. Into not making a scene in front of everyone.

Rhys would probably slather fresh paint over a house with a sinking foundation if he thought it would keep the neighbors from talking. That cowardice, that naked self-interest, pushed David towards the nuclear option.

If Rhys was so worried about what other people thought of him, maybe David should give him a reason to worry.

"Show of hands," David said clearly to the entire room. He turned off the part of his brain that felt pity and let the part of his brain that won case after case in the courtroom get into the driver's seat. "Who here actually thinks Rhys McGowan is doing a good job as High Priest? Who feels comfortable coming to him with complaints? Constructive criticism?"

Nobody moved, but the underlying public sentiment was evident in the way Antoni scowled at the ground, in the way Kitty and Nathan shared a somebody-had-to-say-it-glance, in the way Cameron sighed sadly, not to mention in the way some of the older men who had never cared for Rhys's innovations shook their heads in disapproval.

But David wasn't done.

He didn't start fights he couldn't finish.

"It's an awful feeling, isn't it?" he went on. "Realizing everyone around you only does what you say because they're worried about what you'll do if they don't? You're out of control, Rhys. Everybody knows it."

All the air was sucked out of the room as Rhys took a ragged breath, pressing his palm to his chest as though fighting off a panic attack. His eyes glittered with animal terror, like he didn't know whether to run or to fight or to chew his own leg off.

Antoni and Cameron exchanged a wary look from the perimeter of the circle, but neither said anything. This was an old dance, one nobody but Rhys and David knew the steps to, and getting in the middle of it was likely to be disastrous.

Then, in an almost miraculous display of composure, Rhys straightened up. His expression was smooth as unbroken water.

"David, please step outside the circle," said Rhys.

"I'm not going anywhere."

"You're done for the day." Rhys turned from David and waved him away. Tossed him aside as though he was nothing. Just like he had done all those years ago, when he had walked out on David without any warning. "Nathan can take your place as scryer. He needs the practice."

"You don't get to dismiss me," David said, his control of the situation suddenly slippery. Of all the things Rhys could have done, David hadn't accounted for this. "I'm your second in command."

"You've already ruined the evocation, David," Rhys said, cold as a Siberian winter. "Now get out of here before you embarrass yourself."

"You're the only one embarrassing yourself," David said. This was his oldest vice, his propensity for lashing out. It had gotten him into plenty of trouble as a teen and roused his father's brutal anger, but holding his tongue was a lesson he had refused to learn. It felt too much like defeat. "You're driving everyone to exhaustion, and for what? Your own ego? To prove something to yourself? To God? To the old guard who are never going to respect you no matter how much you order us all around?"

"David," Antoni said, a warning in his voice. If David was thinking more clearly, he might have been grateful for a referee. But he was too far gone to concede.

"Stop talking, David," Rhys said. He was on the edge of breaking; David could feel it. A few more swings of the axe and Rhys would crash to the ground like a tree that had grown too tall too fast. "I'll remind you that I'm your High Priest."

"You aren't a High Priest," David said, leveling the killing blow. "You're just a kid in a crown too big for you. A little boy who's too scared to skip church or come out to his parents."

A rage ferocious enough to chill David's blood passed over Rhys's face.

"You're out," Rhys said.

David almost didn't process the words.

"What?"

"*You're out!*" Rhys thundered, so loud that David jumped in his skin.

The ritual room fell silent.

David had gotten what he wanted; Rhys broken into pieces at his feet, exposed for the unqualified, overleveraged tyrant he was. He just hadn't thought through what might happen to either of them after David won this fight.

"I'm temporarily revoking your membership," Rhys said running the back of his hand shakily over his mouth. David knew this tell; Rhys was moments away from crying. "You need time to cool off. Antoni will act as my second in the interim. This session is adjourned. Everybody go home. We'll try again next week."

Rhys shouldered past Cameron and walked right through the chalk on the ground, breaking the sacredness of the circle. David was left hollow-hearted, so numb he could barely breathe.

Out. He was out. Rhys hated him now and probably always would, and he had taken away the one thing that gave David purpose and structure and friends in the process.

David stormed out of the ritual room, ignoring every person offering him a sympathetic glance or calling out his name. He didn't want to speak to any of them right now. He didn't want to look at them.

David took his coat from Gerald then began the trek back to his car with a horrible burning sensation in his chest. He couldn't move fast enough to outrun it, couldn't put enough distance between himself and the meeting hall he had been banished from.

He hadn't cried since summer, when the demon Baelshieth had been slicing him to pieces from the inside out. Crying was for other people. But right now, it felt very tempting.

He was walking so fast, with his head down against the biting wind, that he nearly collided with a woman walking just as fast in the opposite direction. He clipped her shoulder and murmured a halfhearted apology, then turned around when he got a whiff of her sandalwood perfume.

"David?" Moira said, pulling down her fur-trimmed hood. David's heart twisted. She looked fragile and frightened, so unlike her usual self. But he didn't have anything left in him to offer her. No comfort, and certainly no kindness. "I thought you were in the meeting. Where's Rhys?"

Of course her concern was for Rhys, to the man she had married, and not to David, who was merely an entertaining accessory that could be easily discarded when he became too difficult to deal with. David and Moira weren't bonded by marriage or sex or monogamy or anything else that held weight in the real world.

"He's inside," David said, each word like pulling out a rotting tooth. He couldn't voice what had happened, not now and especially not to her.

"Something bad is going to happen. I can't explain it but—"

David let out a bitter laugh.

"Something bad already happened."

"What do you mean? What's going on?"

His brain was already running through a memorized map of every bar within walking distance, and it would take all his mental energy to force himself to go straight home without stopping for a couple of vodka sodas first. There was no space left for difficult conversations.

"Talk to your husband about it. I can't do this right now, Moira. I'm sorry."

Moira reached out for him as he turned away, her fingertips brushing the bare skin of his wrist, and David flinched as though burned. He didn't want her inside his head right now, and he didn't want to be inside hers. He just wanted to be alone.

David didn't look behind him as he unlocked the Audi, slid inside, and turned up the radio so loud he couldn't hear his own thoughts.

CHAPTER NINETEEN
MOIRA

Moira pressed through the sea of bodies filtering out of the Society hall and into the street, her heart racing so fast she thought it might burst.

Wrong, wrong, wrong, the refrain in her head chorused.

Her mother had always warned her against letting her intuition lead her into panic, but it was hard not to panic when Rhys wasn't answering his phone, and David had looked at her like she was a stranger.

Moira spotted a head of black curls in the crowd and pushed through the throng, repeating an apologetic refrain. She didn't stop until she was standing at the top of the steps that led down into the clubhouse, looking down at Rhys as he ascended them.

Rhys was pale as death, not a drop of color in his lips. The front of his white shirt was stained with sweat and the splash marks of tears. His eyes, though dry, were rimmed with red.

"Baby, what happened?" she asked, out of breath.

Rhys didn't need to ask why she was there, or what had tipped her off to his distress. They had always been tied together by an invisible thread, a gossamer-thin connection that vibrated insistently whenever the other needed help. It had pulled tight the moment Moira had heard of her grandmother's death and Rhys had called her from the stacks at work, knowing in his gut that she needed him, and it was pulling tight now, thrumming with energy.

Rhys wordlessly took her hand and led her down the stairs back into the clubhouse. Moira had never been here before. Meetings were closed to outsiders, and functions like the gala and the winter social took place elsewhere. She had heard vague descriptions of the sitting room from her husband, but he was usually more concerned with sharing the properties of whatever spirit they had summoned than he was with describing the drapes. She had somehow imagined more shadowy grandeur, more sinister opulence, and was surprised to find that the room was small and lived-in, almost drab. The cheap gold sconces and threadbare Persian rugs made the heavy leather armchairs and wood paneling feel particularly secondhand. Ice melted in discarded drinks as though they had been abandoned in haste.

He closed the door behind them, locked it securely, and then pulled Moira into his arms. Rhys hugged her tightly, nestling her head under his chin. For one perfect moment, Moira felt held and *safe*. Like maybe things were going to be alright.

"What happened?" she asked again, closing her eyes and breathing in the scent of her husband: incense and chalk and antique printer's ink. "I got a horrible premonition."

Rhys smoothed his hand down her braids, cupping the base of her skull as though protecting her from injury.

"David and I fought. I revoked his membership."

Moira pulled out of her husband's arms, looking up at him in horror. She felt cold all over.

"You did what?"

"Only temporarily," Rhys said, as though this explained everything.

"Start at the beginning," she said, trying to keep her voice level. It wouldn't help either of them if she panicked. "Tell me everything. Slowly."

Moira listened in silence as Rhys walked her through each moment of the argument. She wrapped her arms around herself, abandoning any pretense at open, welcoming body language. She didn't feel very open and welcoming right now.

She felt frightened. Disappointed. *Angry.*

"He was being impossible," Rhys finished, affect flat. He was completely shut off. Rhys could do this sometimes: smother all human feeling in service to his survival. "He said all those things to humiliate me in front of everyone. So, I told him he's out, at least for a while."

"And you think David is just going to accept that?"

148 ASCENSION

"He doesn't have a choice. I'm High Priest, and I get to choose who I allow into the Society. He can't act like that in meetings. It's for the best for him to sit things out for a while."

"For the best?" Moira asked. "Or for your own comfort?"

Rhys shot her an injured look, shrinking back slightly as though she had shouted. The sacrificial lamb, crawling right back up onto his cross.

Ooh, Moira *hated* when he did this.

"What do you suggest I should have done?" he asked.

"You should have stepped outside and *called me*, done some breathing exercises, had a cigarette, anything but this. David is a legacy initiate, and he was voted in unanimously. He's from a very old and very powerful family, even if he doesn't always act like it. The other members will get unruly without him there, as a figurehead at least."

"I just told you what happened. He tried to make an example of me in front of everyone I'm in charge of. He was way out of line."

"Maybe so. But it's your job as his superior to be the bigger man. I don't believe you've thought this through as thoroughly as you seem to believe."

Rhys huffed out a disbelieving laugh, strapping his arms across his chest. Suddenly, the few feet of open air between them felt like a sprawling chasm.

"You're taking his side," he said.

Something about those four little words broke Moira's last bastion of self-control right down the middle, like a dam splitting under the weight of too much water. Her anger rushed forth.

"I'm taking my own side!" she yelled.

For a long time, they just looked at each other, motionless in the humid, stuffy air of the basement. Moira's heels had sunk into the ancient carpet beneath her feet, but she couldn't move. She could barely breathe.

"Moira," Rhys said. He took a few long strides towards her, his hands coming up to cradle her face, but she took a step back before he could touch her.

"You wanted a queen, didn't you? This is me acting like one. This has to stop, Rhys. You work constantly, you hardly eat, I never see you anymore. And now you're telling me that you started World War III with your boyfriend, one of the most influential occultists in the city, just because he hurt your ego? Now, when we're all under fire? I had two clients cancel on me this week, and Dion is still torn up about giving the reporter that statement to make them go away. A cop showed up to Leda's nightclub to ask her questions last night, did you know that? Are you actually listening to any of us or are you too wrapped up in your own little world?"

"I can't handle this," Rhys muttered, yanking a hangnail out of his thumb with his teeth. "I can't handle David and you–"

"Well, you should have thought of that before you claimed to love us both," Moira said. She was so hurt her chest felt like it was collapsing.

"You didn't let me finish," Rhys said. He stepped forward again, and again, she stepped back. "I just meant that I need you, now more than ever. I need you, Moira, I need you like air, like water, I can't–"

"No poetry, please," she said, holding up a firm hand. It was an echo of her mother, the ultimate sign of female displeasure. "No bullshit. Everything you've done has been for your own ambition, not for any sort of altruism."

Rhys looked at her as though she had hit him.

"How can you possibly say that? Everything I have done since the moment I met you was to keep you safe and make your life better, and anything selfish I want for myself I want to share with you. So what, my ambition is charming until it's inconvenient? I love you, Moira, but let's not pretend you didn't know what you were getting into when you married me."

"I married a good man! You've changed, I don't know what happened, but–"

"I am under so much pressure I feel like I'm going to shatter; there are things on my plate you couldn't imagine–"

"Your self-loathing gives license to your selfishness and it always has," Moira said, turning from him and walking through the halo of dust mites and chalk powder in the air, back towards the surface world. "And until you're ready to own up to that, I don't think we have anything else to talk about."

"Love, stay. Listen to me, I–"

"Let me go, Rhys," she said, voice thick with tears as she shouldered open the door. "I want to be left alone right now."

She had every intention of leaving without looking back, but she couldn't help one glance over her shoulder as she disappeared up the stairs.

Rhys had sunk down into a crouch, folded his arms over his knees, and dropped his forehead onto his arms. He looked like a little boy, abandoned

150 ASCENSION

by whatever parent was supposed to come pick him up from baseball practice. Moira's lip wobbled, but she kept walking, right out the door and up the stairs to the street.

The wind outside was brutal, but she barely felt it, the anger inside her was burning so hot. Without stopping to think whether it was a good idea, she snatched her phone out of her purse and started dialing. She didn't want to go home right now and she *really* needed to be enveloped by so much noise and color that she forgot her own name.

Luckily, she was on friendly terms with someone who specialized in that experience.

"Hi baby doll," Leda said on the other end, voice all velvet and smoke.

"Remember when you said you owed me for helping save your brother's life?"

"Sure do. Who do you need bumped off?"

"Nothing that serious. I just need... I need your help."

"Of course," Leda said, suddenly somber. "What's bothering you? Did one of the boys hurt your feelings or something?"

"Yes, but it's more complicated than that. Can I explain in person? I need..." She took a big gulp of air. "I need a distraction. I need to not think for a little while."

"You came to the right place. Got anything black to wear?"

"I'm not at home right now. I'm wearing..." Moira looked down at her outfit, then let out a delirious laugh. If she didn't laugh, she would just start crying. "Pastels."

"No worries; I've got you covered."

"Can I tell you something?" Moira asked. "Something I'll ask you not to repeat?"

Leda wasn't as close to Moira as Chava or Amari, but she had been fast-tracked into friendship by her connection with David, and by her understanding of the occult. In a skeptical world, it was always easier to seek solace in other believers.

"My breath is bated," Leda said.

Moira glanced at her reflection in a shop window. Twin lines had sprouted between her brows, seemingly overnight, and they didn't go away no matter how much she moisturized. Moira didn't fret about getting older, but she had always assumed her smile lines would come in first. The physical evidence that she might have spent more of her twenties worrying than smiling disturbed her.

"Sometimes," Moira said quietly, like she was confessing something to one of Rhys's priests. "I get tired of trying to be good."

Moira couldn't see Leda's face, but she could hear the mile-wide smile in her voice.

"Then do you want to come over here and be bad with me?"

Moira didn't even have to think about her answer.

"Yes *please.*"

CHAPTER TWENTY
RHYS

Rhys didn't know how long he stayed crouched on the ground, focusing on taking deep, slow breaths to prevent himself from screaming, or breaking something expensive, or stabbing his thigh with that Montblanc pen he had inherited from Wayne. No coping mechanism seemed strong enough to exorcize the emotions from his body.

In one day (no, in mere *hours*) he had destroyed his relationship with his closest friend and then his boyfriend and then his wife. Everyone who mattered in the world hated him, and why shouldn't they? Rhys was a bottomless pit of mindless need, a black hole that pulled anyone foolish enough to enter his orbit into oblivion. Everyone who got too close to him cast him out eventually, even God.

He was no better than a demon.

Rhys got onto his hands and knees on the carpet, which probably hadn't been vacuumed in a small eternity, then rolled onto his back and stared up at the ceiling tiles. They were cheap facsimiles of high-quality copper pieces that were supposed to lend an air of grandeur to the room.

Rhys groaned low in his throat, a toneless death rattle. He was so exhausted and wrung out he couldn't even cry anymore. He could barely breathe, and every breath he took got shallower and shallower as he neared hyperventilation.

He wanted to fix everything he had broken as quickly as possible, but he also wanted to go to sleep on this filthy floor and not wake up until everyone else had forgotten he existed. Maybe, if he awoke to a world where no one remembered him, he could make a better attempt at being a decent human being.

Maybe then everything wouldn't hurt so bad.

In a flurry of self-hatred, Rhys raked his fingernails down his forearm. Hard. His nails were short, but the sharp corners he had hastily neglected to trim caught in his skin, sending searing pain through his flesh and leaving red marks behind. He gasped, surprised by how much it hurt, and then the shame at having done something so embarrassingly self-destructive *again* rushed in.

Hurting himself didn't help him calm down this time, and it didn't make him feel better, but it did remind his body how to gulp down air.

Rhys's phone buzzed in his pocket. He considered throwing it across the room, then realized it was probably Moira, calling to divorce him, or David, demanding that Rhys come get his shit out of the condo before the end of the next business day.

Bracing himself for whatever was to come, Rhys connected the call and put the phone to his ear.

"Hello?"

"Tell me you're not still sitting in that clubhouse sulking," a female voice replied.

Rhys hauled himself up into a sitting position.

"Kitty?"

"It's both of us," Nathan said on the other end. There was the rustling of fabric as he jostled closer to the phone, and a sweet feminine murmur as Kitty made more room for him. Agony shot through Rhys at the tiny act of intimacy, the gentleness of a couple who could go ages without arguing. "Listen, I'll cut right to the chase. We're worried about you."

"And we don't think it's good for you to be alone right now," Kitty said. "Nathan and I were talking, and we figured people don't start acting nasty for no reason. We thought you might need someone to talk to right now, all things considered."

"We're willing to assume goodwill here if you're willing to meet us halfway," Nathan put in, his warmth irresistible. It was sometimes easy to forget that Nathan made a very tidy living convincing tight-fisted entrepreneurs to part with their money. He was almost as persuasive as David, when he wanted to be. "And to express our sincerity, we are extending a peace offering."

Rhys heard the unmistakable click of Kitty's silver Vivienne Westwood lighter, the one in the shape of a heart that traveled around in her purse.

"I don't smoke," Rhys sighed. He had tried to convince Nathan of this many times, which only ever led to Nathan performing a rehearsed monologue about the alleged health benefits of his favorite recreational activity.

"Come by the apartment when you're ready," Kitty said, just as irresistible as her husband. "Door's unlocked. Take it or leave it, but we won't ask twice."

Rhys chewed the inside of his mouth. He didn't want to have any more hard conversations today, and he didn't want to talk about the Society, and he certainly didn't want to pretend that he was fine.

But more than anything else, Rhys didn't want to be alone. And Kitty was correct; right now, he had nowhere else to go.

"I'll be there in twenty," Rhys said.

Rhys wasn't totally sure how he got to Newbury Street. He was dimly aware that he must have driven, even though he couldn't feel his hands or remember turning onto Storrow Drive. He was losing time frequently now, either from anxiety or because of that oily demon darkness that clouded his vision and warped his judgement.

When he came back to his awareness, he was standing on the doormat outside Kitty and Nathan's apartment. Rhys watched himself ring the doorbell, and then Kitty opened the door.

She was holding Moomin, her white Persian cat, to her chest. Moomin blinked golden marble eyes at Rhys, his flat face making him look perpetually judgmental.

Or maybe cats just didn't like people who stank of demons.

"You're right on time," Kitty said, welcoming Rhys into the apartment.

Nathan was sitting cross-legged on the living room floor, grinding up marijuana buds and other fragrant herbs and fashioning them into tidy joints. He laid the joints out in a neat row on the mother-of-pearl inlaid rolling tray. He was barefoot and wearing jeans, and the scene reminded Rhys so painfully of David smoking cigarettes on the floor of his dorm room that Rhys almost doubled over in anguish. Everything that didn't remind him of Moira would probably remind him of David for a while, until he made up with both of them or lost them entirely.

Rhys left his shoes at the door and joined Nathan on the living room floor. It felt like lowering himself into a soothing hot spring, warmth seeping into his muscles and encouraging him to unwind. This sensation had everything to do with Kitty's particular magic.

Kitty had a perfect eye for color and the ability to furnish a space entirely in her head after having only visited it once, but her abilities went far beyond arranging the rooms featured in splashy architectural magazine spreads.

Kitty's power came from her intuitive grasp of how vital energy flowed between individuals and pooled in three-dimensional space, and she could manipulate that energy with a wave of her hands. Her skills had been nurtured by her parents, who ensured she was rigorously trained in traditional feng shui and encouraged her to study architecture at Colombia. Upon graduating, Kitty had garnered a reputation as a corporate assassin, someone who could arrange your boardroom so that your competitor would feel overpowered and willing to sign over their shares. It was rumored that once she had convinced an ailing shipping magnate to name his youngest daughter, not his oldest son, as his successor, simply by redirecting the energy in his office during a fifteen-minute walk-through, then locking the changes in with a single potted plant.

Kitty covered Moomin's face in kisses, making the gold bell around his neck jangle, then set him down in front of his kibble dish.

"You look awful," Nathan said pleasantly to Rhys. "Done shouting and waving your dick around for the day?"

Rhys glowered at Nathan, but he was too exhausted to fight back.

"Yes," Rhys said.

"Good," Nathan replied. Kitty lounged beside her husband, and he handed Kitty a joint, lighting it gallantly after she placed it between her lips. Kitty never lit her own joints, or opened her own doors, or buckled her own shoes. "It was enough to put us off our appetite. We canceled our dinner plans and everything."

"I'm sorry," Rhys said, guilt pouring out of him like a petroleum spill and onto Kitty's pristine cream carpet. "I lost my composure, and I embarrassed myself, and I disrespected the sacredness of the ritual room, and I–"

Kitty held up a manicured hand, her wedding ring winking.

"We're not who you need to apologize to."

Nathan took a couple drags from the joint, tapped off the ash in a crystal dish, and handed it to Rhys. Though pungent, the smoke was surprisingly sweet, and much smoother than David's cigarettes.

"What's in this?" Rhys asked as he exhaled.

"Hibiscus and spearmint and my best flower," Nathan replied. "Don't worry, we aren't going to poison you. David might want to, though."

"Did you bring me out here to tell me that? Because trust me, I already know."

Moomin trotted over, sniffing curiously at Rhys's socked foot. Rhys put his hand out to pet him, but Moomin turned his squashed nose up and slipped away to rub against Nathan. Rhys had never been allowed to have pets as a child, since his mother was allergic to everything, and he knew himself too well to allow himself to get a cat as an adult, no matter how much he admired the clever, independent creatures. He would probably just get distracted with his sorcery and neglect it, and then it would hate him, just like everyone else, and rightfully so.

"You know we both respect you," Nathan said. "Hell, Rhys, we love you. But whatever has been going on with you, it's got to stop. You're really demanding of all of us. I know you do it because you have high standards for yourself, and I know you're under a lot of pressure right now, but you've been acting pretty…"

"Mean," Kitty finished. Something about the simplicity of that word, the connotations of schoolyard cruelty, made Rhys wince.

"I know," Rhys said.

"We're happy to help you out, but we all have jobs, and families, and lives outside the Society," Nathan continued. "So do you. Personally, I think you've taken on too much, and the cracks are starting to show."

"I know," Rhys said, firmer. His face burned with humiliation.

"The Priesthood would be challenging for anyone," Kitty said. "And I don't know what kind of other battles you're fighting. You don't have to talk to us about it if you don't want to, but I suggest you find a way to regain equilibrium. What happened today in conclave can't happen again, especially now that David's gone. I really hope you'll find a way to patch things up and reinstate him soon."

"I'll do what I can," Rhys said.

Nathan glanced over at Kitty, waiting for her input. Nathan was sure of himself, more than capable of holding his own with bullheaded investors, or chatting up anyone at a party. But he deferred to Kitty in all things, and he was more at ease in her presence than he was when alone. If Kitty asked for anything, she got it, and if Nathan needed anything, Kitty usually knew what it was before he did. The Society guys sometimes ribbed Nathan about being whipped (and Rhys knew better than most that whatever Kitty and Nathan had going on probably had at least some element of power exchange to it) but no one could deny they worked together seamlessly. Sometimes Rhys got so jealous of the way Nathan could just relax and let Kitty call the shots that he could barely see straight.

What a luxury, to be able to trust another person like that. What a gift, to know that willing submission was not just appreciated, but celebrated.

Kitty nodded at Nathan, like she was handing him nuclear codes.

"If you feel like the Priesthood is too much for you right now," Nathan said, and the worst thing was, he still sounded *nice*. "I think the most responsible thing to do would be to step down."

There it was, the bombshell Rhys had been dreading.

"I *can't*," he ground out. Stepping down would be a defeat worse than death, it would be the end of everything, utter oblivion. He could never look at himself in the mirror again if he stepped down, much less David, much less Moira. "I can't just give up. I've been working for the High Priesthood since I was eighteen. I asked for this, so I have to handle it."

"What is it worth to you?" Kitty asks. "If it hurts this much? You're the architect of your own misery, Rhys. You can blame other people all you want, you can blame circumstance and stress if you want to, you can even blame God, but at the end of the day, you're the one calling the shots."

If he had been more sober, he might have swatted the unflattering picture Kitty painted of him away like so much smoke. But the weed was starting to kick in, slowing his reaction time just enough that he was forced to chew on what she said before responding. This had probably been Kitty and Nathan's grand plan all along.

It didn't help that Kitty and Nathan, the stoner-connoisseurs of his friend group, probably weren't feeling high at all.

"I fucked up," Rhys said. Despite the fact that this was a near-constant refrain in the back of his mind, he almost never said it out loud.

It felt a little bit like surgery, like lancing a boil.

Painful. Ugly. Necessary.

"Yeah," Nathan said. "But maybe you can still fix things."

Rhys was unable to look Nathan in the eye. How would Nathan, generous even in this moment when Rhys didn't deserve a scrap of kindness, feel if he knew Rhys had used his heart as leverage against Antoni? How would Kitty feel if she knew Rhys had treated her like a chess piece, like some helpless Helen of Troy traded away for the sake of men's egos?

He couldn't stomach himself.

"Do what you have to do to kiss and make up with David," Nathan said. "Just don't burn down Boston in the process, please."

"OK," Rhys said, nodding slowly. He accepted the joint Nathan passed him and took another long, steadying drag. Weed helped immensely with his anxiety, but Rhys would rather die than admit that. He wanted so badly to be able to manage it himself, through sheer power of will. "Thank you. For telling me the truth."

"Don't make me do it again," Nathan said. "I hate conflict."

Rhys huffed, the closest thing he could muster to a laugh. Nathan passed the joint to Kitty, kissing her collarbone as he did so, and Rhys was so envious it hurt.

He had been that happy once, before he had destroyed the only things in his life that really mattered.

Maybe, he could be that happy again, if he earned the right to it.

"And just a heads up," Nathan said. "I won't be around as much to help with the Society for the next month or so. One of the startups I invested in is getting ready to go public, and they're going to need me on call in the run-up."

"The payout should be more than worth the effort," Kitty said, beaming. "You've worked so hard for this, baby."

"I have it timed so the listing will go public at an auspicious hour. Sun conjunct Jupiter, hour of Mercury, day of Mercury, Venus in exaltation."

He rattled off the astrological coordinates so casually, so confidently, that Rhys was taken aback. Nathan had a hobbyist's interest in the occult but typically shirked intensive study. Rhys always assumed he was more interested in the Society for social reasons than supernatural ones.

Then again, Nathan had an uncanny knack for picking businesses to invest in the moment their star started to rise, and he always seemed to know exactly when to cash out or when to hold his shares. Apparently, he had been studying the art of election, or divine timing, for a while now, without gloating about his accomplishments or asking for any help. It wasn't an easy magical discipline to pick up, especially in isolation.

"I didn't know you were so good at electional astro," Rhys said.

"You never asked," Nathan said, with a sad tinge to his smile. He shrugged a shoulder, and then the sadness was gone. "It's alright."

"It's not alright," Rhys said, pulling himself to his feet. His mouth tasted slightly of cotton, and there was a lightness in his limbs, but he still had enough command of his faculties to get home safely.

"Forget about it," Nathan said. Moomin pawed at his pant leg as he stood, and Nathan stooped down to scoop the cat up. "Sure you don't want to stay for another joint? Always happy to smoke you out."

"If I have any more, I won't be able to drive."

"Lightweight," Nathan said with a smile. The fondness in that smile, freely given and completely unearned, was enough to make Rhys's throat tight. He deserved so little in this world, least of all the love of his friends, but somehow, he still had that at least. He shouldn't waste it.

"Thank you both for your hospitality," Rhys said.

"It's one of the many services we provide," Kitty said.

"Say bye to Rhys," Nathan said, lifting Moomin's paw in an approximation of a wave.

Awkward to the end, Rhys waved at the cat, then he gathered his coat and his keys and set off to do something that terrified him more than any ritual, any demon, or any public scandal:

Make amends.

CHAPTER TWENTY-ONE
MOIRA

Moira stood shivering outside The Black Swan nightclub, wishing that she had thought to put on leggings before leaving the house.

The last time she had been here it was with Rhys and David, and she felt more vulnerable in the throng of jostling concertgoers without her two men beside her. The air was thick with smoke, from cigarettes or blunts or candy-colored disposable vapes. Moira shifted from foot to foot, peering over the heads of the crowd to find Luis.

He was guarding the door, arms crossed, face carved from oak. Moira raised her hand and waved, a tiny beacon in the sea of people.

Luis stretched out a hand, hauling her gently through the throngs of college students by her wrist. As she came to a stop in front of the backstage door, Luis rubbed some warmth into her shoulders with his big hands. Warmth pooled in her stomach as well, along with a blush in her cheeks. She didn't often like being manhandled, but when she did, she liked it a lot.

"Leda's right up the stairs," Luis said, opening the back door and giving her a friendly wink. He had cut his dark hair shorter since she saw him last, and it hugged his skull, showing off the silver daggers hanging from his ears. "Need an escort?"

"I think I remember the way, but thank you," Moira said, slipping into the darkness of the club.

A pair of young men tried to follow her, but Luis blocked their way with his body, barking: "She's with the owner. You're not on the list. Back it up."

Moira made her way up the matte black stairs, following the glow strips on the ground to Leda's apartment. Leda tossed open the door with a grin, all long torso and longer legs in her low-cut jeans and a black leather vest.

"Hi!" Leda cooed, leaning nearly double to kiss Moira on both cheeks. Her skin smelled faintly of patchouli. "Come on in."

Moira drifted into Leda's den of decadence, taking in the chaos star spray-painted onto a tapestry on the far wall, and the low-lying furniture. There was a tiny altar set up on a shelf by the door, fashioned from a chipped plate and sprinkled with herbs and spare change. A phallic candle flickered at the plate's center, filling the apartment with the scent of warm wax.

"Sorry for inviting myself over," Moira said. Now that she was here, she wasn't sure if this had been the right idea. She wanted to get closer to Leda, who Moira thought was immensely cool in a slightly intimidating way, but maybe kicking down the door of Leda's life wasn't the best way to do that.

"Don't even worry about it. I'm always happy to host. You sounded upset on the phone. Tell me what's going on and I'll make you a drink."

Moira drifted over to the island that separated the galley kitchen from the living room, perching on a bar stool.

"David and Rhys had a fight."

"What else is new?" Leda snorted. She retrieved a martini glass from the cupboard, along with a bottle of Empress gin from the freezer. "I swear it must turn them on or something. Get a different hobby, am I right?"

"A really *bad* fight. They started arguing in conclave. David accused Rhys of being a terrible High Priest, and Rhys kicked him out of the Society."

"Oh, shit," Leda said, pouring a heavy shot of gin into the glass before dribbling in a bit of vermouth. Then she squirted in a few drops of what Moira supposed were bitters, but could have been some sort of magical tincture, from an unmarked apothecary bottle.

"I ran into David outside the Society, but he wouldn't even look at me, and then I tried to talk to Rhys about it, but then I got upset, and then *we* had a fight, and then I just left him there, and then–"

"Breathe," Leda said, setting the drink down in front of Moira with a clink. "Drink."

Moira obeyed, taking a bracing sip of the dangerously strong cocktail. It warmed her immediately, botanical sweetness blooming in her mouth.

"I knew something bad was going to happen," Moira moaned. "I sensed it, and I got there as soon as I could, but I wasn't fast enough and now–"

"Drink," Leda said again. "There's some moon water in that, it will help calm you down."

Moira cupped the glass and brought it to her lips, taking another swig. Leda poured Moira some water from the tap and set it down on the bar, nodding. Moira drank down all the water without having to be told. She had never enjoyed being ordered around, in the bedroom or otherwise, but right now she could see the appeal of a strong and steady voice telling her exactly what to do so she didn't have to think.

"Good girl," Leda said. "Better?"

"Yes," Moira admitted.

"How are you feeling?"

"I'm worried what this is going to do to the Society, and my patience with Rhys is completely gone. He's been acting so *weird* lately, pushing everyone away and burning himself down to nothing. I don't know why he won't let me help him."

"OK, but that's not what I asked. Quite frankly I don't really care about Rhys right now. He'll be fine, and so will David. You're the one sitting in my kitchen, and you're the one who asked for my help. So once again: how are *you*?"

Moira took a minute to think about it. Then she said, with a resolve that surprised her:

"I'm angry."

She had a hard time letting herself feel angry, mostly because once she opened that Pandora's box it was hard not to explode from all the pent up rage she so often ignored. But right now, that anger was undeniable, sitting in her stomach like heartburn.

"That's fair too. How old are you again?" Leda asked, grabbing herself a frosty beer from the fridge.

"I'm twenty-five in spring."

"A baby!" Leda exclaimed. She whacked the beer bottle against the edge of the countertop with her palm and popped off the cap. "You're too young to be taking care of everybody. Just because Rhys acts like he's ancient doesn't mean you have to. You're nobody's mom. Fuck that vibe."

"I'm worried that if I don't hold things together everything will fall apart."

"Sometimes things need to fall apart to come back together again. All this shit just sounds like the natural consequences of other people's actions. Magical societies are whirlpools of drama that suck in everyone within range, that's why I practice solo. Now come on. Let's find you something to wear."

"Wear?" Moira echoed, following Leda into the bedroom. Leda hit the lights, illuminating a king-sized bed that took up most of the space, strewn with rumpled wine-colored sheets. She kicked a discarded pair of men's work boots out of the way, then hauled open the folding doors of the closet. The shadowy space was crammed with midnight blue velvet and crimson leather and black, so much black Moira couldn't even make out the details.

"It's a goth club," Leda supplied, eyeing Moira's pink sweater vest and long floral skirt. Moira had been trying to emulate a picture of pre-royal Princess Diana when she got dressed that morning and was now regretting it. "You came here to party, right? Blow off a little steam, get back inside your body?"

"Sure, but I don't think anything you have will fit me," Moira said. She wasn't exactly a big girl, but she wasn't tiny either, and she had broader shoulders and a fuller bust than most women her height. Leda, on the other hand, was built like a willow tree, androgynously slender and breathtakingly tall.

"I've got tons of stuff, I'm sure we can find you something," Leda said, already tossing items onto the bed. "I dated a girl about your size a while back, and she left a lot of her clothes here when she got sick of me. Try this."

Leda handed Moira a faux leather mini skirt, then continued to root around in the closet while Moira changed. Miraculously, the skirt zipped up, if only barely.

Next, Leda offered her a halter top with a low back. Once Moira had successfully shimmied into the blouse, Leda rooted around in a ceramic dish of tangled jewelry until she found a bolo tie clasped with a silver moth.

Moira studied the whole ensemble in the full-length mirror, decided she liked it, then spent a few minutes tying her braids up into space buns. Leda scribbled something on a slip of waxy paper, writing out letters before crossing them out and writing them again, each time with fewer and fewer strokes. It looked like she was arranging the shapes left over into a symbol. A many-spoked wheel, maybe, or an asymmetrical star.

164 ASCENSION

"What do you think?" Moira asked, doing a spin to show off the whole outfit.

"So hot!" Leda pronounced. Then she folded up the paper, set it on fire with a match, and dropped the burning slip into a miniature pewter cauldron on her bedside table. Judging by the smudges of ash on the cauldron, this seemed to be its primary purpose. "Almost finished. Stay right there."

Leda snatched up an eyeliner pen from a makeup bag on the floor and stood behind Moira, holding her steady. Carefully, Leda began to draw something on Moira's skin, the touch of the felt pen cool between her shoulder blades.

"What's that?" Moira asked.

"Sigil. Just something I whipped up, nothing fancy. These work better when you charge them with an orgasm or some primal screaming, but fire works just as well to call forth the desired outcome."

"And what's your desired outcome?"

"For you to be the brightest star in the sky tonight," Leda said, adding a few dots and slashes to the sigil. "Not that you need much help. All done!"

"Thank you," Moira said, turning around to look up at Leda. Despite her olive coloring and hawk nose, so different from David's, her downturned eyes were set precisely like her brother's. "I really appreciate you, and I really needed this."

"Don't mention it. Come on, let's get down there!" Leda took Moira by the hand like they had been friends for years, and led her towards the front door. "Your drinks are on the house, just tell the bartender to put it on my tab. Did you bring any singles? I can slip you some dollar bills if you want to tip the go-go dancers. The DJ doesn't take requests though, so don't even think about it."

Despite the day's awful events, Moira giggled as she followed Leda down the stairs towards the thump of electronic music.

For the first time in a long time, Moira felt lighter than air.

Moira spent the evening losing herself in the driving beat of Depeche Mode remixes under the circling spotlights of The Black Swan. She danced for what felt like an eternity, sweating out her anger with her hands lifted above her head as though she were participating in an ecstatic rite. There was a strange sacredness to the scene, vibrating between the artsy boys sloshing their drinks and the sorority girls taking off their heels and the endless combinations of bodies writhing together to the beat. The atmosphere was thick with that electric, thinly-veiled energy Moira felt on Halloween, or in graveyards, or in empty churches. It was the unseen world colliding with her visible reality with a delicious, sizzling friction, opening up whole new realms of possibility.

Moira felt like a maenad, like her pounding heart was a lodestone for all the divinity and debauchery in the world.

Leda presided over it all, the priestess robed in shadows. Everyone seemed to know her, whether they kissed her face in greeting or whispered about her as she wove through the crowd like a snake. David had once jokingly called his sister a cult leader, which Moira had chalked up to a bit of sibling animosity, but now she saw there might be some truth to it. A few of the revelers wore the chaos star, pinned to their jackets on patches, or painted on their skin with ultraviolet pigment, or tattooed in a whirl on the back of their hands. Chaos magic proclaimed that the magician answered to no gods and no masters, but Leda commanded reverential respect even among her most punk peers. Some of that was probably due to the fact that Leda toured as the vocalist for a rock band when she wasn't running the nightclub, which tended to cultivate parasocial devotion. But some of it, Moira knew, must have been fueled by Leda's own potent magic: part Aristarkhov charm, part reckless improvisation, all down-and-dirty power.

"Another backshot, please," Moira said to the bartender, leaning on a stool to catch her breath. She wasn't sure what went into the layered shooter that the bar had dubbed "the backshot" but it was strong, and it tasted like pineapples, and it felt pleasantly naughty to order.

Moira pushed up onto the stool, cooling her heels while the bartender worked. Her feet were starting to hurt, and she had no idea how late it was outside the windowless nightclub, but she didn't want to go home yet. Going home meant coming back to reality, facing her rocky marriage and all the mistakes that had led there. She could waste away one more hour in Leda's poppy field before coming back to her senses.

"That's a strong drink," an approving voice said behind her.

Moira turned as a Latino man who couldn't have been any older than her took a seat at the bar. He wore dark jeans ripped through the knees and thighs, and a cropped T-shirt that flashed his belly button. His chin-length chestnut hair reminded Moira of the posters she used to have in her room of 90s heartthrob actors, and there was a faint sunburn across his nose that suggested he recently spent time somewhere the sun shone through winter.

"It's a grown drink for a grown woman," Moira said smoothly, bringing the shooter to her lips and swallowing it down. She didn't even wince.

"My apologies," he said, holding up his hands with a laugh. "I didn't know I was dealing with a pro."

Moira couldn't help but smile back. He was cute in a messy way, and he was forward without being pushy, two things she liked.

"I'm thinking of trying out for the league next year," she teased. She was a big believer in the social good of a little harmless flirting, and she needed the boost in morale tonight.

"Are you one of Leda's guests?" he asked, flagging down the bartender and leaning over the bar to call out his order. He wasn't very tall, so he had to lean pretty far, giving Moira a clear view of his toned forearms and shoulders.

"Do I really look that out of place here?"

Her companion waited until he was handed his rum and coke, then slipped a ten-dollar bill to the bartender and turned back to her.

"Not out of place. Just magical."

Moira opened her mouth and then closed it again, wondering if she should be flattered or concerned. She had never met this person before, and she certainly wasn't notorious enough in the occult scene to be recognized on the spot. She wasn't even wearing any crystals or zodiac jewelry that might give her away.

"How did you know?" she asked. Her lips tingled as though she had just walked into an electrical storm, like she was edging up against a moment in time that would reshape her in some way, big or small, forever onwards. It felt a little thrilling, and a little dangerous. But she couldn't *not* ask.

Your curiosity will always get the better of you, her mother's voice sighed in her head.

The young man looked at her strangely, almost like whatever he was about to say could only be voiced with effort. He had deep-set eyes, the kind of brown that probably looked amber in sunlight. He was so pretty, prettier still for all his rough edges and the tiny chip in one of his front teeth.

"I saw you," he said.

"You… saw me?" she repeated. Was she mishearing him? Maybe she should cool it on the shooters.

"Dancing," he said quickly. "I saw you dancing. The sigil on your back. It's one of Leda's, right?"

"That's right! How'd you know?"

"She's a friend of the family," he said, not breaking eye contact as he took a deep sip of his drink. "I'm–"

"Moira!" Leda exclaimed, appearing through the crowd. "There you are! I was looking for you. Some of us are going upstairs. Want to come?"

"Sure," Moira said, sliding off the stool and letting Leda take her hand. Before she knew it, she was being pulled away without ever having learned the man's name.

"Bye!" he called, cupping his hands around his mouth.

"Bye!" Moira shouted back, then disappeared through an unmarked door. The noise of the dancefloor fell away as she followed Leda up a flight of stairs.

"You sure know how to pick 'em," Leda muttered.

"What's that supposed to mean?" Moira asked as they spilled into Leda's apartment. "Who was that?"

"I'll let you find that out in your own sweet time."

Moira wanted to demand more answers, but they weren't alone in the apartment. Four of the revelers from downstairs, including a couple who wore the chaos star around their neck in pewter charms, were lounging on the couch. As they chatted with convivial intimacy, Moira watched them touch each other, the fingers that wandered along elbows, the hands that grasped shoulders or settled on hips without a care for how it might look to outsiders. Nothing inappropriate was happening, but the scene was undeniably… intimate.

Suddenly, she felt very warm.

"Are you going to stick around for the afterparty?" Leda asked. She settled her hand on the small of Moira's back and guided her into the kitchen.

"What does that entail?" Moira said, hoping she sounded blasé. She had a pretty good idea of what was going to happen, but it helped if Leda spelled it out.

"A group sex ritual if I have the energy to play ringmaster," Leda said, like she was showing Moira her favorite record, not inviting her into orgiastic excess. "You'd make a sweet little centerpiece for a ritual, if being touched doesn't sound too overstimulating right now? Or you could just watch?" Leda's hand slid up her back, tracing the outline of the sigil on her skin. "Would that turn you on?"

Moira blinked up at Leda in a dumbstruck daze. No one ever asked her what turned her on, except Rhys, who had already memorized all the ways she liked to be touched and talked to in bed like a student studying for their final exam. Even if something like this was technically allowed, and even if participating in this ritual without at the very least giving Rhys a heads-up wouldn't destroy their already fragile relationship, her desire had existed in the boundaries of marriage for so long that she wasn't sure anymore what it looked like in the freewheeling world of casual sex.

Moira felt torn down the middle, like a well-worn love letter folded and refolded so many times it had split.

"Oh, no thank you," Moira said. "I don't–"

Leda removed her hand from Moira's back lightning-fast. For the first time since Moira had met her, devil-may-care Leda looked absolutely mortified.

"God, sorry! I didn't mean to make you uncomfortable! You just said you wanted a distraction and to get back in your body, and I thought you meant – you know what, my mistake, totally heard. Sorry."

"Oh!" Moira exclaimed. This, she realized in a rush of compassion, was Leda's ultimate overture of friendship. To her, sex was just a deeper act of self-giving kindness. "Oh, I see!"

"Don't even worry about it," Leda said, retrieving her phone. She fixed her gaze on the ride app, unable to look Moira in the eyes. "I'm going to call you a car. What's your address again?"

"Leda I'm very touched, honest. I'm not offended."

"OK, thank God. It's just that I…" Leda squeezed her eyes shut, bracing herself. Both Aristarkhov siblings, it appeared, were fearless in the face of everything except emotions. "I just have trouble reading people sometimes. I know I can come on too strong. I wasn't trying to, like, entrap you. I just thought it would be fun. But sometimes I assume everyone is like me and totally cool with these kinds of things, which they're not, and that's fine too."

"I think it's very cool," Moira said quickly. "I just don't know if it's what I need right now. Right now, I think I need to go home and make sure Rhys is OK. And I should probably text David, too. Can I give you a hug instead?"

"Yes," Leda said, with embarrassed relief.

Moira pushed up on her tiptoes and wrapped her arms around Leda, burying her face in the crook of her neck. Leda hugged her tight, like the press of skin to skin and the exchange of body heat was good and holy medicine, and Moira saw in an instant that it was, it really was.

When Leda released her, she was herself again.

"So fun to kick back with you," Leda chirped. "We should do it more often! Good luck with Rhys, and with my little shit of a baby brother. Don't let them be mean to you, OK?"

"I promise," Moira said with a grin.

"Now get out of here before it gets any later! Luis will make sure you get in your car safe."

Moira tossed one more goodbye over her shoulder and then headed down the stairs and into the night, steeling herself for whatever hard conversation was ahead of her.

If there really was an invisible thread tying her to Rhys, she could feel it tugging at her ribs, pulling her back towards him. He needed her, or maybe she needed him. This late at night, with her ears still ringing from the bass in the nightclub, it was hard to tell.

Moira just hoped the ties that bound them together weren't frayed beyond repair.

CHAPTER TWENTY-TWO
RHYS

Rhys had gone straight from Kitty and Nathan's to the nearest bodega, one of those corner stores that stayed open late and sold milk and produce and, crucially, flowers. He bought every cellophane-wrapped bouquet of spray roses left in the shop plus a dozen long-stemmed orange carnations and three bundles of baby's breath. He also grabbed a Saint Jude novena candle for himself, then put it back at the last moment.

It was the only one left on the shelf. Somebody else would undoubtedly need intercession from the patron saint of lost causes more than he did that night.

"Anniversary?" the shopkeeper asked as he checked out.

"Something like that," Rhys replied.

It was nine by the time Rhys got home, and ten by the time he finished setting everything up. Moira hadn't come home yet. He hadn't eaten anything since lunch, so he forced himself to have as many crackers dipped in hummus as his twisting stomach would tolerate, all while alternating wildly between calm acceptance and catastrophic end-times thinking. He reminded himself that they had argued before, that they always worked through it with compassion, but then he started thinking about every argument they had ever had, big or small, until he had to grip the countertop and count backwards from ten to calm down.

Moira still wasn't home. He checked his phone for the dozenth time. She had shared her location with him earlier that night, shortly after leaving him alone with his misery in the clubhouse. There was no text attached, which meant she was still angry, but the location confirmed she was at Leda's, which meant she was safe.

Rhys didn't always understand Leda, but she was in the small circle of people Rhys trusted to take care of his wife under any circumstances.

Eleven rolled around. Rhys ate some more crackers, then almost threw them up in the sink. He wandered upstairs, yanked on a clean shirt – the green one that Moira liked so much – then scrubbed water onto his face, ran a comb through his hair, and splashed some cologne on his neck in the hopes it would make him feel more like a human being.

It did not.

He returned to the kitchen to stand vigil, and dissociated for a little while which was alright, because that meant that he wasn't watching the clock.

Then, at ten till twelve, right when Rhys was convincing himself that he *had* to call her or else he would die, Moira walked through the door.

Rhys just stared at her, words dying on his lips as though she were some Valkyrie vision appearing to a fallen soldier. She was dressed in leather and nylon, her braids coming loose from their buns, her skin nearly bare from sweating off her makeup.

She had definitely been at Leda's.

"Hey," Rhys said, his voice hoarse.

"Hey," Moira replied. She scanned his face with big, wounded eyes, as though she were afraid of whatever he might say next.

Rhys took a single step forward, clasping his hands tight in front of him.

"It's good to see you." Every word felt like he was edging out onto thawing ice, like it might break under his weight and suck him into the frigid black waters below. "I was getting worried."

"I was with Leda," Moira said, tossing her keys into the dish by the door.

"I'm glad you were with a friend. Did you have fun?"

"Yes," she said, gaze guarded. "It was nice to go dancing."

There was more to this story, Rhys knew, but she would not be sharing it with him now. Maybe later, if he made her feel safe enough, she would tell him.

"Moira," he began, clasping his hands even tighter, until he cut off his circulation. He knew what he intended to do, and he knew that it was the only way he could atone for all the things he had done and left undone in all their time together, but that didn't make it any easier. Still, his father always said that marriage was built on sacrifice, and what wouldn't he sacrifice, for Moira? "I want to say–"

"I'm really tired," Moira said, and Rhys's heart deflated like a popped balloon. "I just want to put on my moisturizer, drink some water, and go to sleep. Can we talk tomorrow?"

"Can I..." Rhys ran his tongue over his dry lips, grasping for the right words. "Can I show you something? It will only take a minute."

"Rhys–"

"Please," he said, the word as fervent as a whispered prayer. "You have always trusted me, even when I didn't deserve it. I'm asking you to trust me one more time."

He had asked her this before, not one time but many. Every time, she trusted him, and every time, he ended up proving that her trust had been worth it. He hoped to God this was one of those times.

"Alright," she said. "But only a minute."

Rhys led her down the hall to his study, holding open the door for her as she stepped inside.

He had organized the bodega flowers into vases and pots, arranging and rearranging them until he was satisfied. Honey-colored beeswax tapers and scarlet tea lights and white votives filled the room with soft, flickering light. He had lost count of how many candles he had lit, probably every single one they had in the house. Rhys had even anointed the corners of the room with chrism and done a thorough banishing ritual beforehand, just in case any negative energy was hanging around from his last summoning.

What he intended to do tonight was nothing less than an act of holy surrender, and he felt strongly that anything holy ought to take place in a sanctified space.

Moira drifted over to one of the vases, reaching out to touch the delicate waxy buds of baby's breath. Her expression softened momentarily, but when she looked over her shoulder at him, her eyes were guarded.

"Is this supposed to be an apology?" she asked.

"The start of one."

"It's all very pretty. And I appreciate the effort you put into this, but it doesn't make up for neglecting me for the sake of the Priesthood. And it doesn't change the way you treated David, or the way you spoke to me in the clubhouse, or–"

"I know," Rhys said gently, holding up his hands. "And you're right. Completely."

Moira regarded him with suspicion, the curves of her face shadowed in the candlelight.

"What are you up to, sorcerer?"

Rhys's hands shook, just like they had on his wedding day. He forced himself to breathe, to rid his mind of racing anxieties and simply be *present*. To be an empty vessel, ready to accept whatever was poured into him next, be that Moira's tenderness or Moira's wrath.

"In the Catholic Church," he said quietly. "We kneel at the altar to show submission. We prostrate ourselves in the presence of what is holy, and we offer our hearts as a sacrifice."

"I don't understand," Moira said.

Wordlessly, Rhys sank to his knees.

Rhys gazed up at her, at the lips he had worshiped with his mouth so many times, and at the eyes where he had so often seen himself reflected as a better man, a man worthy of trust and esteem.

Once he said this, once he offered, there was no taking it back. He would lose everything he had worked for since he was eighteen years old, and the course of his life would be diverted forever.

But he would still have Moira. And if this is what it took to keep her, he would do it a hundred times over.

"I'll cede the Priesthood," he said. "Say the word, and it's done."

Moira stared down at him, unmoving as a statue.

"You would do that?"

"I told you once I would do whatever it took to prioritize you," Rhys said. His knees ached on the hardwood, and the tendons in his neck strained from looking up at her, but the ache felt good. It felt like being cleansed. "When it came time to do so, I failed. I'm not fit for the Priesthood, and I'm not fit to be your husband, but I hope that I can still salvage at least one of those things. I'm stepping down."

She had told him once, wriggling away with a grin on her face when he tried to pin her to the bed, that she thought men were prettier on their knees than they were looming over her. Rhys had thought it was a joke, but he understood it now. The tenderness of this thing: his neck bared for her, his will laid at her feet.

Moira's hand drifted up to thread through his hair, fingers winding around the curls as nails scratched lightly against his scalp.

Then, she tightened her grip. Just tight enough to sting, just firm enough to hold him in place as he looked up at her, his throat fluttering.

"No," she said.

"No?" Rhys echoed, his world hazy at the edges. He had seen David like this so many times, bruised and beautiful on the ground with Rhys's hand fisted in his hair, but Rhys had never been the one on his knees before. Not like this.

But if there was one person in the world who deserved to see him like this, debased with love and willing to crawl across broken glass to prove it, it was Moira.

The sensation of Moira's acrylics digging into his scalp while he surrendered to her utterly was electrifying. Rhys's chest felt like it was going to burst, like the space inside him had expanded so much he could fit the entire sky between his ribs.

Was this how David felt, when Rhys pressed down on top of him with his hand around his throat?

"No," she said again. "You don't get to throw your hands up in the air and abdicate responsibility for the hurt you've caused. That's just another punishment, not penance."

Her grip in his hair slackened, and Rhys took in a shuddering breath. He hadn't noticed that he hadn't been breathing. He didn't know where she had learned to do *that*, or if that firm hand had been within her all along, but either way, he didn't want her to stop.

Her nails trailed down the nape of his neck, gentler now.

"If you really love me, you'll fix what you broke," Moira said. "Not just with me. With the Society. With David too."

Moira released him, and Rhys's forehead fell forward against her stomach. He stayed like that for a few ragged breaths, breathing in the scent of perfume and cigarette smoke on her borrowed clothes.

"I don't know how," he said. He slid his hands up her legs and grasped the back of her thighs, looking up at her. "But I will. I swear I will."

"You can start by being honest. What's been going on with you, baby? Please don't lie."

He had to tell her. His armor had already been discarded, he was already stripped bare. It was now or never.

"I'm overleveraged."

"I'm aware."

"No, I mean supernaturally overleveraged," he said, moving to rise.

Something about that, however, didn't feel right. He felt, with a guttural instinct, that he should ask permission. "Can I…?"

"You can get up," Moira said, command coming to her as naturally as any other magic.

Rhys rose to his feet and looked his wife in the eyes.

There had been so many voices in his mind lately: the admonishment of his own guilt, the sibilant whispers of his demanding demons, the wail of his wounded ego throwing tantrums. But in one moment of clarity so crystalline it felt miraculous, Rhys heard himself. His true self, the one that dwelled deep in his heart.

Tell her before you change your mind.

Rhys opened his heart and he let the truth bleed from him.

"I wanted to be good at this job, and I wanted other magicians to respect me. I wanted to be strong enough to save the Society and the protect the people who depend on it. I was desperate, and I was arrogant. I started building up my spirit stable, and at first it was just for a little extra help, but now I'm drowning in demons, and I don't know what to do. They want things from me, Moira, pieces of me that I don't have to spare. Nothing is enough for them. There's too many for me to manage. The moment I stop working, the instant I try to rest, they're there. In nightmares or shadows or even in broad daylight. I've been… seeing things. Hearing voices that aren't mine tell me to push myself harder, to ask for more from everyone else, to not take no for an answer. I think my mind is breaking, and I think they want me broken."

Rhys thought he would feel lighter with all of that out of him, but instead he just felt hollow. He took a shaky breath and waited for her judgement.

Without a word, and without hesitation, Moira embraced him.

Rhys wrapped his arms around his wife and held her tight as he buried his face her shoulder. Relief cracked him down the middle like lightning hitting a tree, and he choked out a sob.

"I'm sorry," he groaned. She always admonished him when he apologized for crying, but this time, she just held him. For some reason, that only made him cry harder.

After a long moment, Rhys pulled away and scrubbed his face clean with his palm.

"I should have told you," he said.

"Yes," she said, reaching up to wipe a stray tear from his jaw. "But I'm glad you're telling me now. Talk me through it. From the start."

Rhys told her everything, rattling off the names of his demons and enumerating the offerings and the petitions they demanded. And then, finally, he told her the whole of what he had done.

"They're with me all the time now," Rhys said, leaning heavily against his desk. The long night –and no doubt all the long nights leading up to this one – was catching up with him. He ached all over. "I'm afraid that they're feeding on something dark inside me, making me do things I never thought I was capable of. I held something over Antoni's head that could ruin him, Moira. I didn't go through with it, but I threatened to blackmail–"

"Antoni's private business is not for me to know," Moira said. "But I don't like that. It doesn't sound like you."

Moira sorted through printed JSTOR articles and scrawled sticky notes on his desk with curious hands. Wheels turned behind her eyes.

"Can you send the demons away?" she asked. Grounding him in theories, pulling him back from the brink with the sturdy rope of scholarship.

"On paper, yes. In practice, not without risk. I've never banished a demon when the boundary between my life and the spiritual world was so degraded. If they're that deeply embedded in my soul, sending them away might tear out pieces of me. Not to mention the fact that most of my magical abilities are being propped up by infernal help right now."

"I wondered how you got so good with a pendulum so fast."

"The spirits are helpful when I can handle them, and I think I *can* handle them, or get a handle on them with time and practice, I just…"

His voice trailed off as Moira levelled a weighty look. Magician's eye, calling his bluff and seeing right into his soul.

"Alright," he admitted. "Maybe I can't handle them at all."

"This is why I told you to stop wading so deep into dark shit," she said, tossing down a grimoire with a sigh. She pressed her hands to her hips, shaking her head as though surveying a God-awful mess. "I wish I could help you more, baby. If you needed divination, or a charm, or even a nasty hex, I could do that. But demons aren't in my wheelhouse. That's David's world."

"I can't ask him. Not after what he said to me. Not after what I did."

"You'll have to see him again sometime. Getting him back on your side is going to take work, probably hard work if I know David. How you do that is not my concern, but I love him very much and he's my friend, so please do it quickly."

"Understood," Rhys said. Moira might have extended forgiveness to him in the interim, but he still had to prove himself worthy of her grace. If he didn't change in a very real way, none of his apologies would mean anything.

"Thank you."

"Are we alright? You and me?"

Moira idly pressed her thumb into the point of the ceremonial dagger on his desk, just enough to divot the skin. She didn't meet his eyes.

"We're alive, and we love each other. That's enough for me for now."

Rhys walked over to his wife and lifted her chin with his knuckle.

"There's something else," he said. "Tell me."

"I love you, Rhys John Michael McGowan," Moira said, slow and weighty, like she was swearing an oath. "But lie to me again, especially about something this big, and you'll wish my love had never found you. Do you understand me?"

"Yes," he said, terrified and utterly rapt. His fingers spread across her skin, cupping her jaw. "Yes."

Moira looked up at him with bright, challenging eyes, not soft in the slightest. This was just another reason Rhys loved his wife; the way she was silk and steel all at once.

"Show me, then," she said, not moving a muscle. Her voice was soft, almost trembling, but what she said next she said with full conviction. "Show me how well you understand."

Rhys dropped his head and kissed Moira, really kissed her, deep and slow. She made a soft sound and ceded to his kiss, letting him run his tongue along her plush lower lip. They hadn't touched each other in what felt like ages, not for the entire night, and now Rhys couldn't get enough of her under his hands.

He had begged for her forgiveness with words already. Now he wanted to seek absolution with his body.

Moira leaned back against the desk and kissed him harder, feeding the fire between them. Rhys's hands found her waist, then slid higher so he could stroke his thumb along the curve of her breast. Her nipples were peaked through the flimsy fabric of Leda's shirt.

"Can I touch you?" Rhys asked.

"You're already touching me," she replied, stubborn to the end.

"You know what I mean. Let me make you feel good." Rhys put his mouth near Moira's ear. Sometimes, being brazen with her was easy.

Other times, when it mattered most, he was more self-conscious. "Let me make you come. Please?"

That simple request unspooled something in Moira, and her body went pliant beneath his hands. She nodded, and Rhys efficiently reached up her skirt and tugged her panties down to her ankles. Moira kicked them across the room, as though she couldn't be rid of them fast enough.

Rhys slid his hand down her stomach and cupped her where she was fever-warm beneath her skirt, the short curls between her legs damp with desire. Rhys wasn't sure if she had been wet all night and had come home with this need already aching inside her. Something about the idea of anything or anyone else turning her on when he wasn't in the room only made him want her more.

"What do you need?" he asked between kisses. He was hard for her already, and there were a half dozen ways he could have her right now that would make him feel good and normal and in control again. But Rhys got the feeling that his submission exercise wasn't over. He got the feeling that this would somehow be better for both of them if he kept the focus on her.

"You know what I like," she said. "Don't tell me you forgot."

"Never," he said, and circled her clit with his fingers.

Moira said his name again, a small, needy sound, and dropped her forehead to his shoulder. Rhys pushed her skirt up higher over her ample hips, and looked down at the naked glory of her. Moira pushed up on the edge of his desk, hitching her knee higher to grant him greater access.

Usually, he would take more time warming her up, but he could tell from the way she was nodding fast and clutching his shirt that she was ready.

Rhys pushed both fingers inside her, firm and deep.

"*Yes*. More," Moira said, so gloriously demanding that Rhys felt a bit out of his own body. He had always seen sex not just as a source of play and pleasure but an act of service, and it was so much better when she spoke to him like *that*.

Rhys pumped his fingers in and out of his wife, gently at first, and then with more force. She pulled him in close and Rhys buried his face in her neck, kissing and nipping mindlessly at her skin. She smelled light Leda's nightclub, like synthetic fog and pineapple vodka and other women and men.

Rhys waited until Moira's fingers tightened on his shoulders and her thighs started to tremble. Then he withdrew his fingers and applied them mercilessly to her clit.

Moira let out a cry somewhere between a gasp and a sob. Rhys worked her though the throes of her orgasm, until she had gone totally pliant in his arms. He wanted to please her so badly. He wanted to be *good*.

When she had finished completely, Rhys kissed her again.

Her face was wet with tears.

"Love," he said, horrified. "I didn't hurt you, did I? What's wrong?"

"Nothing," Moira said, looking up at him with a starshine gleam in her eyes. She let out a breathless laugh. Tears of pleasure, then, not pain. "Nothing at all. I had just forgotten. What you do to me sometimes."

Rhys brought his fingers to his mouth and efficiently sucked them clean. Then he tugged Moira's skirt back down over her thighs and pulled her into a hug. She clung to him tight, a warm, anchoring weight in the cold sea of his ambition.

"I'll do my best to remind you more often," he said.

CHAPTER TWENTY-THREE
DAVID

David spent the day after the argument so furious at Rhys that he came within a stone's throw of a relapse. So furious he actually yanked on his coat, walked himself down to the corner sports bar in the freezing weather, and fished his ID out of his wallet for the bouncer.

But the instant David stepped inside the bar, crawling with college kids and smelling of sweat and pool table felt and spilled Narragansett, he came to his senses. He had worked too hard to stay sober to throw it all away just because his shitty boyfriend pissed him off.

So, David stomped back home, ordered a meat lover's pizza, and ate half of it in one sitting on the couch. He tried and failed to find something to watch on his half dozen streaming services, then threw the remote across the room before burying his face in a couch cushion and letting out a groan.

He hated *everything*. There was no relief from the hot itch under his skin that made him want to drink, or fuck a stranger, or get into a fistfight, or set something on fire. He felt like it was going to consume him.

Then, his phone dinged.

David crawled across the couch to flip open Max's latest message. The texts had slowed to a trickle over the last few days, and David had assumed that Max had heard about David's adolescent behavior in the ritual room and realized David wasn't someone he wanted to involve himself with. But, to David's surprise, Max had something else in mind.

I've enjoyed talking with you this week. Would you like to get dinner with me sometime and catch up in person?

David didn't think twice about his answer, and he certainly didn't feel guilty about it.

Any time, any place.

As it turned out, Max wanted to see him that night, so David arrived punctually to the Seaport restaurant they agreed upon at 7pm. He had missed a call from Rhys on the drive over, which was just as well. David wasn't ready to talk to him again, not yet, and there was no use getting mad behind the wheel and crashing his Audi just because Rhys decided to try and mindfuck him.

David had better things to do that night.

Max had already grabbed their table when David arrived. He was reading over the menu while looking like a wet dream in a knit cardigan.

"David," Max said, so warmly. He gave David a firm handshake, and David was enveloped by the scent of his cologne. Tea, that was it. Whatever he wore, it smelled a little like black tea.

"Nice to see you, Max," David said, feeling deliciously illicit for calling his father's former colleague by such an informal name.

In the conspiratorial glow of the low golden lighting, it was all too easy for this to feel like something more than a professional meeting.

To David, it felt an awful lot like a date.

"How have you been?" Maximilian asked. "Well, I hope."

"Busy," David said. "Which for me is very well."

Maximilian laughed, bright and inflaming as the candle in the center of the table.

"You always had your hands in a hundred things. How are things at the Society?"

David felt the walls of his defenses rise, brick by stalwart brick. He really wasn't in the mood to talk about the Society.

"Transfers of power are always messy. But we're doing fine."

"I heard you and Rhys had some dust-up."

There it was, the bid for information. David considered telling the whole sordid tale, of painting Rhys in the worst light possible, of giving in to the satisfaction of Max inevitably taking David's side.

But venting about a lover wasn't a good look.

"I don't want to talk about Rhys tonight," David said. He resisted the urge to dial up his Aristarkhov charm up, as it didn't seem fair to deploy magical magnetism on somebody he was interested in. David might have been calculating, and he might be his father's son when it came to keeping up appearances, but he did have *some* ethics.

"Fine by me," Max said as the waiter appeared to take their drink order. "You've been living and breathing Society politics lately, I'm sure. What are you drinking?"

"Just sparkling water for me."

"This place has an excellent cocktail list. I'm a Manhattan guy, myself, but they do a nice twist on a gimlet too, if you want something brighter."

"Oh, I'm sober," David said, realizing that Maximilian probably didn't know about his history with alcohol. Would Max be turned off by his inability to pace himself, to drink like a responsible adult? "Me and booze don't really mix."

"Understood," Maximilian said, and that was that. No raised eyebrows, no attempts to cajole him into "just one drink", no pitying glances.

Just acceptance.

"Sparkling water for me as well," Maximilian told the waiter.

"It's fine, you can drink around me. I don't have a problem with it."

"Are you sure?"

"Positive."

"Then I'll take the house Manhattan, thanks."

The waiter nodded and left them to their own easy intimacy, so easy that it almost made David nervous. He was excellent at first impressions, but people usually formed a different opinion of him when they got to know the man beneath the charm. Which was to say, once they realized he was impulsive, vain, and self-interested. David didn't usually have an issue with that; if people didn't like him, that was a matter of their poor taste.

But he *did* want Max to like him.

"I was a little surprised you asked me to dinner," David said.

"Why would that surprise you?" Max asked, with incisive curiosity. It reminded David of his therapist, of her way of cutting to the quick.

"I assumed any questions you had might go through Rhys."

"I'm not here to network. I asked you to dinner because I wanted to get to know you better. I'm not sure how much you remember about the summer I stayed at your father's house."

"I remember," David said.

Max had been a magna cum laude college graduate with endless prospects who, for some reason, chose to pursue the occult. Max didn't come from a magical family. He had been lured in by the siren call of the supernatural like so many other young men seeking purpose and power, and he had written to David's father to request supervised access to the Aristarkhov library while he was visiting Boston. Evgeni, in a lavish display of hospitality, had offered Max one of the guest bedrooms. This was not uncommon; Evgeni traded in information as well as stocks and shares, and he often hosted visiting scholars in exchange for their best gossip. David was used to strange people in his house, usually men in suits who came and went as they pleased, and who kept to themselves until they had bled the library dry of the secrets they sought.

Max, however, was different.

Max had gone out of his way to be kind to David. Sometimes he even asked him questions about school or mediumship in the kitchen while David fixed a quick breakfast and Max sipped his coffee. David had played every interaction cool, or as cool as he possibly could as a sixteen-year-old boy with raging hormones and authority issues and a penchant for soft-spoken, older men.

Max was *kind* to him. Max listened to him. Max never made him feel like a freak or a problem child, and he certainly never crossed any boundaries. They hadn't had very many conversations (Max was there for book and business, not for David) but David had left their every exchange feeling full of light and strangely stricken. David, of course, had suspected that Max was gay. He was never brave enough to ask, but something about the possibility of someone so wonderful sharing something so fraught with David had made him feel less alone.

When David had gotten home from school one early autumn day, still tipsy from the wine coolers he had started emptying into his water bottles, he had been gutted to find that Max had packed up and left without saying goodbye. David had asked his father, in a calculatedly casual manner, about what had happened.

Evgeni had looked right through him, right into the disgusting sentiment at the heart of his question, and said simply, "He found what he was looking for."

"It was always hard to get a word in edgewise when my father was in the room," David said, doing his best to keep the conversation light. "Evgeni kept me on a short leash."

"I was sorry to hear about his death. I apologize for not sending my condolences; I wasn't sure what was appropriate in the situation."

"Don't apologize. My life didn't really begin until he keeled over."

"Strong words."

"I'm a strongly worded sort of person," David said, dragging the conversation back on track with a little flirtation. He didn't want to talk about his father, even more than he didn't want to talk about Rhys.

"Well then, cheers to life beginning," Max said, raising his glass of water with a smile that made David feel naked, in a little bit of a fun way and a little bit of a scary way.

"It's bad luck to toast with water," David said.

"I'm not superstitious. Are you?"

It felt like a challenge, one David was more than happy to rise to. He clinked his glass against Maximillian's and drank deeply.

"You're not superstitious, but you are a magician," David said. "How do those two things coincide?"

"I consider magic a natural science," Maximilian said, latticing his fingers together on the table as his Manhattan was set down in front of him. "Albeit a science we don't know much about. I want to understand it, to contextualize it in the known universe and apply it to modern issues. We all drug ourselves with social media and dating apps and cheap, quick distractions. I spent a lot of my life doing that too, but something about magic always reminds me that I'm real, that life shouldn't be wasted numbing out. I wish there was some way to wake people up, to remind them that they're just tiny players on a much bigger board controlled by forces beyond their comprehension. People used to call that sort of thing the fear of God. I don't believe in God, but I do believe in awe, and I think that's the closest any of us can come to anything holy."

Maximilian took a swallow of his drink, and David watched his throat bob. He ached to taste the dregs of whiskey clinging to Maximilian's lips.

"Magic is my birthright," David said, not caring if he sounded arrogant. It was the truth. "I can't imagine a world without it. It's almost mundane to me now, but it still manages to surprise me sometimes. How did you find your way to Thelema?"

"Accidentally," Max said, leaning back in his seat. He radiated the kind of power that came from absolute security, from not having to grasp or strive to be noticed. Max could probably whisper a request, and the whole room would fall over themselves to obey. David certainly would. "I tried a lot of different traditions, and they all scratched a certain itch, but nothing quite fit. Then I found Crowley. He was such a loose cannon, but the contributions he made to Western occultism can't be denied. His writings are like a puzzle box; you can come back to them a dozen times and find something new to consider on each reading. I guess I was captivated by the potential for learning there. Do you want my cherry? I prefer my Manhattans with lemon."

David was so taken aback by the sudden segue that he nodded. Maximilian deftly plucked the garnish from his drink and handed it to David, who brought it to his lips without a second thought. The dark luxardo cherry was cold and sweet, still dripping with one tantalizing, dangerous drop of whiskey.

"Can I ask you a question?" Maximilian asked.

"Anything," David replied, not caring if it sounded overeager.

"There are a lot of these... rumors swirling around about you."

"My family doesn't have any ties to crime you can prove in a court of law."

"No, I don't care about that," Maximilian said with another one of those disarming laughs. "I was thinking about that old story about the Aristarkhovs, that you all have some sort of supernatural power of persuasion. Is there any truth to that?"

"The Aristarkhov charm," David supplied. "It's true. If you believe in that sort of thing."

"So, you just... tell people what to do and they listen?"

"It's more like I suggest what I would like people to do, and they feel all warm and fuzzy about complying. It's really just charisma on steroids. My sister has it too, but it mostly comes out when she's performing on stage. It makes her fans obsessed with her, or something, I don't know the details."

"Do you use it on people often?"

"Only when I need something done quickly. I won't pretend that I don't use it in the courtroom."

"What about at the Society?"

"There aren't really high enough stakes there to warrant supernatural interference," David said with a scoff. "We're not exactly doing open heart surgery."

Maximilian nodded thoughtfully.

"It does seem disorganized," he said delicately.

"The Society is held together with duct tape, nepotism, and prayers. But it suits me fine. Nobody makes me do homework, and I get to scry as much as I want."

"As much as you want or as much as you're asked?"

"What do you mean?"

Max paused, as though he were afraid of showing too much of his hand. David had never seen him look so unsure before.

"It seems like you're the most competent scryer the Society has. You must be doing the work of three psychics. Do you ever feel overleveraged?"

David hadn't considered that before. Being busy and being recognized for his talents felt so good that he rarely stopped to ask himself if he was getting run down or if he was being taken advantage of, at work or in the Society. And he never turned down a request to scry, not wanting to create the impression that he couldn't be relied upon to perform with excellence every time.

"I'm having fun," David said, which wasn't really an answer.

"Your father pushed you pretty hard. You were excellent then and you're excellent now, but I sat in on some of those seances. I stayed in the house with you both. I know... What he was like."

David kept smiling, even though he felt brittle. He had managed to convince himself that no *one* knew, that Lorena's leading questions and his teacher's sympathetic glances were bullshit, that Evgeni was skilled enough at not fucking up David's face (usually) that their disputes stayed private. David had convinced himself that even if anybody did know, he hadn't needed their help anyway. It was easier then, when help didn't come, to pretend like he had never been hoping for it in the first place.

"I don't know what you mean," David said. That was not a conversation for tonight.

"Right. All I'm saying is, if you ever want to come over to the OTO..." Max's voice took on an atempting, teasing air that was only half a joke. He was trying to lift the mood.

"Nah," David said. "As fun as it would be to be fought over by societies like a shiny magical weapon, I'm good where I am."

"You aren't a weapon," Max said. "Nobody should use you that way."

He said it with so much sincerity, never breaking eye contact, that David felt a jolt of fear. Earnestness always freaked him out, and so did the thought of living in a world where he might not always be tied to the Society, from birth to death.

But then again, Rhys had snipped those ties with his nasty little scissors of bureaucracy, and David was adrift right now, a sorcerer without a society.

It might feel good, to let Max spirit David away to another order where he might be more appreciated.

But that also wasn't a conversation for tonight.

"Anyway, like I was saying, I try to avoid using my charm on my friends," David went on. "Most of the Society members are my friends, and some of them are my best friends, so it's not really relevant there."

"Can we call each other friends?" Maximilian asked.

David resisted a quip somewhere along the lines of *you can call me whatever you want*, and kept the conversation serious. He could do this. He could act like an adult.

"I promise I won't charm you, if that's what you're asking. I'd rather you like me on my own merit."

"Good. Because I do like you, David."

"That's convenient, because I like you too," David said, unable to meet Maximilian's eyes. It should have been an easy thing to say; David had said it countless times before, and most times, he had meant it. But something about saying it to Max made him feel sixteen again, grasping to keep up with feelings that were growing faster than he was.

Maximilian ran his little finger thoughtfully around the rim of his Manhattan glass, a gesture so infuriatingly perfect David thought he might die on the spot. He kept David in agonized suspense for a moment, then said:

"Am I correct in thinking – and please set me straight if not– that you had a crush on me, all those years ago?"

David swallowed hard.

If there was a moment to put all his cards out on the table, it was right now. And David wasn't one for doing things in half-measures.

"I might still have one, if we're being honest."

Max nodded, and for one terrifying moment, it was impossible to parse his expression. What if David had been reading the situation wrong?

In that horrible moment of waiting, a vision of Rhys crept in, freckled and windswept on Nathan's boat, one arm slung around David's shoulders as he laughed.

David shoved the thought away.

"Let me buy you dinner," Max said, as though coming to a conclusion.

"You don't have to do that."

"I want to."

"Careful," David said with a thin laugh. "You're making it sound like we're on a date."

"We weren't before," Max said, so calm that whatever bit of restraint David had left melted. "But we can be now, if you would like."

David smiled at Maximilian wide and unrepentant enough to call down the stars.

"I'd like that very much," he said.

They sat there for three hours, enjoying multiple appetizers and a couple of Manhattans and bottles and bottles of sparkling water for David and a scallop pasta entrée to split. David was having such a good time he didn't even count his calories, and he barely even wanted to drink, not when the sound of Maximilian laughing at his wild college anecdotes was so intoxicating. Max owned up to being disastrously bad at interpreting tarot, which was somehow endearing, and insisted on showing David pictures of his miniature pinscher, which was somehow more endearing. David didn't even like dogs, but he was willing to admit *that* dog in particular was cute enough to justify taking it out for walks at 5am. Then David ended up yanking his chair around the table so he was seated at Max's side, and drew out a quick ceremonial circle on a napkin to demonstrate, with a diagram, that Max's theories about streamlining Solomonic seals held water.

Then, after Max had paid for everything and held the door open for David and settled his hand on his back they jogged across the street to make the light, David stopped by the Audi to catch his breath. He looked at Max under the streaky glow of the city's neon and felt a space open up inside him that he didn't even know was there, a quiet room that he wanted to lead Max right into.

"Do you want to see something?" David asked, heart hammering with hope, with fear, with something dangerously close to love.

"See what?" Max asked.

"Come with me and I'll show you," David replied, unlocking the Audi.

David let them in to the Beacon Hill House through the side door, the one he would jimmy open at 2am in high school to prevent his father from knowing he was sneaking out. He flipped on the lights and led Max through the kitchen and the ground level, pointing out all the renovations he wanted to make to the house.

He didn't know why he had brought Max here, what he expected Max to say, or if he was seeking some kind of approval or not. All he knew was that he wanted to *show* him this place, to make him understand that it wasn't ruined by all the bad memories. To help Max see that David was making something beautiful out of the ugly legacy that had been entrusted to him.

"I can't believe I ever left this place," Max said, craning his head back to look up at the crystal chandelier spinning above their head, as though stirred by some phantom breeze. "It's one of the finest examples of Federal architectural design in the States."

"Why did you?" David said. He was standing what felt like a safe distance away, his hands thrust into the pockets of his coat and the roiling clouds of marble that marked the center of the home below his feet. He felt totally vulnerable, like bravado and sarcasm and all his other weapons of self-defense had failed him. "Leave?"

"David..." Max said gently, so gently that David *had* to keep talking, because if he didn't get it out now he would never say it.

"It just felt weird? One day you were there and we were friendly, and the next day you were gone. And you did it while I was at school, which I never understood. You could have stayed two more hours, you could have at least said goodbye, I–"

Maximilian walked over to David, stepping into the clouds with him. The house breathed and creaked around them, aching to settle.

"I left because your father told me I was no longer welcome in his home. Apparently, I was a bad influence on you."

David let out a bark of laughter that was also a smothered sob. This was too much. Too much tenderness, too much grief, too much magical electricity wrapped around both of them.

"I figured I was the bad influence on you," David said, because he would rather die than be caught crying, but if he was going to break, it would damn well be while making a joke.

"I think it's because I was nice to you," Max said, with a simple honesty that *hurt*, that seared through David like a surgeon's knife. He could almost feel it, Max cutting something rotten Evgeni had infected him with out of his chest with no anesthetic. "And because I encouraged you to go into law like you wanted to instead of working under him for the rest of your life. And probably because I was gay."

"I fucking knew it," David said, unable to do anything but even as his chin dimpled and twin tears spilled down his face. "My sister owes me money."

Max grasped David's chin very gently and tilted his face up so he could see into David's stinging eyes. "I'm sorry I wasn't able to help you. I knew what was going on but I didn't know who to tell. I was young, and I was afraid of what your father would do, to you and to me. But that doesn't make it right. I should have helped."

"I turned out fine, don't *do* that. I was a little shit and he was an asshole, that's all there is to it. There's no tragedy here, it was just life, and I'm *fine*, I'm–"

"Hush," Max murmured, and kissed David on the mouth.

David's hands went right for Max's belt buckle. He knew what came next. He was good at that part, and thank God it didn't involve any more talking. But Max caught David's hands and just kept kissing him, like they had all the time in the world, like there didn't need to be a beginning or an end to what had caught fire between them.

David didn't remember the last time he had kissed someone like this, warm and deep and *slow*, without speedrunning all the steps that always led to the bedroom. It terrified him, but it also felt good, so good that David could have sworn the air in the room heated around him.

Max kissed him over and over again, and David let him, until each press of his lips felt like a stitch in the wound Max had opened inside David.

CHAPTER TWENTY-FOUR
MOIRA

"I know him," Rhys said. Moira was seated at the small tea table in his study where she often took her breakfasts, stitching enchanted knots into an embroidered protection charm while he processed. They were discussing all his unsuccessful attempts to reach out to David, the voicemails and the apologetic texts and the occultism memes that had gone unanswered. "It's only been a couple of days. He needs more time."

"I'm not sure that's time you have to spare," Moira said, pulling the thread tight with her teeth and pinning the embroidery hoop to her lap as she worked on an anchor knot. Rhys took the thread from her mouth and held it taut for her as she tied everything off.

"I'm not in dire straits yet," Rhys said.

Moira glanced warily at the tiny altars he had set up around his room for his various demonic assistants. A jewelry box anointed with candle wax here, a ring dish sprinkled with herbs there, all so easily overlooked as more maximalist clutter.

"Really?" she replied. "Because I thought I heard you get out of bed last night at 3am to come down here and keep the fires burning. You came back stinking like laudanum and sherry."

"Shax," Rhys said apologetically. "He gets restless."

"Next time you see him tell him I don't like him."

"Shax is the reason the university double-paid me for my last week at the library."

"Is Shax also the reason you felt like it was alright to accept stolen money?" Moira said, light and cutting.

"Alright," he conceded. "I'm feeling... frayed. But if I push David too hard, I'll only push him away."

She finished the row of satin stitches she had been working on, then set down her embroidery wheel.

"Alright then. Time for plan B. We're having a dinner party. Occult leaders only."

"David won't come," Rhys said.

"Maybe not. Or maybe curiosity will get the better of him. If you want him to surprise you, you've got to give him the opportunity." "Who else would we invite?" he asked.

"Leda, obviously. Dion, if he's free. Zachary's in the middle of Chanukah so I won't inconvenience him. But we should invite Maximilian too."

"I don't like him, Moira," Rhys ground out. "I don't trust him. He's working for another Society and–"

"And you don't like how close he seems to have gotten to David," she finished. "You're jealous. It's just us two here. You can say it out loud."

Rhys drummed his fingernails on the tea table.

"Maybe I am a little jealous. But David and I have never exactly been in a closed relationship. I know that he wanders, I know that he comes back. It's fine."

"Then what is it?"

"David knew him when he was a kid and that makes me feel.... weird."

"To hear David tell it Maximillian barely looked at him when he was underage. That makes me feel better about the whole thing."

"No, I don't think anything inappropriate happened. It's just a certain kind of history I don't really understand, and that makes the whole situation more... unpredictable. And I'm not convinced Maximilian doesn't have ulterior motives. Call me paranoid."

"I won't call you paranoid, but I will point out bad vibes aren't a good enough reason to ban someone who might be able to help you from a dinner party. And if David's cozying up to him, you better get used to him. Fast."

"What's your read on him? Honestly."

"I think he's polite, and he's smart, and he's got a calming aura," she said. "No red flags on my end."

Rhys breathed out sharply through his nose like a restless bull. Then he gave her hand a squeeze.

"You're right. I need to let the weird feeling go. We'll invite Maximilian. And I will do my best to get along with him."

Moira squeezed his hand back.

"That's all I would ever ask."."

Moira was grateful for the distraction of preparing for the party. It kept Rhys from slipping into a total demon-weary madness, and it kept Moira from worrying herself sick. She tamped down her anxiety flares as she swept out the foyer and scrubbed the oven, and Rhys kept himself busy to the point of neurosis re-washing forks by hand after they had come out of the dishwasher, as though a single spot of soap might ruin the evening. He had barely slept for days, and had once been woken by nightmare so awful he couldn't even tell her about it, he just locked himself in the bathroom and dry-heaved for a few minutes.

Moira tried not to notice the way his hands shook as he prepped the pastry dough. Rhys was going to be alright. She was going to find a way to *make sure* he was alright.

And in the meantime they were all going to have a nice, normal dinner.

David had not responded to her invitation, despite the polite request for an RSVP at the bottom of her best eggplant-colored crafting paper. She didn't hear from him until three hours before guests were supposed to start arriving, when her phone lit up. Moira wiped the suds off her hands then swiped up on David's message.

Hey, peach. How are you?

She tapped out a message with her new acrylic nails. They were eggplant colored, because she loved a theme.

Hanging in there. What a weird winter! How about you?

Rhys walked through the kitchen doorway as David's typing bubbles appeared.

"Is that David?" he asked, voice high and hopeful.

"One second," she replied. "I'm working on him."

Rhys obediently lingered at the other end of the kitchen, too far away to read over her shoulder.

I'm fine, David replied. *Just keeping my head down with work. And I'm sorry I was so shitty outside the meeting hall. I was just trying to get out of there without tearing anyone's head off.*

Moira pulled a big breath into her lungs. He was sorry. He wasn't mad at her, and he was sorry.

I know you were angry. I would have been angry too. But I appreciate the apology. Do you think you're going to be able to come to dinner tonight?

I'm not going to be able to make it, he replied, and Moira's heart sank. *I know you're going to make it a magical evening for everyone else, but I'm not there yet. I want to see you, and I know I need to talk to Rhys, but I need to get my head on straight first.*

He was trying. Actually, as far as David was concerned this constituted a Herculean amount of trying. But the thought of going through the entire night without him made her want to crawl back into bed and sleep through dinner. She didn't want to pretend that she and Rhys were Boston's happiest magical couple, not without the third fulcrum of their triangle there smiling at her over his sparkling water and laughing along with Rhys's jokes.

I understand, Moira typed. *Take care of yourself until I see you again, OK?*

David sent her a saluting emoji, which made her snort even though she wanted to cry.

Then he sent a second message, something he very rarely said out loud and typed even less.

I love you.

Love you too, she typed back.

"Anything?" Rhys asked.

"He's not coming." Moira slipped her phone back in her pocket and returned to the dishes in the sink. "But he's acting sweet. And he says he knows he needs to talk to you soon."

"Small victories," Rhys said. "I guess I should go ahead and put the tarts in the oven?"

"I guess you should."

The pair passed the rest of their prep time in relative silence, weaving in and out of the kitchen as they laid out the slate gray plates, gleaming black silverware, and vases of purple-black calla lilies. Moira had cleared away all her star charts and sheets of drying herbs from the kitchen table, transforming her witch's home office into a room fit for entertaining. Their house was modest, but the table could sit six, and with the overhead light dimmed and candles lit at strategic points around the room, their digs felt chic instead of shabby.

Rhys monopolized the bedroom, changing outfits half a dozen times before he settled on his favorite wine-colored velvet blazer. Moira wore a convincing 1920s replica dress, all drop waist and flirty fringe, and slapped on a smoky eye in the precious few minutes before guests arrived.

When the doorbell rang, Moira made her way down the stairs, Rhys hot on her heels, and prayed Maximilian hadn't arrived first. Watching Maximilian and her husband exchange tight pleasantries in an otherwise empty room sounded miserable.

The door swung open, and the scent of patchouli and lavender-spiked cigarettes rolled into the house.

"Leda!" Moira said. "It's good to see you."

Leda dipped down and gave Moira a kiss on the cheek.

"You two are convivial," Rhys said with a smile.

"Haven't you heard that this is my new best friend?" Leda teased. "Don't worry, I know how to spread myself around."

She leaned down to give Rhys a matching kiss, smudging a little lipstick on his face. Leda rubbed it off with her thumb, in a gesture so familial Moira's heart ached. God, she wished David was here.

"Let me make you a drink," Rhys said, clapping Leda on the shoulder as he led her into the kitchen. "First come, first served."

Leda slipped off her leather duster and hung it on the coat rack, revealing a slinky blouse of darkest indigo. Her throat and fingers were loaded with silver jewelry.

"Where's my darling baby brother? He isn't answering my texts."

"He got tied up at work," Rhys said, not meeting Leda's eyes as he pulled the batched gin and elderflower cocktail out of the fridge and poured her a glass.

"That's unfortunate," Leda said, in a tone that clearly communicated she didn't believe him.

The doorbell rang a second time, and Moira excused herself to go answer it.

Dion stood on her front step, his breath frosting in the air. He grinned at her, broad and inviting. It was so, *so* good to see Dion, a friend that was hers first and everyone else's second, who would always give her the benefit of any doubt.

Dion wrapped her in a hug, and Moira was immediately calmed by the scent of his shop clinging to his clothes. Dion always smelled like dragon's blood incense and the cheap packing paper he stuffed into boxes of online orders. He was in streetwear tonight, black cargos and a boxy button-down open over a turtleneck, but his triple moon pendant still glittered around his throat.

"Thank goodness you could make it," Moira said.

"Don't tell me there's been drama already. That man of yours been treating you right?"

"Yes," Moira said, grateful that in this, at least, she didn't have to lie.

"Good. Tell me if you ever need a love charm to light a fire under his ass."

Dion's affection for Moira had always been brotherly, but she suspected there was also a small crush at play. Dion viewed interfering with anyone's marriage for selfish gain as a betrayal of his professional principles. Even so, when it came to Moira, Dion had joked more than once about wishing he was the man who had gotten there first. Moira appreciated the flattery, and she was touched that Dion trusted her judgment enough to ask for her advice about the tragically timed, not-quite-right women who always seemed to wander in and out his life.

"Dion," Rhys said, poking his head into the hallway. "Welcome! Nice to see you."

"Hi," Leda said, descending on Dion like a lovely vulture. From the appraising gleam in her eyes, she liked what she saw. "The name's Leda. I'm a musician by trade, chaos magician by calling. I don't think we've been introduced. Come over here and sit by me. Rhys tells me you're a Wiccan high priest..."

Leda's voice trailed off as she led Dion into the kitchen, leaving Rhys and Moira in the front hall by the door.

When the doorbell rang a third time, there was no doubt who was standing outside. Moira took a deep breath as Rhys opened the door. She was in no mood for a feud tonight, especially without David here to act as a buffer between Rhys and Maximilian. But Rhys had agreed to temper his pricked pride, so maybe it would all be alright.

Maximilian stood on the front stoop in a crimson sweater, snow gathering like a circlet in his hair. The weather must have turned in the last few minutes, ushering in the seasons' first fall of snow.

"Maximilian!" Rhys said, too brightly. "Come in."

"Max is fine, if you don't mind," Max said warmly. "Thank you for having me over."

"The pleasure is ours," Moira said. He took her fingers in his large hand and dropped a gentlemanly kiss to her knuckles, his eyes sparkling as if to say, *you have a friend in me, should you find yourself in need of one.*

"Rhys batched up a cocktail if anyone is interested," Moira said. She tried not to think about the non-alcoholic version of the drink Rhys had made, labeling it clearly with David's name and stowing it safely in the fridge.

"I'll take a glass," Maximilian said.

"Make that two," Leda chirped from the kitchen. She had already finished her first drink, and she barely glanced up from her conversation with Dion as the rest of the partygoers joined her in the kitchen. Moira considered warning Dion, who she knew was looking for something (and someone) serious, that Leda was polyamorous and polysaturated besides, but she left that to him to find out.

"Are we waiting on anyone else?" Max asked.

"No," Rhys said, gripping his cocktail a little tighter. "David can't make it. It's the five of us tonight."

"Five is a proper number for a gang of magicians," Leda said with a toothy smile. "Come on, let's toast."

"To friends old and new," Rhys said, lifting his glass in the air.

Everyone else chorused out their cheers and filled the townhouse with the sound of ringing crystal before sipping down their drinks.

"Shall we move on to dinner?" Moira asked, even though tiredness was dragging at her skirts. She needed to keep a brave face on tonight, she reminded herself.

This was her party, and she was damn sure going to rise to the occasion.

CHAPTER TWENTY-FIVE
RHYS

Rhys did his best to be an active participant in dinner, even though Moira's bacon-wrapped dates tasted like ash in his mouth. He kept slipping out of conversations as though drugged. A headache had been building behind his eyes all day, either a result of stress or dehydration or the demands of his demons, whose altars he hadn't tended for 24 hours. He was trying to wean himself off, breaking the knee-jerk impulse to make an offering every time Naberius scratched at the nape of his neck with his ghostly talons, or when Vual – who was useful when it came to gaining the favor of others but spoke only in rumbling Egyptian – rattled his strange words around in Rhys's brain.

So far, this effort only left Rhys feeling worn down. He wanted desperately to prop himself up with his elbows on the table, but he sat straight in his chair, since his mother would be ashamed of him for slouching.

"… I'm inclined to believe it's a group of people," Dion was saying. He was sitting beside Moira on Rhys's right, while Leda lounged by herself on the left side of the table. Maximilian was sitting directly across from Rhys at the opposite end.

"It reads more like a solo practitioner to me," Leda said.

"Dion has a point," Max went on. "Marking out a circle nine feet in diameter, mocking up a dummy, and getting though an entire ritual without being caught? You would have to have help."

"Or you would just have to know what you're doing," Rhys said, slotting himself back into conversation. "I've chalked out bigger circles in less time."

Rhys stole a sidelong glance at Moira, hoping his silence hadn't been noticed. She was nibbling halfheartedly on her dill quiche, her own expression a little glazed over. He knew without having to ask that she was thinking about David.

Rhys lost a precious few seconds to the pang that went through him as he remembered David's expression of absolute betrayal in the circle, the way all the light in his eyes had died. When Rhys came back to himself, Max was asking him a question.

"You're sure this isn't someone a Society member shared their study notes with?"

"Not to my knowledge," Rhys said, keeping his tone polite even though he was irritated that Max would default to pointing fingers at any of Rhys's people. "We protect the secrecy of our society."

"So did the Golden Dawn," Max said with a sympathetic smile that edged a little too close to patronizing for Rhys's taste. "Until Crowley broke his oaths and published their secrets."

"Well have you heard anything through the Thelemite grapevine?"

"Nothing filtering down from my superiors, or up from the people who report to me. Although we don't have as strong a presence on the East Coast as we used to. I hope that in time, I can help change that."

"You're planting a new Thelemite order in Boston?" Leda asked.

"More like looking for opportunities to resurrect the old one. We had a stronger presence in town about a decade ago. Without strong leadership, it dissolved. Now the nearest branch is in New York."

Rhys ground his teeth. Max presented himself as a neutral observer of the scene, ready to pitch in for the good of the community at large. But a full Thelemite order in Boston would mean there were two goetic magical groups in the city, not one, and it would no doubt cannibalize Rhys's membership numbers. Thelema was experiencing a resurgence of popularity with young people, who gathered to discuss passages from *The Book of The Law* in their dorm rooms, or burgeoning chaos magicians who, upon doing deeper reading, realized many of the tenets of chaos magic were riffing on principles first codified in Thelema. Even Rhys had to admit that he was indebted to Crowley, since the his go-to English translation of *The Lesser Key of Solomon* featured Crowley's notes. Despite all the controversies, Thelema had a historicity and an sex appeal that was hard to compete with.

"You'll have to bring me up to speed," Dion said. "I don't know my way around Thelema very well. It's a style of magic?"

"It's a religious framework," Max supplied. "Centered on the pursuit of one's highest will informed by love. Thelema is incorporated into the Ordo Templi Orientis, but you can follow Thelema without being initiated into a branch of the OTO. And yes, magic is a part of everything. From ritual workings to everyday life."

Rhys nodded along, the thread of the conversation once again slipping from his fingers. There was a cold, itching feeling crawling down his spine. Shax, requesting more wine?

Maximilian's phone buzzed, and he discreetly responded to a text under the table before slipping his cell back into his pocket.

Angsty heat coursed through Rhys. He just *knew* Maximilian was texting David. David, who couldn't be bothered to answer any of Rhys's calls, but who was firing off texts to another man during Rhys's dinner party.

"Work calling?" Rhys asked tightly.

"Just a friend in need," Max said.

Rhys had a crystal-clear vision of crawling across the table and throttling Maximilian, but he blinked it away and smiled right back.

"Well, don't let us keep you if it's an emergency," Rhys said, taking a steadying swallow of his cocktail. It was too sweet all of a sudden, as though the floral flavors had started rotting in his glass.

"I think he'll be fine," Max said.

"Then you can tell my brother to text me back while you're at it," Leda said.

In the so-quiet-you-could-hear-a-pin-drop moment that followed, throttling Leda seemed pretty appealing too. She wasn't trying to be cruel, but she handled conflict with a brazenness that made Rhys wince.

Beneath the table, Moira sank her acrylic nails into Rhys's thigh. The message was clear: *hold it together.*

The world went on turning without him, conversation shifting once again to the public ritual while his pounding headache worked itself into a migraine. Could he excuse himself long enough to slip into his study and wave some incense around to get Vual to shut up? He was almost positive it was Vual; only Vual made his brain feel like an egg in a microwave.

"I'm still hung up on the motivation," Dion mused, rubbing the stubble on his chin. "It's just so reckless. And without a controlled environment I doubt the spell would have been very effective... Makes no sense."

"Maybe there was a component to the spell we're all missing," Moira offered. "Maybe the public element was essential in some way."

"Yeah," Leda put in. "Or maybe somebody just has a hard-on for attention."

"That does seem like the most likely option," Max said, helping himself to another date. Rhys was grateful the guests were eating; it helped hide the fact that neither he nor Moira had any appetite.

"I'm going to find whoever's responsible," Rhys said, trying to muster his resolve. He had to demonstrate that he was still a competent leader, despite his lapses in self-control. That was part of what this night was about. "I can promise you that."

"Yes, you've made finding this criminal your personal vendetta," Max said. He said something else under his breath as he sipped of his cocktail, something Rhys almost didn't catch. "Some might think you're trying to throw suspicion off yourself."

Sirens blared in Rhys's brain. He didn't know if Max was trying to make a joke, or if the man really was stupid enough to question his morality in his own home, but either way, he wasn't going to stand for it.

"I'm sorry, what did you say?"

"Nothing," Max said. "Leda, I would love to hear more about your practice. Is it really true you host rituals backstage?"

"No," Rhys pressed on, clenching his fists. There was a burning itch building in his fingertips. Magic demanding to be set free. "Go ahead. Repeat whatever you just said."

"Rhys, take it down a notch," Dion said, holding out a steadying hand. "No one means any offense."

"I appreciate that, Dion," Rhys said. Moira was tense at his side, but he didn't dare look at her. If he looked at her, he might realize that what he was doing was incredibly foolish and lose his resolve, and he wanted to see this through to the end. "But I'd rather hear it from Max."

"I'm just saying that we have no way of knowing the extent of your involvement," Max said, speaking slowly, as though addressing a child. "You've been pulling the strings on our public response since day one, including releasing a letter none of us consented to have our names attached to–"

"That wasn't intentional–"

"And you've spearheaded the efforts to root out the responsible party, which is very valiant of you, but no one has taken a look at your own

Society. It only seems fair that you open yourself to the kind of scrutiny you're putting us all under. That's all I'm saying."

Rhys let out a strangled laugh.

"I can't believe this," he said.

"Max, I don't think that–" Moira began.

"The symbols used at the scene of the crime match the ones your people use in their rituals," Max soldiered on. "We all know that."

"You're questioning my competence," Rhys said. That burn was building in his palms and under his nails. His heart beat so fast he thought it might give out, and he felt suffocated, like all the air had been sucked out of the room.

For the first time since meeting him, Rhys saw Max crack. A look of disgust passed over his face, like he could hardly stand to be in the same room with Rhys.

"Let's not play games. Your style of leadership seems in line with a man who would do anything to advance his own power. I've seen it before, in men who never should have been trusted with power to begin with. I've been polite enough not to bring this up as I am a guest in your home, but since we're getting into it, the way you treated David was–"

Rhys threw his hand up, to silence Max with a sharp word, but all the supernatural electricity building beneath his skin rushed out of him unbidden. The lights overhead flickered, sending a flurry of hot sparks fluttering down. Then, with just as much force as if it had been Rhys's conscious intention, Max was sucker-punched an invisible blow.

His head flew back, and his chair skidded a few inches on the floor.

Rhys dragged in a breath, as shocked as anyone else. He was either so deep in the infernal world that his demons would seek retribution on his behalf without having to be told, or he was so strung-out with exhaustion that he could no longer control his own magic. Either way, this was beyond bad.

Max stared at Rhys, his face ashen, his mouth ajar. Slowly, a thin streak of blood trickled out of his nose.

"Maximilian, don't–" Moira said, shoving herself to her feet an instant too late.

Max cut a sigil through the air with his fingers with a growl. A white-hot searing pain shot through Rhys's outstretched hand. It was meant to immobilize, not injure, but it *hurt.*

Rhys had guessed Max was powerful, but he didn't know many sorcerers strong enough to do that much damage without so much as casting a circle or lighting a candle.

Any rationality left in Rhys's mind evaporated. Now, he was acting on pure, blind instinct, cradling his injured right hand to his chest as he splayed out the fingers of his left.

"Eligos, *manifest*," he ordered.

"Don't you dare!" Moira shouted, but Rhys barely heard her. The hissing whispers he caught when he was alone built to a fever pitch in his head, drowning him in a thousand sibilant voices. The pounding between his eyes was so painfully relentless that it almost shoved him out of his body, but Rhys held firm to consciousness.

If it was a fight Max wanted, it was a fight Max was going to get.

The temperature in the room plummeted as a crackling mass of static electricity gathered over the table, making the hair on the back of Rhys's neck stand on end. Eligos promised triumph over a sorcerer's enemies, and he had guaranteed that tiny tragedies befell those who stood against Rhys – flat tires for old school bullies and credit card fraud hitting the leaders of rival orders who spoke badly about him behind his back. Rhys couldn't see the demon within the static the way Moira could – Moira, who was staring at it with horror– but he knew that Eligos was there, and that he was angry, and that he was willing to do Rhys's bidding.

Rhys barked an order in Latin, setting the spirit on Max. Max scrambled to his feet, knocking his glass to the floor with the sound of shattering crystal. He raised his hands into a defensive posture and began rattling off words of power, his eyebrows knitted together in concentration. He was using some kind of warding spell, simple but effective and powered by Max's own magical competence, not the aid of any infernal power.

Fuck, he was *strong*.

The other guests abandoned their seats at the table, rushing back against the walls to clear the blast zone of the fight.

"Is this really the time and place?" Leda snapped. "If you two want to have a magical pissing contest, we can all go outside and I'll play referee, but not like this."

"Max," Dion barked. "That's enough."

Rhys didn't hear them. He was too wrapped up in the spell, too drunk on enchantment. His tongue burned in his mouth, threatening to melt, and his skin was on fire, aching all over.

Rhys drove Eligos forward again and again. The mass of electricity fizzled as it ran against the ward Max had thrown up, threatening to set the tablecloth on fire.

Just a moment more, and Max would break.

Someone slapped Rhys's hands down hard, and the sting shook him from his daze. His pulse roared in his ears as he turned to the only person brave enough to stop him.

It was Moira, scowling in fury with a bottle of murky oil in her hand. She had told him it was a protection oil when he found it in the kitchen cabinet last week. Now he wasn't sure.

"Moira," Rhys said, magic-drunk and delirious. Moira splashed some of the thick, chartreuse oil into her hand and then, quick as a flash, pressed her palm over Rhys's forehead.

"*That's enough*," she said, her voice layered with irresistible command.

A heavy, sick sensation flooded Rhys's veins, making words die on his lips. He tasted bile and metal, and when he tried to pull away from her, he found that all the fight had gone out of him. A monumental force weighed down on him, turning his limbs to lead.

Domination oil, he thought.

"Moira," he gasped as his knees liquified. The room tilted dangerously. He had maybe a few more seconds of coherent thought before Moira's will overpowered him entirely. "Don't do this."

"I need you to stay down, baby," she said, tears of hurt shining in her eyes.

Rhys collapsed at her feet.

Dimly, he heard voices bouncing around the room. It sounded like they were underwater, or like he was.

"Moira, what did you do to him?" Dion asked.

Leda was saying Rhys' name over and over again, but Rhys couldn't answer. When he tried to open his mouth, it stayed firmly welded shut.

"He'll be alright once he sleeps it off," Moira said, sounding broken to pieces. "And now, if you don't mind, I think it's time for everyone to go home."

There was hushed chatter and the sound of coats and keys being gathered, but all the sounds swirled together into incomprehensible white noise in Rhys's brain.

The last thing he saw before his vision gave out was Moira's beaded shoes and the delicate curve of her ankles.

Seconds later, he was unconscious.

CHAPTER TWENTY-SIX
DAVID

David wasn't sulking, but he wasn't in particularly high spirits either. He had spent all morning debating whether to attend the dinner party, and had ended up flaking at the last minute, which he felt bad about. He missed Moira, which made him feel worse, and he missed Rhys most of all, which made him feel miserable. So he holed up in his living room, half-watching *Keeping Up With The Kardashians* while he scrolled mindlessly through his phone.

The last thing he expected was a knock on the door.

David hauled himself off the couch, moving a little quicker than was dignified. The only person who had a code to his building was Rhys. David's treacherous heart betrayed him, kicking up an eager beat.

Maybe Rhys had come to apologize in person. Maybe they could work things out. Maybe–

David opened the door to find Maximilian Markos on his threshold. He looked a bit worse for wear, his wavy hair rumpled. What appeared to be a smudge of dried blood clung to the collar of his sweater.

"Mind if I come in?" Max asked.

David considered asking Max how he had gotten past security, but he already knew the answer was magic, so he just stepped aside. Electronics were more susceptible to well-timed misfirings and enchanted breakdowns than analog devices were, which is why David kept everything truly valuable in a safe in the closet with an old-school padlock on it.

"I thought you were at Rhys and Moira's," David said.

"I was. I figured you might want to hear this straight from me."

There was a horrible apology already brewing in his voice. It cut right through any pleasure David felt at having Max in his home.

"What's going on?"

"Rhys and I got into an altercation. I said some things I probably shouldn't have but he completely flew off the handle. He set a demon on me, David. He would have taken my head off if Moira hadn't stepped in."

"Oh shit," David breathed. "Are you OK?"

"The son of a bitch drew blood, but I'll live." Max grimaced, as though displeased with himself. "Sorry, I shouldn't say that about your boyfriend."

"He's not my boyfriend right now. We're on a break, and he is a son of a bitch sometimes, so no harm, no foul. Let me see."

David was by no stretch of the imagination nurturing, and he didn't know a damn thing about first aid, but he thought he did a pretty decent job cleaning the smeared blood off Max's chin and collar with a damp paper towel, then examining his eyes for any sign of a concussion.

"He did this to me once too," David said, filling the air with chatter. Standing this close to Max in his own home felt searingly intimate, even though they had been sending dirty texts back and forth for days. Sex and its trappings were easier than this: Max's pulse jumping under his fingers, Max's throat bared for David's tender examination. "In conclave, actually. I forget what I said to set him off, but I'm sure it was nasty. He picked a fight, I fought back, he defended himself, and it all devolved from there."

"You set a demon on him?" Max said, scandalized and impressed.

"No," David said, tossing the dirty paper towel in the trash can. "I punched him in the mouth. Split his lip wide open. Probably hurt so bad he couldn't see straight when he summoned his demons, but that didn't stop him. It's the only time we've ever put hands on each other. It nearly got us both excommunicated from the Society."

"Were you together then?" Max asked. There was real curiosity in his eyes, and real concern.

"No. I don't think it would have come to that, if we were. But you know that saying about hate and love being two sides of the same coin."

"I've never believed in that one," Max said, so quietly that David's chest ached. This was all very confusing, and irritating, and he needed to get a handle on himself. That started with getting clear information. Data. David could work with data.

"I need to call him, just – uh, one second. Make yourself comfortable. Do you want a water? I have V8, I think–"

"It's fine," Max said with a laugh as he leaned against the kitchen island. "Just call him."

David retrieved his phone and dialed Rhys.

It rang through to voicemail.

"I think he's down for the count," Max said. "Moira really did a number on him."

"Moira?" David echoed. It was hard to believe. But then again, David knew better than most that if you pushed Moira far enough, she would snap. Her temper was hard to ignite, unless you used the one accelerant that was near-impossible to put out: righteous indignation. "What did she do to him?"

"I don't think she did any long-term damage, but she certainly drained him. She used some kind of dominating oil, I think. Everyone went their separate ways pretty quickly after that."

David dialed Moira, but she ended the incoming call three rings in. He tried not to be offended; if Rhys really was down for the count, maybe she was playing nursemaid. Or maybe she had no energy left for anyone outside her household that night.

Leave it to the married couple to pull rank and put up walls, cutting out the third wheel when the rubber hit the road.

"Let him sleep it off," Max said. He sloughed off his jacket and draped it across one of the barstools. It looked at home there, like it somehow belonged. "He's had a hard night. I wouldn't take it personally."

David pushed up to sit on the edge of the island, leaning back on his palms. He tried to find whatever compassion was left within him, and found his reserves were depleted.

"He barely talks to me unless it's about the Society," David muttered, mean as he liked. "And then he took that away from me too. At this point, he can slip into a coma for all I care."

"You don't really mean that."

"Yes I fucking do."

"Remind me not to cross you, then," Max said with a smile.

"You're not currently in any danger of that."

Max settled his hand on David's knee. The touch was heavy, all splayed fingers and heat, and it betrayed the calm written across Maximilian's features.

David was suddenly agonizingly present in his body, all complaints forgotten. It was Max, not Rhys, who was currently standing in David's kitchen. Max, not Rhys, who was looking at him like he was more valuable than any Society secret.

David and Max had gone out together a couple times now, but no date had ended the way David assumed all successful dates would end. Max had let David smooth his hand over his thigh during expensive dinners and lean over to ghost hot lips across his neck, and David had let Max box him in against the Audi and kiss him breathless in lieu of a goodnight, but they hadn't hooked up yet. Max had access to the sort of sexual patience David couldn't fathom, either because of age or because of temperament. Or maybe, because there was something about the breathless urgency with which David turned all sensuality towards sex that Max was trying to break him of.

That tiny smile at the corner of Maximilian's mouth grew. David had to prod.

"What? Come on, you're look at me like you know something I don't. What is it?"

"You're very passionate when you're angry."

David shrugged one shoulder, doing his best to appear blasé.

"Yeah well, anger is not one of my best qualities."

"I like it. It's honest."

Max's free hand came up to rest on David's other knee, and that was the only green light David needed. He closed the distance between them and kissed Max. He dug his teeth into Max's lower lip and slipped his hand under the hem of Max's sweater, testing his limits, eager to find any boundary and break it.

"Easy," Max murmured, his lips tracing the words against David's mouth.

"Why do you always do that?" David asked, still mouthing over his neck. "If you don't want to do something you can just say so. I'm always game, but I'm not pushy."

"What about my behavior over the last weeks makes you think I'm not game? I'm very into you, in pretty much every way. All I'm saying is, we have all night."

"Bold of you to assume I'll let you stay the night," David said, trying to sound haughty.

"I think I can convince you."

"Show me, then."

Max's hands slid up David's thighs, and then his strong fingers hooked into David's belt loops and yanked him forward on the island. David's knees were spread wider by Max's solid form between them.

"God," David groaned as Max kissed his jaw, his throat, so goddamn *slowly*. He was doing a bad job of maintaining his composure in this situation, but he didn't care. Every nerve in his body was screaming for more closeness, more force. "I've been waiting for you to do that since I was sixteen years old."

Max withdrew immediately, fixing David with a preternaturally perceptive look, right on the edge of mind-reading. That magician's eye Moira always talked about.

"You know I would have never done that, don't you?"

David blinked, still kiss-drunk and eager to get to the good part, the part where he was pressed down into his eye-wateringly expensive sheets with Max's weight pinning him in place.

"Sorry, what?"

"I wouldn't have taken advantage of you like that. You were just a kid with a crush. It was my responsibility as an adult to set boundaries."

"Yeah, well I'm not a kid anymore," David said, irritated by this moralizing in the middle of foreplay. If Max wanted to tie himself up into ethical knots about banging his dead mentor's son, he could do it another time.

"No," Max said, sliding a hand up David's back until his wide palm came to rest at the nape of David's neck. "You aren't."

David felt bridled, like a half-broken stallion, and part of him wanted to shrug the touch off. But another part of him couldn't help but admit that it felt pretty good, being held in place like that, so he kept still.

"I'm happy you took the high road and didn't deflower me in my childhood bedroom," David said, only slightly sarcastic. "But I'll bet my inheritance my first time would have been ten times better if it had been you."

Max arched an eyebrow, and something hungry flickered over his face.

"Then are you going to let me fuck you like it's your first time?" Max asked.

For perhaps the first time in his life, words failed David. He just stared at Max, his blood singing in his veins, his jeans painfully tight.

This offer was, by empirical standards, a little fucked up. Maybe? Was it? All David knew is that it was definitely hot, and it made David feel like his ribs were being cracked open, like this slice of wish fulfillment might feel more right than anything else in the world ever had.

"Yeah," David said quietly. "Yeah, I am."

Max released David and took a step back. For an awful moment David thought he had failed some kind of test, that Max was going to shake his head and start gathering his coat and keys.

But then Max smiled with feral delight.

"If we're going to do this, we're going to do it right. You let me call the shots, and I'll make sure you have a good time."

"What if I want to call the shots?"

"Bullshit," Max said with a chuckle. "Show me the bedroom."

David flicked the lights on when he walked into his room, because he wasn't shy about the body he worked hard to maintain, and because he wanted to see every inch of Max to commit to memory and play back later. Kicking off his shoes and unlatching his watch, David sank down onto the edge of the bed.

"Fine, you win," He said, a little bit bratty. "You've got me here so now what are you going to do with me? Talk all night?"

Max wasted no time pressing David back onto the bed, pinning him in place with his thighs on either side of David's hips. Tension melted out of David's body immediately, replaced by a floaty, buzzy feeling. It wasn't dissimilar to the euphoria that used to wash over him after the first swallow of tequila, but better.

David's hands came up mindlessly to unfasten Max's belt, but Max caught his fingers.

"Don't get ahead of yourself," Max said.

"Why not?" David demanded. "Don't piss me off, Max. I'm thirty years old. I know what I want."

"I know you do," Max said, with a smile so fond David felt like he had already been stripped naked. "But I also know you're the kind of guy who believes people will only stick around if you put out right away and all the time, and I've been trying to show you that's not always true."

"So you *do* want to fuck me," David said with a mean, triumphant grin.

"I would have fucked you in the coat room of the tea house if I thought it wouldn't have sent your High Priest off the deep end and plunged the city into occult civil war," Max said, so calmy, and with so much absolute seriousness that David felt feverish. "But if patience is not getting through to you maybe this will."

Max cupped David through his jeans and squeezed. All rational thought evaporated out of David's brain.

How many times had he touched himself like this, imagining it was Max's broad hands driving him towards the brink?

David thought he was going to lose his mind with exasperation when Max released him, but then Max was kneeling over him, unfastening his own slacks, and David decided immediately that there was no place he would rather be.

Max unzipped his fly and freed his cock, thick and heavy. David took a few seconds to appreciate the sight.

"Start with your mouth," Max said.

Obediently, David parted his lips. This, he knew how to do. He considered himself somewhat of a connoisseur of the act, and he knew the finer technical points of keeping his tongue soft and applying the right amount of suction. But when Max pushed the head of his cock into David's mouth, pressing his fingers into the soft divot beneath David's chin to guide him to open wider, David nearly forgot what he was doing.

"Fuck," Max breathed, his composure flickering slightly, and David's chest ignited. This was what he had been aching for, all these years. To get under the skin of this self-possessed, above-reproach man. To convince him that he had made a mistake by walking out of David's life. "Good, just like that."

Max slowly thrust in and out of David's mouth. David applied himself to giving head like his life depended on it, swirling his tongue and moaning.

He would do anything to hear Max praise him again.

"You're good at this," Max said, and there was that word again, *good*. David was beyond turned on by it, he *needed* to hear it.

And then, Max pulled out. David made a frustrated noise.

Max began unfastening every single button on David's shirt, slow as he liked, and David resisted the urge to do it for him. When each button was finally unfastened, David sloughed off his clothes as quickly as he could manage. This time, when he moved to Max with his belt and slacks, Max didn't stop him. They shed their clothes, kissing with mounting urgency, until they were both naked.

"On your stomach," Max said.

Max slid open the drawer of his bedside table, flicked open the bottle of high-end lube David always kept on hand, and poured a little into his palm. He leaned over David, pressing their bodies together, and put his mouth close to David's ear.

"Tell me if it it's too much, OK? I'm going to take care of you."

Under any other circumstances, those words wouldn't have had much of an effect. David had done this plenty of times before, either in a giving or receiving role, and he knew how to take care of himself either way. But just hearing Max make that promise cracked open David's half-calcified heart. He was hit with a wave of emotion he was too overwhelmed to figure out, and so he buried his face into his crossed arms and focused on breathing.

Max pressed an exploratory finger to David's entrance, circling that tight band of muscle until David squirmed with impatience. Centimeter by agonizing centimeter, Max opened him up. The pressure and pleasant sting intensified as Max worked another finger inside him. He splayed his free hand across David's lower back, keeping him in place. David let out an unsteady breath, his chest full to bursting.

"You're doing so well," Max murmured. "Are you ready for me?"

"Please," was all David could manage.

Max removed his fingers and snapped open the plastic bottle for more lube. David was left so empty, emptier than he had ever felt in his life.

But then the head of Maximilian's erect cock was gliding along him, and all was right in the world.

David knotted his fingers into the sheets as Maximillian eased inside. As Max found a steady rhythm, David ground his hips against the sheets, seeking friction with increasing abandon. He was already halfway there, coming to pieces beneath Max.

"Look at yourself," Maximilian huffed. David looked over to the hanging mirror that he had strategically positioned within view of the bed. There was something about his pupils blown wide with lust and his lips swollen and pink, his wavy hair disheveled beyond repair, that was filthy in the extreme. "Taking it like a star."

Star. That's what Max had called David all those years ago, when Max was to be addressed strictly as Mr Markos. When David had been reckless with his body's limits and his psychic abilities, eager to show off for his father's friend. That's what Max had called him, jokingly at first, and then with earnest admiration, after every successful seance he witnessed.

Nobody had called him that since his father died. Not a single person.

David's orgasm hit him like a punch in the gut, and then the next thing he knew he was spilling all over his stomach and his sheets. For a white-hot second, he actually saw stars.

"Yes," Max hissed, jerking his hips faster. "That's it. You're amazing."

Max let out a groan, thrust so deep David felt it in his ribs, and finished inside him.

David wasn't entirely sure what happened next, because the world was a rosy watercolor blur, but, somehow, he ended up pillowed against Max's chest. David lost himself in the rhythm of the other man's breathing as he drifted back into his body. He listened to Max's pounding heartbeat slow until it had resumed a steady pace.

"I needed that," David said, not quite comfortable enough to meet Max's eyes when he said it. But he said it, and that was a start.

In response, Maximilian pulled David tighter into his arms. The skin-to-skin contact flooded David's system with even more oxytocin, drugging him with pliant trust and an affection that was getting harder to ignore.

"Thank you for letting me give you that," Max murmured. "I meant what I said. You're amazing."

David buried his face in Max's chest, memorizing the moment just in case, like so many other happy moments in his past, it didn't last.

He wasn't a big cuddler, and he certainly wasn't a "sleep over after the first hook-up" kind of guy, but he knew immediately that Max had been right.

He was definitely going to let Max spend the night.

CHAPTER TWENTY-SEVEN
DAVID

David slept soundly through the night, and woke before his work alarm the next moment to the sound of Max's breathing. He rolled over to find Max dozing with one arm under the pillow, his cheeks shaded by his thick lashes.

David's phone vibrated on his bedside table, breaking his reverie. He reached across Max's sleeping form to snatch up the phone and cancel the call, but then read the name on the caller ID. Antoni.

That was weird. Antoni hated talking on the phone, and texted David for everything.

"Antoni?" David answered.

"I've been texting you," Antoni said on the other end. His voice was tight and agitated, like he was watching his favorite sports team get pummeled during a game he had bet on "Where are you?"

"At home," David said, hauling himself into a sitting position. Max mumbled something, then slipped back into sleep. David debated whether to fill Antoni in on the situation and decided there was time for gossip later. "I have work soon; what's up?"

"I need you to call out of work and get your ass to Cambridge. Rhys is out of action, and all active members are voting on his interim replacement in an hour. They won't make a decision without you here."

"They're replacing him?"

"Only until he's well enough to subject himself to formal discipline."

"Discipline?" David echoed. He sounded like a parakeet, but he was having trouble keeping up with the speed Antoni was talking.

"He put supernatural hands on a high-ranking occult official. Maximilian Markos, apparently, at some kind of dinner party. I swear to God, it's like I don't even know him anymore."

"Who's currently in the lead for the Priesthood?" David asked, tossing aside the sheet and rummaging through the clothes on the floor for his boxers. Six months ago, he would have been salivating for a nomination, but since watching the role of High Priest take a toll on Rhys, he was fine sitting on the sidelines.

"Your name has come up once or twice."

"I didn't ask you that; I asked you who was in the lead."

"Uh," Antoni said. He really did sound twenty-three. It was easy to forget that Antoni, who managed vast sums of money and held his own in any magical circle, was barely out of college. "Me."

"Got it," David said, letting out a breath. "Well, congratulations."

"It's not set in stone yet. I still need you to vote."

"I thought I was out of the Society."

"Rhys left me in charge, and I say you're reinstated."

"Message received. I'll be there in a half hour."

Disconnecting the call, David tossed his phone down on the bed and crawled across the sheets to Max, who stirred awake.

"Where are you running off to?" Max asked, voice rough from sleep. If it had been anyone else but one of his closest friends telling him to get his ass to the clubhouse, David would have blown off the request. But Antoni needed him, and friendship still counted for something. David had learned in recent years that oftentimes, it was all that mattered.

"Society business," David said, giving Max a lingering kiss. "Take your time waking up; you're welcome to stay as long as you like. I'll text you?"

"I'd like that," Max said with a wide smile. David kissed him one more time, then threw on a pair of slacks and a button-down and grabbed his car keys.

He made good time getting to Cambridge, and miraculously found street parking. He took the grimy staircase down past the Cantonese restaurant and then ducked beneath the building, rapping briskly on the door. Gerald took his coat.

"I can't believe they got you to come in on your day off," David said, clapping the older man on the shoulder.

"I come when I'm called," Gerald said with a sniff. "And when I'm paid."

The energy in the meeting hall was frenetic. The parlor was packed with every active member, almost twenty-five people, and they were milling to and fro in cliquish groups, smoking cigars and sipping Martinis and gesticulating wildly to make their points. David was relieved to find he hadn't missed the vote. The Society members were still wrapped up in their pre-ballot debate about who should be elected. Judging from the volume in the room, some of the members had very strong ideas about who should hold down the High Priesthood while Rhys recovered.

"David!" Someone called from across the room. It was Nathan, hanging out by the bar with his arm around Kitty's waist.

David joined them and was handed a frosty lime Polar from Cameron. If Cameron had made the two-hour drive up from Connecticut on such short notice, that didn't bode well for the seriousness of the situation.

"It's a madhouse," David said, cracking open his sparkling water.

"This is exactly what Wayne was afraid of happening before he retired," Nathan said. "We all avoided this the first time around because he named a successor in advance, but Rhys didn't think that far ahead."

"He's too stubborn to believe anything could ever take him out," Kitty put in, popping the raspberry floating in her mimosa into her mouth. If Kitty was pounding champagne this early in the morning, that didn't bode well either.

"Yeah well, he wasn't counting on Moira," David muttered.

"I heard she completely short-circuited his system," Cameron said, shaking his head as he packed his wooden pipe with loose tobacco. His brown eyes glittered behind his glasses as he tracked every movement in the room, no doubt marking allegiances and calculating odds. Cameron was perhaps the most cutthroat out of any of them; his natural self-interest just happened to be tempered by the fact that he spent most of his time marinating his brain in Lutheran theology. Teaching at Yale's divinity school had mellowed him, but his membership in the Society, despite his insistence that all he was after was deeper knowledge of his higher self, belied buried self-interest. "I knew she was powerful, but I didn't know she could do *that*."

Antoni appeared in the middle of the room and clapped twice.

"Can I have everyone's attention, please?" he asked.

Only a few of the bickering Society members fell silent. Everyone else ignored him.

David felt it keenly then, how rudderless they were without someone in charge.

Antoni clapped again, surer of himself this time.

"I said, I need everyone's attention," he said, raising his voice like a gunshot. "Right *now*."

This time, it worked. Even the older men, as put out as they were about being interrupted, gave Antoni the floor.

Antoni took a deep breath, and smoothed the front of his shirt.

"It looks like more people who are able to make it are here already, so we should get started. Those who couldn't come forfeit their right to a vote. You all know the drill; one vote per member, no magical interference, and no voting for yourself. The honor code is in full effect here, ladies and gentleman. You're bound by duty to vote for the member you think is most qualified to steer the Society through any waters."

"Can we vote for Rhys again?" Kitty asked, raising her hand.

Antoni glanced over to her, his expression softening.

"Sorry, but no. Rhys is indisposed. He will resume his duties as soon as he's better, and as soon as he's made amends for attacking Maximilian Markos. Any more questions?"

There was a disgruntled murmur among the crowd gathered, but no one else spoke.

"Good," Antoni said. "You've had your time to deliberate and plead your case. Now it's time to vote. Remember folks; cheaters get hexed. And yes, I will use a pendulum to check if I get the feeling there's any foul play."

Antoni took a seat in Rhys's usual armchair as slips of paper were passed out. He worried at the worn velvet on the armrest, his expression a maelstrom. David crossed the room to Antoni and laid his hand on his shoulder.

"You seem upset," David said.

"I'm tense," Antoni replied, yanking out a thread. "There's a difference."

"Do you want it? The Priesthood?"

"I do. So badly. That should mean I don't deserve it, shouldn't it?"

"I don't think Rhys saw it that way."

"And we saw where that got him," Antoni said. He watched people mill about the room, scribbling down their votes in various nooks and corners. "I'm the youngest member. Am I wrong in assuming my name came up because they think I'll be easier to control and edge out?"

David, who didn't believe in the concept of sugarcoating things, nodded.

"Some of them infantilize you. But you're one of the most competent sorcerers we have, and you can be trusted with money. You've got a softer hand than Rhys, but you don't let people walk all over you. Plus, he left you in charge. It isn't unreasonable to elect you in the interim."

Their conversation was cut short by Cameron, who appeared to pass out two stubby pencils.

"May the best man win," David said, flipping his piece of paper around so Antoni could see the name he had written down on his slip.

Antoni Bresciani.

"Same to you," Antoni said, revealing his slip to David in turn.

David Aristarkhov.

Cameron returned with a crystal punch bowl, into which all the members deposited their folded-up votes. Antoni waited until everyone had voted, bouncing his leg in impatience, then took the bowl from Cameron.

"I'm going to read out the votes one by one," Antoni said. "David, mind keeping score?"

"On it," David said, whipping out his phone and pulling up his Notes app.

Antoni pulled the first name out of the bowl, taking a steadying breath before reading it aloud.

"Antoni Bresciani."

David placed a tally mark next to Antoni's name. Antoni received a new slip of paper, his voice carrying easily in the hush that had fallen over the room.

"Antoni Bresciani," he said again.

One of the older men made an irritated noise, but was elbowed into silence by another brother.

"David Aristarkhov," Antoni read out.

The next two names were David's, then a senior brother's, then David's again. David kept dutiful tally, trying to ignore the sweat prickling along his hairline. He didn't want the Priesthood. He wouldn't know what to do with it. But his father was the largest donor the Society had ever known, and David had spent so long ingratiating himself to the established Society members that he was probably many people's first choice.

David kept score as Antoni steadily read through the remainder of the votes. There were a few dark horse contenders trying to edge out a margin against the two clear favorites, but in the end, it was really down to Antoni and David.

"Antoni Bresciani," Antoni said, reading the final slip before folding it up and setting it aside. "David, what's the verdict?"

David counted and counted again, making sure he was correct.

Then he spoke loud enough for the entire room to hear.

"Out of twenty-four votes, thirteen are for Antoni Bresciani. That's a majority."

The room erupted into chaos. Some of the members cheered, while others demanded a recount, while others turned right back to their drinks as though nothing had changed.

David sagged down into a nearby chair in relief. The crown had passed over him yet again.

"Antoni!" Kitty exclaimed, bending down to embrace him. Antoni, who David couldn't remember ever having so much as shaken Kitty's hand, hugged her back tightly. When she drew away, his hand lingered on the small of her back exposed by her cropped blouse, his fingers leaving divots in the flesh like a Rodin statue.

Nathan offered Antoni a firm handshake and a wide smile, and Antoni was soon swallowed up by his well-wishers. David excused himself from the circle of praise with slippery ease, gilding his voice with a little charm whenever anyone tried to call him over or get his attention.

Right now, maybe for the first time in his life, he wanted nothing more than to be invisible.

He fished his phone out of his pocket as he hid in a quiet corner of the room.

"David," Moira said breathlessly on the other end, like she had dashed across the house to answer the phone. "You called."

"Hi, yes" he said. He had been avoiding her since the fight with Rhys, and he felt rotten about that. It was just so hard to untangle the threads that bound them all together, sometimes. "I should have done it sooner. I'm sorry. How's Rhys? I heard about what happened at dinner."

"He's alive. Listen, I know what he did to you was awful, but he would really, really benefit from seeing you right now."

"And how are you, Moira?"

There was a pause on the other end as Moira took a shaky breath.

"I'm… Well, I'd really like a hug, I'll say that much."

"I can make that happen," David said, already moving towards the door. Antoni was in good hands with Nathan, Cameron, and Kitty, and David could pay his proper respects later. Right now, Moira needed him. And so did Rhys, even though he would probably rather die than admit it. "I'll see you soon, OK?"

CHAPTER TWENTY-EIGHT
MOIRA

After putting Rhys on the ground the night of the dinner party, Moira had somehow managed to haul him half-conscious up the stairs to bed. She had collapsed beside him, dead to the world after the night's exertions, and slept until David's call the next morning. Rhys had barely stirred when she answered, but just as she was hanging up, he blearily regained consciousness and looked over to her with bruised eyes.

"Moira," he rasped, struggling against disorientation.

She rolled over onto her side, pillowing her head on her arms as she took in her husband. He looked considerably worse for wear, his curls frizzy and his lips dry and chapped. She felt a little bit guilty for using Lorena's domination oil on him. She felt another bit angry at him for making her reach for it all.

While she had successfully de-escalated the fight, her intentions had not been entirely altruistic. Rhys had embarrassed her and hurt her, and she had wanted to embarrass him and hurt him back.

Now, as his fingers found her own beneath the covers and squeezed, her conflicted heart ached.

"Hi," she said, voice small.

"Hi," he said. "What happened? Where is everyone?"

"They went home," Moira said. "It's the next day, baby."

"Max," he said, awful puzzle pieces slotting into place. "I set a demon on Max. Is he alright?"

"He seemed fine when he left."

"I think I blacked out. I can't remember a lot. Did... Did I hurt anyone?"

"Just yourself. How's your head?"

"Pounding. What did you use on me?"

"Domination oil. Lorena's house special."

Rhys groaned and nodded, scrubbing a hand over his face.

"I haven't gone down that fast since I passed out in the choir risers during Easter mass when I was sixteen."

"I didn't know what else to do," Moira said, but it wasn't an apology. If anything, she was getting mad again. She had felt so *humiliated* last night. He couldn't even hold it together for her for one party, for one hour, even?

Rhys brushed his fingers across her cheek.

"You did the right thing. I'm so sorry for putting you in that position."

"It was really, really scary," she said, hot tears pricking at her eyes. "I've never been scared of you, Rhys, not once in all these years. That can never happen again, do you understand me? We need to cut you loose from those demons as soon as possible. They're turning you into someone I find I don't like much."

Moira sucked in a shaky breath, afraid of starting a fight neither of them had the energy to finish. But Rhys just nodded, accepting her anger without shrinking from it.

"I don't like it either," he said. And then, with a tenderness that made the tears spill down her cheek: "I never want to scare you, Moira, not ever. You know I'd cut my hand off before I raised it against you."

"Then don't raise it against other people."

Rhys's reply was cut off by the sound of David's spare key turning in the downstairs door, and Moira slid out of the bed.

"That'll be David," she said.

"David's here?" Rhys rasped, as if David was the ghost of Christmas past come to torment him into good behavior.

"He's worried about you," she said. "But you've also got plenty of explaining to do."

Moira hurried down the stairs to meet David in the front hall. She all but threw herself into his arms, and he bent down to press his cheek to hers, giving her the skin-to-skin contact she craved.

"You're all messed up about this," he said, pulling her in tighter. "I can feel it."

"And you're worried," she mumbled into his chest. "Even though you're pretending like you're not."

"What happened last night?"

"It was all very fast. Max accused Rhys of being a tyrant and said Rhys should be open to having himself investigated. Rhys took offense and summoned one of those goddamn demons. I don't even think he meant to attack, not at first, but it doesn't matter. He swung first, and Max swung back. I had to use domination oil to stop him."

David whistled.

"That's potent stuff, especially in the hands of a magician like you."

Moira chewed on her lip. She wasn't exactly proud of her behavior, but it felt nice to be praised, and summoning the strength of her intention to heighten the domination's oil effects on the spot had been difficult. So maybe she was a little bit proud.

"He hit the ground pretty hard, I'm afraid."

"He'll bounce back. Bruises build character. Where's Rhys now?"

"In the bedroom," Moira said and began to pull him up the stairs. A fission of worry emanated from his fingers, traveling up her arm like static.

Rhys was propped up in bed, his faded spattering of freckles almost translucent. He looked small tucked into the big seafoam duvet, more like a sickly Victorian child than the man who had started a sorcerer's duel one day prior.

"David," Rhys said. "I didn't expect to see you."

"Yeah well, I heard Moira kicked your ass, so I had to come see for myself," David said.

Rhys huffed out a small, papery laugh.

"She's deadly with that oil. Tell Lorena to stop selling weapons of mass magical destruction to my wife."

"Try not needing to be forcibly neutralized at your own dinner party first," David replied.

He drifted further into the room and settled a hand on Moira's shoulder, rubbing his thumb along the nape of her neck. He was siphoning off a little of her energy to keep himself calm, she was aware of that, but she was happy to share. And the warmth and weight of his hand grounded her.

"I was wrong," Rhys said as though he couldn't go a moment more without ridding himself of his guilt. It poured from his mouth like spring water. "I should have never revoked your Society membership, that was a cruel thing to do. I felt threatened, and so I made an example of you. That's not something you do to someone you love."

"I humiliated you," David said, but it didn't quite sound like an apology. It sounded like he was encouraging Rhys to keep going.

"Yes, but if I can't stand up to fair criticism, then I can't lead well. Moving forward, I'm welcoming all feedback before we reach a crisis point, so you never need to do what you did in the ritual room again."

David removed his hand from Moira's shoulder, just as a pang of trepidation went through him.

"I don't think we're likely to find ourselves in that situation again," he said cryptically, looking down at his shoes.

Rhys tossed back the covers, moving to stand before thinking better of it and sinking back down into his nest of pillows.

"But if we do, we can get through it," Rhys insisted. "I know all the evidence you have right now points to the contrary, but I want to do this right, David. My marriage, my relationship with you, the Priesthood, all of it. I'll apologize to Max, I'll defer to his expertise, I'll even open myself to investigation if that is what this takes. I can be a better man; I swear to God I can. And that starts with fixing what I broke. I'm reinstating you."

"Antoni already did," David said with a wince.

The penny dropped for Moira a moment before it did for Rhys, and she was grateful she was already sitting down. The room tilted at a nauseating angle.

She had no idea what Rhys would do with himself the moment he realized what he had lost.

"Good," Rhys went on, painfully oblivious. "He was acting as my second and I'm happy to uphold his decision on the matter."

"Babe, you're not listening," David said. "I'm *Antoni's* second in command now."

Rhys blinked as though startled by a bright light.

"What?"

"The Society is considering you unfit for service until you're fully recovered and until you've made peace with Max," David said, as mechanically as if he was reading off a court transcript. "They voted in an interim High Priest an hour ago. Antoni will hold the position for the time being."

Rhys leaned back against the headboard with a dull thud, staring off into space for a long time. She expected him to argue, or maybe even to cry in that frustrated little boy way of his. But Rhys didn't say anything at all. Instead, he just nodded slowly, without an ounce left of fight in him.

This was different, she knew, from giving up something he had always wanted in a grand gesture of kingly graciousness. This was a punishment, a rescinding of the good fortune the universe had extended to him.

"Rhys–" David began gently.

"He'll be good at it," Rhys said, still not looking at anything in particular. "He has the right temperament. And he deserves the Priesthood after what I did to him."

"What do you mean?"

Rhys tugged one of his broken cuticles off with his teeth, then mindlessly sucked the blood away.

"I told him if he exposed my secrets, I would expose his. I failed, David. I didn't pass the test. I acted in self-interest when I should have been compassionate. I sought the Grail, and I was found unworthy. That's it. That's where the story ends."

"Wait a minute, you blackmailed him?" David pressed, steamrolling right over Rhys's self-flagellation. "With what?"

Rhys glanced over to Moira, seeking her permission to go on. This was her moment to leave the room and keep her hands clean, should she choose. But if there was one thing Moira knew about herself, it was that she would always choose to know the truth, even when the truth was painful.

Moira nodded.

"I didn't blackmail him, but I threatened to do it, which is just as bad. I told him I would tell Nathan about Kitty," Rhys said.

"Oh, that's *low*," David said.

"What does Kitty have to do with any of this?" Moira asked.

"Come on, Moira," David said, like she was being purposefully naive.

"She honestly doesn't know," Rhys said. "Tell her."

"Antoni has a big-time Thing for Kitty," David said with a sigh. "Unfortunately for all parties involved, I think he's completely in love with her. It's been going on for years."

Moira scoffed. It seemed preposterous that someone as freewheeling as Antoni could hold a torch for anyone, much less prim and proper and *happily married* Kitty, for that long. Besides, Antoni flirted with *everyone*.

He flirted with Moira, and Rhys, and David, and every bartender and barista who crossed his path. It was his way of being friendly.

Antoni rubbed sunscreen onto Moira's back when they were on Nathan's boat, making her giggle with his brazen compliments, and he had responded with a wolf whistle and an impressed "Hey, killer," when he saw Rhys in his ascension ceremony outfit. Once, Moira had overheard him jokingly offer to suck David off, if that would improve David's mood any. Even straight-as-an-arrow Nathan and almost-certainly-ace Cameron were not excluded from the fun and games.

Moira opened her mouth to make this argument, but then she remembered a very important detail. Everyone was included. Everyone except for Kitty.

Moira had only ever seen Antoni respond to Kitty with total earnestness, with attentive listening and sincere smiles.

A memory floated to the surface of Moira's mind. Last Christmas, when Kitty had offered her half-finished eggnog to anyone at the party who wanted it, Antoni had relieved her of her glass. Moira had watched him, in a private moment he probably thought no one saw, slot his mouth right over the coral lipstick print she had left on the glass before taking a sip. It had seemed accidental then, but now, it painted a very clear picture.

Her stomach sank into her shoes.

So, this was what it was like, being privy to the brutal little secrets that made up the inner lives of men.

"He told me then he would step in if I was found unfit to lead," Rhys said. "All he's doing now is keeping his word."

David sighed and sat down on the edge of the bed next to Moira. His right hand drifted out to settle on Rhys's ankle, while his left hand brushed across Moira's stockinged knee.

"You'll get another chance at the Priesthood when you're well, but let Antoni take a stab at it right now," David said. "He's good for it. You know he is. But it sounds like Antoni saw you doing something he shouldn't have. Want to share with the class?"

Rhys nodded, closing his eyes in total surrender to whatever consequences came next.

"I broke the rule of seven. I've been working with too many demons, and I created altars as access points. I hoped keeping the demons on permanent call would make me stronger, but instead, it dissolved the boundaries between their world and mine."

"How many do you have on retainer?" David pressed. "Eight? Ten?"

"Eleven. Well, sometimes twelve. But Paimon doesn't always come when he's called."

Moira expected David to lay into him, or at the very at least lash out with a bitchy remark. But David didn't look irritated, or even mad. Worse, he looked scared.

"That's way too many for one sorcerer, Rhys. Send them away. Let it go."

"He doesn't think he can," Moira put in.

"I didn't mean to hurt Maximilian," Rhys went on. "I spent the day of the party trying to keep the demons at bay. I ignored them and didn't feed the altars. I hoped that would shut them up. But the moment I got angry, they attacked."

"And you didn't ask them to?" David asked.

"No. They're with me all the time now, and I don't know how to get them to leave."

David took Rhys's wrist and turned his hand upright so the pink scar running through his palm shone in the light.

"Baelshieth," David said, and held up his hand to match his flashing star. "The Aristarkhov family demon you pulled out of me last summer. He's still there, in your bones. I'm not saying Baelshieth is the guy who's causing your problems, but I am saying that you already have a tie to the unseen world. You've already sent signals out into the universe that you are a willing host for spirits. It makes you more susceptible to demonic influence."

"I'm possessed?" Rhys said, making a strangled sound of Catholic alarm.

"No, dumbass," David said. "If you were possessed, we could just exorcize you. Hell, a priest could do that. This is more complex. You've made yourself into a walking buffet of energy for these demons. You're using them, sure, but they're also feeding on you. Slipping in through all the cracks and weak spots. And apparently, they're getting strong enough that they don't have to listen to you anymore."

Moira felt small and panicked, just as she had over the summer when pulling her two men back from the mouth of hell.

"Well what are we going to do about it?" she asked. "We can't just sit here."

"I don't know," David admitted. "Rhys, I suggest you focus on getting your strength back up in time for the winter social. That's less than a week from now. It would be good to make a public appearance in a casual setting, then step back into a managerial role as you're able. And you need to make things right with Antoni. In the meanwhile, I'll ask around about the demons. I can see if Max has ever known a sorcerer who got themselves into a similar situation."

"Max?" Rhys repeated, a question in his voice.

"Yeah, uh. You might be seeing more of Max in the future," David said, like he was winding up to throw a curveball. "With me."

It was plain to anyone that the two men were drawn to each other, and they had been spending more time together lately. Moira had felt the attraction fizzling between them in the tea room, but she hadn't thought David was actually going to *go through* with it.

"Y'all are dating now?" she asked.

"I mean, no. Or yeah, but like, not officially. I think."

"Got it," Rhys said with a curt nod. He looked like a strong wind could have blown him over, but to his credit, he kept his expression neutral.

"I'm not breaking up with you Rhys," David said with a sigh. "That's not what this is. You said it was fine if I–"

"I remember what I said, and I meant it. You're welcome to see other people. And if I am found worthy of being one of the people you choose to keep seeing, I will count myself as a lucky man."

Moira couldn't help but smile at her husband. Rhys was inclined towards petty jealousies, and on his worst days, he could be wildly possessive and insecure. But on other days, when his better nature won out, he could be quite the generous romantic.

"Don't fuck with me if you aren't being serious," David said.

"I'm being serious," Rhys said with a sigh. "It's not exactly a bombshell David; you aren't subtle."

"So, you'll play nice?" David pressed, edging closer to Rhys on the bed. This was the dynamic Moira was more familiar with, David wearing Rhys's stony resolve away with teasing until Rhys broke.

"I'll be perfectly civil," Rhys replied.

"And I can bring him with me as my plus one to the winter social? You're taking Moira, so don't be pissy that I found a date."

"I will be so, *so* civil."

"And if you want to fight over me, fine, just make sure you make a big public scene about it, that would be hot."

"Don't flatter yourself," Rhys said. His voice was serious, but a smile tugged at the corner of his mouth. "I already made a public scene with Max, and it had nothing to do with you. Well. Almost nothing."

"He's not a bad guy, Rhys."

"I believe you. But you're absolutely sure this isn't just some weird age-gap power dynamic thing you just need to get out of your system?"

"Not at all. Well, almost not at all."

"I don't want any more details," Rhys said, holding up a hand.

David laughed, that boyish bright sound that Moira's life was so much emptier without, and then he kissed Rhys. It was a gentle weakened kiss, respectful of Rhys's condition and Moira's presence in the room, but it was still lingering and warm.

Moira watched that strange electricity crackle between David and her husband, as strong as the invisible thread of devotion that bound her to Rhys. It was a pretty picture, David with his strong jaw leaning over to kiss Rhys, all bed-mussed curls and hesitant trust. Pretty enough to make her feel warm from the inside out.

Moira knew she was *allowed* to look, strictly speaking. She just usually didn't permit herself the indulgence.

She didn't realize she was staring until David shot her a mischievous look.

"You want a kiss too, peach?"

Moira's face burned.

"Boys have cooties," she said. It was a silly, transparent rebuttal, but it was better than saying nothing. Or worse, admitting that sometimes she *did* enjoy seeing Rhys and David together for horny lizard brain reasons.

David's grin widened, and he reached over and unceremoniously hauled her over, practically into Rhys's lap. Moira squawked out a protest, but she was already giggling, and the giggles only got louder when David seized her face in his hands and covered her face with pecks. She ended up out of breath and flushed with her head pillowed on Rhys's thighs, looking up at her husband while swatting David halfheartedly away.

Rhys's hand came up to caress her cheek, as though he were afraid of being rebuffed. Moira responded by leaning into the touch, rubbing her cheek against his scarred palm like a cat.

Rhys kissed her on the mouth and Moira kissed him back, deeper and deeper until David made a faux disgusted noise and hauled himself off the bed. Rhys threw a pillow at him and then continued kissing Moira, smiling against her lips.

Moira did her best to be present in the moment and ignore the dread tapping at the back of her mind like a crow at the window, begging to be let in.

For all she knew, this might be the only moment of peace the three of them would have for a long time.

CHAPTER TWENTY-NINE
RHYS

Emboldened by his delicate reconnection with David and the fact that Moira, miraculously, didn't seem to want a divorce, Rhys resisted the urge to sulk in bed any longer than strictly necessary. By the next day, he was up, showered, and dressed, with his hair combed. He was still a little woozy, and all the lights in the house were too bright, but he could manage.

He refused to let Moira take any time off work to stay home and baby him, insisting that he could take care of himself.

"I guess since I was the one who used that dominating oil on you, you'll be fine without me here," she said, still wary as she gathered her keys.

"Happy to be dominated by you if the circumstance calls for it," Rhys said, with a flirtation he didn't feel up to following through on but was still happy he could muster. "Now get out of here. I've got plenty to do. I promise I won't push myself too hard."

"I don't believe you," she said, but kissed him goodbye all the same.

As soon as she left, Rhys disappeared into his study to try and burn through as much research as possible. It was unlikely that his personal library – or David's for that matter – hid anything he hadn't already uncovered, but it was worth a try. Maybe there was an elegant solution he had missed, a simple way to untangle his demons from his soul.

Eventually, his phone dinged, pulling him from his reference text, which offered no more insight into his conundrum than the first book had, or the second. Rhys sucked in a breath when he glanced down at the screen.

It was an email from Antoni, politely but clearly outlining his current standing with the Society. He was encouraged to make an appearance at the winter social, but it wasn't recommended that he return to weekly Society meetings until he was fully recovered. As far as his conduct the night of the dinner went, he was expected to make a sincere personal apology to Maximilian Markos, and to refrain from any other outbursts that might cast the Society in a bad light. He could still vote on Society policy, but his powers of veto and ability to pass executive orders were revoked. Any bad behavior during his convalescence would result in immediate expulsion from the Society.

Antoni had signed the email *Antoni Bresciani, acting High Priest of the Society for Theurgic Work and Hermetic Study.*

Rhys rubbed at his aching eyes. It was somehow harder to accept this reality, seeing it spelled out in black and white, than it had been when delivered with care and a kiss from David.

Rhys flipped to the texts he had missed while unconscious. There were three messages from Leda, sent over a series of hours.

Hey hotshot; that was some pretty impressive spellcasting. How are you holding up?

Sorry for bringing up David at dinner.

Are you still out of it? Want me to smuggle some whiskey into your sickroom? I'll tell Moira it's tea 🐱

As the cherry on top, his mother had texted to ask him to nail down his Christmas visit plans. Rhys took a moment to compose a text to Leda (*Hey! I'm alive. Sorry I flew off the handle. I'll explain when I see you next. No whiskey necessary at present*) and was halfway through brushing his mother off with some platitude about being excited to see her, when the doorbell rang.

Rhys had zero witch's intuition, but this pricked his brain in a strange way. Moira had a key, as did David. Anyone else who wanted to see him would call first to make sure he was at home. Even the mail carrier had been instructed to leave his international orders of spell-crafting materials in the package box at the door.

Rhys stalked through the hallway, running his fingers through his curls, and opened the door.

Max stood on his doorstep.

"Mind if I come in?" Max said pleasantly. Rhys couldn't tell if Max was looming slightly, or if he just took up more broad-shouldered space than Rhys, who was all narrow bones and a whopping five feet seven inches in stocking feet. Rhys wished he was wearing his shoes with the extra two inches of lift, even though he doubted it would help him feel any more prepared for this conversation.

"Maximilian," Rhys said, stumbling into formality as he tried to get his bearings. "I didn't know I was expecting you."

"You weren't," Max said, with that apologetic smile that was all Greek island warmth. It was hard to say no to Max when he smiled at you like that, which only made Rhys want to say no to him more. "Is Moira out?"

"She is. You're welcome to come back when she's home from work."

"No trouble. I was hoping to catch you alone. Could we talk?"

This, Rhys knew, was not an overture he could decline. Any rudeness would read like outright hostility, which would shatter whatever chances he had left of regaining the Priesthood, not to mention his chances of proving to Moira that he could keep his word, or proving to David that he wasn't a petulant child who didn't know how to share. But he really, *really* did not want to be alone with Max right now. Not with the humiliation of what he had done at dinner still burning in his veins, and not when he was diminished and weak and no doubt sallow as a consumptive heroine in one of Moira's gothic romance novels.

"A ward is as easy to break as any lock is to pick," Max said with a laugh. "It's simpler to just let me inside."

A joke, something to lighten the mood. But Rhys didn't like how quickly Max had identified that Rhys had the front door warded. The doorframe had been slathered with holy water, dust from Moira's dried wedding bouquet, and three droplets of Rhys's own blood during the first full moon after they moved it. The ritual had been sealed with an ironclad oath that Rhys and all the powers of heaven and hell would do anything to protect the house and the cherished woman inside. It was a powerful ward, and it should be all but invisible.

Max was sharper than Rhys thought, and probably a more adept sorcerer than even their impromptu duel had suggested.

"Please come in," Rhys said, stepping inside. "Do you mind if we talk in the study? I was just... getting through some backlogged work."

"Of course," Max said, following him into the room.

It made Rhys itchy, seeing Max standing by his desk in his cozy fisherman's sweater, hands tucked casually into the pockets of his pants. Rhys wanted him to leave. But no matter what he wanted, what he *needed* to do right now was make peace.

"Max," Rhys said, leaning a little more heavily than he should have on Moira's embroidered chair at the breakfast nook. "I want to extend my deepest apologies for the way I acted at dinner. That was completely out of line. I wasn't myself, but that's not an excuse. I have every intention—"

"Don't worry, you didn't hurt me," Max said, attention drifting as though he was already bored. He leaned over to take a closer look at the books open on Rhys's desk, then had the audacity to flip through a chart of planetary hours. Rhys bristled. He *hated* people touching his books without asking, even David. Only Moira was allowed to, because Rhys trusted her gentleness and had taught her how to properly handle the delicate pages.

"I was just double-checking some planetary transits," Rhys lied.

"Really? Because it seems like you're deep into some serious research. Looking for something?"

That burning sensation of foreboding just kept building in Rhys's body, settling in the bottom of his lungs. It wasn't unlike the feeling of the seawater that had rushed inside him that summer he was eight, when he swam too far out on the Cape and swallowed a dangerous amount of water before his father dragged him back to shore.

Rhys's hand drifted up to rub a warming circle on his sternum.

"No rest for the wicked," he said. "I still need to pull rituals to fill Society members' requests. Some demons are better for mortgages than marriages, you know how it is."

"If it isn't out of line to say, some rest might do you good. I heard Antoni Bresciani stepped in as High Priest."

"Interim High Priest," Rhys corrected quietly.

"David told me you two are close friends. And Antoni is younger, right? That's got to sting a bit, having a man you mentored succeed you."

"Antoni is my magical equal and better than I am with numbers," Rhys said, smiling through the fact that yes, it did sting, very fucking much. However, no matter how broken his relationship was with Antoni at the moment, he would not speak ill of the other man. He would not lie to save his ego. "He'll do an excellent job until I'm back."

"You're up for re-election, then?"

"I will be. As soon as I'm ready."

Max rocked back on his heels, surveying the room. This was Rhys's inner sanctum, decorated with all his favorite items. Max's eyes roved across the framed pinned butterflies and the vintage postcards taped up next to Rhys' diploma and even the stuffed meerkat David had gotten him in some overblown apology after a stupid college argument. Then they settled on the tiny altar shoved in a corner of his bookcase.

Max nodded, as though he had found what he had been looking for.

The burning in Rhys's chest kicked up to an aching sear.

"Crocell?" Max asked, pointing out the altar as though there was any way Rhys could have missed it. "He's a pretty heavy hitter. I'm impressed."

Rhys realized a split-second too late that while he possessed no psychic intuition and no witch's foresight, he *did* have a stable of demons who were committed to keeping him from harm. Parasitic as they were, his demons would find a way to raise the alarm if Rhys was in any kind of danger.

The burning in his chest wasn't heartburn.

It was a warning.

"Out. He needed to get out of this room. He needed to call Moira, or David, or Nathan. Anyone who would answer.

"Crowley was a Golden Dawn initiate before he planted his own order," Max mused. "And if I'm remembering right, your Society traces its origins back to one of the splinters of the Golden Dawn. We're practically stepbrothers, magically speaking."

"I suppose so," Rhys said stiffly. His eyes darted to the door.

Max quickly identified another altar in the room, that pewter jewelry box whose purposes Rhys thought were so cleverly obscured.

"Looks like there's some blue candle wax on that… Stolas, right? How many demons do you have on call?"

Rhys had been caught in Max's net like one of his butterflies, and now no matter how hard he flapped his wings, there was nowhere to go.

Rhys traced a summoning seal in the air behind his back with shaking fingers, calling on Vual. He grasped for that thrumming energy in the atmosphere, wrapping his fingers around the glimmering echo of his demon and dragging Vual closer. A traced seal wasn't strong as chalk on hardwood, and Rhys had never been good at spontaneous summoning, but it still might work in a pinch. Vual brought an amiable atmosphere into any room, encouraging friends and foes alike to treat Rhys with preferential favor. It might discombobulate Max long enough for Rhys to convince Max he had it all wrong, it might buy Rhys enough time to–

Max cut a banishing pentagram through the air with his fingers, quick and brutally efficient. The thread of energy Rhys had been pulling on dissolved as Vual disappeared back into the infernal world, beat back for the time being.

"Any further act of aggression against me will result in your immediate expulsion from the Society," Max said. "I don't think you want that. If you intend to beat me, you're going to have to knock me out cold, and I really don't think you want to do that either. Take a breath. I'm not here to attack you."

Rhys could probably push harder and get Vual back under his control, but without the structure of a summoning seal beneath Rhys's feet and the amplifying power of a spoken incantation, Max would just banish Vual again and again. As many times as it took for Rhys to get the message.

"How many demons do you have on call, Rhys?" Max asked softly. Why did he sound sad?

Rhys stammered, unable to conjure any convincing lie, and Max simply nodded.

"There was a girl, back in Seattle," Max said. "A woman, really, almost as old as you. So bright. Determined to succeed at any cost. She believed she was strong enough to juggle multiple spirits, and at first, she was. But the strain got to her. Eventually the demons started... twisting her. Compelled her to steal and lie, among other more personal trespasses I won't mention here. It took half the Seattle OTO to dissolve the tether between this woman and her demons. Agonizing ritual. Took us days. She recovered, but she never set foot in a summoning circle again. Couldn't stomach it."

Rhys finally found his voice.

"That's unfortunate. But I'm not sure what her situation has to do with me."

Max smiled at him with knowing, which made Rhys want to pick up the nearest geode and hurl it at Max's smug face.

"It doesn't take an expert, or even someone who knows you very well, to see that you're underwater. Don't tell me how many demons you're wrangling, that's fine. But I can clearly see it's more than seven. Sometimes, superstitions are rooted in truth. And no matter how badly you want it to be true, you're not a god. You're only human, and you're drowning."

"Why did you come here, Max?" Rhys demanded. He wanted to cut to the chase, to whatever brutal, metal-warping crash this conversation was hurtling towards.

"I'm here as a friend–"

"We're not friends," Rhys said, the words coming out of him in a spiteful flash of heat. "You've been undermining me ever since you got to Boston, and then that wasn't good enough for you, so you had to *mesmerize* David, just as I was finally starting to get him to trust me again."

The words were too honest, too damning, as good as throwing in the towel on his dignity.

Rhys felt the last little bit of ground he had to stand on give way underneath him.

"Any broken trust between you and David has nothing to do with me," Max said, so calmly that Rhys wanted to scream. "This work is dangerous. I think it becomes so familiar to all of us that we forget that. It's your body and your soul on the line, every time you step into the circle, and sometimes, even the best defenses fail. There's a darkness inside all of us, and it calls to those demons just as much as any summoning seal does. If they get their claws into that darkness and start feeding on it, they're incentivized to create more, to push us to become people we never imagined we would be. Is this making sense to you now?"

"I don't want your pity," Rhys said. Deflecting with pride was far easier than admitting that Max had seen right through him. Right into his ugly corroded heart.

For the first time since arriving, Max looked frustrated.

"I'm not trying to insult you, I'm trying to *help* you."

"This is my mess to clean up, Max, my sins coming home to roost. While I appreciate your interest, this is none of your concern. I got myself into this, and I can get myself out of it."

"I just told you I've presided over a bond-breaking ritual before. I can do it again. If you would just trust me, I can untie the knots binding your demons to you. You can start fresh and build from the ground up, secure in the knowledge that any mistake you make is yours and that any victory you win is also yours. I can give you back control, Rhys."

Rhys had been leaning on his demons since he was eighteen years old, using them to help him gain admittance to college and advance through the ranks of the Society. He used them for things as weighty as warding his home and as flippant as getting out of library late fees. He didn't know who he was without them, and he didn't know if, when stripped away, he would like the man he was underneath.

But he didn't like himself now and hadn't for a long time. He had sacrificed more than just sherry and cinnamon sticks and pieces of his vital energy on those altars. He had sacrificed himself, and his strongly held beliefs about right and wrong. He had very nearly sacrificed his relationships.

Maybe, the peace he found on the other side of this dark, narrow tunnel would be worth the loss. Maybe, he could mend the rifts he had opened between him and David, and Moira, and Antoni, and everyone else who mattered. Maybe, the people he loved would still find him worthy of respect, even stripped of all his infernal aid.

"At least let me try," Max said, exasperation in his voice.

"And what do you want in return?" Rhys asked. There had to be a catch. There always was, with magic.

"I know your role in the Society is in flux right now, but you still have a lot of influence. If you propose changes, people will probably listen to you or at least take them under consideration." Max took a deep breath, and Rhys tensed for a blow. "I think we have more than enough evidence that the Society, as it stands, is not tenable in the long-term. Your recruitment numbers have taken a hit, many of your members are nearing retirement age, and you're hemorrhaging money. I know about the audit, Rhys. And we all know about the scandal in the paper."

"And?" Rhys asked, exhaustion hitting him in a wave.

"If you allowed the OTO to annex some of your resources, even if it was just using the Society ritual room from time to time or taking some of your grimoires off your hands, that would allow you to bring your expenses under control. Any further transition could be done gradually–"

"Of course," Rhys said, fighting the urge to sag down into the chair. "This is what you're actually after. You don't want to help me. You're trying to get me to sign off on a takeover."

"Technically, you don't have the authority to sign off on anything right now, and I'm not proposing a takeover. I'm just asking you to use your influence to make the others see that the Society is dying a slow death, and that you all have an opportunity here to staunch the bleeding before it gets any worse. Do that, and I'll happily help you."

"I told you no the first time, at tea."

"The first time I was offering a favor. Now I'm offering a bargain, if that makes it easier to accept. A fair trade. There's no shame in taking it, Rhys."

"I don't think you're getting it," Rhys said, feeling a strange power build within him. It had been so long since he drew upon this power, unaided by demons or caffeine or sleeplessness, that he almost didn't recognize it at first. But then he realized: it was his own indomitable power of will, anchored by moral certitude. It was the fire inside him that never went out, the one he had been born with.

"Aren't I?"

"I'm only in this pit because I put my own ego ahead of everything else, ahead of my friends and my partners and even the good of the Society. If you think, for one second, I'm going to do that again now, when we're all in such a precarious position, you must be out of your mind. I know the Society is an old boy's club riddled with debts and infighting, but it saved me when I had nowhere else to go, and I'm not selling it out. Not for all the money and power in the world, not even if I was on death's door. So no, I can't accept what you're offering."

Max's gaze shuttered, and Rhys saw clearly that they had reached the end of their conversation.

"I hope you'll reconsider. And if you don't, I wish you well dragging yourself out of that pit you've gotten yourself into." He sauntered past Rhys towards the door, pausing to take in the room in one last long, somber-eyed gaze. "Because from where I'm standing, you've dug a pretty deep one."

And with that, Max was gone, already halfway down the outdoor steps with the front door clicking softly shut behind him.

He stood stock-still for a moment, his hands cold and his heart wrapped in the thorned vines of agony, then fished his phone out of his pocket and began to dial Moira. She needed to know that Max was eyeing the Society like a carrion bird eyeing a carcass, that his self-interest had finally emerged from the earth after germinating in the darkness. She needed to know...

Rhys caught himself before he hit the call button. He could practically hear it, the irritation in Moira's voice when she realized he was calling her – at work no less – to advance his grandiose conspiracy theories about someone he perceived as a rival. David was likely to take it even worse, as an affront against the man in whom he had found a sort of comfort that Rhys could never offer.

Any attempt Rhys made to bring either of them into his anxieties would only drive a wedge further between them, especially since he couldn't quite articulate how threatened he had felt with Max in the room, how flayed open and inspected.

Besides, Rhys had hurt Moira and David enough already.

Max had only done what any sorcerer in his position would have done, what Rhys himself might have done in other circumstances. He had leveraged what he had to offer in exchange for what he wanted in return, and that was no crime. That was a bargain, a barter, the foundation of any human economy.

Rhys set his phone face down on the table and pinched the bridge of his nose. He had to focus. The winter social was days away, and he still wasn't operating at full capacity. He wanted to draw a bath and sulk until the water went cold, and he wanted to walk outside in the biting air until his nose and fingers were numb, and most of all, he wanted to crawl back into bed and sleep until Moira got home, then pull her into bed with him and fall asleep again, but none of those were solutions.

He ran his hand down his face, scrubbing his palm against the stubble on his jaw, and leaned back over his desk. He snapped the book he had been scouring shut and then picked up another one, flipping it open to the relevant chapter.

When he had trouble believing in anything, not even God and certainly not himself, he could still summon a belief in books. A belief in the written word, in the power that centuries of human scholarship had to bring order and meaning to the agonies of a modern life. When everything else failed him, books did not.

As Rhys ran his fingers down the dusty page, scanning the lines of text for revelation, he mouthed a silent prayer that just one more time, a book might be his deliverance.

CHAPTER THIRTY
DAVID

David didn't appreciate Rhys's tenure as High Priest until it was over. Yes, Rhys had been demanding and intractable, and he had gone off the deep end in those last few weeks of his reign, but it was only in his absence that David realized how indulgent Rhys had been.

Without showing too much outright favoritism, Rhys had made ample space for David's bone-deep need to show off and his tendency to wiggle out of admin. Rhys had given David plenty of time in the circle, more time than he probably deserved, and he had brought him into all his meetings as a trusted partner, even when David had offered nothing but sarcasm. He had never even chided David for texting under the table during budget planning or rolling his eyes when asked to pick up more work.

All these things too, were acts of love.

Rhys's love, David had come to realize, was a stone worn smooth by oceanic devotion. It had a weight to it, a heaviness David sometimes resented, but it was undeniable. When Rhys McGowan loved you, he showed it by moving a hundred mundane mountains: remaking the bed every week because David had never figured out how fitted sheets worked, or clearing the Society schedule so David always had access to the ritual room without having to ask, or being the designated driver every time, even after David had stopped drinking, just because getting David home safely at the end of a long night brought him satisfaction.

Love, for Rhys, was a practice, very much like prayer, something to be done every day, with quiet consistency and attention to detail. There were glimmering moments of elation, heavy glances and heady conversations and kisses stolen between cigarettes, and there were also moments of absence, bereft days when Rhys's energy was stolen away by his work. But most often, Rhys's love was the rhythm of those waves crashing against the rocks again and again, relentless and reliable.

It was the sort of love that David, steeped in unpredictability and far more comfortable in the fiery passion of on-again-off-again love-hate cycles, couldn't quite fathom.

That sort of love felt ancient, like it was older than Rhys, older than David even.

Antoni, for his part, did a good job picking up the pieces as High Priest. He followed the paper trail Rhys had left of caterers and florists ahead of the winter social, and he kept the gears of the Society turning smoothly. Like Rhys, Antoni knew when to keep silent, watching the room for shifts in group sentiment, but unlike Rhys, he also knew when to speak, adding his enthusiasm and decisive expertise to the conversation. Most importantly, Antoni knew when to smile.

David enjoyed working with him, but the friendly professionalism of being Antoni's second was nothing compared to the glory of being the hand-picked successor at Rhys's side, a trusted advisor by day and chosen consort by night.

As far as things with Max were concerned, David didn't have a single complaint. Max let David pay for nothing, a bit of lavishness that was in no way sensical considering the size of David's inheritance, but he enjoyed playacting being in some way dependent on this generous older man. They chatted about travel, and art, and dead occultists, all those things that could be so boring when not enlivened by the spark of attraction, and they went for long walks together until their cheeks were bitten pink from the cold and they were out of breath from laughing. Max held David down when they had sex until David's conscious mind winked out into perfect oblivion, and he held David close afterward in a way David always insisted he didn't need but had come to look forward to.

The only thing Max didn't seem to be able to help with was Rhys's demon trouble. David tried asking a few times if Max knew anything about what Rhys had gotten himself into, but Max always hedged, seemingly disinterested. He always assured David that Rhys was smart enough to help himself, and that it wasn't David's responsibility to play supernatural nursemaid, and did David want Indian for dinner or hot pot?

David let it go. Their relationship was still casual, which was how David usually liked to keep things, a fledgling connection that might grow into something more, or might not. He didn't want to push too hard, not when Max had already agreed to attend the winter social as his date.

The night of the social, David and Max arrived slightly early, just in case Antoni needed someone to set up punch glasses or direct the caterer. The historic Ipswich mansion Rhys had rented out for the event was lit from within with a festive glow, flanked by the blue-black sea beyond the cliffs. As David stepped through the front door, obediently dropping his car keys onto a nearby tray, he saw that he was not, in fact, needed at all.

The house was decorated from top to bottom, with boughs of holly hanging from the doorframes and crimson ribbons adorned with golden bells hanging from the eaves. Servers circled the room offering small bites and cranberry spritzers – alcoholic and zero proof – on silver trays.

Antoni was locked in a dire-looking conversation with one of the servers, so David left him alone. There would be plenty of time for saying hello later, after the party was safely underway and Antoni had surrendered himself to whatever direction the night took. The only other one of David's friends who was there was Cameron, chatting away with one of the more tenured Society brothers about what sounded like theologian Dietrich Bonhoeffer, a conversation David had neither the heart to interrupt or the knowledge to join.

When Max slipped away to find him a sparkling water, David was left without anyone to talk to. He felt a little bored and a little awkward and he kept glancing over his shoulder in the hopes of seeing Rhys and Moira walking through the door.

There had been contact since his visit to the McGowan-Delacroix household – a chatty call from Moira, and articles on demonology shared by Rhys via email. Rhys was very much like an overeducated alley cat when he wanted to apologize for something: he would send links throughout the day like birds deposited on David's front stoop, strange little peace offerings. And there *was* peace, tenuous though it felt. They had both taken bites out of each other in the ritual room, taken enough time to cool off and realize how badly they missed each other, and agreed to try and move forward. But David knew himself, and he knew Rhys.

Things would not feel totally repaired until they were in the same room again, probably with their hands on each other.

David broke into a grin when he noticed a baby grand piano tucked away in the corner.

David sat at the piano, adjusting his bottle-green suit, and plucked out the opening chords to a languid rendition of "Silver Bells". He found most Christmas music either trite and saccharine or dirge-like and onerous, but he did have a soft spot for "Silver Bells".

David hummed for a few bars, finding the key, and then started to sing. His voice was his oldest companion, from humming himself to sleep as a child or talking out loud as he studied frantically for the bar. The familiarity of it, the color and the timbre and the resonance vibrating through his chest, soothed him.

The song was almost over before he thought to look up, just in time to see Rhys and Moira meander through the door. Moira's arm was threaded through her husband's as he leaned down to point out the ribbons above their heads, igniting her smile. She was wearing a figure-hugging red velvet gown that evoked Monroe, and Rhys was shower-fresh and wide awake in a sharp black suit. Silver filigree rings gleamed on his fingers, and his curls even looked trimmed and set.

David's heart clenched.

When Rhys saw David at the piano, he slowed to a stop. Moira followed the line of his sight and gave David a little wave. Then she kissed Rhys, murmured something in his ear with her hand cupped around her mouth, and drifted off towards the punch bowl.

David didn't believe in the whole locking-eyes-and-the-world-stops thing, but time really did slow to a crawl as Rhys crossed the room, hands tucked into his pockets, a hopeful smile on his face.

"Hey," Rhys said.

"Hey," David responded. "I wasn't sure if you were going to feel well enough to come."

"Oh, Moira didn't deal any damage she couldn't patch up," Rhys said, that smile deepening in the corner into a perfect dimpled shadow. "Besides, I'm not going to miss a party I planned. Especially not if you're there."

David envisioned himself crossing the distance between them, seizing Rhys's face in his hands, and kissing him like the finale of one of those romcoms Moira was always telling him about. But then a hand settled on his shoulder, and he looked up to see Max at his side, a sweating can of La Croix in his hand. David smiled at Max and then turned back towards Rhys, who looked troubled.

David was caught, for just an instant, between the two forces of nature he had gotten into bed with.

He could practically feel it: the lifegiving heat of the sun beating down on his shoulders while he looked right into the heart of the ocean: cold and infinite and somehow all the more welcoming for it.

"Max," Rhys said, stepping forward and offering a handshake. "Good to see you."

"Good to see you as well," Max responded, giving a firm shake. "Glad you're up and at 'em."

Rhys held Max's hand for a second longer than was strictly necessary, but then he dropped his hand and his gaze, the bid for dominance over.

"Right as rain," Rhys said.

David could practically see Rhys running the mental calculations about how to proceed through this social interaction in the most cordial way possible. You could say a lot about Rhys, not all of it charitable, but you could never say he wasn't polite.

This was no doubt a hard puzzle to solve: how to interact with David, who he had recently kicked out of the Society, in public, with Max right there, as David's formal date.

David probably should have thought this scenario through a little better before throwing everyone in the same room together and hoping for the best.

"I should go find my wife and make sure she's got her drink," Rhys said, finishing the calculation a beat later than most people but still sticking the landing. David was proud of him. "I also need to congratulate Antoni on the beautiful job he's doing hosting. I just wanted to say hello before the night got away from us. I'll see you both later?"

"Sounds great," David said, both to give Rhys an exit from the conversation and to indicate that he had done a good job of upholding etiquette.

David thought that would be the end of it. But then, Rhys tucked his knuckle under David's chin and kissed him quick and sweet on the mouth, just like they were saying goodbye without an audience.

With that, Rhys was gone.

Max gave David an amused look as he passed him the sparkling water.

"I've never met someone so tightly wound. He's like a tin soldier."

"He just spends a lot of time in his head, that's all," David said, coming to Rhys's defense as automatically as flinching when burned. He would be first in line with a laundry list of Rhys's shortcomings, but had always bristled if he heard anyone insinuate that his boyfriend was odd or, God forbid, off-putting.

Max raised his eyebrows.

"No offense meant," he said.

David smiled lasciviously at him. Flirtation was David's favorite form of de-escalation.

"It's kind of hot though, you acting jealous."

"I don't understand Rhys, but I'm not threatened by him. And I'm not feeding your little love triangle fantasy."

"What fantasy?" David said, mock innocent.

"Play another song," Max said, nodding towards the piano. "That's what's actually hot here."

"What's so hot about ivory and wood?" David scoffed.

"Me enjoying you enjoying doing something you're obviously very good at. Play."

David smirked as he leaned languidly into the opening bars of "What Are You Doing New Year's Eve?" He would never say no to the pleasure of an encore, and being celebrated by Max's approving gaze with the ghost of Rhys's kiss still warm on his lips felt pretty good too.

CHAPTER THIRTY-ONE
RHYS

Rhys did his best to focus on the party, on having *fun*. After running himself into the ground trying to keep the Society afloat, siphoning off bits of his vital energy to feed rowdy demons, and getting the wind knocked out of him by Moira's magic, he wasn't exactly feeling festive.

Still, it was hard not to appreciate the twinkling lights, the ring of Nathan's laughter across the room as he made Kitty shriek with glee, the way Moira's cheeks glowed with mirth. She stuck close to his side, snaking her arm around his waist as though he might wander off, and he latticed his fingers through hers, as though to tell her that he wasn't going anywhere.

Cameron, knowing that the Society's budget only allowed for well liquor at these events, snuck in a flask of 1972 Full Proof bourbon. He had a knack for temperance to rival any saint's, but when he did indulge his vices (which included pedantry and poker and brown liquor), he only drank the best. Rhys gladly accepted a surreptitious swallow of the bracing liquid, which tasted of vanilla and char. Cameron tried to warn Moira about the burn, but Moira – who had cut her teeth drinking highballs and juleps in Georgia – put away a tidy swallow without so much as a wince.

"Good God, woman, did you even taste it?" Cameron asked with an approving chuckle.

"I can taste it just fine on the way down," Moira said, grinning right back.

Rhys tried to be present in the moment, to soak up all the light coming off his wife and enjoy the rapport of his friends, but he still found himself scanning nervously around for Antoni. Catching up with David could wait. Antoni, however, was another matter. That was a bridge Rhys hadn't crossed yet, and one he would probably have to build with apologies as he went.

As it happened, Rhys didn't have to go looking for Antoni. Antoni found him.

"You three look like kids passing a joint around a high school dance," Antoni said. He was wearing a brocade jacket with showy golden buttons. Perfect for a High Priest, Rhys thought with a pang.

"Moira's drinking me out of house and home," Cameron said, sloshing the bottle invitingly. "Want a nip?"

"What is it?" Antoni said, already bringing the bottle to his mouth.

"Better than the Evan Williams they're serving at the bar, that's what."

Antoni kicked some of the bourbon back, then grunted to clear his throat.

"That's good stuff. Sharp suit, Cam. Moira, pretty as always. Even you cleaned up nice, Rhys. Looks like you finally learned how to comb your hair."

Rhys accepted the jibe for what it was, a gesture of good faith.

"And it looks like your party went off without a hitch," he responded. "You've done a wonderful job."

"All I did was follow the notes you left behind," Antoni said. To Rhys's surprise, he held out his hand, as though their friendship hadn't been irrevocably fractured. Rhys clasped his hand and stepped into the one-armed embrace Antoni always greeted him with, punctuated with a thump on the back.

"I'm glad you're alright," Antoni said near his ear, low so nobody else could hear. "I was worried about you."

Rhys wanted to die. He had been an absolute tyrant to everyone, but especially to Antoni. He didn't deserve grace.

"Can I speak to you privately?" Rhys asked. "Just for a minute?"

"Of course," Antoni said. "Everybody else, keep drinking. I'll catch up with you in a sec."

Antoni led Rhys over to a large potted poinsettia. It was situated in a quiet corner of the room and offered modest cover for a conversation.

"I need to apologize to you," Rhys said, and once he wrenched those words out like a rotten tooth, the rest bled out from him easier. "That night in conclave… I don't know what I was thinking. I held things against you I never should have. I've been an dick, I know that. You've been nothing but a friend to me since we met, and I took that for granted. What I'm trying to say is you don't have any reason to trust me, but I swear your secret is safe with me. I won't breathe a word to Kitty."

"That's alright," Antoni said. "I will."

"Pardon?"

Antoni looked over Rhys's shoulder to Kitty, who was draped across her husband and smiling at him like he was the sun in the sky. She was wearing a black silk dress that skimmed her toes and an elaborate updo decorated with tiny crystal snowflakes.

"I'm tired of running around with my tail between my legs," Antoni said, with more resolve. "And while I appreciate your apology, I never want anyone to be able to hold something like that over me again. Nothing's going to come of saying how I feel, but that doesn't really matter. Kitty deserves to know, and I deserve to be the one to tell her. I'm not going to be able to move on from this until I do."

"What about Nathan?" Rhys said, slipping right back into the role of confidant. "Do you want me to speak to him for you sometime next week, or distract him while you talk to Kitty?"

"Well, he can't kick my ass at a public party, can he?"

Bourbon threatened to crawl back up his throat, and Rhys swallowed hard.

"You're talking to her tonight? Here?"

"Sure," Antoni said, with the shrug of the young and reckless and damn near invincible. "If I'm going to get my heart broken, it might as well be with a glass of champagne in my hand. I guess I should thank you for giving me the wake-up call I needed."

"I wouldn't put it that way," Rhys said, guilt welling up in him.

"Neither would I. But I am choosing to look on the bright side." Antoni gave him a smile, all teeth and poison sweetness. "That said, I swear to God, Rhys, you pull some shit like that again and I will break your nose. Got it?"

"Got it," Rhys said.

"And I expect you to tell me what the hell you were doing summoning Paimon."

"No story to it. I was arrogant and I thought I could tame him. Tale as old as time."

"That's fair. Stupid, but fair. Now at least try to enjoy yourself, for once. You look like you've got a stick up your ass. No ruining my party with a sour face."

"If it's any consolation," Rhys said with a fond smile, "you make an excellent High Priest."

"Does that mean you're not going to fight me for the title?"

"Not on your life, Bresciani."

"Works for me," Antoni said, polishing off his champagne. "I haven't had a good challenge in ages. Now get back out there. David is looking for you."

Rhys glanced over his shoulder. David was subtly scanning the room while Max told some charming anecdote, his hand resting lighting on David's back. There were a few raised eyebrows from the other Society members who expected to see David attached to Rhys's hip, but most people were happy to meet Max. Unorthodox relationships were more common in the magical world than in the mundane one, and most of David's peers understood that he wasn't the settling-down type. No matter how captivated David was with Rhys or how devoted he was to Moira, his heart would always remain open to new connections.

Rhys understood that better than most. He had even given his blessing.

So why did he feel like he was chewing on glass?

"Go," Antoni said. "And don't start a fight during an event with my name on it, capisce? I may end up holding one of the shortest tenures as High Priest on record, but I won't have my reign sullied with scandal."

Rhys clapped Antoni on the shoulder, then strode over to David. Max had disappeared, maybe to go find more sparkling water, so Rhys laced his fingers through David's and started leading him briskly through the crowd.

"Where are we going?" David asked.

"Someplace quiet," Rhys said. "You and I need to talk."

The second story of the house was technically off limits, but Rhys unfastened the velvet rope from the staircase and ushered David up the steps all the same. They found their way to a window at the end of the upstairs hallway, overlooking the churning ocean waves below.

"So. Are we even?" Rhys asked, glancing sidelong at David. He was never sure how to go about these things. Sometimes, if Rhys played a conversation too somber, David would feel lectured at. Other times, if Rhys came on too flippant, he would be hurt Rhys wasn't taking him seriously.

"How so?" David asked.

"I kick you out of the Society. You bring Max to the social. Does that make us even?"

"Babe," David said with a sigh. "I wasn't trying to hurt you."

"Not even a little?"

"OK," David conceded, shrugging one shoulder. "Maybe a little. But I got your attention, didn't I?"

"Is that all Max is? A way to get my attention?"

David pressed his lips together, slouching with his back against the window so he could look Rhys in the face as he delivered the damning blow.

"No."

Jealousy reared up in Rhys like a snake poised to strike. He breathed slowly through his nose until it settled down, coiling up small.

"I know. And I'm glad you're enjoying him. Hand to God, I am. It's just... an adjustment."

"Nothing has to change between us," David said, like he had already thought it all through and come to his own solution without running it by Rhys. Rhys hated when he did that. "Obviously I still want to be with you. But it was never going to be wedding bells and two-point-five kids for us; you know that."

Rhys knew, rationally, that David was being reasonable. David had never wanted to get married, even when that was an option, and had always been brighter, happier, *better* when they were more monogamish than monogamous. Rhys knew, rationally, that it was unfair to hoard the love that David and Moira gave to him so freely, and that he shouldn't try to hold them down and clip their wings. That would result in nothing but resentment: blood and feathers everywhere.

But Rhys also felt, irrationally, that David Aristarkhov was his, his to have and hold, and his to hurt and heal.

"I know," Rhys said, voice thick.

"Is that what did it, the first time around?" David asked, spinning his finger in the air like they were on some merry-go-round that never stopped turning. "When we first tried to make this work? I was awful, I know I was awful. But I was awful for months, a year even, and we were still together. Then one day I came home, and you were just gone. Moved out. I didn't even read your stupid note, I was so pissed."

Pissed, Rhys knew from the fragments of hearsay he had picked up from other people, was putting it lightly. David had gone on a bender so dark and absolute that it took Wayne showing up at his apartment, banging on the door until David let him in, and all but forcing David to spend Christmas with Wayne and his wife in the Alps while he pulled himself together. David had apparently spent most of the trip sulking by the fireplace drinking frangelico coffees, making only occasional appearances at family dinners, and trudging behind Wayne on frigid, mandatory wellness walks across the resort.

Rhys had been so guilty that he hadn't eaten for days. Then, when he forced himself to wolf down some of his mother's honey ham and green beans on Christmas Day, he had promptly and quietly thrown it all up in the bathroom.

"The check," Rhys said, his chest collapsing.

He had spent a year wondering if David had ever read his note, then numbly accepted the reality that David probably had not. It hadn't been a good note, no matter how many times Rhys rewrote it, and it wasn't close to an acceptable parting message. But he had hoped David had glanced at it, at least.

"What check?" David said.

"The North End," Rhys said, words coming in the wrong order. He hadn't expected to have this conversation tonight. He hadn't expected to ever have it at all. "The check for that dinner. The night it was snowing."

They had been at one of those overpriced spots in the Italian district, dragging dinner out over two and then three hours as David picked at his food and ordered a second bottle of wine.

Rhys had drunk one large glass. David had drunk the rest.

They had been talking in circles, edging up against a half dozen different fights before retreating from them with a subject change. Rhys had a hard time remembering the details of these disputes. They were probably about petty Society squabbles, or semantics, or what to do with their weekend. All excuses not to address the open wound at the center of their relationship: David drank too much, and when he drank he was selfish and snide, and Rhys had long ago surrendered to a growing bitterness that had turned him controlling and cold.

It was breathtaking, how bad a good relationship could get in the span of two years.

When the check finally came, Rhys had sighed in relief. Now, at least, they could go home and drop into unconsciousness with their backs turned to each other in bed. They could stop pretending that they weren't slowly poisoning each other, at least for the night.

David had patted himself down only to realize, with a too-loud laugh that rang through the restaurant, that he had left his wallet in the car. He slid the check across the table to Rhys, waving his hand in dismissal.

"David, I can't pay this," Rhys had said, voice as low as possible so nobody else in the restaurant would overhear. He had had this nightmare before; all eyes on him in public, nothing in his bank account, David unimpressed with his poverty. Only this time, it was happening in real life.

"Don't worry about it," David had replied, still too loud. "I'll get you back."

"This check is three hundred dollars," Rhys replied, covering the slip of paper with his hand as though that might make it go away. "I don't have that kind of money on me right now."

Of course he didn't, because he never did, because David paid for everything. David paid for dinners and trips and drinks and rent, a display of lavish generosity that had been dazzling to Rhys in the beginning but had slowly started to feel like golden shackles around his wrists. David barely felt it, he just swiped the card and signed the receipt, but Rhys made very little money of his own as a student, and none of their shared expenses were in his name.

Rhys had worried about the power differential from the beginning, and David had insisted it was all just numbers on a computer, nothing of any real weight. But now Rhys was sitting across from a man who, on paper at least, owned him entirely, and who couldn't even be trusted to get through a single dinner sober. A man who was currently looking at Rhys like he was nothing more than an annoyance.

"Walk back to the car, then," David said, sliding him the keys to the Audi. Rhys wrapped his fingers around the metal, forming a fist. The keys bit into his palm, nearly breaking the skin. "It's right around the corner. I'll wait here."

David, in his haze of merlot, had forgotten that they had parked a half mile away. Rhys didn't remind him. He just stormed out into the cruel night, finding to his utter misery that the globs of dirty ice on the street were being quickly blanketed over with fresh snow. Rhys trudged in his too-thin shoes and his secondhand scarf back to the car, nearly slipping twice, and retrieved David's wallet from where he had left it in clear view on the passenger seat.

By the time Rhys made it back to the restaurant, his fingers were numb, and his heart was iced over, and he had decided, with brutal finality, that he was going to leave.

David clapped when Rhys returned, as though he were an intrepid knight who had retrieved the Grail, then brushed the snowflakes from Rhys's eyelashes and paid the check. He had chattered about banalities on the way home, drunk enough to mostly just be talking to hear himself talk, and David didn't seem to realize that Rhys barely spoke a word to him the rest of the night.

Two days later, Rhys was gone.

In the hallway of the historic home, a considerably older, stone-cold sober David huffed out a disbelieving laugh.

"You're serious? We didn't even fight."

"We didn't have to," Rhys said. "I just... recognized that things had gotten too bad for me to stay."

"And you might have been right about that," David said, voicing a conclusion that had probably taken him years of denial and thousands of dollars in therapy to come to. "But you didn't have to do it like that. It was—"

"Cowardly," Rhys filled in, providing the conclusion that had taken him years of regret and countless hours bruising his knees in confessional booths to come to. "I was scared, so I ran. It had nothing to do with you not wanting a ring, or a white picket fence. That's what was in the note."

David chewed the inside of his mouth, and Rhys prayed that he would accept this honesty, unflattering as it was.

"I probably should have read that note," David said after a long while.

"Probably," Rhys said. He smoothed his hand over David's jaw, then cupped the base of his skull. "I fucked this up once, and I'm trying to do it right this time. So please give me a little grace if I'm not totally sold on you dating a man who is much older than you."

"Easy, morality police, he's only six years older than me," David said, arching a challenging eyebrow. That infuriating smile was back on his lips, an invitation towards confrontation, or consummation. "I'm four years older than you. An evil college senior preying on the unsuspecting virgin freshman. Should we call Dateline?"

"I was an adult, and I went after you first, not the other way around. I weighed the risk and accepted the consequences."

"Which is exactly what happened with me and Max."

"And he's fine with you being my boyfriend at the same time he's yours?" Rhys said, following the inviting thread of David's teasing. "He's not going to be angry I pulled you away while he's here as your date?"

"Max doesn't mind sharing."

Rhys dropped his hand to David's belt, unfastening the metal so quickly the latch bit him.

"So, he won't mind if I have you while he's downstairs? Is that right?"

David grinned bright as the sun, bracing himself against the sill of the window. He didn't need to say a damn word for Rhys to know he was getting exactly what he wanted.

"If I have to see you with him, I'm going to send you back to him ruined," Rhys said, because he knew a little meanness would get David off, but also because it felt good to voice his own ugly possessiveness, in this stolen, momentary reprieve from always being the reasonable one. He should probably find a better outlet for any emotion that frightened him other than sex or spreadsheets, but for now, it was a system that worked.

Rhys unzipped David's expensive slacks and slipped his hand beneath David's briefs.

"You're a terror," David said, then hissed through his teeth as Rhys grasped him. David was already hard, his flesh hot to the touch.

Rhys stroked David roughly, skipping the pleasantries and any semblance of sweetness. David's head tipped back, exposing the tanned curve of his throat. Rhys dug his teeth into that throat as he worked David over, not caring if he left marks.

David was his, goddammit. His to own and his to love and his to bruise. Even if that made Rhys wicked, even if that meant he would never see heaven.

He needed to remind David of this irreplaceable, sparking friction between them, the give and take that would always exist, no matter if they were separated or not, probably even continuing after they both were dead.

David canted his hips against Rhys's hand, whining as he approached the edge. Rhys produced a handkerchief from his pocket and wrapped it around David's cock moments before David climaxed, spilling into the silk.

"Christ," David panted, buttoning up his pants. "What's gotten into you? Not that I'm complaining."

Rhys folded the soiled handkerchief and tucked it back into his pocket, already smoothing his jacket and turning to go.

"Hey, hey," David said, voice a stone's throw from supernaturally charming. "Don't run off yet."

David kissed Rhys, his mouth warm and pliable, and Rhys couldn't help but fold. He gave way under the barrage of tenderness and kissed David back, all intentions to play the cruel dominant evaporated. Maybe, at the end of the day, he was the desperate one: desperate to be so needed that someone would actually obey him.

What was a dominant but someone enslaved to their desire to be of use?

"Come to Vermont," David said against Rhys's mouth.

"What's in Vermont?" Rhys asked, dipping his head to press a soothing kiss over the red spot on David's neck. He would be embarrassed for leaving the mark in the morning, but he wasn't right now. Right now, that mark felt like a gift David had happily received.

"My family's country house. I'm going to spend Christmas up there. Imagine it. You, me, Moira. We can have breakfast by the fireplace and hike around the grounds and spend hours in bed. No Society bullshit, no investigation, just an escape, three hours from the city where no one can bother us."

"Who's coming?" Rhys asked, even though he already had an inkling of the answer.

"Leda, of course. And Max. He didn't have any other plans; what was I supposed to do? Come on, it will be fun. We can all get to know each other better. He's willing to play nice, and so am I. Will you try?"

Rhys considered it. Running away with Moira and David to a palatial estate north of Boston did indeed sound tempting, and he had grown to appreciate Leda's company, abrasive though she could be. He knew he should probably get out of the city that was starting to feel like it was trying to eat him alive. A quiet place to get a handle on all the demons he was juggling would be nice, too. Physically removing himself from his study and its many altars might be just the thing to wear away the ties that bound him to his spirits. He had tried force of will, and sheer deprivation, and a dozen rituals besides, but distance was one thing he hadn't deployed yet.

And Max... He could work harder to get along with Max.

"I'll talk to Moira," Rhys said. "But if we do come, I absolutely have to be back in Boston by Christmas Day. I promised my parents."

"I would never dream of upsetting Arthur and Mary Ann," David said solemnly, hand over his heart.

"I should get back down there. I'm supposed to be putting on a good face and showing everyone how sane I am."

"Good luck with that," David said, sliding his hand across the plane of Rhys' stomach as he slipped past and he strode down the hallway.

Rhys let David go, pausing for a quiet moment to compose himself. Then, he strode out towards the landing of the stairs and watched the proceedings below. David was back at Max's side, murmuring something in his ear that made the other man smile wickedly. Moira was dancing with Nathan, one of their awkward, giggling, swaying numbers that always seemed to happen after they had both had a couple of drinks. And Antoni...

Where was Antoni?

Rhys searched the ballroom, and found Antoni perched on the edge of a chair in a dark corner, one of Kitty's hands pressed between his own. He was speaking in a low, urgent manner, and Kitty was staring at him with open marvel.

Rhys watched the confession, his heart twisting. Even when Antoni had everything to lose, when the High Priesthood was in his grasp, he was still willing to do the right thing. Rhys wished he had that decency. He wished that he was composed of anything but a hurricane of dark, demanding emotions that clawed at everyone around him.

Maybe David had been right to call him a terror.

Maybe, at the end of the day, he was terrible at being a person.

But he was trying to learn what it meant to exist in the world without doing damage to his surroundings, what it felt like to hold the ones he loved without squeezing so tight that he choked them.

And maybe Vermont would be the reset he needed. Maybe out there, in the wilderness, he could meet a different version of himself.

Straightening his tie, Rhys descended the stairs into the ballroom.

CHAPTER THIRTY-TWO
MOIRA

The invitation to Vermont was barely out of Rhys's mouth before Moira accepted. She was drowsy in the passenger seat, knees tucked up under her, high-heeled shoes forgotten in the trunk, but she stirred to life as soon as she heard the words "family home". David's idea of a modest country retreat was probably a small mansion with fireplaces she could drink brandy in front of while watching horses frolic outside. And, if she was being honest, her townhouse with its many demons had started to feel claustrophobic. Fresh air would be good for her, not to mention Rhys, who could only benefit from removing himself from the stressful swirl of Boston,

"Oh, Rhys can we go?" she pled. "We've got to. It would be wonderful."

"You think so?" Rhys asked, a smirk on his face as he glanced sidelong at her from the driver's seat. He was navigating the winding, dark coastal roads back towards Boston with meticulous care, like she was the most precious cargo in the world.

"I know so," Moira said, caught in that sleepy twilight where everything felt romantic and full of faultless promise. The party had gone without a hitch, and she was going home with a stomach full of champagne and brie tarts, Nathan's lime and neroli cologne and Kitty's pink lipstick clinging to her skin from goodbye hugs and kisses. She had bonded with Cameron over their shared love of Marlon Brando movies, and she had waltzed with David so much that the entire ballroom had been spinning by the end. And best of all, there was light in Rhys's eyes again, brightest of all when he looked at her. "When do we leave?"

The day of the trip, Moira stuffed her suitcase full of knit dresses, chunky sweaters, and vintage costume jewelry, then loaded up the car. Rhys offered to drive, so she could fully appreciate the breathtaking scenery out the window.

Winding roads lined with spruce and pine rolled past as they crossed the Vermont border, and about an hour out from their destination, the frozen ground became blanketed with snow. Rhys started the drive chatty but fell quiet the further they got from the house and his altars. He smiled brightly whenever she glanced over at him, but she knew he was worrying about being away from his demons for so long. Moira snapped photos through the window of does and turkeys, losing herself in cooing at the animals outside, until Rhys took a turn and said, "I think this is it."

Moira glanced up from her phone and gasped.

Calling the house a cabin would have been the understatement of the century. An edifice of gleaming russet wood sprawling over gently rolling hills, it featured a staggering number of windows and chimneys. The house grew even larger as they approached up a long brick-cobbled drive flanked by decorative hedges.

As they trundled to a stop, David strolled out of the door, looking like a Ralph Lauren ad in his burgundy sweater and camel-colored slacks. He held out his arms, beckoning Moira over.

She tossed open her door and scurried into his arms, practically purring as he gave her a squeeze. He felt like deep peace and contentment, threaded through with anticipation. He must have a fire burning indoors; she could smell it on his clothes.

"I missed you," she said.

"I missed you too, peach," David replied, turning the collar of her coat up against the cold. "Rhys, let me help you with that."

He walked over to where Rhys was wrestling Moira's overstuffed suitcase out of the car, doing his best to act like it wasn't too heavy. David lifted the suitcase easily, pausing only to bend down and give Rhys a kiss.

"Thanks," Rhys huffed, his cheeks slightly pink.

"You OK?" David asked. "You look peaked."

"Just a headache. I was looking at the road too long."

"We'll get you a Tylenol. Come on in," David said, bumping open the front door with his hip.

Moira's jaw dropped as they walked inside the great room. The house was decorated like a well-loved hunting lodge with overstuffed leather furniture, knit Afghans tossed over couches, and cushy rugs underfoot. Gleaming hardwood floors were accented by soaring exposed beams overhead. The room was devoid of the expected decapitated deer heads and mounted antlers, for which Moira was grateful. Dead animals always distressed her, but David knew that, and he must have had the foresight to have them put away in storage.

Leda was lounging on the sofa in ripped jeans and a massive black cardigan, deep in an animated conversation with Maximilian, who was warming his hands by the fire.

"Ecstatic states are the quickest route to spiritual power," Leda was saying. "Dear old Crowley knew that."

"Crowley also died in dissolution and ruin," Max said. "Because he didn't know his limits."

"All I'm saying is the occasional acid trip does the body good. Rhys, Moira, you made it! I was worried about you driving through the snow in that ancient Lincoln."

"The car held up just fine," Rhys said, accepting Leda's tight hug. She was slightly less tall out of the platform shoes, but she still had to bend down to embrace him. Moira was greeted with a flurry of cheek kisses.

"Max," Rhys said, taking the initiative and extending his hand. Rhys had promised to be nothing but pleasant for the duration of the trip, and Moira believed him, but it was good to see that promise in action.

"Rhys," Max said, accepting his hand and giving it a firm shake. "Glad you made it safe."

"Let me show you your room," David said, guiding Moira and Rhys up a mahogany staircase and into a well-outfitted guest bedroom. There was a cozy hunter green armchair in one corner, a four-poster queen bed, and a merry woodland scene of rabbits in repose hung over the headboard.

"I'm glad you decided to come," David said, arranging Moira's suitcase on the bed just so, like he needed something do with his hands. "It wouldn't be the same without you both."

"I'm surprised you invited us," Rhys said, snaking his arm around David's waist. "You don't even like Christmas."

"I like an excuse to get my favorite people together and forget about my diet for a few days."

"I don't want to hear a word out of you about that damn diet this trip," Moira said with a laugh. "I'll make you slow down and enjoy the pleasures of life if it kills me, *including* dessert."

"I won't fight you too hard on it," David said, brushing his lips across her shoulder and leaving a sizzle of playful energy behind. "Leda is looking forward to linking up with you again and I think between the two of you, I won't stand a chance.

"And Max?" Rhys asked.

"All is forgiven, OK? There's no bad blood in this house." David dropped a reassuring kiss to the corner of Rhys' mouth. "I'll give you two a bit to get settled in, we're in the great room when you're ready. Fair warning, Leda's got a gleam in her eye that tells me she wants to play a game. Pray it's checkers and not shooting apples off each other's heads at the archery range."

"You've got an archery range?" Moira exclaimed.

"It's only a half-acre big, don't get excited," David said. "Anyway, get cozy, my house is your house, all that stuff. Dinner's at seven, no need to dress for it."

David disappeared down the hall, leaving Moira batting her eyelashes at her husband in their room.

"You like it here," Rhys said with a smirk.

"Oh, I don't like it, I *love* it. Did he say an archery range?"

"There are stables, too. I'm sure he would show them if you asked."

"It's so much fun having a rich boyfriend-in-law."

"It makes me happy watching you two have so much fun together," Rhys said. Moira threaded her fingers lovingly through his hand, then paused over his forehead. David was right, he *did* look peaked, and he was running hot.

"How's your head, baby?"

"Honestly? Pounding since the Vermont border. But I expected this. It's just withdrawal. If my demons can't get to me through the altars, they'll try to irritate me into driving back home and feeding them. But I'm not going to do that." Rhys took his wife's shoulders in his hands, squeezing. "I'm going to have a very nice time with you, and David and Leda *and* Max, and I'm going to ignore this headache until it goes away. I'll find a way to distract myself."

262ASCENSION

"I can help distract you," Moira said, wiggling her shoulders in a come-hither way. Everything about this house felt luxurious and romantic, and like she might want to break it in with her husband.

"We don't have time," Rhys said with a chuckle, but he drew her closer all the same.

"Says who? David told us to take our time and make ourselves comfortable. I'm just doing what I'm told."

"I'm so sure," Rhys said, leaning down to trace his words against her lips in that way that always drove her crazy, mere millimeters from a kiss. "You're just being the world's best guest, is that it?"

"Yes," Moira said, shoving him playfully back onto the bed. Moira, who didn't usually take aggressive initiative in these sorts of things but was willing to try anything once, crawled atop him, bracketing him in place with her knees. Rhys stared up at her in wonder, lips slightly parted, as beautiful as she had ever seen him.

"What are you doing?" he asked, still laughing, but slightly nervous now. He didn't move a muscle.

Moira pushed his hands up above his head, lacing her fingers though his own and squeezing while she held him down.

"Enjoying you," Moira replied. "Aren't I allowed to just gaze at my husband when it pleases me?"

Now Rhys looked caught between desire and panic, his chest rising and falling with quick, shallow breaths. Like he couldn't fathom being something someone simply *enjoyed*, instead of something that was *needed*, that had a function and a purpose and a place. There was so much wild light in his eyes, like a hundred candles burning at once. Longing squeezed Moira's heart even as arousal curled warm and inviting in her stomach.

"I think you would look so handsome tied up," she said, because she had always thought it and never been brave enough to say it, and there was no better time than now. "You should let me try it one of these days."

Rhys opened his mouth, words on the tip of his tongue, and then Leda hollered up the stairs: "I'm opening the wine! Get down here before it's gone."

"Give us one moment, Leda!" Rhys barked back. Then he turned Moira, severity melting from his features as he spoke sweetly. "You and I are going to finish this conversation later. And I'm not saying no. Maybe we can find a better use for that dominating oil while we're at it."

Moira nipped Rhys's nose as she released him, and he pulled her out of bed with him, smiling over at her a little starry-eyed. He looked so young like this, open to love and unexpected pleasure.

"Let's get down there before Leda comes up here to retrieve us," he said, leading her out of the room. It was hard for Moira to keep her eyes on the stairs under her feet and not look back at her husband, close and warm behind her.

Maybe things would be alright after all. Maybe they would all find their way through this stressful season into perfect harmony, and no one would have to cry or bleed or shout to get to the other side.

Leda was in the giant kitchen, rummaging around in the wine fridge for a bottle. Moira was surprised to find there were a dozen different bottles chilling.

"You keep this place stocked?" Moira asked David, who was fiddling with knobs on the La Cornue oven as though he had never seen a gas stove before. The interior of the oven was lit, showing a tinfoil-covered ham and a casserole dish of something that looked like it involved cheese and vegetables. Moira was charmed that David, who knew how to make exactly eight calorie-calculated large-format meals for himself, had even attempted to cook.

"Just with sparkling water," David replied, scowling down at the range. He swatted the side of it, like it was a misfiring car radio. "Leda brought the booze."

Rhys came up behind David and turned a single knob to the correct temperature. He may have never even been in a room with a kitchen appliance this expensive before, but he knew how to cook under virtually any circumstances.

"Moira, Riesling?" Leda asked, pulling a pale-yellow bottle from the fridge.

"Yes please," Moira said, retrieving a wine glass and holding it out. "I knew I could trust you to be in the charge of drinks with dinner."

"I couldn't stand the thought of us all standing around awkwardly without a little liquid courage in our systems," Leda said, leaning down and lowering her voice. David rummaged around in a cupboard on the other side of the kitchen for a Tylenol for Rhys, so they had a little privacy. Leda poured one glass for Moira and one glass for herself. "David notwithstanding, of course."

"Come on, Leda, I doubt you've ever been scared of anything in your life."

"I'm not kidding. Do you know I still get the worst stage fright, after all these years? Sometimes I just freeze up, right before I'm supposed to go on."

"I find that hard to believe."

"Stick around a while, I might surprise you."

Moira took a sip and found that, despite Leda's palate skewing more towards cold pizza and beer, she was good at picking out wine.

"Why do you think you still get scared?" Moira wondered.

"Veteran musicians always tell you not to confuse applause with love, but I think we all do, to some extent," Leda said. "Nothing else in the world feels as good as a packed venue of people screaming your name, and trust me, I've tried a lot of other pick-me-ups. But I get worried about letting people down. Like if I play one wrong note, they're going to realize that there's no god underneath the greasepaint and hate me for it."

"Human fallibility is endearing," Moira said. "Besides, who wants to be a god anyway? Sounds like too much responsibility to me."

"You really are as clever as you are pretty," Leda said, in the warm-wide open space between friendship and flirtation that Moira was learning she loved. "I'm glad you came. And between you and me, as much as I love my brother, we don't always know what to talk about when it's just the two of us."

"*Leda*," David wailed, and Moira could clearly hear it, the fact that David was seven years younger. "It's smoking. The oven is smoking. I burned the ham."

"You can't have burned it," Leda said. "You literally just put it in. I watched you."

Rhys peered into the oven, squatting down to assess the situation like one of the competitive bakers on the reality television shows he liked so much.

"It's not the ham," he announced. "You dripped some glaze onto the heating coils. It will stop smoking in a second, just don't open the oven door."

"Oh, thank God," David said, as though Rhys had, through simple observation and common sense, saved Christmas.

"Is David burning the house down?" Max asked, appearing from the great room. "Let me know if I should call the fire department."

"Don't even joke," David grumbled, but he softened when Max leaned over to kiss his cheek. David murmured something to him, and it sounded like *Maxim*, a pet name that was also, if Moira was reading things right, an of honorific.

"I think it will all be fine," Rhys said. "I'll take that glass of wine now though, Leda."

"Fab," Leda said, splashing a double helping of wine into Rhys's glass. "Max, Riesling?"

"Yes, please," he said, holding David by the waist while he took his glass from Leda. Then, to Moira's delight, Max extended his glass to Rhys for a toast.

"To health, wealth, and harmony in the new year."

"To health, wealth, and harmony," Rhys repeated.

They all clinked their glasses together, toasting in unison. Then Leda put back half her glass in one swallow, smacked her lips, and said:

"Now, who here wants to play a game?'

CHAPTER THIRTY-THREE
RHYS

Rhys had never been one to lean on alcohol too heavily when it came to managing his anxiety, but his nerves were so shredded that he found himself reaching for glass after glass of the Riesling Leda had opened, then the Chardonnay she opened after that.

He had hoped going completely cold turkey would weaken his demons. Prior to the trip, he had considered packing travel altars to take with him, and had even started filling Altoid tins and sunglasses cases with pinches of herbs, before leaving it all behind in his study. Bringing the demons with him to Vermont would defeat the purpose of going at all.

He was strong enough to ride out the withdrawal, he had decided. He could resist the press of irritated demons scratching claws down the window of his mind. He could do it.

Now, six hours out from his last hit of demonic power, Rhys was slowly losing faith in himself.

Sometimes, something as simple as time and distance was enough to make even the strongest enchantment fade. Rhys just wasn't sure this was one of those times. Judging by his pounding head (which had only worsened after taking an aspirin), his dry mouth, and the stutter in his heartbeat, it probably wasn't.

Rhys took another swallow of his wine while Leda explained the game, hoping his expression was pleasant, not pained.

"This is the oldest game in occultism, so old it doesn't even have a proper name," she said from her spawl on the couch. They had moved into the great room, discarding shoes and empty wine bottles as they went. "Some might call it chicken, or a pissing contest. I like to call it one-upmanship."

"Games usually have rules," Moira teased. "Got any of those?"

"Let her monologue," David said into his wine glass of sparkling water, eliciting a chuckle from Max, who sat with his arm around David's shoulder. Rhys wasn't terribly bothered by this closeness, and that seemed like a step in the right direction. Admittedly, Rhys's skin felt a bit like he had stood too close to a roaring fire for too long, but that had nothing to do with David's hand on Max's knee and everything to do with the fact that Paimon liked to make Rhys feel like he was in a fiery furnace when Rhys didn't give him enough attention.

"Alright, alright," Leda said, swatting at her brother. "I'm getting to it. Basically, all you need to know about the game is—"

Leda's cell rang, and she answered in her throaty alto.

"Hi, baby, how are you doing?"

It was impossible to tell which "baby" Leda was talking to, and Rhys's ears pricked up in curiosity despite the fact that eavesdropping was a sin. As far as Rhys could figure it out, Leda was somehow romantically or sexually involved with her head of security, her bassist, her ex-therapist and the therapist's wife, and some rope top who lived in Bushwick. Rhys could barely balance his wife and his boyfriend.

Leda made pleasant listening noises for some time, but then her sounds became lower and more dour, with a crease appearing between her dark brows.

"No, I'm going to be in Vermont for two more days. We talked about this, remember? I know you were hoping we could go to the holiday market together tonight, but I just don't have the time... Now, that's not what I said, I didn't mean it that way, alright?"

Gesturing for everyone to carry on without her, Leda stood and secluded herself in a private corner, her shoulders hunched forward as she continued her conversation.

Rhys had every intention of giving her privacy, until he noticed that she was surreptitiously wiping tears off her face.

Rhys cast a glance at David, requesting permission, and David shrugged as if to say, *you can give it a try*. Emboldened by alcohol, Rhys drifted over towards Leda, just in time to hear the end of her conversation.

"Let's not make any big decisions until we're back in the same room, OK? I'm sorry again. I love you. Have a good Yule."

Rhys touched Leda gently on the shoulder and she half-glanced at him, carefully scrubbing at her face so as to not disturb her heavy eye makeup.

"It's fine," she said, voice too tight to be honest. "Just poly scheduling bullshit. You get it."

Rhys made a knowing hum, both because he was intimately acquainted with how badly you could damage your relationships if you didn't manage your time well, and also because he wanted to encourage her to continue talking.

"Eon is bent out of shape because they thought we were going to spend Yule together," she huffed. "I thought we'd come to an agreement that I was going out of town this year and that they were going to go out with their friends instead, but maybe I could have been more up-front... I just wasn't sure if I was going to be here or with Luis, and I didn't want to disappoint anyone, but then I waited too long to tell anyone anything because I'm a flake, and then I fucked off to Vermont thinking everything was copacetic, and apparently Eon didn't even know I had left town until Luis told them, and now *everyone* is mad. So. That's my Christmas so far."

This was the biggest download of personal information Leda had ever given Rhys, and perhaps the longest sentence she had ever spoken to him. She had always struck him as untouchably cool, if occasionally edgy for edgy's sake. While that was still true, Rhys had just uncovered one more indisputable fact about Leda.

Like him, she was anxious.

"Fucking up is just a lesson," he said. "You can either bend over for the universe's cat-o'-nine-tails, take your lashes, and move forward as a better version of yourself, or you can scream and cry and refuse to learn anything. Either way, it still hurts. But the growing pains can also be pleasurable, if you're willing to surrender. It's like a Saturn return death and rebirth thing."

Rhys was positive he was making zero sense, especially after three glasses of wine. Whatever he had just told Leda didn't sound like comfort or even good advice; it sounded like what he jolted awake to scribble in his journal in the middle of the night after an esoteric dream. More philosophical chatter that made him a bummer at parties. He was probably already boring her.

But Leda didn't look bored. She looked electrified.

"You are a real *freak*," Leda said, like Rhys was the untouchably cool one, like it was not an insult but instead the highest compliment. Rhys flushed scarlet. "Alchemizing your own suffering by getting off on Daddy Universe teaching you a lesson? That's next level."

"And at any rate, I'm sure this is a misunderstanding you can smooth over," Rhys said, doing his best to recover from the compliment.

"Yeah," Leda said, not sounding very sold on the hope. But she seemed to appreciate it all the same. "I'm sure you're right."

Leda brought her hands together in a brisk clap, striding back towards the group in the center of the great room.

"Sorry about that, folks," she said, eyes dry, secrets safely stowed in the confessional of Rhys's heart. It was as though she had never been crying. "Anyway! Game!"

"Rules first," Moira pressed. As take-it-as-it-comes as she was in most other aspects of her life, Moira was a stickler for proper gameplay. She refused to play even the most elaborate board game until she understood all the rules, *all of them*, which she then enforced without mercy. Rhys had never had the head for strategy games, and he was bored by anything involving dice, which was fine by him, because occultism and pop punk and the dog-eared copy of *Dune* he re-read every summer were nerdy enough. Also, he didn't find the stereotype about all polyamorous people being obsessed with Settlers of Catan funny at all.

"The best part about the rules is that there are no rules!" Leda exclaimed triumphantly, as though this might delight them all. Moira wrinkled her nose in disapproval. "Everyone gets a chance to show off one of their magic tricks, and the most impressive manifestation of power is the winner."

"That's barely a game," Max said.

"It's a game, alright," David said. "Leda's *favorite* game. We used to play it all the time in Russia. We nearly set the attic on fire once."

"But I still won that round," Leda said proudly. "Don't worry, no pyrotechnics this time."

"But so much of our power is invisible," Rhys said. "You usually don't even know if a ritual has worked until weeks later, and even the most powerful sorcerer can't turn water to wine or lead to gold in front of your eyes. We bend the laws of nature, not break them. What are we supposed to do that's impressive?"

270   ASCENSION

"That's up to you and your creativity," Leda said, retrieving her lighter and a cigarette from her back pocket. "I'll kick us off."

Leda lit the cigarette, pulled a drag deep into her lungs, and then blew the smoke into the nearest empty wine bottle. It curled in blue-gray tendrils inside the glass, suspended as though by magic – or perhaps precisely by magic. Then Leda pressed a kiss to the bottle, murmuring an enchantment against the glass.

"Ever play spin the bottle?" she asked as she sank down onto the rug where Rhys and Moira sat. She beckoned for Max and David to join.

"I'm not playing that kind of game," Rhys said quickly. There was no way playing spin the bottle ended well. The last thing any of them needed were more reasons to get jealous over each other, or more romantic entanglements.

"I will," Moira chirped, hoisting her glass of wine. She had put away just as much wine as any of them, but she was the smallest, and wine always went to her head faster than liquor or beer. "There's no one here I wouldn't kiss."

"That's very sweet of you, Moira," Leda said. "But it's not kissing I'm after. The only thing we're going to get naked about right now is the truth. Watch this. Show me our lovely host, bottle."

Leda gave the bottle a nice, wild spin, so quick that it was impossible for her to control where it ended up pointing.

A few moments later, the mouth of the bottle landed squarely on David. He arched a skeptical eyebrow.

"That one was easy. Give it a harder one," David said.

"I was just establishing a baseline."

"Will the spell still work if you aren't the one doing the spinning?" Rhys asked.

"Of course. My magic is watertight."

"Then you shouldn't be the one touching it. What if you tampered with it? What if somehow this is just sleight of hand?" Rhys was walking through all possible weak spots in Leda's enchantment not because he enjoyed being pedantic (not often, anyway) but because it gave his brain something to do besides focus on the splitting pain in his skull. It was getting worse, somehow.

"Now you're thinking like a magician. You give it a go, then. Ask it anything you want."

"Alright," Rhys said and squared his shoulders. He picked up the bottle, which was warm from Leda's touch and, undeniably, from magic. A good sorcerer could tell something was enchanted just by touching it: the item was always a faint degree warmer than the air in the room. "Let's ask something I don't even know the answer to."

And then Rhys just sat there with the bottle in his hand while everyone look at him. His thoughts were coming embarrassingly slow, dulled by pain. Or maybe anything would feel sluggish compared to the lightning-fast way he could usually calculate contingencies.

"I don't know what to ask," he said, feeling stupid.

"It doesn't matter what you ask," David said. "This is just the control."

"Uh, OK," Rhys said. He was getting the phantom smell of smoldering myrrh, or maybe burning plastic, even though he had double-checked that David had turned the oven off. Ghostly scents were a telltale sign of gathering spiritual energy, whether it was the scent of seawater and roses that accompanied apparitions of Mary, or the stench of sulphur that preceded demonic manifestations. His demons were pressing him towards psychosis, but they only won if he broke. Rhys tried to focus, grasping for a benign inquiry. "Show me anyone in the room who's an only child."

Rhys gave the bottle a spin, and it came to a stop pointing at Moira. She clapped her hands, delighted, but then let out a little gasp when, inch by inch, the bottle began to move again.

"Look at that," she breathed. "Leda, you aren't pulling any strings, are you?"

"No ma'am," Leda said. "Let's see where it lands."

The bottle made a half rotation around their little circle, then came to a stop pointing at Max.

"Was it lonely?" David asked, propping his chin in his hands and looking at Max with open fascination. "Not having any siblings?"

"You tell me. Were you lonely, all those years by yourself?"

"I had Leda for a little while. And the servants and the tutors."

"I don't think household staff really count as friends, David," Max said. He reached out to sweep a stray wave of hair out of David's eyes, a gesture so tender that Rhys felt physical pain in his chest. It was either the tenderness, or a psychosomatic reaction to being this far from his altars. Rhys wasn't sure which one was worse. "But I'd like to hear you talk more about it, sometime."

Rhys cleared his throat. He might be willing to share a house with David and Max, even tolerate them acting coupled-up, but he wasn't about to stand for all this eye-gazing and gut-spilling. He practically had to pry childhood details out of David with a crowbar the first time they were together. It had taken Rhys months to even learn of Leda's existence. It was hard not to take offense at how quickly David had opened up to Max.

"I think I made my point," Leda said. "Even when I'm not touching the bottle, it still works."

"That's a neat trick," Max said, playfully provocative. "But I've seen better."

"And what are you bringing to the table, Mr. Markos?" Moira tittered. "Big talk for a man who hasn't shown us what he's got yet."

Rhys tried not to wince as he remembered Max shutting down Rhys's summoning of Vual with a wave of his fingers. He had seen Max in action twice now, once at dinner and once in his study, and both times Rhys had felt foolish and small.

Still, that didn't mean a third time would result in Rhys's humiliation. Maybe, if he paid attention, he might even learn something.

Max finished the rest of his wine in one swallow, then stood and crossed to an oak bookshelf in the corner of the room. He held aloft an old novel bound in cloth. "What about bibliomancy?"

"Ooh," David said. "It's been ages since anyone's done *that* in front of me."

"Bring me up to speed on what bibliomancy is?" Leda asked.

"It's a very old divination technique," Moira said, fanning herself with her hand. She always got overheated when she drank. "Pulling out messages from randomly chosen passages in a book. Folks sometimes use Bibles, to receive a word from God. My meemaw used to do her devotional every morning with a bibliomancy."

"I don't have such lofty aspirations, but it sounds like your grandmother was a sharp sorcerer," Max said with a warm smile, which made Moira smile back at him. Everything about Max was warm, in such stark contrast to Rhys's dark energy and hard angles. Rhys tried not to hate him for being pleasant and gregarious, for making Moira smile, for making David happy. "But I've always been pretty good at this particular trick. Moira, would you mind being my magician's assistant?"

"I'd be delighted," she said, pulling herself to her feet and walking over to where Max stood. When Moira took his hand she did a little bow, like she was a showgirl on a Vegas stage.

"Beautiful," Max said with a laugh, twirling her on the spot so her skirt flared around her. "All I'm going to need you to do is hold the address of your childhood home in your head nice and tight for me. Just focus on the street name and house number. Can you do that?"

"Easy enough," she said, closing her eyes and lacing her fingers together.

Max trailed his fingers along the deckled edges of the book, taking a deep, grounding breath. The room fell silent as he worked to find his center of power before letting the book fall open in his hands.

"67?" he asked, indicating the page number.

Moira's eyes flew open in surprise.

"Yes, that's right!"

"So, we've got the number, now let's get the street name. I might have to spell it out letter by letter, or I might get lucky, and the correct noun is already in the book."

Max began flipping through the book without looking down at the pages, slowly at first, then faster and faster, scanning the pages at lightning speed with his mind's eye. He muttered an incantation under his breath as the fluttering pages stilled, then he ran his index finger down the typed words until it came to a complete stop.

"Does the name Lillian ring a bell?" Max asked.

"Lillard!" Moira exclaimed. "I lived on 67 Lillard Lane!"

"Close enough," Max said, snapping the book shut and returning it to the shelves.

"You looked her up ahead of time, you must have," Leda said.

" I didn't," Max said. "I might not be as adept at charms as I'd like to be, but I'm good with a book."

Rhys got the distinct sense that Max was being modest, that he could probably do a lot more than he let on. It made sense: Max and Rhys had both started studying magic in college, but Max had a decade of experience on him. Was there a world in which he could accept guidance from Max? Most importantly, was there a world in which that guidance didn't come at the cost of Rhys's pride and the integrity of the Society?

For the dozenth time, he ached to tell David and Moira what Max had offered him. For the dozenth time, he bit his tongue.

"I never had the knack for that, no matter how hard my meemaw tried to teach me," Moira said. "I would try, but I only ever got verses about plagues of locusts or donkey penises."

274 ASCENSION

"Christianity is so weird," Leda muttered, and David made a noise of assent.

"You've got lots of other talents," Rhys reminded his wife as she came to sit beside him. "You should read Max's natal chart and show him how good you are with the stars."

"Oh golly, those charts take hours to calculate and interpret correctly, sometimes days, and I'm not exactly clear-minded at the moment."

"I'm sure there's something else you could do?" Max said with gentle encouragement. He seemed so kind, so different from the conniving, arrogant sorcerer who had asked Rhys to lay the Society at his feet only days ago. The cognitive dissonance made Rhys' head hurt. "You read tarot, don't you? Now *there's* something I'm bad it."

"Show him what you can do, peach," David said, nudging her with his foot from his sprawl on the other side of the circle. As Max leaned in to listen to Moira's introductory lecture about the cards, David cast Rhys one of their private looks. It was imminently approving, tinged with a smile behind David's glass. Rhys might feel like there was a swarm of bees in his brain, but apparently, he was doing a good enough job playing nice that David was pleased with him.

Rhys arched an eyebrow back, as though quoting one of David's favorite movies: *What, like it's hard?*

David's smile deepened just as he cut his eyes away, pretending that they weren't openly flirting. For a moment, Rhys felt at peace, and the pain travelling down his vertebrae abated long enough for him to lean over on an elbow to watch Moira at work.

"We'll start with something easy," she was saying as she pulled the cards from her purse. "Just a one-card pull to help me lock onto your energy. Then you'll be able to try and stump me with a specific question. Sound fair?"

"Very," Max said.

Rhys watched as she shuffled at lightning speed, losing himself in the familiar curves of her heart-shaped face, all round cheeks and a smart, sharp little chin. He was so dazed with wine and infatuation that he almost didn't glance down at the card she pulled, the one he could see better than Max.

It depicted a man with his arms full of swords sneaking away from an encampment where soldiers slumbered unaware.

The Seven of Swords. Betrayal. Deception. Treason.

A microexpression of distress crossed her face, and then she deftly slid the card she had pulled back into the deck with a fluidity that would have shamed a stage magician.

Moira cut the deck with a flourish, giving herself a lightning-quick peek at a few of the cards within easy reach, and produced the Eight of Cups instead.

"You're going on a journey," she said, her interpretation so vague as to be mostly meaningless but delivered with enough confidence that Max would probably buy it. "To get where you're going, you're going to have to leave some old dreams behind. Does that sound right?"

Rhys tuned out the rest of the conversation, his head splitting with pain. He desperately tried to catch David's eyes, but David was wrapped up in some kind of sibling conversation with Leda that was mostly in Russian, so Rhys was left with his own terror while Moira placated Max.

Moira was lying. Moira never lied when it came to tarot, not unless the truth was so dangerous that it demanded to be hidden.

And she had certainly never been wrong, not in the entire time he had known her.

Either someone was deceiving Max, or Max was deceiving them all.

A disembodied whisper hissed in Rhys's ear, so harsh he couldn't make out the word with confidence. But it sounded like *adversary*.

"You're up, McGowan." David asked, oblivious to his torment. "Show us those scary High Priest powers."

"I don't think that's strictly appropriate," Rhys blustered. He needed to get out of this room with Moira's hand clutched in his own to go whisper-plot in a dark room. He didn't know the entirety of what she had seen in the cards, but he knew it wasn't good.

"Come on, fair play's fair play," David said, in that tone that could easily bulldoze anyone without a big enough personality to push back. "You come into my house, and you won't even do a little magic trick for me and my guests? That's not very sporting."

"David, he doesn't feel well," Moira said, voice unexpectedly sharp. She was panicking too. "Let him alone."

David and Leda just blinked at them, baffled as to why the fun had suddenly been sucked out of the room. But Max was staring squarely at Rhys, waiting for his next move. There was no mirth in Max's eyes now, no warmth and good humor.

276   ASCENSION

He was sizing Rhys up as if evaluating his weak spots.

"I thought you felt fine," David said. "Listen, it's just a game, we don't have to–"

"I'm good," Rhys said, drawing himself to his feet even though he felt like he might collapse. This was not the time to roll over and show his belly. He didn't know what Max was up to, but he was confident he didn't want Max to discount him as a threat now. Rhys unbuttoned his shirt cuffs. "I'll play."

"You're not at full capacity," Moira said. "David can go next instead."

She was correct, but she also didn't know exactly how high the stakes were in the room. Max had made it clear that the Society hung in the balance of their rivalry. Rhys had no intention of letting Max believe he was too weak to defend his own order.

So Rhys ignored his wife, which historically had been a bad idea, and rolled his sleeves up past the elbow.

"*Manifestus*," he ordered, splaying his fingers in front of him.

He was fuzzy on what, exactly, he was ordering to manifest, which was a rookie mistake. Good spellcasting required clear intention, focus, and vitality, none of which Rhys had in supply at the moment. But he needed to impress, to really bring the house down on this whole ill-advised trip. At the very least, he had to buy time so he could figure out what the hell was going on.

"*Manifestus*," he said again, trying to grasp the proper spirit name. Moments ago, he had been calling on Naberius, but now Shax seemed closer. Or was it Stolas making his eyes sting and his sinuses burn? There were just so many to choose from, and Rhys's neurons were firing through mud. Rhys wasn't sure if it was the alcohol or the anxiety or the lingering effects of Moira's knock-down drag-out magic, but he knew he wasn't bringing his best.

Still, he had to try.

He had failed at so much already, lost so much. He couldn't stomach losing again.

"Now," Rhys snarled, curling his fingers into a fist.

The sound of electricity dying whirred through the house as every light winked out. The room was plunged into shadow, windows black with the sun long-dead outside. Leda produced her zippo and lit the large three-wick candle on the coffee table, while Max put a hand on David's shoulder and stood, every inch of him alert.

Rhys gazed at him across the ring that had been created by their bodies, his makeshift magical circle. Salt and chalk were ideal, but when it came right down to it, the blood and bone of supernaturally-touched people would do just as well to trap a spirit. Max stared right back, his dark eyes blazing. It felt as though they were the only two people in the room.

"Is this what you wanted?" Rhys demanded, bringing his free hand up to wipe at the wetness dripping down his lips. Blood. He tasted blood. His nose was bleeding.

"Go on, then," Max replied, as cold as the frost clinging to the windowpanes. "Finish what you started."

Rhys's skin buzzed, his demons pressing in on him from all sides. Their presence was so powerful that the air nearly choked him, like he was breathing in smoke. Sense slipped from his grasp as that infernal hissing in his ears got louder, building to a chorus. When he had started this ritual, Rhys had been begging for a manifestation. Now, he just wanted it to end.

But there was no way out but through.

"Max," David said. "What are you–?"

Rhys cut his hand through the air mercilessly, spitting out the final Latin chant that would force the spirit to join them fully. He rushed the invocation, but even though it felt like pulling teeth, even though it ached like he might be spitting up blood at any moment, he finished the damn thing.

For a long moment, there was nothing, just the sound of his hammering heartbeat and labored breathing in his own ears. Rhys stood there in the dark, feeling increasingly idiotic with every passing second.

"I–" he began.

"Shh," Leda said, her face eerie in the candlelight. "Listen."

A scrabbling sound echoed from down the hall, growing louder as it approached.

If Rhys didn't know any better, he would have thought it was the sound of claws on hardwood.

A large black dog trotted into the room, red tongue lolling between pearly white teeth. It was roughly the same size and shape as a borzoi, but more muscular through the shoulders, broader in the snout. It stood stock-still in the entryway to the great room, panting as though it had just run a long distance.

"That's…" Rhys stammered. He couldn't get the words out. His anxiety kicked into overdrive, turning to trembling nausea.

"You keep dogs out here, David?" Leda asked, extending her hand to the dog to invite it over for a friendly sniff.

"That's not a dog," David said, pulling her back by the wrist.

The dog didn't seem interested in Leda at all. It just stared at Rhys with impossibly black, reflective eyes, as metallic and colorless as a scrying mirror.

"What is that?" Moira said.

"A m-manifestation I've only ever read about," Rhys stammered. "The black dog. I. Um. In Faust, and in older legends, it–"

"Demons appear as black dogs when they're ready to make a deal for a sorcerer's soul. We call them mephistos," Max supplied, chillingly calm. He was staring at Rhys with open disgust, or perhaps pity. "Are you really so willing to do anything for power?"

"I didn't ask for it to appear," Rhys said, edging up on hyperventilation. "I didn't want this, I would never–"

"This isn't fun anymore," David said, real terror in his voice. "Send it away. It can't have you. We're not doing this."

Rhys raised a trembling hand, moving through the quick, cutting motions of the lesser banishing ritual. But he didn't move fast enough, and the dog turned and lumbered away just as quickly as it had come, its footsteps receding eerily into the house.

Static crackled along Rhys's skin, growing to an intense buzz that made him want to claw his skin off. He went through the motions of the lesser banishing ritual again, and then again, but to no avail. That tension kept building, wriggling down his spine like an electric eel.

"It's not over," he said, voice wavering. "Everyone get down."

"Rhys, I'm scared," Moira said. "You opened the door, just close it. Why can't you send it away, I–"

The electricity reached a screaming fever pitch. Rhys wrapped his arms tight around Moira, pulled them both down onto the floor, and braced for impact.

A winter storm so ferocious and sudden it could have only been supernatural lashed against the windows and rushed down through the chimney. Rhys's teeth rattled at the arctic blast, but he held Moira fast. Leda stood stock still until Moira yanked her down into their heap of bodies. Max and David huddled together, and David slammed his hands over his ears, yelling out expletives that were snatched away by the wind.

Above their heads, masses of black shadows swirled together. The flickering candlelight cast horrific shadows against the wall, of bodies with too many limbs and necks bent at strange angles. An ugly rumbling sound very much like laughter echoed through the great room, and even stalwart Leda yelped at that, burrowing deeper into Moira's neck. Rhys clutched them both, eyes turning towards the heavens to witness what he had wrought.

In his arrogance and his weakness, he had flung the door wide open to not just one demon, but his entire spirit court. He had invoked not just the devil, but all the unfettered powers of hell.

And now he and everyone he loved was trapped inside the house with them.

"God, forgive me," he breathed.

CHAPTER THIRTY-FOUR
DAVID

The backup generator kicked on, and the lights overhead flickered to life. David was sprawled on the ground, half in Max's lap, and Moira and Leda cowered against Rhys. There was no sign of the demons that had been marching through the room moments before, but David knew from the ache in the base of his skull and the cold sensation dripping into his stomach that they were far from gone.

The demons had merely made themselves scarce for the time being, probably receding into the darkest corners of the house.

"What the *fuck*, Rhys?" David demanded. He didn't have the energy to be nice about this, and moreover, he was scared shitless. "A mephisto? You know what those things are capable of. You've seen what making a demon deal did to my family, to me! Was one ancestral curse not enough for you to deal with?"

"I didn't call for a mephisto," Rhys snapped, clambering to his feet. He had scrubbed the blood from his face, but there was still a rusty smear down his neck. "Do you think I'm stupid? I was just trying to summon one demon, but I couldn't focus, and I got distracted–"

"Obviously!"

"Max was antagonizing me–"

"Oh my God, are you *seriously* going to try and make this Max's fault?" David said, not just meeting Rhys' volume but doubling it. Fighting with

Rhys was not the most productive thing he could be doing in that moment, but it was a distraction from the fear crackling through his veins like radio static. "You did this Rhys, you and no one else! Now your whole fucking retinue is running rampant in my house."

"You were the one who insisted we play that stupid game!"

"Hey, easy," Leda snapped. "No need to get pissy just because you can't keep your demons on a leash."

"This isn't about you!" David said, gunning her down in the crossfire. "Stay out of it, OK? I can handle this."

"Obviously not," Leda scoffed, examining her nails. "This party is a bummer."

"Would it kill you to take something seriously for five seconds, Leda?" Rhys demanded. He sounded about fourteen years old, and David felt fourteen too, ready to wrestle Rhys to the ground and throttle him.

"You do *not* to talk to my sister like that. Especially not when you're in my house."

The air was split by a piercing whistle, breaking up the quickly devolving fight. Shaken from his anger, David turned to see Moira with two fingers in her mouth. She who was standing before Max, staring him down while he stared right back. Neither one of them were smiling.

"I think things have gotten a little out of hand–" Max began diplomatically.

"I don't want to hear another word out of you unless you're answering a question," Moira said, each word dipped in ice. David had never seen her so angry. It was somehow more frightening than any demon. "Seven of swords. Do you know what that card means?"

"No," Max said, scowling up at her.

"It means you're a liar," Moira said.

"What are you implying?"

"I'm not sure I know yet. But we're not leaving here until you tell me."

Max stared her down for a long while, waiting for her to relent. When she didn't, Max simply stood and gathered his coat and keys.

"It's been a stressful night," he said, voice perfectly calm. David had always loved that voice, but now, instead of sounding reassuring, it sounded like placation. "None of us are thinking straight right now. It isn't safe to stay here in this weather, especially if the generator gives out, and there's very little we can do against a houseful of demons by ourselves. I propose we go home, get some sleep, and regroup with backup."

"Look outside," Leda said, unimpressed by Max's attempts to captain a sinking ship. "Storm's still raging. You can't drive in that."

"David can. He learned how to drive on iced roads in Russia. We can all take my car back to Boston; that's just one vehicle to dig out of the snow. If we get going soon, we should make it in one piece." Max turned to David with those kind brown eyes, a crease of insistence between his brows. He sounded irreproachably sincere. "Please come with me. I just want us all to be safe."

David considered going with him. It would feel so good to let Max bundle David up in his scarf, to be the hero who drove them all safely back to Boston, to abandon the house and its demons to whatever darkness wished to devour it. But something didn't feel right here. Moira had planted a seed of doubt in David's mind, and if there was one person whose judgement he trusted above all others, it was hers.

"Answer Moira's question first," David said. "Then we can go."

"David. Come on, this is–"

"Answer her," David said, laughing even though nothing was funny, even though he was starting to get nervous. "Just answer the question, Max."

"I never wanted to hurt any of you," Max said holding his hands up in a gesture of surrender, as though bracing for violence. All of David's hope left him in a deflated rush.

"What have you done?" Moira asked, her face a maelstrom of fury.

"I was only fulfilling my obligations to my order," Max said. "I had nothing to do with the trouble you folks have found yourself in this winter, and I have never wished ill upon any of you, but I'll admit that when I released that letter I hoped–"

"*You* released the letter?" Rhys demanded, striding forward. Leda caught him by the arm, holding him in place with her kickboxing-hardened biceps. He looked like he had half a mind to claw free, then claw Max's face off. "You published a private document with my name on it, with *all* our names on it, and you made me feel like I was losing my mind? I was convinced I had sent that email in my sleep!"

"It had nothing to do with you personally, although I admit I was concerned about your leadership capabilities," Max said.

"How the fuck do you even get access to my email, I–"

"Just because you don't know the spell for something doesn't mean I don't," Max snapped, and now he was getting irritated. David knew he should probably step in and play referee, get the story straight, try to make some sense of what he was hearing, but he couldn't move. His ears were ringing, high and tinny.

"Okay but *why*?" Leda demanded.

"All societies crumble the same; through infighting and scarcity of resources. I saw the writing on the wall. I was only expediting a process that would otherwise be drawn-out and painful."

Rhys started yelling, releasing a torrent of words David barely heard. He felt like he was floating above his own body, watching himself take the barrage of betrayal on the chin the same way he had taken his father's blow. He couldn't breathe. He didn't remember how.

"—ignited a city-wide Satanic panic!" Rhys was shouting. His feet slipped against the hardwood as he struggled to break free from Leda's grasp. David was dimly aware that he should help his sister, that he was probably the only one in the room besides Max strong enough to pin Rhys down if it came to that. He had done it before, but only ever in play. He never wanted to have to do it for real.

"Please don't be dramatic," Max said. "I didn't do–"

"What about Moira! What about David and Dion and Leda and everyone else in the city? You fucked with livelihoods, Maximilian!"

"I'm truly sorry for that, I am," Max went on, desperation rising in his voice. "I was just trying to put a little heat on you, and make you see that if there was a natural opportunity for the OTO to absorb the Society and share resources, everyone would benefit, and we could fix the optics problem together, and–"

Rhys let out an insane peal of laughter, as though he had just discovered the formula for the sorcerer's stone.

"Oh my God, I was right about you from the start!"

Max's expression darkened, and then, for the first time in David's memory, Max lost his composure.

"Sorcerers are a dying breed," he shot back, loud enough to make Moira jump. "Every year, another order schisms, or dies, or is consumed with scandal. All I have ever tried to do is unify us under one umbrella so we can cultivate real power and better protect ourselves. If this whole debacle proves anything it is that no matter how civilized society pretends to be, people are still more than ready to burn witches when they need someone to blame."

"So that was your plan the whole time?" Rhys went on. "Infiltrate us, destabilize the community, instate yourself as leader?"

"You're not listening to me. I came to that meeting at the tea house for altruistic reasons. It wasn't until I saw how obviously underwater you were, how worn down David was from carrying every single summoning, and how much debt you were in that I decided on a mercy killing. I know you're a smart man, and I know you understand sense. Why choose dissolution and obscurity when there's more strength in numbers? All I ever did was try to save this Society you obviously love so much."

"And you lied to me," David said, voice barely audible. Max looked at David, the anger on his face breaking like a storm cloud. He strode over and spoke in a low, urgent voice, like he needed to get all the words out at once.

"Please listen to me. Yes, I released a statement that was not mine to release, which I am willing to take responsibility for. But I never lied to you."

"And getting into my bed was just part of following orders from your higher ups, is that it? Screw the Aristarkhov heir and win him over to the OTO?"

"Nobody asked me to do any of that. I would have never brought you into the OTO unless you wanted that for yourself. Everything I've ever told you about how I feel is true. I admire you, and I respect you, and I couldn't stand to see you taken for granted by the Society or treated poorly by your High Priest–"

"Rhys treats me well."

"Rhys *wastes* you," Max said, gripping David's hands. The touch burned, heavy as lead, but David was powerless to pull away. The anger was catching up with him though, building inside him and begging for release, even if it had to burst through his skin. "You're one of the most extraordinary magicians I've ever met. You're a generous friend and an even more generous partner, and more importantly, you're a good man. I want to see you celebrated, not sequestered away in a basement running spiritual interference for magicians who can barely pronounce their Latin, called to heel by a man who confuses love and control–"

"*Tell the truth!*" David thundered. He didn't hear it until it was out of him, how every word was dipped in solid gold charm, absolutely irresistible in its intensity.

Here was the truth of the matter, when you got right down to it: David Aristarkhov was much more powerful than he let on, and he was certainly capable of doing more with his inherited gifts than winning court cases. It wasn't that he was afraid of the power inside him, it was that he resented it, just as he had resented his father for the way he had swanned though life on money and might and no merit at all, picking up whoever he wanted along the way before discarding them like cracked baubles.

David never spoke loud enough to crowd out someone else's will – not because he didn't know how, or because he was too good to stoop so low. He never charmed anyone like this because above all else, even when it backfired, he wanted to be liked, and he wanted to be able to trust that people liked him for who he was, not the illusions he could spin.

But right now, he didn't care if Max liked him at all.

Max stared at him, eyes shining with hurt and confusion and utter, total submission.

"I love you, David," he confessed. "I think you're one of the last great enchantments left in this world. I love you so much it hurts to look at you, sometimes–"

"Stop it," David whispered.

"I love you, and you can send me away but that won't make it stop, and that's the truth, it–"

"Get out of my house," David said, wrenching his hands out of Max's grasp and breaking the spell.

The room was silent as a tomb for a long while. Max looked as though he had been slapped, like David had committed the highest violation against him, which in some ways, David thought miserably, he had.

David bit the inside of his mouth as tears stung his eyes, staunching the flow with pain. Aristarkhovs didn't cry.

"David," Rhys said quietly. He turned to find Rhys standing at the window, his arms wrapped around him as he peered out into the night. "Look outside."

David strode over to the window, and his heart fell into his shoes.

The storm had already blanketed the ground with snow, and it was raging so ferociously that David could hardly make out the outline of the cars parked in the drive. Icy wind blew sideways, battering the home. Any visibility that may have remained was smothered by indistinguishable fog.

"It's a whiteout," Moira said. She tucked herself in at David's side and he put a tight arm around her, soaking in her body heat and the sensation of her fear.

"No one is leaving tonight," Max said, staying exactly where he was a safe distance away from all of them. He wasn't looking at David. He was looking at nothing at all. "And that storm's not stopping until we banish those spirits."

In the quiet that ensued, David could make out what sounded like papery whispers drifting towards them from the darkest recesses of the house.

CHAPTER THIRTY-FIVE
MOIRA

Moira wasn't a smoker, but she wished she was as she watched Leda, David, and Rhys light up, volleying theories back and forth as they burned through the last of David's pack of Parliaments. Having a little something to take the edge off while they all tried to figure out what to do about the demons and about Max sounded appealing, and sipping water wasn't cutting it.

They had been at this for twenty minutes, and had found nothing close to a viable solution. And the house was only getting colder.

Moira nodded at her husband in a silent request and Rhys raised his eyebrows before handing her his half-smoked cigarette. Moira took a ladylike drag, like a pageant girl sneaking a smoke backstage before making her public debut, then handed the cigarette back to Rhys. The nicotine gave her a bit more clarity, but it made her nervous heart hammer faster, so it all came out in the wash.

Max had not been offered a cigarette, nor a glass of water, because, as David had succinctly put it, Max no longer had rights.

"You're sure we can't call Dion?" Rhys asked the room.

"Dion wouldn't know what to do with a demon if you handed him a grimoire," Moira said. "It's not his area of expertise."

"Zachary?"

"Zachary might know what to do, but I've still got no bars. What about you?"

Everyone in the great room checked their phones before making disappointed noises. Cell service was spotty out here on a good day, David had explained. Throw a vortex of ice and malevolent energy into the mix, and all bets were off.

"If we can figure out what the demons want, we might be able to find a way to fix this," Leda said. She had been brave enough to poke her head down some hallways and take a quick survey of the house. The backup generator was powering the wing they sat in, but many of the other parts of the building were still dark. And those dark rooms, Leda had informed them, felt *wrong*.

"I think what they want is pretty clear," Rhys said. There were bruises around his eyes like he hadn't gotten proper rest in days, and he was holding a dishrag to his nose, which wouldn't stop bleeding. "They want to twist me into someone who will feed them no matter the cost, or, barring that, bargain for my soul. Either way, I'm the one they followed here. I'm the one who's responsible for this."

"You fucked around with dark forces, and you found out what the cost was," David said from his seat next to Moira on the couch. He had his hand on her ankle, refusing to stop touching her even for a moment. At this point, Moira wasn't sure if she was grounding him, or he was grounding her. "It's a long and storied tradition. There have got to be other sorcerers who went through this and made it out alive."

"I should have listened to both of you," Rhys told his partners. "I was arrogant, and I refused to ask for help until it was too late."

"And you didn't take help when it was offered to you," Max grumbled under his breath. He was sitting in the great room's leather wingback chair, as far away from David as possible. He had spent most of the last twenty minutes scowling out the window in silence.

No one else seemed to hear him, but Moira had been watching Max like a hawk since she pulled his tarot card.

"What was that?" she asked.

"Ask Rhys," Max said. "This isn't my mess. But I did offer to clean it up."

"What's he talking about, baby?" Moira asked.

Rhys sagged down onto the arm of the couch. He didn't look like he had another hard conversation in him. Leda, who had wedged herself into the windowsill and was smoking while keeping an eye out for a break in the snow, put the pieces together first.

"Tell me you didn't turn down a solution to all this suffering just because of your ego," she groaned.

"It wasn't just because of ego," Rhys said. "Max came by the house. He figured out what was going on, and he told me he could sever my ties to all my demons. Permanently."

"And you actually considered that?" David asked, staring at Rhys as though he had been body-snatched. "Rhys, you've spent your entire adult life building up your demonic stable. Some of those spirits have been tied to you for damn near a decade. The entire time I've known you, mastery over them is all you've ever wanted."

"What does that matter when it rots me from the inside out?" Rhys muttered. "Why gamble my soul just to gain the world?"

"So, there *is* a solution," Moira said, thrusting a hand towards Max. "Make him help you. God knows he's got amends to make."

"It wasn't a bargain I was willing to make," Rhys said. "Max offered to help only if I agreed to annex the Society to the OTO. I couldn't do that to the people who trusted me. We might be small and broke and riddled with infighting, but I believe in this organization. If it goes down, I'm going down with it. I told Max no. And I didn't tell you all about it because I didn't want you to think I was letting jealousy get the better of me again."

Moira had never seen David look at Rhys with such unbridled love, such ferocious pride and tenderness.

"You're not as bad as you make yourself out to be, do you know that?" David asked Rhys. Then, he turned to Max and jabbed a finger at him. "And *you* are a piece of shit."

Moira swatted his hand down. She wanted to lay into Max just as badly as David did, but there was no point in them eating each other alive before the demons did.

"There'll be no bargain and there'll be no annexation," Moira said. "Max is going to help us for free."

"I'm not exactly feeling very much like helping any of you right now," Max said, crossing his arms. He was probably expecting her to beg or fawn or at least butter him up to convince him to lend a hand. But Moira was plum out of tolerance for the wounded egos of men.

"David, charm him again," she ordered.

David blinked at her in shock. He probably thought she was bluffing, but she was not. She had been pushed too far over the last few months, and she was mad and scared, and what wouldn't she do, to save her husband's soul?

"Moira, that's–" David began. He looked like a deer caught in headlights, like the total breaking of Max's will might break David too. Moira wasn't actually sure what sort of toll a thing like that might take on David, or how long he could maintain total control over another person, so she pivoted.

"Fine. If you won't make Max help us, I will."

Max looked her up and down.

"And how exactly does a tarot reader intend to do that?" he muttered.

"I was willing to use domination oil on my own husband," Moira said, colder than the storm outside. "What makes you think for a second I won't use it on you?"

Max stared her down for a long moment, but Moira didn't so much as blink. Let him try to wait her out. He would be sorely disappointed when he realized how stubborn she was.

Finally, Max dropped his eyes to the ground, the universal sign of mammalian submission.

"I knew a young woman in Seattle who got in over her head with Valefar, a duke of hell," he said. "He overtook her completely. It took me and six other magicians working in tandem to dissolve that tether. Do you know how hard it is to sever one spiritual tie, let alone a dozen? You're going to need salt, lots of it, and candles, and the expertise of someone who's presided over a working like that before."

"Let me guess, that person is you?" Leda sneered.

"Yes. But I'm not making any promises. If I had the time to prepare a ritual, to seal off the room, to choose other magicians to help, we would have a better shot at this. As it is, we're going to need everyone in this room firing on all cylinders."

"And what do you want in return?" David demanded.

"Nothing," Max said, finally meeting his eyes. Moira was a good judge of people's character – better than good, she had a damn near supernatural talent for it. Max had flown under her radar, and she was cross with herself about that, but now she saw the reason she had never felt unsettled around him before now. When he spoke, he told the truth, even if it was only partially, and when he looked at David, it was with something dangerously close to real love. "Just promise me you'll take care of yourself, and I'll leave you alone."

David said nothing for a long while, just chewed on the inside of his mouth. Hard, like he was trying to dig something out of the flesh

Finally, David nodded and spoke.

"Leda, salt is in the kitchen. Moira, there should be candles underneath the sink and in the hall closet. Rhys, you're with me; do whatever Max tells you to do. I want to set a world record for the fastest exorcism known to man and then I never want to see you again, Maximilian."

Max merely nodded, the picture of courtesy, but Moira caught the tightness in his mouth, the pained flash in his eyes.

"I can make that happen," Max said.

CHAPTER THIRTY-SIX
RHYS

Maximilian Markos was the last person on Earth Rhys wanted to be taking orders from, but desperate times called for desperate measures. So, he did as Max instructed, working with Moira to lay out a circle of salt large enough for an adult to lie down in on the hardwood floor. They encircled that outline with another ring of salt, with enough space between the circles for people to stand. Rhys watched as Leda placed lit candles at strategic points around the circle, and as David took down Max's dictated ritual on his Notes app, not missing a detail.

Rhys's heart thrummed against his ribcage as he carefully filled in gaps in the circle of salt. Rhys hadn't been inside a ritual ring since the summer, when he had dragged David back from the brink of death by offering himself in David's place. Rhys could still feel that unholy heat searing his chest, could still taste the blood and bile in his mouth as his body rebelled against onrushing possession.

He was not eager to get into a circle again.

Max had yanked off his sweater and was down to shirtsleeves, like he anticipated having to physically fight something off.

"For this to work," he said, adjusting the placement of the candles, "Rhys is going to need to be cooperative."

"I'm cooperative," Rhys said, bristling. Moira, who had been helping him sweep up excess salt, put a steadying hand on his elbow.

"You say that now, but you might feel differently when you're in the circle. It's imperative that you comply with whatever Moira tells you."

"*I'm* leading the ritual?" Moira said.

"Rhys loves you," Max said, a simple statement of fact. "He'll be more inclined to listen to you than to me. And if your spellwork at that dinner party was any indication, you have a talent for domination magic. That will serve you well when you're ordering demons around. I'll support you in every way I can, as will David and Leda. But if you aren't comfortable doing this, I won't make you."

"I'm comfortable," Moira said, not to Max, but to Rhys. Rhys squeezed her hand, overcome with a powerful love and a powerful fear. He might be willing to risk his own skin every week in the ritual room, and he might trust David to hold his own in a circle as well, but that didn't mean he liked the idea of Moira stepping into one.

He had to keep his faith in her. She was strong. She could do it.

"Good," Max said, giving her the quick nod and formal half-bow of one sorcerer welcoming another into the circle. Moira, seemingly grasping this small ritual on instinct, bowed back.

"Tell me how to help him," David said, like that was the only thing that mattered in the world, like David would open a vein and bleed if that was what it took. Rhys felt sick to his stomach, he loved him so much.

"You'll be acting as scryer, to help us see what's happening on the astral plane, that way Moira can keep her focus on Rhys," Max said. "Moira will stand here, at the north head of the circle. David, you take east; Leda, the west. I'll hold down the south."

"Got it," Leda said, taking her position between the two circles of salt. She stretched her arms, wiggling her fingers to summon every drop of magic from deep within herself. "Now what do we do?"

"We kill the lights," Max said.

Cold trickled down Rhys's spine.

"Why?" he said. "Darkness is a demon's playground. The lights are keeping them at bay."

"We don't want them at bay," Max replied. "We want them close at hand, so we can banish them the moment we're able. The outer circle of salt should protect us from the worst of their scare tactics, so don't step outside of it for any reason, any of you."

Max stepped into his place between the two circles of salt. Moira followed suit, planting her feet as she became their north star.

"What about the mephisto?" Rhys asked. He hadn't been able to stop thinking about those black, empty eyes. "I know how to deal with the other spirits, but I've never even seen a mephisto before."

Max gave him a strange, weighty look.

"Only you'll know what to do about him, and it will only be when the time is right. Now, take your place in the inner circle."

Rhys swallowed hard but he did as he was told. He looked into the eyes of his lovers and friends, seaglass green and walnut brown and crow black. Finally, his gaze came to rest on Max, who passed Moira David's phone to read from.

"Your pronunciation doesn't have to be perfect," Max said. "Just give it your best shot."

"I know how to pronounce Latin," Moira shot back. "And I love my husband enough to do better than my best, thank you very much."

Rhys's chest burned with admiration. This was Moira operating at one hundred percent, tender and vicious in equal measure, completely unashamed of herself and her abilities.

If Moira could be brave, so could Rhys.

"Leda?" Max said. "The lights."

Leda flicked the great room lights off, plunging the room into the flickering glow of candlelight. The temperature in the room immediately slid downwards at least ten degrees as she hurried back to her place.

"They're coming," Moira said, eyes lit with premonition.

"Good," David said, rolling up his sleeves to reveal his *Monas Hieroglyphica* tattoo. "I'm ready to be rid of the little bastards."

Moira fixed Rhys with her steady gaze, then raised one hand in the air in a sign of benediction and began to recite.

Rhys spun to face the sound of hissing coming from one shadowy corner of the room, then his eyes snapped up to follow the sound of keening laughter from above. He could make out nothing in the darkness, despite the eerie way the sounds echoed through the room, but judging by Moira's wide eyes and David's steely grimace, the demons were congregating.

"David, talk me through this," Leda said. Rhys was grateful, as always, for her willingness to speak up and ask questions.

"I'm spotting three black masses, four humanoids, and at least one animalic manifestation in the room with us now," David said.

"Two animal manifestations," Moira corrected. "Don't you see that messed-up deer by the sofa?"

"Focus on the Latin," Max said. "No need to double-check your scryer's work."

Moira wrinkled her nose at him.

"I'm getting tired of you, Mr Markos," she said, but she turned her attention back to the phone screen and resumed her chanting.

Rhys did everything he could to focus in on his wife, waiting for the spell to take effect. When the bonds that tied him to his spirit court began to dissolve, would he feel it? Would it hurt?

"Come on," Rhys said under his breath. Sweat trickled down his neck and into the stained collar of his shirt. He might not be in control of his demons anymore, but that didn't mean he couldn't address them. "Do something already."

He quickly regretted leveling that challenge. White hot pain shot through his ocular nerve, and before he knew it, he was on the ground on his hands and knees.

Rhys's vision went black at the edges, and he was hurled forward into a vision that blocked out everything else in the room.

He saw himself as though in a dream, seated on a black marble throne with a crown of gold set with blood-red rubies on his head. He was flanked by torches, bathing his stern features in firelight. At his right was a wooden chest, and as he plunged his hands into the chest and retrieved a fistful of silver medallions, they spilled over his feet.

Rhys shivered, every extremity bathed in cold. He was sucked deeper into the scene, until he found himself occupying his own body, gazing out into his throne room. Before him, dozens of occultists kneeled, his Society friends and former Society High Priests, even figures from history– John Dee and Samuel Mathers and Solomon himself. They had all come to pay homage to him, the sorcerer above all sorcerers, the king in darkness.

It was everything Rhys had ever wanted, and it was just out of his reach, glimmering like a heat haze.

Rhys hadn't understood Max earlier when he warned him to remain cooperative. He had already made up his mind to banish his demons; he had clear reasons for doing so and real people he wanted to protect in the process. But tumbling in this vision of all that power and glory was more intoxicating than he had ever anticipated. He didn't just want to sit on that throne, he *desired* it, and that desire burned through him like covetousness, like lust, like an ambition so sharp it would cut anyone who came near it.

"I'm not ready," he ground out. It was all too much, too ultimate a final decision. "I can't let it all go. Not yet."

Moira was saying something in a pleading tone of voice, but Rhys couldn't hear her. He was too rapt by the vision, too wrapped up in the sensation of cool metal in his hands and that crown, heavy on his head. Moira spoke again, sterner this time, but her words were snatched away by his own blood roaring in his ears.

You can have everything, a symphony of voices whispered in his ear. Some chittered, some hissed, some purred, but they all spoke as legion. *Let us in, and we will deliver your wildest dreams to you.*

In the fantasy, Rhys gazed upon the faces of his deferent admirers. Even Antoni was looking at him with terrified adoration.

It was only then that Rhys realized that Moira was nowhere to be seen in this fantasy. Neither was David. Rhys was entirely alone, with no queen at his side or prince leaning over his throne to advise him.

In the vision, Rhys was exactly the man he had been constructing for a decade. A man who had sanded down his accent so he could more easily pretend to be at home among his wealthy college friends, a man who had refused to let either his grades or his occult studies slip even if it meant sleeping four hours a night, a man who had attacked every ritual with a ferocious determination to succeed until he was, unequivocally, the most powerful sorcerer in the Society. Until he was High Priest. A man without peer or equal, a man feared by those too envious to love him, a man who wore holiness like a fur coat and wielded the powers of hell like a weapon.

A man entirely alone.

Accept us, the cascade of voices said again. The sound slithered over his body like a brood of serpents. *Do as we ask, and we will serve you well, sorcerer.*

Moira could have been screaming herself hoarse at the moment, and Rhys would have never heard her. All he heard was that voice, sinuous and beguiling, weaving in and out of his ears.

The choice was clear. Choose to walk the path of infamy alone or turn his back on everything he had worked for.

Rhys lived under no illusions; he knew exactly what he was. He was a bottomless pit, a yawning maw of pride that swallowed up everything and everyone that got in his way. He was cruel and calculating, more often in love with his own ambitions than he was with any human being.

When you got right down to the heart of it, Rhys McGowan was a monster of his own making. And he didn't deserve any of the love he had been shown.

In the vision, Rhys rose to his feet. All the occultists kneeling before him cowered, pressing themselves closer to the ground.

He reached up and took the crown from his head, turning it over in his fingers. The metal was cold to the touch, the peaks of beaten gold so sharply pointed they could draw blood. He sank into all that desiring, letting it fill him from head to toe. He memorized the shape of it, the weight of it, the way it burned in his belly.

Then Rhys reared back and dashed the crown to the floor, watching it shatter into a thousand glittering pieces. He was ripped out of the vision as though by a clawed hand, and found himself once again in his own body, panting and sprawled on the hardwood floor.

"He's made his choice," Max said. Rhys blinked, the room around him coming into bleary focus. Moira had her hands up, chanting with a furrow between her brows, while David and Leda held down their energetic points. "First hurdle crossed. Everybody lock in. Things are going to get rough."

"Rough how?" Rhys demanded, his voice coming out in a rasp.

The wind outside picked up, rattling the shutters as it tore against the house. Rhys could see his breath in front of his face.

"The ties that bind have been dissolved," Max said, his voice carrying over the racket. "Your demons have no master now. You need to send them away, Rhys."

"I'm not exactly flush with power right now," Rhys snapped back.

"Come on, McGowan," David said, his green eyes darting around as he tracked the demons through the room. "Not afraid, are you?"

Rhys knew from David's tense stance and bloodless lips that David himself was terrified, but he also knew that David was trying to keep Rhys focused and fighting by appealing to their long-standing competitive streak.

He had never loved David more.

"Alright," he responded, damn near shouting to be heard over the wind. "But I'm going to need them to hold still long enough for me to banish them."

"On it," Leda said. "David, direct me."

"Manifestation on your left, eleven o clock," David said.

Leda cut a sigil through the air with her fingers, probably one of the dozens of homebrewed magical symbols she kept in her back pocket. Slowly, something materialized on the physical plane, in the form of a stormy cloud of shadows hanging over Rhys's head. Leda grunted with exertion, both hands thrust into the air as she struggled to hold it in place.

"Work fast," she ground out.

Rhys formed the sign of the cross over his body as he began the lesser banishing ritual of the pentagram, which should have been sufficient to banish any demon, but as the black mass above him grew, his heart sank. The weight of that mass bore down on him, oppressive and malignant, and for a moment, he couldn't figure out what was wrong.

Then Rhys realized, with crushing horror, that it was not just one demon swirling above him, gnashing its teeth and hungry for his soul.

It was all of them.

"Max–" Rhys began, voice thin with panic.

"I know. I see them. But you have to try."

Rhys tried. He tried to execute the crispest and most laser-focused lesser banishing ritual of his life, pouring every last drop of himself into the spell. But as he drew his pentagrams out in the air and invoked his divine names, the mass didn't diminish. If anything, it only seemed to get darker, larger, more angry.

His eyes found Moira's across the circle. Her fingertips were shaking with the effort of keeping the ritual going, but she was doing magnificently.

She nodded at him, urging him forward. He was out of options, and he was out of strength, but maybe there was one more route to salvation open to him. It would take the kind of faith he hadn't been able to muster in ages, but for Moira, he could try.

Rhys closed his eyes in the circle, dropping his hands from their authoritative sorcerer's stance. He forced his mind to clear, blocking out the cold and the fear and the all-consuming weight of his demons bearing down on him.

If he did this, there was no coming back. If he asked for aid and actually received it, he would be tying himself to the only power that frightened him more than infernal spirits, a power that would ask everything of him and accept only his best, with the highest discipline and utmost purity of intention.

There would be no demon-summoning for Rhys after this. Not now and perhaps not ever.

Rhys grasped in his heart for something more demanding than ambition and more potent than greed: perfect submission.

He waited until the emotion consumed him, crashing over him like ocean waves, and then he pressed his hands together in prayer.

"Saint Michael the Archangel," Rhys breathed. "Defend us in battle."

Rhys's stomach trembled as the scent of sand and sweat and sweet herbs invaded his nose, and he was nearly blinded by the golden light that flashed through the room like an atom bomb. He didn't know if anyone else in the circle could see that light, if it stung their eyes and scorched their retinas with pure, unbridled glory the way it did his. He was nearly driven to his knees by the force of it, by the overwhelming power that rushed through the room.

The swirling mass above Rhys's head shrieked like a swarm of insects enveloped in a cloud of pesticide.

"Be our protection against the wickedness and snares of the devil," Rhys said through gritted teeth, determined to finish the prayer even if it killed him. "May God rebuke him, we humbly pray; and do thou, O Prince of the Heavenly Host, by the power of God, cast into hell Satan and all the evil spirits who prowl about the world seeking the ruin of souls."

The black mass above Rhys's head broke into pieces, torn apart like a hare in the jaws of a hound, and their piercing cries of agony nearly split Rhys's eardrums. He clapped his hands over his ears, crouching down to shrink from the cosmic turmoil above his head.

"*Amen!*" he shouted, willing this to be over and done with for good.

When he opened his eyes, the light was gone, and the darkness above him had winked out of existence.

There were no sounds except the labored, terrified breathing of the other magicians in the room. It was only this quiet that made Rhys realize the punishing storm outside had evaporated. The snow was now falling so lightly it made no sound.

Rhys looked out to window to see a black smudge in the white landscape. The mephisto demon waiting patiently for him, looking at him down that long snout. As though it had been driven from the house but would not take its final leave of them until Rhys made his choice.

Rhys shook his head at the mephisto. There would be no deal struck today, or any other day, no matter what the demon offered in return.

The mephisto cocked its head, then turned and trotted off towards the woods. It disappeared totally into the dark, leaving no footprints behind.

Leda broke the silence first.

"Thank fuck," she said, bending over to brace her hands on her knees. She hauled breath after breath into her lungs, wiped to the point of exhaustion. David blinked the otherworldly gleam from his eyes and then hugged his big sister, nearly lifting her off the ground.

Rhys all but collapsed onto the ground, lowering himself awkwardly onto the hardwood. Moira crossed the circle of salt and joined him. Rhys was wrapped in that familiar cloud of rose and sandalwood perfume, and the sweet animal musk of her skin below that as she twined her arms around his neck. He breathed her in, holding her close.

"You did wonderfully, little goddess," he murmured against her cheek.

"So did you," she whispered back. "I thought I saw something, there at the end. Some kind of light. Was that—"

"Yes. I'll explain it later," Rhys said, putting a hand out for David.

David clambered down onto the floor with Rhys and Moira and draped his arms around both of them. Rhys heaved an adrenaline-shaky sigh, pressing his face into David's chest. And then, to Rhys's surprise, Leda walked up to him, gripped his shoulders hard, and leaned down to kiss the top of his head with a proud smack, like he was her little brother just as much as David was.

Rhys was so wrapped up in the near-death euphoria of it all that he didn't even look up to see if Max was still in the room. When he glanced around, he found Max watching them from a safe distance, his arms crossed across his chest as though to ward off any misunderstanding about him being a part of this. But, if Rhys was not mistaken, there was a small smile of triumph on his face.

Rhys nodded at Max.

Max nodded back.

CHAPTER THIRTY-SEVEN
DAVID

None of them stayed in Vermont long after that. The cheery Christmas atmosphere had been shattered by demonic forces, and after being snowed in with no power, everyone was eager to get back to the comforts of the city. David felt sullen about having his grand designs for a holiday with all his favorite people ruined, even if it had all turned out alright in the end. And he felt Max's betrayal as sharply as a knife through the heart, avoiding eye contact with the other man as they packed up their guest bedroom. When Max reached for him as he passed, an apology on his lips and his suitcase half-packed, David didn't even acknowledge him.

He should have seen it. He should have paid better attention, instead of following the wild impulses of his stupid heart. Nobody ever liked him so much without an ulterior motive.

David gave Leda a big hug in the front yard before she rode away.

"I'm so glad we're talking again," he said, because he had no words to express the enormity of the gratitude he felt for all the times he and Leda had saved each other over the years, from fathers or demons or their own self-destructive tendencies.

"Me too," she said, giving him the same wink she had given him to cheer him up when they were children. "But why is it that every time we hang out someone is on the brink of death? Let's just, like, go to the movies next time."

"Deal," David said.

"Ciao," she said, and smacked a kiss to his cheek, no doubt leaving a smudge of black cherry lipstick. With that, she hopped onto her motorcycle and sped away down the winding back roads of Vermont.

David scooped Moira up in a hug that made her toes leave the ground, then kissed her on both cheeks, like a spell of protection. Rhys smiled, a glimmer of his old self shining through like winter sun through storm clouds, then he leaned in and kissed David. It tasted like an apology, and a promise of better days to come.

"I'm sorry I've been so intolerable," Rhys murmured. Moira politely wandered a little further towards the Lincoln, tapping away at her phone so as not to eavesdrop. "I should never have let things get so bad. I should have stepped down sooner, and I should have been kinder to you."

"You're not wrong," David said. "But I also shouldn't have said all those things to you in conclave, either. About your parents and stuff. That was low."

"I think we're more than even now," Rhys said. "But I am sorry about Max. Truly."

"Well, men are trash," David said, with a blithe sarcasm that only made him feel empty. He cast a glance over his shoulder to Max, who was loitering by his own car, turning his keys over and over in his hands. David had already informed Max that he would be driving himself home, using one of the beamers from the garage to return to Boston. "I'll bounce back."

"I love you," Rhys said.

"I love you too," David said, pulling him into one last hug. "Now get out of here before you freeze to death. Take good care of Moira for me until I see you both again."

Rhys opened the door to the Lincoln for his wife, slid into the driver's seat, and then carefully began backing the car down the drive.

That left David and Max alone outside the house, looking at each other like strangers.

"Drive safely," David said, his hands thrust deep in his pockets, standing an easy eight feet away. That was about as much goodwill as he could muster. If Max tried to sweet talk him or apologize, David would explode.

But Max did neither of those things. He just walked right up to David, like he wasn't frightened of him at all, and leaned down to press the lightest kiss to David's cheek. David imagined himself shoving Max away but instead he just stood there, his chest tight, his heart in his throat.

"Be well," Max said quietly, and that was all. He turned and walked back to his car, then pulled down the drive without looking back at David.

He waited until Max's range rover disappeared into the trees before he turned back to the garage.

The drive back to Boston was long, cold, and lonely.

The Vermont trip had been his first attempt at holiday cheer in a long time, and that had been a spectacular failure, so he fell back on his old ritual of working right up until the holidays and then spending Christmas Eve by himself. In the past, he would have spent it watching 90s action movies while draining a magnum of red wine, but he was a new man now, so that meant that the wine had been replaced with sparkling water.

On Christmas Eve, David cracked open a Perrier, draped himself across the couch, and tried not to think about Max, or Rhys and Moira for that matter. The holidays were busy for families, and even though David desperately wanted to show up on their doorstep like a feral cat meowing for table scraps and scratches behind the ear, he resisted the urge to insert himself into their marital bliss.

He was the boyfriend, not the husband. The friend, not the lover. He needed to remember his place.

But just as he was settling in to watch *Desperado*, his phone rang.

"Hey, Rhys," David answered, trying not to sound overeager. "What's up?"

"What are you doing right now?" Rhys asked. He was bright and clear, flush with confidence.

"Nothing," David replied, snatching up the remote to turn down the sounds of gunfire and agonized screaming from his surround sound system.

"Are you sulking in that million-dollar eyesore of a condo?"

"What else would I be doing?" David said snappishly.

Rhys laughed on the other end.

"I thought you might have had plans! You know, with other human beings? Then I remembered that you're weirdly misanthropic about holidays. Listen, come by the house. Moira and I miss you. And no one should be alone on Christmas."

"Technically Christmas isn't until tomorrow."

"Don't be such a lawyer about it."

"I'm really fine," David said, his instincts towards rugged individualism kicking into overdrive. "I don't want to interrupt your holiday with your wife."

"My wife loves you, and you're my boyfriend. Why wouldn't you be welcome in our home?"

"Because it's *your* home, you and Moira's, your little married-person feathered nest. I don't want to overstep or overstay my welcome."

"Is that what you're worried about?" Rhys asked. David had believed that if they ever had this conversation about him sometimes feeling like a third wheel it would turn into a fight, but now Rhys only sounded curious. "Listen, if either of us never need any space we'll tell you, and I would hope you would tell us the same thing. But you're not an inconvenience. And it's not the same without you."

David made a noncommittal noise, loathe to let Rhys know how much hearing that meant to him.

"If it makes you feel less weird about the whole thing, Antoni will be dropping by later too. He wants to talk to you."

"What about?"

"Show up and maybe he'll tell you. Just put on an ugly Christmas sweater and get over here."

David didn't own anything ugly or Christmas-themed, but he did own plenty of cashmere, so he pulled on a buttery black turtleneck and a somewhat festive blue herringbone blazer, splashed on cologne, and drove to Jamaica Plain. The small townhouse where Rhys and Moira lived had been positively bedecked, with boughs of greenery hung over the door and twinkling white lights outlining the roof. David took a moment to just look at the house when he arrived, taking in the scene. He didn't really go in for all that holly-jolly stuff, but he had to admit that there was something appealing about a house waiting for him, filled with warm yellow light and the voices of people who loved him.

He shook the thought away before he could get too sappy about it.

He knocked on the door and Rhys appeared, looking like an Irish-American Christmas card in a lambswool sweater and with his old Saint Michael medallion sparkling between his collarbones. Or maybe it was a new one; David remembered the medallion as tarnished and this one gleamed bright silver. Rhys kissed David soundly on the front stoop for all the world to see.

"So happy you made it," Rhys said, and he really did sound happy. David tried not to acknowledge how good it felt, to be wanted like this. Opening his heart to people had led to nothing but catastrophe recently, and he was still leery about letting Rhys back in fully after all their recent disputes. But he found himself pulled by the hand into the cinnamon and pine-scented house.

Moira appeared from the living room, wearing a green wrap dress with a sprig of mistletoe pinned into her hair with a red ribbon.

"David, you're here!" she exclaimed. His arms were open to her before he even knew what he was doing, and moments later she was snuggled in his embrace. She had swapped out her usual perfume for something that smelled like sugar cookies in a hot oven.

"Mistletoe," he teased, brushing his fingers over the greenery in her hair. "Very forward of you, Ms Delacroix."

"It's good luck to kiss me," she said, and David obliged her, pressing his lips to her temple.

"Is Antoni here yet?" David asked, glancing around.

"In the living room," Antoni called, and David found him seated on the antique couch Rhys had rescued from a roadside sale, perfectly at ease with a snifter of port in his hand. Apparently, something had happened between Rhys and Antoni when David wasn't looking that had smoothed over the rift between them.

"What are you doing here, Bresciani?" David asked, pulling Antoni into a one-armed hug. "Doesn't that giant family of yours do a bang-up feast of the seven fishes?"

"Everyone decided to take a Caribbean cruise this year," Antoni said. "I would have just spent the entire trip holed up in my cabin seasick as a dog. Rhys and Moira were good enough to invite me over. Come over here and have a seat. I've got a proposition for you."

"Business first," Rhys said, handing David a wine glass of sparkling water sweetened with a splash of cranberry juice. "Then, with that out of the way, we can have apple cake. I've been baking up a storm."

"He wouldn't let me lift a finger in the kitchen," Moira said proudly. Perhaps, David hoped, the scare in Vermont had finally put Rhys's priorities in order. "But trust me, you're going to want to hear what Antoni has to say."

She curled up in an armchair, tucking her stockinged feet up under her, and Rhys perched on the edge of the couch nearest David. Antoni took a long swallow of his port, then leaned in towards David.

"I heard about what happened in Vermont," he said. "I'm sorry about Max."

"The only person to be sorry for in this situation is Max," David said coolly. "In case you haven't noticed, I'm a catch."

"Sure, sure," Antoni said with a roll of his eyes. He would get details out of David later, probably when David was pinned under a barbell with nowhere else to go. David had been meaning to check in with him about the tax audit anyway, to see if Antoni had any luck convincing the government to let them operate in peace. "Nathan said he and Kitty are starting to get calls from magicians who are interested in the Society again, but not like they were before. Looks like Max did some real damage with that letter."

"No damage would have been done if I was more careful," Rhys said. "It's amazing how all it took was one person applying pressure for cracks to spread through the Society."

"I think you mean through you," David corrected.

"That's what Rhys and I have been talking about," Antoni said. "Now that he's feeling more like himself, and eligible for the Priesthood again."

So that was Rhys's angle. Invite David over and butter him up to win his vote. Society scheming, at least, was familiar. It was easier to process than freely given love and affection.

"Got it," David said. "Rhys, at this point, I'll do whatever it takes to avoid more controversy. Quite frankly, I'll vote however you tell me to."

"I don't want your vote," Rhys said, settling his hand on David's knee. "And I don't want the Priesthood. Not all of it, anyway."

"That position is the only thing you've wanted since I met you."

"Things are different now. There are things I care about more than the Priesthood. You, Moira, my own health and sanity. I obviously cannot be trusted with unchecked power, so I'm not going to accept it."

"So... Antoni is taking over?"

Antoni's dark eyes sparkled, a sure sign of a scheme brewing.

"Not exactly. What we're proposing has never been done before, but we think it could work."

"So, what, exactly, are you proposing?"

"A triumvirate," Moira put in, holding up a trio of fingers. "Three leaders, sharing power equally."

Now, David was really listening.

"What, you, me, and Antoni?" he asked Rhys.

"That's the idea," Rhys said. "I know you saw everything that happened in Vermont, but I'm not sure if you actually knew what was going on behind the scenes. You didn't happen to see a bright light there at the end, did you?"

"I saw a lot of things. It's not my job to ponder signs and symbols, it's my job to scry. So there was a light, so what?"

"How much do you know about archangels?"

"I avoid them," David said. "They're lawful-good nuclear reactors. Not my style."

"Right. Unlike a demon, an angel actually cares about your ethical conduct and moral character. They'll come when they're called, especially in times of desperation, but if you want to cultivate a long-term relationship with an angel, you have to play by their rules. And that means, at the very least, that you work with angelic energy exclusively."

"And promising to cultivate that sort of long-term relationship," David said slowly. "That's something you're thinking about doing?"

"It's something I've already done," Rhys said, toying with the medal in the hollow of his throat. "It was Michael I called on, and Michael who saved me. I'm bound to him now, and he's going to expect me to act honorably moving forward."

David stared. He couldn't fathom a Rhys who didn't move through the world flanked by demons, a Rhys who didn't drive himself to the brink of exhaustion summoning all the forces of hell. David didn't really believe in heaven and hell in the classical sense, and he wasn't big on God, but he couldn't deny that there was a dichotomy of energetic currents that kept the universe humming. The Society specialized in wrangling the darker currents in pursuit of their goals, but Rhys, apparently, had surrendered himself entirely to a force just as powerful and just as frightening, but which played by entirely different rules.

"You really gave it up," David said. "All that power and you just–"

"I wouldn't say I gave up power completely," Rhys said, a cunning smirk pulling at the corner of his mouth. This was the Rhys David knew, still present amidst the moral clarity and dedication to reform. "I'm just going to have learn how to harness a different type of power. But I won't be summoning demons any time soon, not even to demonstrate a technique in conclave."

"What about Baelshieth? He's a demon. Did your scary Catholic angel magic nuke him too?"

"No. That's a blood tie, more difficult to forge and complicated to break. He's still with me, I can't explain it but I can feel it. I believe that Michael could have done something about him, if he wanted to. But I get the sense that Baelshieth is my dragon to slay."

"And I'll help you with that," David said.

"We all will," Antoni swore as Moira made a humming noise of agreement.

"Antoni is the most adept among us when it comes to spirits," Rhys went on. "And I'm pretty good with the bureaucratic side of things, and the research. I can handle the paperwork and the translations and the sourcing of new spells, if Antoni will lead the rituals and manage the money."

"Where does that leave me?" David asked.

"Every empire needs a mouthpiece," Antoni said, waggling his eyebrows.

"Everybody loves you David," Moira put in. "You're an occult household name. If you can handle the social side of things, the events and the outreach and the public relations, I think you all could build something really solid here. Together."

"I've been thinking about what Max said in Vermont," Rhys said, spinning his wedding ring. "About me wasting your talents and taking your work for granted. In that, at least, he was right. I'm sorry for that. I want to celebrate you for what you can do in the circle, but I don't want to burn you out, and I want to trust you with more responsibility, if you're willing to take it on. Also, you've offered to infuse cash into the Society a dozen times, and I've never let you. I know I have hangups with money, I'm working on it, and I still don't like it when you pay for everything when it's just to two of us. But this isn't about the two of us, it's about the Society. So, if you really want to, I'll let you kick some money Antoni's way to he can tie things up with the IRS."

David's mind whirred. David had a rebellious streak a mile wide and wasn't built to sit behind a desk and flip through dusty tomes. But Rhys certainly was, and Antoni could hold his own in the ritual room any day. If David could be left to his own charming devices, empowered to entice new blood into the Society and make shining appearances at public events as the Society's legacy golden boy, if he could actually get over his aversion to being seen trying at something he might fail at before he got good at it…

"Say yes," Moira urged, jabbing him with her foot.

"I'm thinking," David said, catching her by the ankle before she could poke at him again. Excitement surged through her and into David, overpowering any hesitation he felt.

"Come on," Rhys put in. "Say yes. It won't work without you."

"You had a hand in this didn't you?" David asked Moira.

Moira held her thumb and forefinger close together, indicating that she may have helped, just a teensy bit. Knowing Moira, it was probably more than a bit.

She was cut out for the Society, after all.

"Alright," David said with a nod. "Let's do it."

Moira let out a squeal of delight as Rhys and Antoni both clapped David on the back, talking over each other in congratulations.

"But I want an ascension ceremony," David said, raising his voice over all of them. "With all the bells and whistles, and a party afterwards. And I want new business cards. And redecorating privileges over that cave of a High Priest's office."

"You can have whatever you want, David," Rhys said, a wide smile on his face. In that moment, David felt that perhaps, Rhys was right to trust him with power. Maybe David wasn't inherently irresponsible, and maybe, he might even find that he enjoyed having more responsibilities, so long as he had the freedom to fulfill them on his own terms.

"Happy to hear it," David said, taking a swig of his mocktail. "Now somebody give me a slice of cake."

CHAPTER THIRTY-EIGHT
RHYS

Christmas Eve was a delight, with Rhys, Antoni, David, and Moira sitting up late into the night, eating too much cake and drinking too much port, and sketching out a hundred dreams for the Society. They argued and came to consensuses, divvied up responsibilities, and encouraged each other to share their ideas with no fear of being shot down without being fairly heard out. Moira perched on David's lap and detailed her strategies for forging stronger bonds with other occult leaders while Rhys made them all sobering tea, and David kept an arm bracketed around her waist so she wouldn't slip while he leaned forward to move pieces of brainstorming paper around on the coffee table. When Antoni left at one in the morning, he pulled Rhys into a tight hug at the doorway that spoke volumes without anything having to be said.

They were forging a new path together, one built on cooperation and trust and most importantly, daring.

Rhys woke up the next day flush with potential and filled to the brim with good cheer, until he remembered that it was Christmas Day. He was expected at his parents' house at 11am sharp.

His heart banged against his ribs like a battering ram as he buttoned up his crispest shirt and even reached for a tie before he got frustrated with fumbling the knot and abandoned it.

"No matter what Mary Ann and Arthur say," Moira told him as she retrieved the length of green silk and tied it perfectly around his neck, "your people will be here for you afterwards."

"Thanks," he had said hoarsely, then let her kiss him until he felt half like himself again.

Moira was set upon by Rhys's little sisters the moment she stepped foot in the modest Southie home where he had grown up. She was fabulously popular with all three of them. Veronica, who was enrolled in trade school to become a dental technician, thought she had a good head on her shoulders; Dolores, who was eighteen and had just barely squeaked out a respectable score on her SATs despite her lousy reading comprehension, adored the fact that she ran her own business; and Brigitte, the baby of the family, who was currently making a name for herself as a sophomore baton-twirler at her Catholic high school, thought Moira's vintage clothes and Southern slang and art school degree were the height of cool.

"Moira!" Brigitte cheered, throwing open the door and hugging Moira around the waist. Her frizzy red curls had been pulled up with a festive velvet scrunchie.

"I'm right here too, Bee," Rhys said as he stepped across the threshold.

"Yeah, yeah," Dolores said, appearing from the kitchen with a smudge of powdered sugar on her nose. She looked the most like Rhys, with the same pale freckled skin and dark hair, but she was stocky like her mother. "What'd ya get me for Christmas?"

"Nothing at all if you keep running your mouth." Rhys turned towards his oldest sister, who was curled up on the couch under a blanket with her nose in a book. "Hi, Veronica."

Veronica blinked a few times as though startled out of a private world. She was the changeling of the family, and looked nothing like either of her parents, with her watery blue eyes and flaxen hair.

"Oh, hi John Michael."

"What are you reading?" he asked, glancing at the cover of her secondhand paperback. "*Wuthering Heights*, huh? Isn't that a little heavy for the holidays?"

"I think it's romantic," she said dreamily, probably still away on the moors with Heathcliff and Cathy. "Tragic, but romantic."

"Oh sugar, I've got to get you onto some proper dark romances," Moira said. "I'll email you a recommendation list. Don't tell your mom, alright? Are you more of a mafia girl or a monster girl?"

"Is that my favorite daughter in law?" Mary Ann called from the kitchen. She emerged a with a gingham apron tied around her waist, her curls piled up out of her face. Rhys had never known his mother, even at her most harried, to be caught without her mascara and lipstick on or without her hair pinned up. He had ribbed her about it once in middle school, and she had given him the most somber look and explained that self-respect was one thing the world could never take away from you, and that it showed in the way you carried yourself.

"I'm your only daughter in law," Moira laughed, and hugged Mary Ann. Rhys's mother was not a big hugger, not even with her own children, but Moira was so endearing that she always got greeted with a hug. Arthur appeared a moment later, wiping his hands off with a dishrag. He had probably been glazing the ham, or placing the easy-rise rolls on parchment paper, or doing whatever else Mary Ann would allow in her kitchen domain.

"Good to have you, John Michael," he said, pumping Rhys's hand before clapping him on the back. He was in good spirits today, as formal as ever but still jovial. Arthur was a traditionalist when it came to the holidays and expected pristine hygiene and punctuality and decent dress from all his children at the Christmas meal, but it was only because he cared so much.

Mary Ann said something that made Moira let out a peal of laughter, and Rhys's heart constricted at the sound. Everything in his world was absolutely at peace, ordered and calm once again. He was loved by his parents, he was accepted by them, and his wife was adored by everyone in his family.

Everything was perfect, and he was about to burn it all to the ground.

"Who wants to eat?" Arthur said, already ushering Moira and Rhys into the kitchen. "Ham's just about cooked. Come on in and sit down."

Rhys got through dinner with the requisite smiles and friendly chatter and even managed to say grace without his voice breaking. Then, when the plates had been cleared and Moira had strategically drawn the girls into the living room for a cutthroat game of UNO, Rhys bit the bullet. This was, in part, what he had come here to do.

He had promised David. He had promised Moira. It was well past time.

"Can I talk to you both for a minute?" he asked.

Mary Ann looked up from scrubbing the dishes – by hand, since they had never been able to afford a dishwasher – and Arthur stopped sweeping up and pushed his reading glasses into his greying hair. He sat down at the table, the very same table Rhys had used to do his homework at, since the room he had shared with Veronica was too small for a desk. This was where they had all been sitting when he broke up with his first girlfriend (they had only ever gone on three dates, but it had still felt like the end of the world) and when Rhys opened his acceptance letter to Williams. Everything important that had ever happened in this family happened at that table, and Rhys had always imagined doing this here, if he was ever able to work up the courage.

"You can always talk to us," Arthur said, so kind that Rhys wanted to douse himself in kerosene and light a match. His father worked himself to bone at the electrical company, but he always had time for his son. "What's on your mind?"

Rhys's mother abandoned her rubber gloves and took a seat, giving Rhys her undivided attention.

"I need to tell you something," he said, already disassociating.

"Go ahead, John Michael," his mother said encouragingly.

"Actually Ma, I prefer to go by my middle name." Somehow, ripping off that little Band-Aid was easier than ripping off the bigger one. "Most other people call me Rhys. It would nice if you did too."

Arthur just nodded, looking faintly confused but otherwise unbothered. The lines around his eyes and mouth had deepened, Rhys noticed. When had his parents gotten so old? How had he managed to go this long without having this conversation?

"Fine by us, Rhys," he said.

Something about the sound of his father saying his chosen name spurred Rhys into further action. The words tumbled off his tongue before he had another moment to second-guess them.

"That's not what I wanted to tell you. I'm bisexual."

Mary Ann just stared at him, and for one horrible instant Rhys thought he might have to actually define the word for her. But then she put her hand on top of his, nodding sagely.

"We've had an inkling for some time," she said.

Rhys felt like he had just been slapped in the face.

"You *knew*?"

"You're our son. Of course we knew."

"And you didn't tell me?" Rhys said. The world was spinning too fast.

"Not our business to tell you if you don't want to tell us," Arthur said. "But you were never very good at sports."

Rhys bristled. His father was supportive, but he also always had a note or two for Rhys's improvement.

"I was good at baseball," Rhys said.

"Decently good," his father conceded.

"We thought, of course," Mary Ann said, stepping in before the two men lost themselves bickering, "that things changed, after you met Moira and settled down."

"Bisexuality doesn't work like that," Rhys said, trying to keep calm and remember the talking points he had rehearsed with Moira. "Just because I'm attracted to Moira doesn't mean I'll never be attracted to another person. It doesn't mean that I can't..." Rhys cleared his throat. This was the hard point, the pinnacle he was working up to. "Be in love with men or women. Or anybody else."

"And that's fine," Mary Ann said, squeezing his hand. "You know it's not our place to judge you for the way God made you. I don't care what Father Mulligan says; I know what's right. David loved Jonathan didn't he, as his own soul?"

In any other world, this would have been a win, and even now, with another huge secret hanging over his head, Rhys felt grateful tears prickle at his eyes. He wanted to stop the world right here, in this moment of acceptance, and live in it forever.

He wanted it to be over. He never wanted to have to come out to his parents again.

Unfortunately, that was exactly what he needed to do.

"Do you remember David Aristarkhov? My..." Rhys swallowed. "Roommate sophomore year?"

"Of course," Mary Ann said. "Tall blonde boy, right? Very charming. You said he moved out of state once he graduated."

"Not quite. And he wasn't my roommate. He was my boyfriend. Actually, he sort of still is."

A storm cloud settled over Arthur's features, making him impossible to read. Rhys hated when his father got like this. He might have been confused, or angry, or sad, and it would be impossible to know which until he spoke.

"Sort of. What does that mean?" Arthur asked.

Confused it was, then.

Rhys withdrew from his mother's touch and clenched his hands together in his lap. It would be easier, he decided, to pull away first, in case she wrenched her hands away when she heard his confession. Rhys wasn't sure he could handle that.

"Not sort of," Rhys said, forcing himself to look his father in the eye. "David is my boyfriend. We got back together six months ago. I love him the same way I love Moira."

There was a long beat of agonizing silence. Rhys's parents looked at each other, and Arthur shook his head in bafflement, indicating that he was way out of his depth.

"How does that work, exactly?" Mary Ann said slowly.

"It works because we work on it," Rhys said, finding his momentum. "We take care of each other, and we look out for each other, and we do our best to respect each other's time and feelings. It's no more simple or more complicated than any other relationship."

"But at your wedding," Arthur said. "You swore to be faithful to Moira. How does she feel about this?"

Rhys glanced over his shoulder into the living room, where Moira was hammering Dolores with a quadruple play that left Dolores with a fistful of cards.

"Moira and I talk through everything. We make it work. And she loves David too, in her own way. The three of us just… go together."

Arthur nodded slowly, looking off into the middle distance. Rhys sat stock-still, waiting for his father's condemnation or acceptance.

In the end, he didn't get either.

"This is going to take us some time to process," Arthur said. "But we appreciate your honesty."

Rhys' ears were ringing, as though a bullet had just whizzed by his face. Relief and despair battled it out in his stomach, making his gut churn.

"That's very fair," he said.

"Is there anything else?" Mary Ann said, putting on a brave face even though she was looking very pale. Rhys wasn't sure either of his parents could withstand another shock, and he wasn't sure he could stay upright long enough to deliver it, so he decided to table the occultism conversation for another time.

"No," he said, his voice barely above a whisper. "There's nothing."

"Then why don't you get out there and play a round of cards with your sisters? They've missed you something awful," Arthur said. Then he propped his chin in his hand, losing himself in thought as he stared off into the distance, and the conversation was over.

Rhys stood on shaky legs and wandered into the living room, where Brigitte was crowing about being down to only two cards. He leaned down over Moira and kissed the top of her head.

"How did it go?" she whispered.

"We all survived," he murmured back.

He might not live in a perfect world anymore, but for the first time in his life he lived in an honest one, and that, for the time being, would have to be enough.

CHAPTER THIRTY-NINE
MOIRA

Every year, Rhys insisted that he didn't want a birthday party, and every year, Moira ignored him. She had heard too many stories about the anticlimactic parties of his youth, always four days after Christmas, when all the money had already been spent on the few presents his parents could afford. She considered it one of her personal callings in life to make sure that every single one of Rhys's birthdays after meeting her were worth remembering.

She arranged for catering so neither of them would have to cook, then filled the house with burning candles and winter greenery. It was a spread suited to Rhys's tastes: dark and moody, with plenty of spruce boughs and dripping red wax and stark white camellias. Rhys protested at every stage that it was too much, but she saw him smile when she uncovered the platter of thinly sliced meats and imported cheeses, and she caught him running his thumb in admiration along one of the camellias. He even dressed for the occasion, wearing all his silver rings and a smudge of eyeliner.

Moira invited all his closest friends. David, of course, and Leda and the Vos. Antoni and Cameron arrived together, carpooling in Antoni's chrome-trimmed Chrysler 300, and soon the house was filled with the sounds of clinking cutlery and laughter. Moira had opted for a more casual feel, with no assigned seating, and encouraged everyone to mill about the lower level of the house with their drinks and plates in hand.

318   ASCENSION

Moira watched the party with deep satisfaction, paying attention to every smile – genuine, if a little overwhelmed – that crossed Rhys's face. For the first time in what felt like ages, Rhys was fully present when he was at home with her, and he was home more often than he was away. He had tried to bend the rules to grant her an honorary Society title, which she had refused, but he had instead gifted her a golden signet ring engraved with the Society's acronym on Christmas Day. Apparently, he had it commissioned months ago, to thank her for all her support as his queen. She proudly wore it during the party.

The night passed in a blur of laughter and red wine and good company. Leda ended up telling wild touring stories to the delight of both the Vos, and Antoni sat in a nearby armchair goading her on by demanding more dirty details. Later, Moira overheard a conversation between Rhys and Kitty in the kitchen that answered most of the lingering questions she had about that particular dynamic.

"All I'm saying is that there was a delicate balance going on that you disrupted," Kitty said, airy even in her criticism as she poured herself a glass of water. Rhys watched her with concern while Moira lingered just out of sight in the hallway. "I've always maintained my friendship with Antoni while gently encouraging him to seek romance elsewhere. If I thought he needed a firmer hand, I would have set him straight. I'm a big girl, Rhys."

"I know that," Rhys said. "And I'm sorry for meddling. I just thought there was something else going on, like you were attracted to him or–"

"Who says I'm not attracted to Antoni? If I wasn't married, he could probably get me to break my rule about not dating men under twenty-five. But I've already made my match, and I wouldn't risk Nathan for the world. I love what you and Moira and David have, but it's not for everyone. I like to keep the fence around my house shut, if you know what I mean. And while we're getting into this, did you seriously think Nathan didn't know? He's not stupid. But unlike you, he doesn't view sentiment as a weakness, and, most importantly, he trusts me."

"Sounds like you're very lucky to have him, and it sounds like you three have it all figured out," Rhys said, nodding his head in deference with a smile. Moira admired the way Kitty put him in his place without losing her cool, not for a second.

"The next time you feel like white knighting for a woman's honor," Kitty said, briskly patting his cheek, "how about you talk to her first?"

"Yes ma'am."

"Good. Now get out there and enjoy your party, birthday boy."

Moira grinned and disappeared down the hall before Rhys could catch her snooping.

As the night wore on, Cameron pulled David and Rhys into an enthusiastic round of poker, and even Moira found herself bluffing like her life depended on it at the card table. Rhys tapped out after a hundred bucks wagered, but Cameron took David for whatever he was willing to bet, and ended up cleaning David out of half a grand before Moira called the game, not wanting to see her kitchen turned into a casino. Cameron leaned back in his chair and counted his money with a self-satisfied air. David threatened to finance a career in professional poker if Cameron ever got tired of teaching undergraduates about exegesis.

When Moira brought out the cake with help from Leda, who lit the candles with her Zippo, and David, who led them all in a rousing chorus of "happy birthday", Rhys flushed red as a beet. Kitty took pictures for posterity, or perhaps, for a little blackmail of her own.

After gift-giving (and even more embarrassed but appreciative noises from Rhys), folks started to drift home. Moira hugged all her guests at the door, and once Leda finally headed out, Moira followed the sound of David's voice back into the kitchen.

"Tell me what you want," he was saying.

"I've got everything I want," Rhys said with a laugh. "I have you and Moira, I got through coming out to my parents, I had a very nice birthday party *and* got some wonderful gifts. You don't have to do anything else."

"Come on, the Breitling watch was just a warm-up. You nearly killed yourself between the High Priesthood and what went down in Vermont. I want to make this year memorable."

Rhys held his hand out to Moira as she entered the room, and she perched on his lap, draping a hand over his shoulders. David was leaning against the edge of the kitchen table, facing them both.

"I forbid you from getting me anything more," Rhys said, faux stern.

"Yes, sir," David replied, flirtatious.

Rhys used the hand he wasn't using to steady Moira to tug David in for a kiss. It was quick and brazen, and left the indentation of Rhys's teeth in David's lower lip.

"I want a kiss too," Moira pouted.

"Then come and get one," Rhys said, more playful and at ease than she had seen him in a year. Moira, feeling bold, threaded her fingers through Rhys's hair and tugged, tilting his face back so she could capture his mouth in hers more easily. When she pulled away, Rhys's eyes were bright with desire, and David was staring at her with shock and delight.

Moira came back to herself, suddenly self-conscious. David's wit could be cutting, and her slowly blooming interest in bossing Rhys around in the bedroom was not something she wanted him to poke fun at.

Happily, he had no off-color comment to make.

"At least let me buy you a new Lincoln," he went on, nudging Rhys with his knee. "Or a little trip to Lake Como, nothing extravagant."

"Absolutely not," Rhys said, with a toothy grin. "I would be absolutely furious with you."

"But I like it when you're mad; it keeps things fresh."

Moira let out a groan and swatted at David. Her hand was still on David's chest when he leaned in to steal another kiss from Rhys. This happened to be the exact moment Rhys tightened his hand on her hip, digging his thumb into the soft juncture between her thigh and her pelvis, and Moira let out a soft, surprised gasp.

Moira realized a moment too late David could no doubt feel her pulse of arousal. Moira could count the number of times he'd seen David blush on one hand, but if he wasn't mistaken, there was heat in his cheeks now.

Moira snatched her hand away.

"Oh golly," she fretted. "Sorry, I didn't mean to–"

"It's alright," he said with a laugh, rubbing a circle over that spot on his chest. He couldn't stop looking at Moira like she was a newly discovered wonder of the world. "It didn't feel bad. Just sort of... tingly. Velvety? Warm. It's hard to explain."

"Do either of the psychic wonder twins want to let me know what's going on?" Rhys asked, still in good spirits.

Moira and David just stared at each other for a long while, recalibrating. She didn't shrink back from his searching gaze. She just looked right at him like he was one of those boys she had grown up with who bet ten dollars she wasn't brave enough to dive from the top of the local waterfall into a swimming hole. She looked at him like she was going to clean him out of his lunch money, and maybe rock his world in the process.

"Your wife is all hot under the collar for you," David said, but didn't look at Rhys. He was still looking at Moira, like he was running rapid-fire calculations before coming to a conclusion. "I can feel it."

If Moira was right, and David was thinking what she was thinking...

David glanced down at his smartwatch and pulled up his calendar, which was the most David thing he could possibly do in this situation.

"I don't need to be anywhere until eleven tomorrow. I could stay over, if you wanted me to." David gave Rhys his most charming smile, pulling on deep ancestral magic to seduce boyfriend. "Do you want to go upstairs?"

"What, now?" Rhys asked, smile faltering in confusion. He was never the quickest on the uptake about these sorts of things. "But tonight is one of my nights with Moira, I–"

"And I'm happy to share," Moira piped up.

Rhys just stared at her like she had started speaking ancient Sumerian.

"You're... You're not–"

"I am."

"But... David is gay," he said. While he might be putting up a scandalized façade, Moira knew her husband well enough to know this sort of transgression held a certain appeal, and the wild light in his eyes gave away the fact that he was just as turned on as she was right now.

"I'm gay, but I'm a good sport," David said, catching her eye.

She caught his drift right away. They didn't have to become directly involved with each other, but exchanging a little energy in the heat of the moment wouldn't be the worst thing in the world.

"You can't be serious," Rhys said. "You two planned this. It's a joke; you're just messing with me."

"When have I ever joked about what I want?" Moira said. "And why shouldn't we all get exactly what we want, especially after all we've been through together?"

"Even that?" Rhys said, his black eyes wide, his pupils blown. She loved him most when he was like this, barely held together at the seams, bursting with desire.

She had fallen in love with her husband precisely because he wanted the world, and if there was anything that he didn't currently possess that was in her power to give to him, she would give it to him, no questions asked.

Besides, if her smutty romance novels were any indication of what she might like, she was going to enjoy herself immensely.

"Do you guys want to have a threesome?" David said, cutting right to the chase.

"Yes," Rhys and Moira said simultaneously.

CHAPTER FORTY
RHYS

Rhys's own bedroom shouldn't have felt foreign to him, but as he stepped inside with Moira's fingers laced through his own and David close behind, he felt as if he had never been there before. Had the bedspread always been that shade of green? When had the lace doily on the chest of drawers started to yellow? He busied himself fiddling with dimmers on the bedside lamps until David's hand came up against his back, thumb pressing into the sweet pressure point below his shoulder blades.

"You seem nervous," David said. "We don't have to do this if you don't want to."

"I want to," Rhys said, the words coming out with more bluster than he intended. David had run laps through the casual dating circuit in the city of Boston, and Moira had been reading feminist literature about yoni power and radical intimacy since college, but Rhys was not quite so liberated. It was Rhys who had the hang-ups, Rhys who had been baptized in Catholic guilt before he was old enough to do anything more about it than cry.

But he couldn't deny that, underneath all the hand-wringing, he wanted this. Badly.

"Alright," Rhys said, voice tight. "Um, OK. How to begin? Why don't we all just take a deep breath and–"

"Hush," Moira ordered, kissing him deeply. Rational thought evaporated right out of his brain. She was soft beneath his hands, but her voice was *firm*.

Rhys was dimly aware that David was behind him, helping him out of his jacket. David leaned down to press a kiss to the nape of Rhys's neck, and the sensation jolted through him like an electric shock. David's mouth on his skin and Moira's plush lips against his own… It was almost too much to bear.

"OK," Rhys said again, breaking the kiss. If he wasn't careful, he would start babbling. "Wow. OK."

"Shut up, Rhys," David said, with so much love in his voice.

Rhys shut up.

He sat on the edge of the bed and watched in silence as David slipped off his expensive shoes and unfastened Moira's necklace, leaning down to say something inaudible in her ear. She nodded with a grin.

Rhys wondered if he was doing something unthinkably stupid right now. He wondered if this night would topple the knife's-edge balance of their triangular relationship, all because he had let the boundaries between them blur. He wondered if he had let himself get too greedy with love.

But when Moira reached out to smooth his hair as David eased down beside him on the bed, spreading a hand across Rhys's thigh, all potential consequences flew out the window.

He might be working on reforming himself, but he was still, at his core, a greedy man.

Rhys looped one arm around David's waist and used the other to draw Moira into a crushing kiss.

David nipped at his neck while Moira lavished kisses on his mouth, and then Moira's fingers were in his hair while David deftly undid the buttons of his shirt. Rhys kissed them both with abandon, losing himself in every shuddering breath.

It was bliss.

David smoothed his hand down Rhys's stomach and then lower still. When David cupped him through his chinos, Rhys bucked against his touch, all pretense at self-composure gone.

"You're desperate for this," David teased. "Just look at you."

"You're gonna be a talker, aren't you?" Moira said.

"You do your thing, and I'll do mine," David responded, arching a playful eyebrow as he unfastened Rhys's fly.

"God," Rhys groaned, wondering what the hell he had gotten himself into and never wanting it to end.

"Kiss me, baby," Moira said, her gentle order giving him something to focus on. David's mouth wrapped around Rhys's cock the same moment Rhys's lips met Moira's, and something short-circuited in his brain. He moaned against Moira's kiss, and she held him tighter, trailing her long nails down his bare chest as David worked him over expertly.

"Somebody help me with this dress," Moira said, already half-out of her tight cocktail dress as she tried to wiggle it down over her hips.

David stopped what he was doing long enough to yank her closer by her ankle and then tug the dress past her ass. Moira dropped the dress on the ground, revealing Rhys's favorite lingerie set, the sheer baby blue one.

"You're sure you two didn't plan this?" Rhys said, mouth dry.

"Scout's honor, we did not," David said. "Although I'm not sure we could have come up with anything better."

David began to unbutton his own shirt, and Rhys took the cue to slip out of his own clothes. Moments later, they were all gloriously naked in bed together.

"Come here," Moira said, lying back against the pillows and letting her knees fall open. In the warm light of the bedside lamp, her skin seemed to glow, and her eyes sparkled with delight.

Every inch his goddess, every inch his queen.

Rhys stared at her, his chest constricting. He wanted to commit every detail of this moment to memory, just in case the universe conspired against him once again to shatter the good and precious things in this life the moment he touched them.

"Go get her," David said softly into the juncture of Rhys's neck and shoulder, as gracious as any prince.

Rhys leaned over his wife, kissing her with the desperation of a shipwrecked man seeking fresh water. When he slipped his hand between her legs, he found her inner thighs slick with anticipation. Her skin was hot, like she had been sunbathing all day, like she was the sun itself. She wiggled closer to him, canting her hips up against his erection.

"Please," she whispered, and the last of Rhys's resolve fractured right down the middle.

Rhys slid himself inside his wife as Moira dug her nails into his back. Their bodies slotted together perfectly, reunited once again.

David knelt behind Rhys, kissing the freckles on his shoulders as Rhys stroked in and out of Moira. Her fingers twined into the pillows above her head, but she didn't shut her eyes. She looked right up at him, bearing perfect witness.

There was the soft sound of a drawer opening as David helped himself to the lubricant in the bedside table, then the unmistakable pressure of David's finger pressing against Rhys' entrance. Rhys took his finger inside with a shuddering gasp, but then every muscle in his body relaxed as he slowly fucked his wife in time with the rhythm David set.

When David pressed a second finger inside him, curling in just that way Rhys liked, Rhys could have cried, it all felt so good.

It was incandescent, luminous, like a white-hot star exploding in his chest.

Rhys lost himself in the sensation for a whole two minutes until he tensed, suddenly worried about what David might think of seeing him with Moira, what Moira might think of watching David with him. Was this too depraved, too hedonistic, too selfish? Were they only doing this to make him happy? What if they didn't want to be doing this at all?

"Don't get shy on me now," David said with a chuckle. Then, a little gentler. "You feel alright?"

Moira's eyes searched his with a tenderness so vast he felt like he might drown in it. Rhys pressed his forehead against her own and breathed with her for a few heartbeats, letting her comb gentle fingernails through his hair. He waited until his pulse slowed, until the spike of anxiety had cleared.

Then he looked over his shoulder so David could drop a quick kiss to his lips.

"Yes," Rhys said, and he meant it.

David hummed his approval, then eased his cock inside Rhys.

Rhys groaned, driving deeper into Moira, and she wrapped her legs tighter around him, digging her nails into his shoulders harder than ever before. The pain was clarifying, cleansing, like the ache in his knees after praying or the burn in his shoulders after holding his arms up during an hour-long summoning. David bit a red crescent moon into his shoulder as he fucked him, and Rhys knew he was going to be walking around tomorrow marked by both of them.

Somehow, impossibly, that just got him harder.

David braced a hand between Rhys's shoulder blades and pushed him down further, harder into his wife, and Moira practically purred at the increased pressure.

For the first time in a long time, the bottomless pit inside Rhys didn't feel so empty anymore. He felt filled to the brim with light, with the kind of contentment he only ever felt in hard-won, fleeting snatches after achieving something monumental. But right now, he wasn't chasing any goal besides his own pleasure and the pleasure of the only two people he had ever really loved.

"Baby," Moira panted, rolling her hips beneath him. Her thighs had started to tremble. "I'm close. I'm going to–"

David wrapped a steadying hand around Moira's ankle, probably to keep her where he needed her to be while she rode out her orgasm, but it was David who let out a bruised, needy sound the instant he touched her.

"*Christ*," he swore, his cock kicking inside Rhys.

Moira came with a sharp cry, and David followed her moments later, spilling inside Rhys. The sound of both was almost enough by itself to drive Rhys over the brink, and he buried himself deeper in Moira, tucking his face into her shoulder. David wrapped a hand around the nape of Rhys's neck, applying just enough pressure to remind Rhys that he was still here, that he was present and involved despite Rhys currently being sheathed to the hilt in his wife, and that – fucked up or not – was what did it for Rhys.

He finished with a groan, filling Moira with heat. She let out a breathless giggle, probably still seeing stars from the force of her climax. Judging by how hard David was breathing, and how heavily he was sagging against Rhys, David probably was too.

Predictably, David was the first one who spoke.

"Where did we end up on me spending the night?" he said, sounding like he had just run a mile.

"You're welcome to stay, if it's alright with Moira," Rhys said. How he was stringing together words right now, he had no idea.

Moira made a blissed-out sound of assent.

"Good," David said. "Because I don't think I can drive after that. I'm… going to shower."

This was not uncommon for David. He wasn't a big cuddler, unless you caught him in a certain mood, and he hated being sticky after sex.

"You alright?" Rhys asked, settling down next to Moira. She draped a leg over him and tugged the sheets half over their bodies, already drifting in the hazy twilight between wakefulness and sleep.

"Oh, I'm totally fine," David said. "I'm just... discombobulated."

"I didn't hurt you, did I?" Moira asked, lifting her head up drowsily off the pillow.

David barked out a laugh, like she had just said something preposterous.

"Hurt me? No. No you did not. But I think you permanently fried a few neurons."

Moira ginned, very pleased with herself, then went back to drowsing. This was usual for Moira, who *was* a big cuddler, and who Rhys had seen, on multiple occasions, fall asleep minutes after sex.

Rhys twined his arms around his wife while the sound of the shower filtered in from the master bathroom.

"Hey," he said softly, stirring her from her afterglow. "Thank you. For everything."

"Pretty good birthday present, right?" she teased.

"Yes, but I didn't mean for that. I meant for being so brave and kind and clever. For being with me, every single day."

"You're a sap," Moira said, but she was smiling.

They lost themselves in the mundanities of pillow talk until David returned from the shower, his cheeks pink from the heat, a towel wrapped around his hips.

"Shower's all yours," he said, and then dropped the towel, with complete unselfconsciousness, and stepped into his boxers. Moira rolled her eyes, but she threw back her covers with a similar lack of shame and sauntered towards the shower.

"Rhys, are you coming?"

Rhys and Moira showered together, Rhys luxuriating in every single drop of water on her skin, her heat and her closeness, the tiny noises of pleasure she made while he lathered her up with her vanilla body wash. When they emerged, unknown minutes later, David was already dozing in bed, one arm under the pillow, one knee splayed out in that hanged man position he slept in. Rhys took a breath and marveled at the sight, David asleep in his bed, Moira pulling on her pink silk slip, the two of them sharing his most intimate space with perfect ease.

Moira scooted into bed next to David and dropped a sweet kiss on his forehead. David wrinkled his nose at the display of affection, but he smoothed a gentle hand over her hip which, for David, was tantamount to an "I love you too".

Rhys swore, in that moment, that he would never jeopardize what the three of them had ever again.

"Rhys, I can feel you staring," David said, not even opening his eyes. "If you're going to have a Catholic guilt episode, save it for the morning, please. I'm wiped."

"It's not that," Rhys said, leaning down to pull on his briefs and a pair of sweatpants. "I'm just... admiring you both."

"Get on over here," Moira said as she tucked her braids into her satin bonnet.

She tossed back the covers, and Rhys joined her on his usual side of the bed. She snuggled down between the two men, letting out a contented sigh.

"I'm buying you a California King," David murmured, his words muffled by the pillow.

"No, you're not," Rhys said, but there was a smile in his voice.

Rhys turned out the lights and slept the deep, dreamless sleep of a man truly at peace.

CHAPTER FORTY-ONE
RHYS

Rhys woke with the sun, largely because Moira and David were taking up most of the bed, but he wasn't irritated with either of them. Instead, he felt deliriously happy to wake to Moira wrapped around him like a clinging starfish, David still out cold with one arm draped over Moira and the other wrapped around the pillows he was hoarding. Rhys managed to rise without waking either of them, then he went downstairs and fished the puff pastry out of the freezer, diced up some feta and chives, and got down to cooking breakfast.

Moira made her way down the stairs just as the tarts were coming out of the oven. Rhys handed her a mug of coffee sweetened with cream and his homemade orgeat syrup.

"Good morning, little goddess," he said. "David still out?"

"Like a light."

"That's not true," David said, appearing in the kitchen doorway wearing last night's slacks and one of Rhys's Henleys. It was, strictly speaking, one of David's Henleys that Rhys had stolen and then "forgotten" to get rid of after the original breakup. It still fit him well. "I never sleep in."

"Morning to you too," Rhys said.

"Did you cook us breakfast?" David asked, raising an eyebrow. "Wow, you really are whipped."

"A simple thank you will get you a long way."

"In that case," David said, snagging a tart and leaning down to press a kiss to Rhys's mouth, "thank you."

He gave Moira a kiss on the cheek, then slid past her with his hand resting lightly on her waist. Moira's fingers came up thoughtlessly to brush against his, probably saying something in that silent language of theirs.

"So," David said, helping himself to coffee and taking a seat at the kitchen table. "How's everyone feeling after last night?"

Moira and Rhys exchanged a glance, attempting to gauge each other's reactions.

"Good," Moira said.

"Great," Rhys put in.

David grinned at him in a way that clearly telegraphed he didn't regret a thing.

"Me too."

And that was that. They had proven they could trust each other with a deeper level of intimacy, that they fit as well together in bed as they did in a summoning circle.

Moira sat next to David and pulled up the news app on her phone. Rhys wiped down the counters, enjoying the meditative quality of completing these small domestic tasks while his lovers sipped their coffee.

"Anything new from the *Inquirer*?" David asked, reading over Moira's shoulder. "Or have they gotten bored of playing witchfinder general?"

Moira scrolled and then scrolled some more.

"Nothing new that I see. Oh no wait: here in the arts and culture section"

"Arts and culture?" Rhys echoed, tossing the dishrag in the sink.

David peered at the phone, skimming at lawyer speed, then let out a laugh.

"Oh babe, you're gonna hate this."

"I can't believe it," Moira said. "Well, actually I can, and I'm not above saying I told you so."

She held her phone out to Rhys, and he bent down to read the headline.

RISD Student Pleads Guilty to Defacing Public Property.

"No way," Rhys said, snatching up the phone. David was laughing at him, and Moira was rolling her eyes at him, but he barely noticed. He read the article, feeling more foolish with each passing sentence. The "ritual" in Boston Common was not done by one sorcerer, or by many. It was an unauthorized art installation by a senior from the Rhode Island School of Design who wanted to use occult motifs to challenge societal expectations, or something like that. The student had come forward on their Instagram account, publicizing their artistic process and hopes for a public reaction to the piece. They had gotten off with a fine and a slap on the wrist.

Rhys handed the phone back to his wife, feeling dazed.

"The next time one of us tells you that you're overreacting, listen the first time," David said. "Now have some coffee before you keel over."

"But I didn't... I mean, how was I possibly supposed to know that–"

"It's done with," Moira said. "No rewriting the past, only doing things differently in the future. I'm curious to know how the other magicians are reacting to the news, though. David, anything in the backchannels?"

David retrieved his own phone and pulled up the handful of Occultism Discord groups he was a part of, mostly to keep an eye on trending topics and to screenshot unverified personal gnosis he found particularly unhinged and pass around the group chat of younger Society men.

"Looks like the interest is dying down. Most people agree this isn't that surprising, considering that weird paper mâché doll and the fact that none of the symbols in the art installation were one hundred percent accurate. Other than that, it's the usual stuff. Some chatter about the levels of hauntings in Boston spiking recently. I hadn't noticed that, but I haven't been doing many seances over the last few weeks."

"Oh?" Moira asked, leaning in to spy on his phone.

"It's probably nothing," David said. "Just bored occultists stirring the pot. But if there's any truth to it, that makes your interest in channeling the dead all the more fun."

"Now that things have calmed down a bit, I was thinking maybe we could go to that graveyard you mentioned and go ghost-spotting. Next week? I'll pack us a lunch."

"I'd love that," David said.

Moira and David lost themselves in theories as to why, exactly, some dead souls remained tethered to the mortal plane, while reaching over each other for tarts and more sugar for coffee

Rhys leaned back in his chair, and as he watched the two loves of his life, a pain so sweet sang through him that he felt as though his heart had been pierced by swords.

Maybe this time, he hoped, the good things would last. Maybe happiness didn't need to come hand-in-hand with heartache, at least not this time.

When Rhys McGowan was fifteen years old, he had gone looking for the sacred. His entire adult life had been one winding and crooked path towards anything that felt divine, whether in the darkness or in the light. He had mistaken many things for divinity along the way. The pursuit of power, the hardline structure of organized religion, the shadowy temptations of the occult. He had tried and failed many times to grasp for God.

But as Rhys sat there in his kitchen, watching Moira and David gossip over the food he had prepared for them, Moira's brown eyes alight with interest, David's mouth curving into a smile, Rhys felt that this might be a glimmer of the thing he had been ceaselessly searching for.

He felt, perhaps for the first time in his life, holy.

EPILOGUE

RHYS

During the first Society meeting of the new year, Rhys stepped into the center of a brand new ceremonial circle chalked onto the stone floor of the ritual room and breathed in the scent of smoldering resin.

"I'll be demonstrating this technique by myself today," he said, addressing those gathered in the circle. He was grateful for every familiar face, and that he had lived long enough to see a new year dawn with all of them. "No scryer needed."

Intrigued murmurs rippled through the room. David, who Rhys had begun to insist take longer rests between scrying sessions so he didn't burn out, grinned at him from across the circle. Antoni watched with rapt interest at David's side, already trying to commit the new symbols chalked on the floor to memory.

Rhys swallowed hard and settled into the silence, into the wellspring of power he found at the center of himself. He had prayed for nine days before attempting this summoning, not to mention fasting all morning. He had been trying to live a better life lately, a life more deeply rooted in compassion and courage, a life where he didn't turn to deceit or manipulation at the first sign of trouble. He had been trying to be a better husband, a better boyfriend, a better friend and better son.

Rhys put his hand out, not in a gesture of domination or in a plea of supplication, but in a sign of benediction.

"Saint Michael," he said, voice clear as a church bell. He wasn't using traditional liturgy today. Today, he was relying on himself, on his own nerve and power of will. On his own faith. "Come."

The atmospheric pressure shifted as the air around him whirred like locust song and warmed like a sunbaked desert day. Antoni's lips parted in terrified reverence as that whirring grew to a fever pitch. Kitty stumbled back a pace, gripping Nathan's hand, and Cameron muttered a fast prayer under his breath as an undeniable presence began to gather in the room.

The circle had not been chalked to trap an angel – who would be foolish enough to attempt that? – but to make the space hospitable to a heavenly guest.

Heat and vitality flowed through Rhys, and he knew he had constructed the circle correctly.

As the angel appeared in a ripple of light in the center of the room, some Society members gasped, or clapped, or shed tears of awe.

David, however, had no eyes for the angel. He was looking at Rhys, green eyes burning bright like Rhys was the sun at the center of the universe, like David had never in his life been prouder of him, like he couldn't wait to get Rhys alone.

Rhys grinned back at him, all teeth and triumph.

It was going to be a good year. He could feel it.

THE CHARIOT

Chariots have speed and energy, so can carry you forward, often very quickly. They can also take you upwards into heaven, as we see in Ezekiel's vision from the Old Testament. The Chariot image usually faces you head-on, so it can be cocky and ostentatious, but many of us need some of that confidence. Still, it's not always straightforward: in many card iterations, the Chariot is drawn by the mysterious figure of the Sphinxes. Sphinxes are well-known for their riddles, so your forward motion won't necessarily be instantaneous or easy. Chariots were included in a victory parade, especially in Ancient Greece and Rome, and they are useful in battle.

The Chariot is a card of success.

THE HIGH PRIESTESS

The High Priestess is full of mysterious imagery. She conveys an inner power – not masculine might or anything that overpowers – but energy in deep currents and dark places. She is an initiator, and she sits in front of a veil emblazoned with pomegranates which are the fruit of Persephone, the Greek goddess who spends six months of the year in the Underworld. She has transcended the mysteries of life and death. She is the patron saint of "I can't explain why" when we try to explore our motivations. She sits between the black and the white pillars of the Temple and is quite comfortable holding that space in between. Finally, behind the veil – behind everything – are the waters of the unconscious.

With her, you will go deep, find out something surprising and learn from your intuition and your instincts.

THE HANGED MAN

An enigmatic card. The Hanged Man hangs upside down and assumes a strange position, but he doesn't look unhappy about it either. Some traditions call him a traitor and compare him to Judas Iscariot, but that doesn't always seem like the right interpretation. Maybe it's this and more. The Hanged Man follows his own course and doesn't need approval from anyone, but he is also watching and waiting, taking a neutral position as he languishes in an in-between state. He calls back to the Norse god Odin, who hung from the World Tree, waiting to receive the magic of the runes.

The Hanged Man doesn't mean that things are easy but it's an encouraging card: avoid making rash decisions and be wise, and everything should be alright.

ACKNOWLEDGMENTS

Returning to a series for a second installment is a particular joy and a particular challenge, and the people who supported me in this process made getting *Ascension* down on the page a joy more days than not. The Angry Robot team remain a joy to work with, and I particularly want to thank Amy, Caroline, Eleanor, and Des for their tireless work on shaping and marketing this series, as well as Eleonor Piteira and Alice Claire Coleman for creating drop-dead gorgeous covers.

This novel went through so many subplots until I finally found the straightest path into the heart of the story, so thank you to my suite of creative friends for hearing out every plotline and helping me sort through them all. Elias, Ellie, Sydney, Koren, Maddie, and all the rest: thank you for contributing your clever brains and patient support.

To Laura, who swooped in during the developmental editing stage to bring the muddiest parts of the story into clarity and remind me that this series is ultimately and always about power and love, thank you. And to Kit, who kept me steady while consistently challenging me to be braver, smarter, and more vulnerable with this book than the last; you're the most clever sorcerer I know.

The writing process was supercharged by the energy of readers I chatted with online and met at live events on tour. We read to feel not so alone, but many of us write to feel that way too. Whenever I get discouraged about my work, your enthusiasm fills my well. I can't wait to continue sharing this series with you with Moira's story in *Divination*. Until then, keep yourselves well, and practice safe spellcasting!

ABOUT THE AUTHOR

S.T. Gibson is the British Fantasy Award nominated and Goodreads Choice Award nominated author of the Sunday Times bestsellers *Evocation, A Dowry of Blood* and *An Education in Malice*. A graduate of the creative writing program at the University of North Carolina at Asheville and the theological studies program at Princeton Seminary, she currently lives in Rhode Island with her fiancé, a spoiled Persian cat, and vintage blazer collection.